FREED KINGFISHER

THE SLAVE-SOLDIER SERIES

R. LAHAM

OLIVER HEBER BOOKS

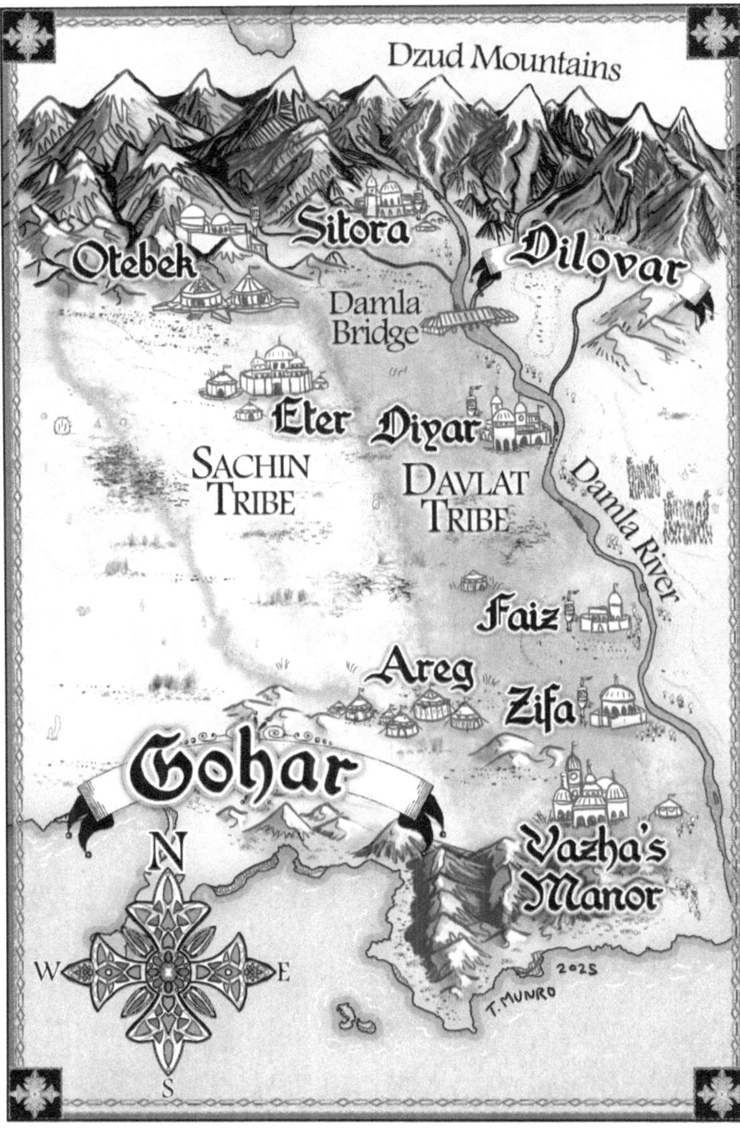

Dzud Mountains
Otebek
Sitora
Dilovar
Damla Bridge
Eter
Diyar
SACHIN TRIBE
DAVLAT TRIBE
Damla River
Faiz
Areg
Zifa
Gohar
Vazha's Manor
N
W
E
S
2025
T. MUNRO

PROLOGUE

Eastern Gohar
Year 222 of the Dark Age

Wrapped in a thick wool blanket and crouched beside the fire, Zolto watched as two Gohari mages-in-training weaved and bobbed in the long grass of the steppe. Even though his vision was weak from age, he saw enough to make him smile. One of the trainees was his great-grandson, Berk, who'd been singled out by one of Anzor's red-clad mages. The entire clan had gasped at the revelation that frail, wheezy Berk had the Essence. Zolto chuckled to himself and shook his head. *They didn't believe me.* He'd been telling them so for all sixteen years of the boy's life. Being an elder, a "beg," should have lent his words more credence, but starvation broke down even the sturdiest cultural norms.

Now, however, the famine in Gohar was slowly ending. The Manzakars of Anzor had brought their mages to the steppe, and the rain fell more often these days. The soil was richer and life returned—wheat and barley sprouted across the plains. Sheep, goats, and cattle grew plump. Herds of horses had even been spotted grazing amidst the wild tulips and poppies, which grew in abundance. Zolto was old, but not so old that he remembered ever seeing Gohar like this.

Berk approached, panting, and dropped down next to his great-grandfather with a plop. He'd donned a Gohari mage's attire, which had not been worn since the Akmaral War, including a sheepskin vest adorned with eagle feathers and long, leather strips that were beaded and hung down to the ankles. Berk swept the short, conical hat made of a patchwork of fabrics and owl feathers from his head and set his spell book down beside him. "I'm exhausted. Who knew conjuring was so draining?"

"Indeed," Zolto said, his eyes heavily crinkled with amusement. "Bringing forth life is not meant to be easy."

Berk leaned back on his hands and stretched his long legs toward the fire. As his breathing slowed, he peered at the old man through the plaits of dark hair that hung in his face. "Beg Zolto," he said, addressing the elder respectfully, "I don't think I've ever seen you smile so much."

Zolto reached into the sack resting at his side and pulled out a large, fan-shaped bone—a horse's scapula. Unlike the other bones in his sack, this one had not been scorched by fire and was not inscribed with the curvy, dotted Perchuhi script. It had belonged to a warrior horse of exceptional speed that had died by a Manzakar's lance. He said, "For the first time in over two centuries, there is finally something to smile about." He held the clean bone to the flames, his skeletal hands twisting it slowly, deliberately.

Berk sat up, his eyes fixed on the darkening scapula. Zolto watched as a crack splintered across the bone's edge and snaked down toward his hand. His smile widened. Another crack appeared on the opposite side and descended toward the first in a stuttered creep. Zolto's smile dissipated. When he finally pulled the bone away from the fire, Berk was practically in his lap.

"What? Beg Zolto, what do you see?"

The elder ran his callused, gnarled finger across the singed, still-hot ridge of the bone, then down along each of the cracks. His eyes saw without seeing. His voice, when he finally spoke, sounded like the rustling grass. "Betrayal."

CHAPTER I

Anzor
Year 222 of the Dark Age

Tikran's eyes glazed over as he listened to Lord Gennadius, Chancellor of the Exchequer, read from the annual financial records, droning on through royal expenditures, payments made to the Crown, debts owed to the Crown... Tikran couldn't stop his leg from bouncing with restless energy. He wished he were anywhere at that moment other than in the great hall, trying to pay attention to the endless deliberation on taxes, maintenance of bridges, financial penalties...

When Commander Naran burst through the doors unannounced, Tikran practically leaped out of his chair with joy and relief. The big Manzakar strode over and embraced Tikran fiercely, indifferent to the strange looks from the lords and durais of the king's council as he squashed the king of Anzor to his chest.

"Finally back from the cold Gohari north," Tikran said, grinning. "Is all well?"

In response, Naran handed him a Dilovari arrow. "We have a problem on our hands, Tik," he said, his scarred face solemn. "Found this—and others like it—just outside Sitora. My men and I have been working our way along the Dzud Mountains and can confidently say there's no sign of any crossings, by Haldorans or otherwise."

Tikran's chest tightened as he took the arrow and turned it over in his hands. Unquestionably Dilovari, it was two feet long with a shaft made of birch and fletched with eagle feathers. The bodkin arrowhead was tapered and made of forged, hardened steel —a tip meant to pierce armor. If there was no sign of crossings, Bilguun was sending troops into Gohar for a different reason...and willfully violating the renewed truce between the kingdoms of Anzor and Dilovar.

"That didn't take long," Tikran muttered, then turned to Lord Haydar. "Six months was not enough time for him to replenish Dilovar's Essence? It's not enough that he likely has the most powerful mage on the Continent?"

Haydar drummed his fingers on the table. "It's definitely aggressive of Bilguun, I will say that much. I think a visit to Dilovar might be in order."

As the council murmured in agreement, a tingle of surprise ran from Tikran's head to his feet. For nearly a year—ten months, to be exact—Tikran had been king of Anzor, and he hadn't expected problems from Dilovar so soon. He found himself torn between two very different emotions: On the one hand, he had enough to worry about domestically, within Anzor and its colony Gohar, that adding this to his list of problems made him want to vigorously prune the royal gardens with his saber.

On the other hand, *Damir.*

He remembered the day King Bilguun's royal physician and head mage left Anzor as if it were yesterday. *Gut-wrenching.* Damir hadn't said goodbye privately; he'd avoided it, in fact. They had said their farewells in front of the entire court, shook hands like two men who hadn't fought in battle together, who hadn't cried in each other's arms, who hadn't found pleasure in each other's bodies...

"Your Highness?"

Tikran blinked back to the present. "I'm sorry. Yes?" Flustered, he rubbed the back of his neck. "Don't call me that. Please. I hate it."

Haydar cleared his throat. "King Tikran, I think the first order of business must be to find you a head mage. I think that will be very important when you speak to Bilguun, so he doesn't think he has the advantage."

"Yes," Tikran said, feeling oddly defeated. "I agree." He didn't want to drag some poor Gohari kid with the Essence into service for him, but he understood that many would be honored to serve him and that it was hardly by force. Still. Using the Essence as leverage or worse, as a weapon against another kingdom felt wrong in every possible way. But it was a necessity now, especially considering Damir. Was Bilguun's audacity because his head mage had divulged sensitive information about Anzor? Damir had been deeply involved in the rebellion and knew everything from the layout of Anzor City's Citadel to Manzakar military tactics. While Tikran desperately wanted to believe Damir would never betray him, current evidence was not in the doctor's favor.

"After your birthday celebration, we will send mages and troops into Gohar to find those with the most powerful Essence and bring them to you," Haydar said.

Oh, no. His birthday celebration. Tikran made the mistake of looking at Naran, who snickered out loud. He could already hear the taunts: *A birthday party for the boy king!* Tikran grit his teeth behind his flat smile. As Haydar had repeatedly pointed out, it was more for the morale of the Anzori people than it was a celebration of Tikran himself. But many Manzakars' birthdays were unknown, since they'd been brought to Anzor as slaves. Tikran had "celebrated" his birthday as a cadet by getting an extra hour on the training grounds while the others headed back to class. But there had been no *party.* Only blue-blood Anzori children had birthday parties.

Tikran rubbed his eyebrow. "Of course. My birthday. When is that, again?"

Haydar grinned. "Tomorrow, Your—er, King Tikran. You'll be twenty-four, in case you've lost count."

He had lost count. Twenty-four. Why did he feel twice that age?

The council resumed its discussion regarding taxes, then Tikran listened to the land trespass grievances of several lords, as well as the supplications of three clergymen. After declining their request to build yet another temple to Cenk in Anzor City, Tikran was ready to be done. He looked at Haydar, feeling like a schoolboy waiting for the magister to dismiss him. He could tell Haydar was trying his best not to roll his eyes or smile as he said, "We're done for today, Your Highness."

Thank Cenk! Tikran was so relieved he didn't feel the need to chastise Haydar over the whole "Your Highness" thing. He rushed to his chambers, threw off his formal Manzakar's uniform, and slipped into his training one, hoping to hurry to the royal stables then the hippodrome as imperceptibly as possible—which wasn't imperceptibly at all. He was king, for Cenk's sake. While he'd managed to convince Haydar that he didn't need a bloody retinue everywhere he went because, lest anyone forget, he was a Manzakar, he knew that the Aslans still tried to keep an eye on him. Even though he still wore his Manzakar uniform daily, he didn't exactly blend in, particularly once people recognized him. Then it was all the bowing and kneeling and "Your Highness" and more bowing. It was far worse than being the celebrated Manzakar, the Caged Kingfisher.

As Tikran hurried through the Citadel to the stables, he snuck through alleyways and away from the busy streets. To avoid as much attention as possible, he dressed as a regular Manzakar, with the loose end of his white turban covering the lower half of his face. As he maneuvered through a dim and narrow backstreet, he heard the soft whimper of a child. He paused to look toward a cluster of barrels and spotted a little Gohari girl sitting against them, her knees drawn to her chest, her head buried in her arms. She looked to be six or seven years old, barefoot and wearing what used to be the plain linen tunic of a house slave. Tikran had officially abolished slavery two months prior, but because many of the former slaves had no money or education, they remained bound to their owners, their situations unaltered. Tikran had been working on changing that—he wanted every ex-slave to be given some monetary compensation and, if desired, an apprenticeship in a trade. He knew from experience that child slaves were especially vulnerable and he sought to provide them with housing and education, funded by the Crown, or even possibly return them to their families in Gohar. Of course, all of this was an administrative, financial, and logistical challenge that would take time, but Tikran was impatiently pressing the stubbornly reluctant council and Exchequer to put things into effect.

The child startled when she saw him and clambered to her feet, her eyes wide with fear. Her dark hair was in a messy braid down her back and her ruddy cheeks were stained with tears.

"Don't be scared," Tikran said, letting the cloth of his turban fall away from his face. "I just heard you crying. Are you okay?"

Her lip trembled and she shook her head. She pointed further down the alley to a puddle that lay amidst shards of broken ceramic. "My lady sent me to buy a jug of blackberry wine and I tripped..." She let out a sob and a hiccup. "She's going to whip me."

Tikran kept his expression calm and said to the child, "No, she won't. Let's go get another jug, shall we?"

"Sir," she stammered, "I have no more money."

Tikran smiled, holding his hand out to her. "I'll buy it for you. What's your name?"

"Aya," she said. She took his hand hesitantly and they walked back to the marketplace. Tikran pulled the turban across his nose and mouth, nervously hoping he could get the job done without too much attention. Aya led him to the shop where she had bought the wine and Tikran uncovered his face again. Beneath a bright orange awning, he addressed the vintner, a rotund Anzori man with a silver mustache wearing a red felt cap. "I'd like to buy a jug of blackberry wine, please."

The man's eyes widened as he looked at Tikran. "By Cenk, you look like…" His jaw dropped. "Your Highness?"

Tikran smiled tightly. "I'd prefer not to draw attention to myself, please."

The merchant blinked rapidly. "Of course, my king," he said as he spun on his heels and hurried into the dim coolness of the shop and down to the wine cellar. A few minutes later, he reappeared and handed a full ewer to Tikran.

"Thank you," Tikran said. "I'll be sure you're compensated for your troubles."

Carrying the ewer, Tikran followed Aya to a pretty terraced home with blue shutters. He crouched down before her and handed her the vessel. "Be careful now and don't trip, Aya," he said with a wink.

Her eyes were enormous in her small face. "Are you really the king?"

"Yes." Tikran held a finger to his lips. "But let it be our secret, okay?"

She beamed with delight. "Yessir. Thank you so much, Your Highness."

He watched her walk into the house, the ewer balanced on her head, and hurried back into the alleyways. Former child slaves like Aya needed the protection of the Crown, and he was determined to see it happen. It may not have been a priority for the council, but it was a priority for him.

He finally entered the hippodrome and exhaled, relieved and surprised he'd managed to make it without being mobbed. Training with Naran, Coxani, and the other Manzakars was the best part of his day. He rode through the portico to find his two best friends already in mock combat, wielding sabers on foot. When they saw him, their faces lit up, and Tikran hopped off his horse, grinning, feeling the tension of the day leave his body.

"Tikran," Coxani said, giggling behind her hand, "you have an audience." She raised her eyes deliberately behind him.

His smile faded as he turned to see dozens of aristocratic

Anzori women sitting in galleries overlooking the arena, their jewels glittering in the light. Each lady's eunuch hovered near, holding a colorful parasol aloft, over his mistress's head. *What the...?* Tikran frowned. "Why? Did something happen?"

Coxani widened her eyes at him. "Yes, something happened. You just made it legal for the Anzori and Gohari to intermarry. Which means you've officially made Manzakars—including yourself—fair game. All those Anzori women who lusted after the Caged Kingfisher have a chance with you now. And as if that wasn't enough, you're the *king*."

Oh, shit. Tikran's heart plummeted. He certainly hadn't anticipated that to be a side effect of repealing an awful, archaic law that forbade the mixing of Anzori and Gohari bloodlines. He turned back to his friends, groaning. "Why won't people just leave me alone?"

Naran slapped Tikran's forehead. "Because you're the king, jackass."

Tikran's hackles were raised. "I didn't ask for this."

The yellow-haired Manzakar set a firm hand on Tikran's shoulder, a playful smile on his lips. "There are some beautiful women up there. If I were you, I would use this as an opportunity to scratch a certain itch, if you get my drift."

"*Naran.*" Coxani scowled. "Their intentions are not innocent, I promise you."

"No kidding. The fact that they're sitting up there all of a sudden is enough proof that their intentions aren't innocent," Naran replied, laughing heartily.

"Holy Cenk, stop." Tikran rubbed his face. "I want nothing to do with any of them. I'm going to keep them out of the hippodrome during training starting tomorrow." He sighed. "For now, let's just pretend they aren't there."

Coxani must have noticed Tikran's shoulders slump and his smile vanish. She said, "Well, since they're not going anywhere this afternoon, let's put on a show, why don't we?" She asked the attendants to hang three sets of gourds and birdcages. She turned to Tikran and Naran, smiling. "I shoot Naran's. Naran shoots Tikran's. Tikran shoots mine."

Tikran couldn't help but smile. "Coxani..." It was the game that had earned him his Manzakar name—Tikran of the Caged Kingfisher, which, at his coronation, had been changed to Freed Kingfisher.

"Cowards," she said as she hopped onto her horse. "I will win this, so help me Cenk."

Naran jumped into his saddle and wiggled his eyebrows at Tikran. "At this rate, Coxani is going to get all the women."

"She can have them," Tikran answered moodily, climbing back onto his horse and riding after them.

CHAPTER 2

The man looking back at Tikran from the polished silver mirror was both familiar and strange all at once. It had been that way for a while now, but especially tonight, the night of his birthday celebration. He'd absolutely refused to wear the former king's ceremonial dress, insisting that, as a Manzakar, a commander's uniform worked fine. But Haydar had new formal wear made for him nonetheless, starting what Haydar called a new "warrior king" tradition. In addition to the Manzakar's blue jacket with the standing collar over loose breeches, Tikran wore a black silk mantle draped over his shoulders that hung down to the heels of his curved-toe boots. A custom-made ceremonial saber, its slightly curved, sweeping blade made of steel and gold, bore a black jade grip and hung from an intricately tooled sword-belt around his waist. He wore the same turban as the Manzakars except his was the same black as his mantle. He had been clean shaven and his hair hung in loose waves. His burn scar just peeked above his collar, now a fibrous, shiny, pale pink.

Tikran blinked at his reflection. The stranger in the man before him was striking. He was someone who commanded respect and adoration. But when he saw himself in that same man, a crawling discomfort overtook him. *I'm a fraud.* He was no king. He felt like a boy playing at king. He wanted to rip off all the silly adornments and go back to being himself, whoever that was. A Manzakar. A soldier.

A slave.

He flinched.

"Tikran, are you all right?"

The reflection of a young woman who looked like Coxani appeared behind him, and he turned, his eyes wide. A green velvet kaftan molded to her figure, layered over a wispy white silk tunic and loose pants. She wore a black silk sash tied around her waist and her hair fell in glossy dark curls down her back and over her shoulder. "Coxani, holy Cenk. You're gorgeous," he said.

She smiled widely, her green eyes shining. "I was just about to say the same thing about you. You have got to be the most beautiful king Anzor has ever had."

"I'm definitely the brownest," he said with a chuckle. "I feel like a clown."

She took his hands in hers. "You really don't see what everyone else sees, do you?"

"I guess not." He wrinkled his nose. "I don't want to go to my so-called birthday celebration. Do you think they'll miss me if I don't show up?"

She laughed. "I'm thinking yes."

"It's going to be awful."

She squeezed his hands in sympathy. "I agree that it's probably going to be uncomfortable for you, especially with all of Anzor's eligible women in hot pursuit of you."

He winced. "I'd rather get a good flogging."

She held up a finger. "I recommend a glass of xew before you go out there."

"Well, good thing I'm king, then, because I have three decanters of it sitting on that sideboard over there," he said without enthusiasm.

Before she could reach the table, an attendant had poured two glasses of the strong liquor. "Thank you," Coxani said, taking the glasses and handing one to Tikran. "Let's toast to you, Freed King-fisher," she said.

"No, no." He shook his head. "They're going to be toasting me all night. Let's toast to you, Dolphin." He smiled. "May you be happy, always."

They emptied their glasses and Coxani said, "That should help you relax a bit." She raised herself up to her toes and kissed his cheek. "I'll see you out there. Chin up."

Tikran took several deep breaths after she left. Within a minute, Haydar opened the door and raised an eyebrow at him. "Ready, lad?"

No. He straightened and lifted his head. "Let's get this over with."

As he entered the great hall, a voice cried, "His Highness, King Tikran of the Freed Kingfisher!"

A sea of luminescent faces watched silently as he walked in. The flames of many tall candelabra illuminated the intricately carved, gilded columns and ceiling. Overhead, the stained glass of the clerestory windows shimmered with vibrant color. All the aris-tocrats of Anzor stood before him in their finery, glittering with gems and gold and silk brocade, their eyes fixed on him. Tikran felt like he was outside his body as he watched the Anzori lords and ladies bow to him in homage. Even after ten months, the experi-ence continued to feel unreal. He made his way to the throne and lowered himself into it, which was apparently the sign that people could begin socializing again. Tikran finally exhaled, glad that the throne sat on a dais so he could be somewhat removed from the crowd. Unfortunately, his relief was short-lived.

"Tikran," Lord Haydar said, leaning down to speak in Tikran's ear, "there are people who would like to meet you. A lot of people."

He was grateful for Coxani and her foresight with the xew as he stood and braced himself for the compulsive bowing and flattery. Conversations floated around him as he greeted lord after lord and answered questions politely, albeit vaguely.

"Two thousand of the king's Manzakars. By Cenk! I'll be

honest, Your Highness, I was certain your little uprising would be squashed terribly..."

"Delger's outrageous poll tax, not to mention the astronomical tariffs..."

"If I may ask about Your Highness's diet? Do you consume fish regularly? I have heard it helps maintain one's health and virility—not that Your Highness needs the help..."

At some point, Lord Ruslan, one of the more vocal Anzori lords who had been suspiciously silent during the overthrow of Delger, approached Tikran, a polite but haughty smile on his face. Tikran forced his mouth to smile back. *Great. Just what I need right now.* Ruslan was in his early thirties and athletic, often boasting about his "intense" exercise regimen. Tikran struggled with a petty urge to challenge the lord to the sport of his choosing just to knock him down a few notches. *Let's test the effectiveness of that regimen against a Manzakar, shall we?*

"Your Highness, happy birthday," Ruslan said, bowing his head.

"Thank you, Lord Ruslan," Tikran answered, noticing the excessive number of rubies that adorned the lord's yellow turban and matching tunic.

"You've been very busy since your crowning, haven't you?" Ruslan said, smiling despite the edge in his voice. "Repealing laws left and right. I will say that I agree with some of your decisions, particularly those involving taxes and trade. But your social policies are quite extreme and somewhat vexing to the Anzori aristocracy."

Tikran shifted so that he stood with his legs apart, his hands folded in front of him. "Extreme? Which policies do you speak of? Perhaps the one that required children born of mixed Gohari and Anzori blood to be killed? Oh, wait—that was Delger's policy." Tikran's smile was more of a grimace now. "Do the Anzori find the abolition of *that* law particularly vexing? Or perhaps the one that forbids them from enslaving other human beings?"

Ruslan maintained his false smile more easily than Tikran, no doubt from years of practice. "Surely you can see how overturning centuries of social customs can be jarring, Your Highness?"

"I think you mean inconvenient and uncomfortable." Anger flared in Tikran's chest. "But the inconvenience of being unable to treat another human being like property or of being related to someone with dark skin is surely nothing compared to the achievement of restoring the dignity of an entire race of people, no?"

Contempt flashed briefly in Ruslan's eyes. "The Manzakars may have earned their freedom. But what of the other Gohari slaves? You have created a poverty crisis in Anzor. Under slavery they were fed and housed and mostly well-treated. Now they have nothing. I'm certain many of them resent you for it."

"I'm in the process of fixing that," Tikran said through his teeth, any remaining pretense of congeniality gone.

"With what funds, Your Highness?" The disdain returned to the Anzori lord's expression, blatant now. "The funds needed to defend Anzor against its enemies?"

How about we use the rubies in your outfit, asshole? Tikran wanted nothing more than to plant his fist in Ruslan's face. Before he could speak, however, Haydar was at his side, smiling that broad, white smile of his. Tikran was envious of Haydar's uncanny ability to look like he was genuinely smiling regardless of what he might be feeling.

"Lord Ruslan," Haydar said, "my apologies for interrupting your conversation, but there are countless lords and ladies awaiting King Tikran's attention."

Ruslan flashed that fake smile of his again. "Of course, Lord Haydar." He met Tikran's eyes quickly before sweeping a bow. "Your Highness."

As they walked away, Tikran muttered, "Good timing. I was fighting the urge to bash his face in."

Haydar cleared his throat. "You're king of Anzor, Tikran. No bashing faces."

Tikran found himself once again floating from conversation to conversation, trying to push Ruslan's words from his mind. He lost count of the number of daughters and granddaughters he met, all golden-haired, wide-eyed beauties who smiled so much that Tikran's mouth started aching as he tried mirroring their expressions. At least they also talked so much that he couldn't have gotten a word in edgewise even if he'd wanted to. It allowed him to be silent and wish he were somewhere else. But by Cenk, he heard some strange things from their mouths.

"...and it will be so refreshing to see caramel-skinned children running around..."

"I've always wanted the best life for my sweet Inzhu, and now she's free to get a job, although Cenk knows what that would be, since she can't read..."

"...personally have only ever seen myself married to a Manzakar, even before it was legal. They are the only ones worthy, you know?"

He realized that the buzz from the xew was wearing off and turned to Haydar urgently. "My lord, I need more alcohol. Please."

Haydar barely restrained his smile as he gestured to a servant carrying goblets brimming with wine. "Temper yourself, Your Highness," he said in a low voice. "The Anzori won't take kindly to a drunk king."

Taking a proffered goblet, Tikran wanted to roll his eyes. He was already utterly out of place among the men of the council and constantly felt undereducated, boorish, childish... What had made them choose him to be king? The suspicion that it had a lot to do with his naivety haunted and infuriated him. He took several large swallows of wine, feeling mutinous.

This party would end soon. It *had* to end soon.

He found himself drawn into a conversation with Lord Gennadius' seventeen-year-old granddaughter, who subjected him to her thoughts on marriage as he shifted from leg to leg restlessly.

"...clearly sacred, between a man and woman who are meant for each other, or you know, because it would strengthen one's family's political power..."

He was convinced there wasn't enough wine on the Continent to keep him afloat when Haydar rescued him. Sort of. "Lord Prem would like to speak to you. He says it's of the utmost importance. He also requests Naran's presence."

Naran. He could use some solidarity at the moment. Tikran politely excused himself from his current conversation and followed Haydar to Lord Prem, who was standing with a young woman and a boy. He remembered (without Haydar's reminder) that Prem had been the deciding vote in Delger's deposition and what had swayed the council in Tikran's favor.

"King Tikran," the white-haired lord said, "I can't tell you how grateful I am that Your Highness repealed that awful law. It has saved my daughter Dinara's life, as well as Kadyr's life."

Tikran was finally paying attention. He looked at Dinara, who was a pretty Anzori woman around his own age, and Kadyr, who was a boy of about eight or nine, with dark skin and hazel eyes.

Naran came to stand beside him, looking like a Manzakar commander if Tikran had ever seen one. Between his dashing aura and impressive stature, Tikran couldn't fathom how every woman in the place wasn't throwing herself at the Stalking Lion. He imagined it was Coxani's intimidating presence that kept them at bay.

"Lord Prem," Naran said, bowing briefly, a broad smile on his face. "A pleasure."

"Commander Naran," Lord Prem said. "I was just telling His Highness how grateful I am that he repealed the law forbidding the mixing of Anzori and Gohari bloodlines. It has saved my daughter and grandson's lives." He nudged Dinara and Kadyr toward Naran. "Dinara is finally free of service in Cenk's temple, and Kadyr doesn't need to hide among my household slaves anymore."

Bemused, Naran looked at the boy then Dinara, who swallowed nervously, peering up at him with large blue eyes. She said, "Commander, Kadyr is your son."

The blood drained from Naran's face even as his expression remained steady. "My lady...?"

Oh...shit. Tikran desperately wanted to turn and look for Coxani, but his eyes were glued to the disaster unfolding before him. His hand curled convulsively over the hilt of his ceremonial saber. He heard himself say, "Commander Naran, the boy has been living in hiding since his birth. His mother has been confined to a temple. The boy is yours."

"I THINK HAVING MOST of the same rights as the Anzori is a step in the right direction," Coxani said to a group of Gohari women and former classmates about the recent change in the laws. "But a Gohari woman can still be made an Anzori lord's courtesan if the lord so wishes it, regardless of her preferences. That must change."

Ola, her former headmistress, let out a laugh. "Coxani, there's no chance that law will ever change. Having their courtesans taken away would make powerful men very unhappy."

Coxani pulled back her shoulders a fraction. "I think, with Tikran as king, it could very well happen."

A pert-nosed woman with luxuriant red hair spoke up. "In any case, I enjoy my time as a courtesan. I'm not sure I would want it to change."

Growing increasingly irritated, Coxani said as evenly as she could, "Well, then, you may remain a courtesan regardless of the law. The need for change in the law is for women who *don't* want to be courtesans." She wanted to add *you selfish idiot* but bit it back.

"Captain Coxani, you look ravishing tonight."

She turned to see Lord Revaz, his eyes bright, smiling at her in admiration. Lord Revaz had been a windfall to the rebellion. As one of the first Anzori noblemen and king's advisors to join the cause, he'd helped rally more Anzori support and Manzakar troops to fight with Tikran. He'd also helped her keep away from Commander Nasch, Delger's commander-in-chief and, much to her chagrin, her former husband. Revaz had been elevated to the position of Chief Justiciar and she saw him only occasionally when they were both included in the king's council. Now, Revaz stood before her, looking like the picture of the Anzori masculine ideal, with his charming smile, thick blond hair, and penetrating blue eyes. She excused herself from the women's conversation and said to Revaz, "And you look very handsome, Lord Revaz. How are you?"

"I can't complain," Revaz said. "Anzor has been making positive strides since Tikran became king, and I am carefully optimistic for the future. And you, Captain? How has life been treating you?"

She smiled. "It's been good to me. I've been busy training and helping the former slaves as they transition to free citizens. At some point, I would like to go into Gohar and assist it in establishing self-governance. But for the moment, I'm content." Tikran had offered her a multitude of titles and positions, but she'd needed time to process...everything. She wanted to settle into her new role as captain of the Manzakar flight archer unit and figure out what she wanted to do with her life now that the laws were swiftly changing.

"That's wonderful to hear." He cleared his throat and gave her a jaunty smile. "I wanted to let you know that you are officially relieved of your duties as my courtesan."

She laughed. "It took you ten months to decide I was so terrible at them that you had to get rid of me?"

His cheeks reddened a little. "Hardly. I'd happily keep you on."

She wasn't sure how to answer. She searched his face. "Why?"

"Because I enjoy your company."

"And what would we do now that there isn't a dangerous husband to hide from or a rebellion to foment?" she asked playfully, a hand on her hip and an eyebrow raised.

He shrugged. "Whatever you wanted." She looked down, even more unsure of what to say, and he added, "Perhaps you could teach me some flight archery. I, in turn, could teach you to play polo. It's all the rage with us silk-stockings, you know."

"Ha! That sounds perfect," she replied, her discomfort falling away. Her eyes focused past him for a moment and she saw Tikran and Naran standing together, their backs to her. "Lord Revaz, would you excuse me? I want to harass a couple of friends while they try to look important."

He laughed and bowed. "Of course."

She made her way around clusters of conversation, her eyes on her boys. As she approached, she saw that they spoke to Lord Prem and what appeared to be his daughter. The woman had an arm around a boy, Gohari by the looks of him. She wondered what it was all about when Naran crouched before the child, taking his hand. The boy smiled, flashing a deep dimple in one cheek, and Coxani's heart stopped.

No.

She came to a sudden halt, transfixed by the sight before her. Her eyes drifted to the young woman, who was gazing adoringly at Naran, her eyes glistening with tears.

Oh, Cenk.

Coxani took a few steps to the side so that she could see Naran's face. He looked like he'd been struck by lightning yet managed to smile kindly at the boy as he spoke. Then Coxani looked at Tikran's face and her worst fears were immediately confirmed. Tikran had that look, the one he got when he spoke of injustice; his brow slightly knit, small, tense wrinkles around his eyes, and a jaw that compulsively flexed. He saw her and froze. She quickly turned and strode from the great hall.

Coxani rushed to her palace suite. Tikran had offered her a house, but she chose to reside in the palace instead. Gohari women could not yet own property and she wanted to wait until it became reality. She wanted to *own* her house legally. Naran owned a house and had been hinting at having her move in, but she'd demurred. It wasn't that she feared a scandal—she'd stopped worrying about that long ago. She cared about Naran, but...things in Anzor had not changed enough for her to be ready for something serious—with anyone. In her chambers, she threw on her training uniform and hurried to the royal stables. She needed to think, and there was no better place than on the back of a galloping horse.

She rode to the hippodrome where several Manzakars still trained. Tikran had been born mid-winter, it occurred to her as she breathed deeply, the cold air burning her lungs. She had no idea when her own birthday was.

She did a few laps, deep in thought. The boy was clearly Naran's. And now that the law against intermarriage and the mixing of bloodlines had been repealed, Prem could come clean about the boy's true identity. The young woman appeared to be Naran's age. She could now escape Cenk's temple, but her reputation was certainly tarnished. *I know plenty about that.* As an aristocrat, she likely didn't have any desire to face life on her own, and finding a lord to marry her would be difficult, unfortunately. What made most sense for her was to marry the father of her child, who now happened to be respected, admired, and, after Tikran, the commander of Anzor's Manzakar forces. Lord Prem clearly understood that, and the woman herself seemed eager enough.

Perhaps most significantly, Lord Prem had been one of two votes that had tipped the scale in the rebellion's favor. Losing his support would be dangerous, as there were plenty of Anzori noblemen who were displeased with having a Manzakar king.

Well. There you have it.

She was too shocked to cry, a feeling of eerie calm settling over her. She did not want to speak to Naran tonight. Or even tomorrow. She just wanted to disappear. Where could she go where they wouldn't find her?

Chief Justiciar Revaz.

She rode back to the Citadel and through the streets until she reached Revaz's city home. He was likely still at the party, but she would wait. A Gohari servant let her in, seated her in the garden, and asked if she wanted something to drink. Coxani said, "Xew, please." *A lot of it.* The xew was brought and she had thrown back a bit more than a glass by the time Revaz arrived. His eyes widened when he entered the garden and saw her.

"Coxani, both King Tikran and Commander Naran are looking for you," he said.

"I don't want to deal with them right now, please," she said. "I need someone to talk to who isn't either of them."

Revaz pulled up a chair next to her and sat. "What's this about, then?"

"I don't want to talk about it."

"Ah." Revaz folded his hands in his lap. "Is there anything I can do to help?"

The xew was definitely working. She dropped her head to his shoulder, relaxed by how he still smelled of ginger and bergamot. She heard herself say, "Why are men so stupid?"

This elicited a snorting laugh from him. "This is about a man, then." When she was silent, he said, "Perhaps one of the men looking for you?"

"It doesn't matter. All men are stupid."

"That sounds like the xew talking."

She lifted her head, feeling a spark of anger. "We women live within these intolerable constraints. We must be well-mannered, and pretty, and obedient, and get married, and have children. Men get the world. Is it too much to ask that they not bed every woman in sight?"

Revaz's eyebrows were at his hairline. "This is definitely getting personal. You're obviously speaking of one particular individual. I've gotten to know Tikran fairly well these past ten months and I doubt you speak of him. So I must assume you speak of Commander Naran."

She snapped him an angry look. "Would you stop being the bloody law enforcer for five minutes?"

He stifled a smile. "It's my job." She groaned and hid her face in her hands. He said, "Coxani, if I may, I think you should talk to him about your feelings."

"There's no point," she said. "He got Lord Prem's daughter pregnant years ago. They had to hide the boy. The law has been repealed. And Lord Prem is the reason that any of us are alive."

Revaz rubbed his chin as he pieced together what she was saying. Finally he said, "I see."

"I haven't slept with him," she blurted, her mouth moving even as her mind screamed at her to stop talking. *Holy Cenk, why am I telling him this?* "I haven't been ready. I'm scared. It's a long story."

Revaz went fully red. "I...am certain you... Perhaps we should stop drinking." He took her glass of xew and tossed its contents in a rosebush. After taking a deep breath and staring down at the ground for a moment, he said, "I stand by what I said earlier. You should talk to him."

She shook her head, the alcohol goading her past her embarrassment. "I'm not ready." After a beat, she said, "You've been very good to me, my lord. Without you, the rebellion likely wouldn't have succeeded."

"It would have succeeded eventually," he said. "The rebellion was inevitable."

She tilted her head to look up at him. Her mind was foggy but she spoke the next words deliberately. "May I kiss you?"

The color in his face did not subside. He looked utterly wrecked. "Coxani, you've been drinking and seem vulnerable at the moment. It would be—"

"Holy shit, you simply *can't* be this perfect," she said, her voice gruff and laced with frustration. "Would you *shut up* and just answer my question?"

He sat there, stunned, his mouth open and eyes wide. Then he muttered, "Yes. My answer is yes." His eyes were on her mouth as she gripped his shoulders and pulled him toward her. Her kiss was gentle and his response tentative, as if he wasn't sure she actually wanted him to kiss her back. She looped her arms around his neck and pressed herself against him, finally feeling him relax into the kiss. As she let out a small sigh, a voice interrupted.

"My Lord Revaz?" A eunuch cleared his throat, standing half turned at the entrance to the garden. Coxani and Revaz lurched apart. The eunuch kept his head turned away. "Forgive me for interrupting, but...the king is here."

CHAPTER 3

Revaz appeared at the door looking flustered. A stray lock of hair escaped his usually impeccably coiffed hair and his face was rosy. "Your Highness."

Tikran sucked in his breath. *You've got to be kidding me.* Only one person could possibly cause a man as composed as Revaz to look so unnerved. She had to be there. He said, "Lord Revaz, I apologize for bothering you at this late hour, but I was wondering—"

Coxani poked her head out from behind Revaz, scowling. "I don't want to talk to him."

Tikran exhaled. "He's not here, Coxani. It's just me. May I escort you back to the palace? I promise you won't have to deal with Naran."

Coxani nodded, turning briefly to thank Revaz for letting her hide, however briefly, with him. Her eyes were bloodshot but Tikran doubted it was from crying. He knew her too well. She must have had quite a bit of xew. They mounted their horses and headed back to the palace in silence. Eventually, she said, "How did you know where to look for me?"

"Revaz sought you out at your first choosing party. You spent a lot of time with him during the rebellion. I've gotten to know him better these past ten months and he speaks of you often." He looked at Coxani. "You're clearly good friends and I suspect the man is in love with you."

"I don't think so," she muttered. "I think he's in love with the idea of being in love with me."

Tikran shrugged. "In any case, I thought you might seek refuge with him."

She looked at her hands. "Has Naran married Prem's daughter yet?"

"Coxani, Naran is under no obligation to marry anyone."

"But Lord Prem—"

"Hang Lord Prem," Tikran said in a low voice. "I want the man on my side, but I'm not sacrificing my best friends' lives for his support." She looked at him then, her eyes brimming with tears. He said, "Oh, no. Please don't start crying now."

"Okay," she said, gulping back her sob. After a deep breath, she asked, "Where's Naran?"

Tikran sighed. "I told him that I thought I knew where you were, but that if I was right, it meant you didn't want to talk to him. I told him to go home."

"Is he okay?"

"No." Tikran pursed his lips. "But he will be, once you talk to him."

"I can't—"

"Not tonight, Coxani. You need to get some sleep." He rubbed his face. "Holy Cenk, what a night."

When they finally got back to the palace, Coxani stood before him, her eyes enormous. "Tikran, can I please stay with you tonight? I don't want to be alone."

"Of course," Tikran said miserably. It wasn't that he didn't want her around. Quite the contrary. But it bothered him that she only wanted to stay with him because she was upset over Naran, and not solely because she wanted his company.

In his bedchamber, she stumbled as she kicked off her boots, threw off her jacket, and climbed into his bed, falling into the softness with a groan. Tikran rubbed his face for the fifth time that evening, at least. *Well, shit.* She was clearly in the mood to torment as many men as possible—Naran, Revaz, and now him. He removed everything but his breeches, extinguished the light, and flopped down on the couch across from the bed. He clamped his eyes shut and said, "Naran's madly in love with you, you know." He said it almost as much for his benefit as for hers.

She grunted. "Too bad the man can't keep his breeches on."

"It happened nine years ago."

"He was old enough to know better."

Tikran chuckled. "Neither one of us has the right to criticize him, Coxani."

She was quiet for a moment then mumbled, "You're more right than you know."

He blinked in the darkness. "What does that mean?"

"Good night, Tikran," she said softly.

He frowned, wiggling in an attempt to get comfortable on the brocade-upholstered settee. He wanted to dwell on her words but exhaustion crept over him and his eyelids drooped. He was asleep within seconds.

After what felt like five minutes but was actually a good five hours, he was awakened by Coxani's frantic gasp. "Tikran!"

"Wha—?" He nearly fell off the couch, still half asleep.

"Someone is banging on the door," she said, diving beneath the covers.

He stood and stumbled toward the door, muttering, "Aren't you a Manzakar? What are you afraid of?" He opened the door to see Naran, his nostrils flaring, lip curled over his teeth, and shoulders around his ears, looking very much like his namesake. Tikran was suddenly wide awake, his fight-or-flight instincts kicking in. He ducked just as Naran's fist swiped over his head. Tikran lunged shoulder-first into Naran's gut and the two men flew out into the corridor, slamming against the stone wall and grunting in unison. Naran growled, hurtling Tikran back into the bedchamber with brute strength, then attempted to pounce on him. But Tikran was both nimble and very familiar with Naran's fighting style. He leaped out of the way then flung himself across Naran's back.

"Stop it, you idiots!" Coxani screamed, hovering over them. "Stop it now!"

Naran grappled his way back on top and pinned Tikran to the ground with his hands and knees. Rather than continue fighting, Tikran opened his hands. "Naran. Have you lost your mind?" he said, panting.

Moving a knee to Tikran's chest, Naran said, "You really have the nerve to take Coxani to your bed after putting me under house arrest?"

"He didn't take me—" Coxani paled. She looked at Tikran. "You did *what?*"

Tikran bared his teeth at Naran. "You were going to tear up the city looking for her. You needed to calm down. I told you I knew where she was."

"And you wouldn't tell me." Naran leaned harder. "Instead, you put Manzakars on me."

Tikran's voice was strained from the weight of Naran pressing down on him. "I could tell...she didn't...want to talk...to you."

"Naran, get off of him," Coxani said brusquely.

Naran didn't relent. "You want her for yourself, you self-right-eous bastard."

Coxani smacked Naran's arm. "I said get *off* him."

There were Aslans in the room now. They grabbed Naran and pried him off Tikran, who stood unsteadily, rubbing his chest. "Let him go," Tikran said. "I can handle him."

The soldiers obeyed and released Naran, who immediately threw his fist into Tikran's face, landing a solid punch to the king's left eye. The Aslans once again jumped in and restrained the big Manzakar as Tikran reeled.

"Tikran, Naran, Coxani." Haydar stood before them, glowering. "In my office. *Now.*"

THE THREE MANZAKARS sat on a couch sullenly. Coxani sat between the two men, folded on herself tightly, as if trying to get as far away from the both of them as possible. Tikran held a cold, poulticed washcloth to his eye, his face burning with shame. Haydar stood before them, his arms crossed and expression fierce.

"I don't think I need to tell you how embarrassed I am by your behavior," he said. He looked meaningfully at each of their faces. "All three of you. I vouched for you. I've spent a good part of my life vouching for you. And you are doing a spectacular job of discrediting me."

"Lord Haydar, it was all my fault," Coxani said. "I was upset and drank far too much and—"

"Coxani, you are excused for the moment," Haydar said. "I will summon you shortly. I need to speak to these two privately."

"Yes, my lord." Coxani stood and left the chamber without looking at either of the men beside her. Naran watched her leave, his face lined with desperation.

Haydar waited a few beats after the door shut before turning on Tikran and Naran. "A king and his commander brawling like boys in the schoolyard—over a girl. What in Cenk's name were you thinking?"

Tikran winced. *When he puts it like that...* "Lord Haydar, Coxani was understandably distraught—"

"It was between me and Coxani," Naran said in a low voice, his eyes flashing angrily at Tikran. "You were meddling where you didn't belong because you're jealous."

Tikran sat upright. "Jealous? Of you?"

"Yes," Naran said, his lip curling. "She ultimately chose *me*. I don't think you believed she would, but she did, and you can't handle it, Caged Kingfisher. Yes, I said *caged*. Because you're still in that cage."

Tikran lowered the washcloth and made a fist. The next words out of his mouth were both cruel and untrue, but his anger flared. "Maybe I *should* insist you marry Lord Prem's daughter, then. It sure would make my life a whole lot easier. I'd get Coxani, Prem's unwavering support, and you'd learn to keep it in your breeches."

Naran spoke through his teeth. "You had your chance with her. She doesn't want you. And enough with the whole keeping it in my breeches—you've screwed up just like I have, so stop acting like you're better than me."

Tikran furrowed his brow. "What are you talking about?"

"Naran," Haydar said firmly, "please leave. I need to speak to Tikran alone. But don't wander too far, because I want to speak with you afterward."

Naran wasted no time standing and striding out the door, letting it slam behind him. Tikran's eye throbbed painfully as he tried to parse Naran's words. Haydar rubbed his face. "Tikran. Putting Naran under house arrest was wrong."

"I was trying to protect Coxani," Tikran said. "And Revaz, for that matter. Naran would have broken every bone in that man's body if he'd discovered Coxani at his house."

"That doesn't change the fact that you abused your power as king to meddle in Naran and Coxani's affairs," Haydar said. "Your reasons might have been entirely noble, contrary to what Naran believes, but it still doesn't make it right."

"They *were* noble," Tikran insisted. "I'm not jealous of Naran. Well, maybe a little. But I'm certainly not trying to take Coxani for myself. I want them both to be happy. It's all I've ever wanted for either of them."

Haydar looked him in the eyes. "Tikran, you need to snap out of this. Too much depends on you taking charge of your role as king and you have yet to do it. You need to remember how you got here, what compelled you to react to the world around you. All the strides we've made can be undone in the blink of an eye without a leader who embraces his position with everything he is."

"Maybe I'm not ready," Tikran said, feeling wretched.

"Lad," Haydar said, "you need to find the will to be ready, and soon. The world won't wait patiently for you." He let out his breath. "I have a couple of things to take care of before we meet with the council. I suggest you speak to Naran before I do."

But Tikran was still angry. His friend had said things that had both wounded and confounded him. He stood and left the room, the now-warm washcloth dangling from his hand. He hadn't walked entirely down the corridor before he saw Naran leaning against the wall, his arms crossed, a foul expression on his face. Tikran's body immediately tensed for a fight. As he approached, he said, "Naran. What I did was wrong. I'm sorry. And I want you to know that...we just slept."

Only Naran's eyes moved. After a moment, he said, "I know. Coxani gave me the what for."

"Listen," Tikran said, "I admit to being somewhat jealous of you. But not because Coxani chose you. I've only ever wanted happiness for the both of you. I'm jealous because you have someone like her who loves you so entirely." He frowned. "And because you don't have to be king. You get all the admiration and glory without the weight of the entire kingdom and beyond on you."

He saw Naran's expression soften. After a long silence, the yellow-haired Manzakar said, "I'm sorry about your eye."

"Yeah. I probably deserved it," Tikran said, finally relaxing his muscles. "I'm a complete disaster."

"We all are," Naran said, dropping his head against the wall. "The reason we are where we are is because you managed to get it together enough to get us here."

Tikran snorted. "Right. Whatever that means. You don't need to flatter me."

"When have I ever flattered you?" Naran looked down at the floor. "It's been you all along, Tikran. Your outrage, your passion. None of this would have happened without you. And I know you feel overwhelmed and hopeless. But you got us here. I believe—we all believe—you can get us beyond."

"Yeah, well. I'll have a black eye for a bit of that, won't I?" He tried to smile as he walked away, feeling desperately alone.

WITH A BIG PUFF, Coxani dropped down to a bench in the royal gardens. She'd just come back from apologizing to Lord Revaz for her unforgivable behavior the previous night. *What was I thinking?* Every time she remembered insisting on kissing him, she cringed in mortification. He had been gracious, as always, if a little sad. *I'm a terrible person.* And then, to make matters worse, she'd crawled into poor Tikran's bed, as if he didn't have enough to worry about. She was the reason the king of Anzor currently had a black eye. *Good grief, Coxani.* She was a complete mess.

Now, she waited for Naran. She had agreed to speak to him after she'd briefly ripped into him for pummeling Tikran. She had thought about what she would say and had made up her mind. Now she had to follow through, despite those devastating amber eyes. She saw him walking past a row of pomegranate trees toward her and she took a deep breath. She could see the anticipation in his face as he sat on the bench beside her. Speaking quickly, she said, "Naran, I behaved poorly last night. I want to apologize for making everything so much harder for you."

Naran fixed his eyes on hers, making her resolve waver. "I need you to understand something, Coxani," he said. "I love you. Nothing will change that."

Coxani looked down at the ground. Meeting his gaze was more difficult than she'd imagined. "When Kadyr smiles, he's the spitting image of you. I can't imagine what that poor boy—or his mother—had to endure to keep his identity secret."

"I can't either," Naran said. "And all the while, I got to live my happy-go-lucky life without a worry in the world. I feel immense guilt."

"What will you do?" she asked softly.

"I've committed to supporting them both," Naran said. "And I'll be as involved in Kadyr's life as I can."

"I'm sure Lord Prem would prefer you marry Dinara," she said, looking at him.

Naran shook his head. "There's only one person I'd consider marrying, and she's sitting right next to me."

A lump formed in her throat. "I'm sorry, Naran. I won't ever get married," she said, realizing she sounded cold. She couldn't help it —she would not give him false hope. "But perhaps marrying Dinara is a good idea. It certainly would make things easier. And it would ensure Lord Prem maintained his support for Tikran."

"Coxani, look at me," he said, shifting his body toward her. Reluctantly, she met his eyes again. "I love you. Madly. Forever. I don't want to marry Dinara, no matter how much easier it makes anything."

She couldn't decide if she wanted to smile or cry. "I think," she said carefully, "that you need to spend time with Kadyr and adjust to this change in your life without my influence. I have asked to go to Dilovar with Tikran. I've been wondering what to do with myself, and this is an opportunity."

He stared at her intently. "I want your influence in my life."

"Many years ago, I promised myself that my life would never revolve around a man," she said. "Not a lover, or a husband, or a master. I need to figure out what I want my life to mean, now that I'm no longer a slave." Naran's pain was palpable, and she felt a sharp pang in her chest.

"If you need to do this, I won't try to stop you," he said softly. "But nothing will change. I will still want you as much as ever in a few months, years, or decades."

"I have to go," she said abruptly, the urge to start sobbing overpowering her. Without looking back, she rushed out of the garden, wishing she wasn't so complicated and difficult, wishing she could just be happy as a wife and mother—like a *normal* woman.

CHAPTER 4

Damir leaned against the doorway with his arms crossed, watching as Dorji, a fellow mage, walked the freshly acquired Gohari children very slowly through a spell. There were three of them, two girls and a boy. They did not have strong Essence, but they had enough to ensure life was fruitful in Dilovar. The girls were very young, no older than seven or eight, and the boy looked to be around twelve. Something about the boy's eyes, the way he quirked his mouth when he got the spell wrong, reminded Damir of Tikran, and he found himself rubbing his chest over his heart as if it would ease the pain that resided there.

Dorji turned, saw Damir, and said to the children, "This is Master Damir, the head mage and King Bilguun's royal physician."

The boy's face lit up. "You fought in battle with the Caged Kingfisher, didn't you?"

Damir nodded his head once. "I did."

"What's he like?" the boy asked, gazing at Damir in awe.

What's he like? Memories flooded back to Damir in flashes, as they often did at the most inopportune moments—Tikran's joy, his anger, his despair. Tikran loosing his arrows at lightning speed; sobbing quietly over Mago; standing at his trial, his hands bound, face fierce and unrelenting. Tikran's scent, like Gohar's long grass after the rain; his strong, callused hands; the way his nose wrinkled when he laughed; how he purred and relaxed his entire body when his shoulders were rubbed. "He's a brave and skilled warrior," Damir said, his voice wavering as he tamped down the intrusive thoughts.

"I hope to be just like him someday," the boy said.

Damir and Dorji exchanged looks. Of course the Gohari children had bad cases of hero-worship for the king of Anzor, the Manzakar who'd fought against Anzor's persecution of the Gohari. Would these future mages of Dilovar ever be truly committed to defending the kingdom—particularly against Anzor, Dilovar's historical enemy, now that the Caged Kingfisher ruled?

Freed Kingfisher. It was a brilliant change and no doubt Haydar's doing. Damir smiled to himself every time he imagined Tikran's coronation. The man who absolutely hated attention had become king. There was no escaping the constant scrutiny of the kingdom now. Damir spent far too much time wondering how Tikran was faring and if he'd found a new head mage. He also wondered if Tikran thought about him a fraction as often as he thought about Tikran. *Bloody constantly.*

"Master Damir, His Highness wishes to speak with you." An attendant stood at Damir's elbow, whispering quietly so as not to disturb the mage's lesson.

Damir walked to the king's personal library, where Bilguun was steeped in books. His thirst for knowledge was a quality that Damir shared and admired in the man, albeit one of the only ones. Damir bowed deeply. "Your Highness summoned me?"

"Hmm?" Bilguun lowered his spectacles. "Yes, Damir. Please sit." Damir obeyed and the king of Dilovar sighed. "Six months in Gohar, and we only managed to find three children with some Essence. It's not nearly enough. Surely you, too, see that?"

Folding his hands in his lap, Damir said carefully, "It's not enough for what, Your Highness?"

A smile slowly spread across Bilguun's face and he chuckled. "You're chastising me, Damir."

"Not at all, my king," Damir replied. "I'm merely pointing out that these three young apprentice mages are enough to keep Dilovar flourishing long after the older generations have gone. But I think you know that, which begs the question, what are they not enough for?"

"And I think you know the answer," Bilguun said gruffly. "We can't defend against Haldor with that. We can't defend against anything with that. We're sitting ducks." He slammed a book shut. "I have been sending troops into Gohar to find more nomads with the Essence. I have no choice."

Damir's mouth went dry. "You're breaking the truce?"

"Yes," Bilguun answered. "Anzor is in a state of flux, and no doubt fractious. Now is the time to assert ourselves. With any luck, we can find more Essence before Anzor's new king notices anything is amiss. And even if he does..." Bilguun shrugged. "He is in no position to win a war."

Anzor's new king. Damir inhaled sharply. Bilguun suspected Damir was much more powerful than he'd let on, and the Dilovari king was correct. The truth was, Damir hadn't thoroughly explored the extent of his Essence, mostly out of fear. What he'd done in Gohar while fighting beside Tikran...was more than he'd ever tried.

But Bilguun knew of it. Everyone knew of it.

He said, "Your Highness, perhaps we don't need to break the truce with Anzor. Perhaps we already have what you need."

Bilguun removed his spectacles, his dark eyes piercing. "Show me, then, Master Damir."

———

THE RIVER, black and icy, wound its way between the snowy mountains and through the valley that stretched out before Damir. He glanced over his shoulder at Bilguun, who sat on his horse several paces away, surrounded by several of his advisors and at least twenty soldiers. They were there to see what Damir could do with his Essence, other than grow food, light fires, make it rain, and apparently move earth. It had been Damir's idea. He wanted Bilguun to know that he was much more powerful than anyone thought, in the hope that the king would stop violating the truce with Anzor.

Because a war with Anzor would be devastating.

Of course, he didn't want Bilguun to know *exactly* how powerful he was—Bilguun would no doubt want to use Damir's powers against Dilovar's enemies, and the blood of thousands of innocents would be on his hands. There were certain powers better left untouched, hidden deep within him. He closed his eyes briefly, taking several breaths, and crouched along the bank of the river. He'd never tried this, but sensed he could do it. He removed his gloves and touched the damp earth right at the water's edge, kneading it with his fingers. The earth beneath him shuddered and the river began to stir, undulating in waves that steadily swelled higher. Damir was getting splashed now but he hardly noticed. He stared blankly at the suddenly turbulent river, focusing on the Essence as it flowed through him. He moved the earth beneath the water in sharp spikes until the waves themselves were leaping upward, cresting white, reaching heights of fifteen feet. He then dipped his other hand in the river, anticipating the searing burn within his fingers as the water froze. The ice quickly crept across the river as Damir continued to pull at the riverbed, making it rise sharply just as the waves turned to ice. They creaked and sighed as they surrendered, solidifying into tines, one after another along the length of the river, seaming it in half.

Damir pulled his hand from the earth. Even though he hadn't killed anything as far as he could tell, his hand ached. His other hand was frozen with the river. Once again, he called his Essence, this time for heat, slowly pulling his hand free of the melting ice. Bilguun stood next to him, a small smile on his face as he surveyed the barrier of crystal blades that separated one bank from the other.

"Why did you keep this from me?" Bilguun said, his voice low.

Damir shook his head. "I didn't keep it from you, Your Highness. I simply didn't think it was useful. My job thus far has been to create and sustain life in Dilovar, both as a mage and a doctor."

"The waves of earth you created against Delger's Manzakars... These pikes of ice, splitting the river in half... The fires you can blaze..." Bilguun narrowed his eyes at Damir. "These are useful in war. Very useful."

Damir bowed his head. "I'm happy to be of service, Your Highness." He was lying. He wasn't happy at all. *I'm a doctor, for Cenk's sake.* He'd spent most of his life terrified and repulsed by his powers, determined to use them only when necessary, and only for a good cause. But to pacify Bilguun, Damir would do what he had to do.

Even if that meant becoming a weapon of war.

CHAPTER 5

Anzor City, with its glistening spires and stone streets, left Tanith speechless. As she walked through the king's palace, she marveled at its high, painted ceilings, mosaic floors, and enormous windows. The panes were decorated with fragments of colored glass and created a spectrum of vibrant light that danced across the walls. *I wish Ayym could see this.* The entire Citadel was beyond anything she had ever imagined. She felt like her presence blemished the place.

As two hulking Manzakars led her into the great hall, she held her breath. Several noblemen sat at a vast table, the murmur of their voices echoing. The throne, gilded and intricately carved with droplet patterns, was empty. *I requested an audience with the king, didn't I?* No one in the room looked like a king. Not that she knew what a king should look like. Mantles and crowns and scepters, no? A bearded man with a dazzling smile approached.

"Madam Tanith, I presume?" he said, bowing his head politely.

Madam? As if she were nobility. *Ha!* She smiled stiffly and reciprocated the bow. "Just Tanith, my lord." It was disorienting, interacting with people who were clearly Gohari but behaved so completely Anzori.

"I'm Lord Haydar," he said. "Let me take you to see His Highness."

She followed, her eyes finally landing on a Manzakar seated in a random chair amidst the lords, one leg drawn up on the seat with an arm draped over his knee, presenting his profile as he gazed sullenly into space. Was this the king? He turned his head to look at her and she saw the three-inch-wide purple bruise encircling one eye. She also noticed that, enormous purple bruise or no, he was remarkably handsome. He had penetrating brown eyes (or eye, since one was nearly swollen shut); a perfectly sculpted Gohari nose, mouth, and jaw; and smooth, tan skin that glowed with the flush of health and youth. When Haydar stopped before him, she realized that this soldier who looked like he'd lost a fist-fight was, in fact, the king. She kneeled and bowed her head.

"Your Highness, this is the woman from the Sachin tribe who has powerful Essence and has been masking it," Lord Haydar said by way of introduction. "The mages have confirmed that she has it. Her name is Tanith."

Keeping her head bowed, she heard the king shuffle and arrange himself to face her. "Please...have a seat, Madam." He sounded utterly uncomfortable. She stood and looked at him as he seemed to debate on the correct posture for the occasion. He was definitely uncomfortable.

She sat on the edge of a chair. "Thank you, Your Highness, for having an audience with me."

"Yes, of course," he said, rubbing the back of his neck. "Lord Haydar told me you were seeking the position of head mage."

"Yes, I suppose... but I, like most Gohari, feel like I owe you my life for what you did. I just thought my gifts could be useful to you." Did she imagine it, or did his face color a little bit? *Archil, but he's young!* She stifled a smile. For some reason, the stories she'd heard made him sound more confident, more decisive, more...mature. And he likely *was* more confident when he was in the arena or on the battlefield. But being king was different, wasn't it?

"I only did what was just," he said, and she could tell by the way his knee bounced that he wanted to dash out of the room. He seemed to look her in the eyes, but didn't. He was looking at her ear. Or maybe at something over her shoulder.

She either had to get to the point or burst out laughing. She said, "I knew your mother." All discomfort fell from the young king's face. He looked her directly in the eyes now. She continued. "She had powerful Essence. I felt it from far away. Unfortunately for her, she wasn't powerful enough to hide it. So I went to her and warned her that the Manzakars would come for her. They'd been scouring Gohar for the Essence, and she was like a beacon." She could tell he was struggling to appear impassive. "I met you and your sisters. You were but a small boy. I told Gamze—I offered to take you. To hide you. At the time, I had no idea what my Essence could do. I just knew I had it and that I could mask it. She refused but thanked me. I can't blame her. I was a stranger. But just a few days later, we heard of her death. I returned to see what became of you and your sisters, and your father had sold you. He reassured me that the girls would be fine."

King Tikran was leaning forward in his seat, his eyes fixed on her face. "What *can* you do?"

She shrugged. "I imagine it's the same as the others. I helped feed several clans, more when possible. Calling rain was dangerous in the steppe, as it drew Anzor's attention. So I stuck with the earth, and what was beneath."

He suddenly rose from his chair and, to her astonishment, kneeled before her. He asked softly, "What *else* can you do?"

Can he know? She sucked in her breath and closed her eyes. "Terrible things."

When Tikran first laid eyes on Tanith, he saw a Gohari woman with light-colored eyes. Her complexion was a light olive, fairer than most Gohari, and she looked to be around thirty or so. She had a scattering of freckles across her cheeks and nose, beneath the thin, brown tattoos of a Gohari warrior. Her thick hair was plaited and adorned with beads or feathers. She wore the nomad's attire—a long sheepskin vest over a tunic, breeches, and soft leather boots. A frayed sack was slung across her chest and she gazed at him in puzzlement.

The moment she told him that she'd tried to help his mother he knew she had to become one of his mages. He didn't even need to see her use her magic. If she was able to mask her Essence, it certainly meant she was powerful. He only knew one other person who could do that. Then as she sat before him, he realized her eyes were a very faded blue, almost gray. *Almost like Damir's eyes.* And when he'd asked her what else she could do, her answer had been Damir's verbatim.

Terrible things.

No. Not just one of his mages.

Tikran stood and held his hand out to her. "Madam Tanith, will you be my head mage?"

Her eyes widened as she took his hand and stood. "Please, I insist you call me Tanith. Just Tanith. And while I would be honored, of course, I'm not schooled in magic, Your Highness."

"I will call you Tanith if you call me Tikran," he said. "And being schooled in magic is really only for those who need spells to invoke the Essence."

"Your Hi—Tikran," she visibly cringed as she said his name, as though uttering it without a formal title offended the gods. "You should know that I don't even know the extent of what I can do. I'm afraid some of those things are not meant to be done."

"We have an entire library here with books on the Essence. This will be your opportunity to explore safely," Tikran said. "I know a man as powerful as you. He's shown or told me the things he can do. Maybe I can help you."

She continued to hesitate. "I just don't know."

"What can I do to persuade you?" Tikran asked. "Bring your family from Gohar. They can live in the palace with you."

"That's kind of you, but I have no family." Her tone was very matter-of-fact. "They all died of the plague years ago."

"I'm sorry," he mumbled. "Tell me, then. How can I convince you?"

She shifted her weight from foot to foot and looked away. "Red isn't really my color."

Tikran grinned. "What *is* your color, then?"

She almost smiled. "Black."

"Lord Haydar," Tikran said to the durai, "Can we have a black mage's robe commissioned for Mada—Tanith?"

Haydar bowed. "Right away, Your Highness."

Tikran put his hands on his hips and raised an eyebrow at Tanith. "Is it settled then?"

She took a deep breath. "I suppose so." She looked around nervously, her hands worrying the frayed end of her sack. "I feel wildly out of place here."

"I've been here ten months and I still feel wildly out of place," Tikran said with a chuckle. "Let's install you in a suite. I'll have the attendants bring you a bath, then the tailor can take your measurements for a new wardrobe. Afterward, you can dine with me."

She nodded. "Thank you."

After leaving Tanith in her chambers with a bevy of attendants, Tikran walked back to the great hall feeling oddly enlivened. He'd found himself a head mage easily and she had powerful Essence. That alone made him feel lighter. But more than that, he dared to hope he'd found himself a companion, someone to talk to who wasn't an advisor.

Someone who didn't have other people who were more important to them.

Someone who wasn't the enemy's head mage.

He made sure they would dine alone in a private part of the royal gardens, beneath a grapevine-laced pergola. He had the chefs prepare the most popular Gohari dishes—roasted bustard, lamb with rice, pickled cabbage, and eggplant stew. No doubt she could use a good meal, slight woman that she was. He rubbed his chin. He needed a shave. And a change of clothes. As he hurried to get ready, he was keenly aware of how desperate he was for the camaraderie he'd had with Naran when they were younger, and Coxani before Naran had begun taking up all her time. He'd had it with Damir, too, but the sexual—and political—tension between them had overshadowed their relationship most of the time they'd spent together. Perhaps this new head mage would slake his thirst for friendship.

He was waiting for her when an attendant led her into the garden and under the pergola. She was dressed in a silk embroidered gown and her plaits, feathers, and beads—except for a single pair of black and red beads—had been removed. Her hair now framed her face in voluminous, untamed curls. Tanith was not conventionally beautiful; her most remarkable feature was the color of her eyes. Tikran bowed his head and smiled. "Feeling any better?"

She shot him a withering look. "No. Not only do I now feel out of place, but I'm wearing someone else's clothes."

This made Tikran laugh. "I'm sorry. I promise it will get better. At least that's what I'm told. Maybe some Gohari cuisine will make you feel more at home?" He gestured to her chair, pulling it out for her. She sat and he joined her as the attendants brought out the platters of food and filled their glasses with xew. He held up his glass. "To a collaborative relationship." Her smile was rigid as she clinked his glass and drank.

"By Archil," she said, her voice coming out as a wheeze. "That's strong enough to knock out a horse."

"It's an acquired taste," he said. "And it's definitely not something to swig. Don't the Gohari have a strong liquor?"

"Oh yes," she said. "Several. It was the only way to escape the fear and hunger for many under Delger's reign."

Tikran looked down at his full plate of food. "I can't imagine what you went through. All of you."

She ate her lamb and rice slowly. "Well, once I discovered what my Essence could do to the earth and water, things got better for me and my clan. I wish I had been brave enough to discover it sooner."

"When did you discover it?"

She sighed. "I knew I had the Essence my whole life. But I was afraid the Manzakars would find me, so I masked it and didn't attempt to use it until I was eighteen, about one year before I tried to warn your mother."

He did the math and was caught off guard. "You're thirty-six? I thought you were younger...I mean, you look younger."

She nodded solemnly. "It's infuriating. It's very difficult to command respect when everyone thinks you're younger than you are."

Tikran tilted his head. "You know, had I told an Anzori woman she looked younger than her age, she would have giggled and blushed."

Tanith scowled. "Anzori women have never tried to lead warriors against Manzakars."

Tikran raised his eyebrows. "And you have?"

"Of course. I'm a warrior. But the truth is, nearly every Gohari between the ages of fifteen and fifty has fought against the Manza-kars to some extent." She took a sip of the stew's broth. "I still have a visceral reaction to seeing so many Manzakars everywhere. It's taking some getting used to."

"I can imagine." The xew had relaxed him, so he asked, "From what little you saw, what was my mother like?"

Her expression softened. "Gamze was beautiful. You look a lot like her. She seemed incredibly strong. Fearless. I only saw fear in her eyes when she spoke of you and your sisters. She knew the Manzakars would come for her. She was not afraid for herself. But she was very afraid for you."

"Had she been using her Essence to feed us?" he asked. "I don't remember ever seeing..."

"Yes," Tanith said. "And after she died, your father didn't know what to do. He'd relied heavily on her to feed your family."

"I remember being especially hungry the months after she passed," Tikran said. "It makes sense now."

"I remember you and your sisters," she said. "Goodness, were the three of you beautiful. But you especially, with your big brown eyes and black curls."

Tikran's neck grew hot. "Not that it did anyone much good. I would trade them in for my mother's Essence in a heartbeat."

They ate in silence until Tikran felt her eyes on him. He met her gaze. "What?"

Tanith's lips quirked. "You know, I can make a poultice for you that will make the bruise heal faster, if you like."

"Oh." The heat spread from his neck to his ears. "Thank you. It's fine. It'll heal eventually."

Looking at him sidelong, she said, "Dare I ask what happened?"

Tikran sat back. *Why not?* Something about this woman loosened his tongue. He felt safe telling her things. Maybe it was the tenuous connection to his mother. Of course, the xew helped too. "My commander-in-chief has been my friend since we were little. Recently, we both had relationships with the same woman. Not at the same time. Consecutively. I was first, he was second—with my blessing, by the way. Anyhow..." He told her about the party, Naran's illegitimate and illegal child, and Lord Prem's support of the rebellion. At this point in the story, he was naming names and hardly cared. "Coxani definitely understood the situation and ran off. I suspected I knew where she was going and knew that, if I was right, it meant she didn't want to talk to Naran. He was losing his mind looking for her so I put him under house arrest."

Tanith's face was resting in her hand and her eyes were wide. She looked like a schoolgirl hearing the latest palace gossip. "You did *what?*"

"Yeah." He scratched the back of his head. "A mistake, I admit. But perhaps the bigger mistake was letting Coxani sleep in my bed."

"Holy shit," Tanith muttered. "You were asking for it."

He let out a laugh. "Agreed. Nothing happened between us, mind you. She just didn't want to be alone. But the next morning we were awakened by a banging at the door, and..."

"That's how you got the black eye," Tanith finished for him. "I can't say that I blame him."

"I know." He forked a piece of lamb without the intention of eating it. "I fucked up."

"Are you still friends?"

He chuckled. "I hope so. I think it would take a lot more than a few hours of house arrest to end our friendship."

They talked some more about Gohar as they finished their meal and, as they rose from the table, Tikran said, "You eat like a bird, Tanith. You hardly had anything."

She patted her belly. "Constant hunger makes the stomach shrink. But the food was delicious. I'm sure I'll be nice and plump come spring."

He walked her back to her chambers and said, "Tomorrow I can introduce you to the other mages and show you the library. Would you like that?"

She gave him an inquisitive look. "I would, but... Don't you have kingly things to do?"

He rolled his eyes. "Yes, I'll have to do those things too, but I'd rather show you around."

"All right, then," she said with a smile. "See you tomorrow, Tikran."

As he strolled back to his rooms, he realized that he was the happiest he'd felt since becoming king of Anzor.

THE CAGED KINGFISHER, *Hero of Gohar and King of Anzor, is lonely.*

Tanith sat on the stupidly soft bed, her mind reeling. When she'd decided to offer her Essence to the king, she couldn't have fathomed any of this would happen so quickly. She knew Tikran was in his early twenties, but she hadn't expected him to be so...*young*. She hadn't expected the position of head mage to be thrust upon her so soon, nor had she expected him to seek out her company—and seem to enjoy it. Perhaps most confounding of all, she hadn't expected to enjoy his company as well.

She couldn't remember ever letting the unbearable weight of her past slip from her shoulders. And yet tonight she had, for at least an hour. The man who'd had dinner with her was a far cry from the man she'd first approached in the great hall, his face downcast, his body language like that of a petulant child who'd been forced into something he didn't want to do. To complicate matters further, she couldn't reconcile either one of those men with the legend of the Caged Kingfisher, the rebel Manzakar who had led a small faction of dissidents against two thousand of the king's best soldiers and won.

She rubbed her face. It made sense for him to be so multifaceted. How else would he have accomplished so much?

Tugging the gown's straps from her shoulders, she shimmied out of the itchy Anzori dress and climbed into the bed. She lay on her back, a hand behind her head. *If only Ayym could see me now!* This, all of this, was more than she had ever hoped for. So much more. She'd grown up like most Gohari—hungry and angry. She'd learned to wield a bow with the best of them and she'd injured plenty of Manzakars. She'd come to accept that her life was going to be one big tragedy. She'd resigned herself to it. But now, fortune favored her. Who knew why? She had to collect her thoughts and plan her future. *Head mage of Anzor.* She had the king's ear, by Archil!

He shaved before dinner.

She closed her eyes and breathed deeply. King Tikran, she had to believe, was much craftier than she was giving him credit for. She didn't doubt he was lonely or that he might have enjoyed her company. But she knew ambition well. Tikran had ambition—and had to be cleverly playing everyone around him.

Including her.

CHAPTER 6

Tikran found Tanith sitting in a corner of the library, poring over some enormous tomes, her brow knit. She had been his royal mage for two weeks, and in that time had become something of a friend. He looked forward to talking to her after a long day of making decisions about troop deployments to Gohar and arbitrating boundary disputes between noblemen. What did he care if one lord had a fraction more land—with no identifiable resources—than another? *Are these rich assholes seriously bickering about this?* It wasn't like a tiny crust of land was making enough money for it to become a point of contention between two insanely wealthy lords. It certainly wasn't enough to bring before the king. No, the only thing that drove them was ego. And their egos were driving Tikran mad.

In any case, he was free of those things now. He could put them out of his mind until tomorrow. Tikran approached slowly so as not to startle her. "Mistress Tanith, are you busy?" he asked softly, with a smile.

She looked up and upon seeing him, said, "I was just reading about the Essence's effect on water. Did you know the more powerful among us can turn it to ice?"

Tikran's heart sank. "No. I didn't know that." Damir would

certainly have known it, would have been able to do it. Why hadn't he said anything?

"Tikran." Tanith was looking at him inquisitively. "Are you okay?"

He forced his face to relax. "Yes. I was just wondering if you knew how to do it?"

"I've never tried." She looked around. "Should I try it now?"

He nodded. "Let's go into the garden. There's plenty of water out there."

In the shade of an apple orchard, they sat together at the edge of a pool. Tikran raised an eyebrow and said, "Well, let's see it."

He could tell she was excited and nervous. Her cheeks were rosier than normal, her eyes brighter. She took a deep breath and dipped her fingers into the pool. Her gaze became absent, her breathing slightly labored. Tikran heard a small cracking sound and looked down. The ice invaded the pool quickly, creeping up the spout and freezing the water as it spilled mid-gush.

"My hand is stuck," she said. "Wait. I can...wait." After a few seconds, the ice melted around her hand enough for her to wiggle free. She looked at Tikran, her eyes wide. "By Archil!"

Her enthusiasm was catching. He said, "I'm sure there are a lot of things you can do that you haven't discovered yet."

Her breath came quickly. She was clearly surprised by her own ability. She said, "I've only ever used my gift to help people. It never occurred to me that I could use it for other things, like..." She hesitated. "...cooling my drink."

Tikran laughed aloud. "I guess that's definitely one of the ways it can be used. Surely you know about your ability with fire?"

She inclined her head. "Of course. It's one of the first things we figure out."

"Why is that?" Tikran asked curiously.

"Because it's the easiest to do," she said, a hint of mischief in her smile. "We humans generate heat. A lot of it, depending on the occasion. All we need is a bit of tinder."

For some reason, Tikran suddenly generated some heat

himself—in his breeches. He wasn't even sure why. Half a minute ago he'd felt abysmal, imagining all the things Damir hadn't told him, all the things Damir had likely chosen, instead, to tell Bilguun. But his body rarely listened to his brain. It was probably because of the playful implication in Tanith's tone and the fact that he hadn't had any sexual outlet in nearly a year. Good grief, he hadn't even had the time—or energy—to take care of things alone. He went to bed every night exhausted, passing out the moment his head hit the pillow. Then he awoke to find his body more than ready, only to be instantly interrupted by attendants and advisors and whoever else thought it was okay to burst into the king's bedchamber at six in the morning. He should put a stop to that nonsense. He was king after all. *Why didn't that ever occur to me?*

On the inside, he was still a soldier—following orders instead of making them.

He blinked hard several times and turned back to Tanith. "I was wondering if you wanted to take a break from doing whatever mages do to ride and shoot some arrows?"

She rose, wiping her wet hand on her robe. "I would love that. I've never gone so long without riding a horse before. Or, for that matter, shooting arrows."

After Tanith changed into breeches, Tikran took her to the training grounds outside the city. He expected to see Coxani there, but the field was empty. He frowned. Coxani had not been herself lately, and he knew it was because of the situation with Naran. She'd asked to go to Dilovar with him, and he'd agreed, on the condition that she talk to Naran. He suspected his friend was going to be a mess without her.

"Are you up for some friendly competition?" Tanith asked.

Tikran grinned. "Always."

She pulled her bow from its sheath and pointed at one of the targets of coiled straw wrapped in burlap standing before them, looking like it had seen better days. "Whoever hits dead center first wins. But it must be at a full gallop...and backward." She turned and indicated the big oak tree. "We can loose arrows once we're at a full gallop and past the tree there."

It was then that Tikran seriously assessed Tanith as competition. She had clearly been raised on a horse. She rode elegantly, as though the horse was an extension of her own body. Her bow was of an impressively high draw weight, and she'd told him she'd led Gohari warriors against Manzakars. She *could* be a challenge. Maybe. She may have been thirty-six years old, but she was still a warrior of the steppe.

He nodded at her. "Let's go, then."

At her signal, they kicked their horses into a gallop quickly. Tikran felt rather than saw the tree go by and immediately pulled an arrow from his quiver. He nocked the arrow to the bowstring, drew it taut to his cheek, twisted at the waist to aim at the target, and released.

Nock... Draw... Anchor... Aim... Release...

His arrow hit dead center first. Tanith's was right behind, by a fraction of a second. She was good. She was *very* good. He reined his horse around. "By Cenk, Tanith, maybe I should make you a Manzakar commander rather than a mage."

She came to a stop beside him, her eyes blazing. "They weren't kidding about you, were they?" Her hair was doing its best to escape the thong that held it. Her cheeks were flushed and her brow furrowed. "Did you go easy on me?"

He began to laugh. "I swear I didn't. I was afraid you might actually win. What would happen to my reputation then?"

"Let's go again," she demanded.

They went three more times. Tikran won three more times. She looked furious. With a smile on his face, he said to her, "Tanith, you have your Essence. Let me have my skills as a fucking archer, would you?"

She looked startled, then tossed back her head and laughed. It was Tikran's turn to be startled. He'd never seen her laugh before. He'd never even really seen her smile, other than the polite, wary, tight-lipped smiles she gave everyone. It was as though she was suddenly a different person entirely. She no longer looked like the world-weary Gohari woman he'd seen when Haydar had first introduced her. Her face transformed with that laugh, becoming something unexpectedly alluring.

Grinning at him, she said, "Fine. I concede this time. But I will tell you, I was the best archer in southern Gohar. Or so it was said."

"I believe it," he replied honestly.

After an hour of non-competitive target practice, Tikran suggested they take a break and sit under the oak tree. He tried not to think of all the fond memories he'd had under that stupid tree with Coxani and refocused his thoughts on the woman who was currently before him, looking more like a giddy young girl than a seasoned Gohari warrior or a royal mage. He said, "So tell me. Do you miss Gohar?"

Her smile faded a bit. She looked out across the field, leaning back on her arms. "Yes, I do." After a moment of silence, she said, "I was married at twenty-three. My husband, Shams, was brave and kind. I got pregnant. The child was born dead. A few years later, Shams was among a group of warriors who were killed by Manza-kars. I barely had time to spread his ashes to the wind when the clan was struck with the red plague. My mother and sisters died within days."

Tikran dragged his fingers through the grass, back and forth, back and forth as she told the story. He stopped now. "I'm so sorry, Tanith," he said softly. There were simply no words. She looked off into the distance, the sunlight hugging the curve of her cheek, the slope of her neck. Tikran stared, fascinated. Something in her poise, her aplomb even in the face of tragedy, was intriguing. By the time she looked back at him, he had stopped gaping. He said, "You know, I don't consider myself religious. At all. But I do believe that...they aren't gone. They are in every living thing around us."

She inclined her head, smiling at him. "That's definitely the Gohari in you talking." They sat in comfortable silence for a few minutes, then she said, "The Dilovari mage who fought with you against Delger's Manzakars. He could mask his Essence as well?"

"Damir," Tikran said, stifling the feeling of longing that welled up at merely uttering the doctor's name. "Yes, he could."

"He must be very powerful as well, then. What compelled him to fight with you? He must have had a stake in the success of the rebellion."

Tikran tightened his lips. She'd gotten right to the heart of the matter, hadn't she? He hesitated. "I'll be honest, I'm not sure. I want to trust it was because he believed in the cause. He is half Gohari, after all, and saw what Delger was doing to Gohar very clearly. But then I discovered he'd been communicating with Bilguun the entire time and...I wonder if his reasons were truly noble."

She was gazing at him fixedly, as if trying to decipher something. "You're very hurt by it, aren't you? You must have been close to him."

"Yes." He looked down, feeling that familiar ache in his chest. "He treated my numerous, never-ending injuries. He fought by my side against Delger's armies. He risked his life for me and my friends. But after he left to return to Dilovar, I started to think he may have shared sensitive information with Bilguun."

"What makes you think so?" Tanith tilted her head.

"Bilguun's recent actions are evidence enough. In the end, however, it doesn't matter," Tikran said, the pangs in his chest sharpening. "He's Dilovar's head mage. I'm the king of Anzor. That about sums it up."

Tanith fell quiet.

"We should get back," he said, standing and offering her his hand. "I've been gone too long. I'm sure I'll get mobbed by attendants and secretaries the second I walk into the palace."

DAMIR LOOKED up at the sky, assessing the rain clouds. *It'll do.* He glanced back at Prince Orxan of Dilovar and his men. "You're certain you've cleared the area of people, Your Highness?"

Orxan nodded. "If there's anything out there, it's just lost sheep and unlucky wildlife," he answered with a chuckle.

Looking out over the plain, Damir took a deep breath. His hands had been aching for days as he'd tested the limits of his Essence. Even when nothing died, the ache persisted. Perhaps it was the sheer violence involved—crumbling earth to raise craggy hills, agitating river water, and turning its waves to blades of ice... But it wasn't just the ache that concerned him. It was the fact that the more he attempted to do these things, the more he *wanted* to do them. It was something beyond a mere fascination with the magic; it was more sinister. He didn't like it all.

He lifted his hands, feeling the air as it flowed between his fingers. He focused on the Essence as it rushed through him and called the wind. What was a breeze became stronger, whipping about him, leaning the trees and flattening the grass. He looked up at the clouds, his eyes watering in the gusts of wind. He began to spin the air on itself in an upward motion, toward the dark clouds above. Soon the clouds themselves began to churn, rotating faster and faster as the spinning air tugged the moisture down.

A funnel of clouds dipped, reaching for the ground like a nebulous finger. Although it touched the ground far away from Damir and the other men, they all felt like they were being drawn closer to it. As it ripped through the plain, its column became dark with debris. Dust and dirt got into their eyes as they covered their faces.

Orxan was yelling something, waving his hand. Damir understood. *He wants me to stop.* As he turned back to his violent creation, he found himself instead thickening the funnel's width. His hands ached but it was a delicious throb now, growing more and more satisfying as his tempest grew. *I have to stop it.* He squeezed his eyes shut, forcing the magic to withdraw. He heard himself groan at the pain as the funnel pulled from the earth and back into the sky, eventually melting evenly into the blanket of clouds above. The wind died abruptly, eerily.

Damir sank down to the ground, feeling drained, his hands throbbing. He felt Orxan's hand on his shoulder. "Damir, are you all right?" The prince frowned at the sky. "That was some dangerous conjuring. No doubt my father will be pleased."

Damir grimaced, his entire body aching. "Prince Orxan, I'm not sure—"

"You look downright sick," Orxan said, slipping a hand under Damir's arm and lifting him to his feet. "Let's get you back to the palace."

Damir rode back to the palace with Orxan, feeling terrible. He looked at his hands. This was some dark magic. How could something that was meant to bring life take it away so easily? Why did it feel *so good* to destroy? He opened and closed his hands, swallowing. He was strong. He could learn to control the urge to destroy.

He *had* to learn to control it.

CHAPTER 7

The steel blade of Naran's saber shone in the diffused winter sunlight as Kadyr gripped it by the hilt, waving it around and grinning from ear to ear.

"Easy," Naran said with a chuckle, closing his hand over the boy's. "It's very sharp. You wouldn't want to hit anyone or yourself with it."

Kadyr looked up at the man he'd recently discovered was his father with awe. "Can you cut someone's head off with it?"

"Yep," Naran answered. "With one good swing."

"Have you ever cut someone's head off with it?"

"No. And I'd rather not have to." He released Kadyr's hand and let him just hold the weapon steady. "I could teach you how to fight with a sword, if your mother allows it."

"Mama!" the boy yelled, swinging around.

Naran laughed and grabbed the hilt again. This time he pulled the saber from Kadyr's hands. "Careful. I think we need to find you a smaller, less menacing sword."

Kadyr ran back to where his mother and grandmother were seated in the shade of Prem's estate gardens. Naran followed, sheathing his sword. "Mama, Naran says he can teach me how to fight with a sword! Will you allow it?"

Dinara smiled. "I don't see why not."

The boy turned to beam at Naran as Dinara's mother, Lady Prem, stood and said, "Well, Kadyr, how about we wash up before supper and let your parents have some time alone?"

Naran cringed inwardly. On the outside, however, he smiled placidly. Besides, they wouldn't be truly alone—a eunuch was ever-present, hovering in the background. Kadyr was disappointed but went with his grandmother without a fuss. Naran sat next to Dinara on the bench.

"He's a great kid," he said. "You did good with him."

"It really wasn't me," she admitted. "I was at the temple most of the time. I credit Dilay, one of my father's former Gohari slaves, with raising him so well. After he was born, she was his nurse-maid. Besides, I think he has his father's temperament."

Naran blinked. How did she know anything about his tempera-ment? He'd remembered the single intimate moment spent with Dinara after wracking his brain. He had been eighteen and a newly initiated Manzakar, and they were together no more than fifteen minutes, if that. He'd been wandering the Citadel that night, intending to sneak into the city. He happened across two Anzori girls, one of which was Dinara. They were giggling uncontrollably, and Naran guessed that they had somehow managed to escape their eunuchs. When he greeted them, Dinara's friend nearly swooned. Manzakars were the heartthrobs of Anzor and Naran had taken full advantage of that fact. While her friend hyperventi-lated, Dinara smiled at him boldly. She ordered her friend to hurry back to their escorts and that she would follow. The friend obeyed and, the moment she turned the corner, Dinara approached Naran with clear intent. They found a dark alleyway and were done in the nick of time, just as the eunuchs were nearing.

And that was it.

He forced a smile. "You flatter me, but I think you're mistaken."

She smiled, lowering her eyes. "Oh, the daughters and grand-daughters of Anzori lords know everything about you Manzakars. We were obsessed with Manzakars long before the law was repealed. I suppose the forbidden aspect of it made it even more enticing. We would get all the details about you from servants and slaves, and we would play games where we would choose a Manzakar..." She stopped, blushing. "In any case, we knew things."

"I see," Naran said, smiling despite himself.

"We knew the Caged Kingfisher was shy," she said. "Although he was—still is—the most favored Manzakar among the girls."

Naran rolled his eyes. "Yeah, yeah, we all know that."

"But you're right after him," she said.

"Second always to Tikran," he said, smiling and shaking his head, feeling that familiar twinge of envy.

"Well," she said, shyly looking at him. "You were always my first choice."

Naran tugged at the collar of his jacket. It was cold outside and yet he felt overheated. "I'm truly flattered, my lady."

"I thought about you often," she said softly.

He looked at her, guilt sour in his mouth. "You *had* to think about me. You had a daily reminder."

She shrugged. "Well, yes, but despite Kadyr. I've always loved you, Stalking Lion."

He doubted that was true—she didn't know him. She was likely confusing love with lust. "Eh, Dinara—"

"Yes, I know it's ridiculous," she said, placing her hands at her sides, on the stone bench. "When I realized I was pregnant, I kind of...made a big deal of you in my mind, created a star-crossed lovers' story to ease the pain of it all. It helped me stay sane."

Naran hung his head. "I'm so sorry, Dinara."

"If I remember correctly, I was as willing as you were," she said, the redness returning to her cheeks. "If not more so. We were both young and stupid."

"And horny," Naran added with a crooked smile.

She laughed. "Yes. Most definitely that, too." She placed a delicate white hand on his. "Listen, Naran. I know my father is going to push you to marry me. He's all about reputation and social standing, and in his mind we have to pay the price for our mistake. But I want you to know that I do not expect the same from you and will not hold it against you if you choose otherwise."

Naran tilted his head to look at her. "Really? Even after I turned your life upside down?"

She smiled. "You gave me Kadyr. He's amazing. And I would argue I did half of the turning my life upside down myself."

Naran sat up straight and looked at her in admiration. "You women never cease to amaze me with your strength." Then he frowned. "But what will happen to you?"

She looked down into her lap. "I'll be fine. I'll likely be shunned from some ladies' gatherings, but nothing too serious."

"But will you be able to marry? Have a normal life?" Naran gripped the edge of the bench tightly with his fingers.

She began to reply when Lord Prem appeared around the manicured hedges, walking back from the manor.

Naran stood. "My lord."

Prem looked at his daughter. "Dinara, go inside and help your mother with Kadyr. I would like to have a private word with Commander Naran." Dinara did not look pleased, but obeyed nonetheless. Naran watched her leave as Lord Prem turned to him, his wrinkled blue eyes penetrating.

"Commander," he said. "Please sit."

Naran sat. He really wished he could take off his jacket. He was sweating profusely. "Lord Prem. I want to thank you for—"

"Naran," Prem interrupted. "I understand what you must be feeling."

There was a time when Naran would have believed it. That time was not now. He tightened his jaw as he bowed his head. "Thank you, my lord."

Prem slowly lowered himself on the bench next to Naran. "Commander, we all make our fair share of mistakes when we're young. Believe it or not, I remember being young. I'm incredibly lucky that I emerged unscathed from many of those mistakes. However, had one of those mistakes followed me, I'm certain I would have done the honorable thing and married the young woman in question."

I'm sure you would have. "My lord, I'm often on campaign. Marriage between us doesn't make sense. Dinara deserves better."

Lord Prem sighed. "That hardly matters, Naran. This is about her reputation. This is about *my* reputation."

Naran met the old man's eyes. "I'm in love with someone else."

A hint of a smile hovered on Prem's thin lips. "As I said, that hardly matters. So long as you're discreet..."

Naran felt bile rise into his throat. "Is that...doing the *honorable* thing, my lord?"

Prem chuckled derisively. "You're still very new to Anzori high society. In time, your priorities will change, if only out of necessity." He stood. "There are still many Anzori aristocrats who believe having a Manzakar king is shameful, that only an Anzori blue blood deserves the crown. I am not one of them. Don't force me to reconsider, Commander."

The scars on Naran's back prickled—something that happened often these days when he was unpleasantly startled. "That's a pretty blatant threat, my lord," he said.

Prem smiled. "Indeed. I understand you are heading back to Gohar's northern frontier soon. Perhaps you should take that time to think on it. When you return, I will expect an answer." He looked back at his sprawling estate. "Let's join Dinara and Kadyr for supper, shall we? I hear the chef has prepared his specialty in honor of your visit—roasted boar in a mustard caper sauce."

Naran stood, feeling like he might vomit. "Sounds delicious."

Riding out into the hippodrome, Tikran approached Naran with a challenging grin. His friend had just unseated three of their fellow Manzakars with his blunted lance and was riding around restlessly, waiting for his next opponent.

"Commander Naran, I challenge you to the lance," Tikran said.

Naran shook his head, his eyebrows drawn beneath his helmet. "I will knock you on your ass, Your Highness," he replied. "I don't care that you're king of Anzor."

"I certainly hope you don't care," Tikran said. "What would be the fun in that?"

Naran grunted, turning and putting some distance between them. Tikran immediately sensed Naran was in a foul mood, which meant he'd be harder to defeat.

"Hey," Tikran said loudly. "Is something bothering you?"

Naran said, "Yeah, Caged Kingfisher. You're bothering me."

Tikran blew out his breath. "*Still?* I thought we sorted things out."

"No," Naran said. "You becoming king has been a real pain in my ass."

Tikran's horse became restless, sensing its rider's energy. "I didn't ask to be king. You can't hold that against me."

"I sure can," Naran said, raising his shield and lowering his lance.

Something about Naran's anger sent a thrill through Tikran. It reminded him of their years as cadets, when their greatest concern was winning some silly competition. It was still a silly competition, but they were different people now—their faith in humanity had been diminished. They'd been beaten and tortured; they'd been blackmailed and deceived. Their hearts had been broken. They had gotten to know the enemy, who was just as human and flawed as they were.

Without any warning, Naran charged, his lance slightly couched along his forearm. Tikran swung around in the nick of time and the rounded tip of Naran's lance smashed against the iron leaves of Tikran's shield with teeth-chattering force. Tikran circled back, this time fully grasping the magnitude of Naran's anger. It *had* to be about Coxani, although he'd genuinely believed they'd cleared the air over the unfortunate incident on his birthday...

Both men rushed forward, and at the last minute Tikran

flipped his lance, changing his grip. He then lifted the weapon over his head, intent on stabbing over Naran's shield. It wasn't that easy. It was never that easy. Naran parried the blow and they both rounded back, panting like wild dogs. At this point, Manzakars, grooms, and spectators had paused to watch the match between their king and his commander.

It was then that Tikran decided to lose. He wasn't entirely sure what was fueling Naran's anger, but he sensed winning this battle would do no good. So as they charged each other again, Tikran shifted his lance and shield, opening himself up just enough.

Naran swung his lance to the side at the last second, roaring angrily. "No! Fuck! Why would you do that?"

"Because I don't want to fight you like this," Tikran said between breaths. "What's going on, brother?"

His nostrils flaring, Naran growled. "I told you I would knock you on your ass, and I meant it. Fight or lose." He rode a distance and turned back, charging immediately. Tikran used his shield arm to punch the tip of Naran's lance aside and thrust his weapon at Naran's torso, but Naran deflected the blow with his shield. Tikran raised and twisted his shield to protect the back of his head—just as Naran's lance smashed against it.

At this point, Tikran was fuming. *It's going to be like that, is it?* When Naran rushed him again from the opposite side, Tikran once again brushed the tip of the lance away with his shield and, as Naran rode past, took advantage of a gap that was left unprotected by Naran's shield to thrust the blunted tip of his lance directly into Naran's side. Naran grunted at the impact and swayed in his saddle. When the big Manzakar reined around, the look on his face was savage.

Tikran threw down his lance. "Are we done now?"

Naran dismounted and drew his saber. "No. You won't win this time."

"I'm done fighting, Naran."

"You just know I'll beat you at swordplay."

Tikran exhaled noisily as he slipped from his saddle. "Can we talk about what's bothering you instead?"

Taking two long strides, Naran loomed over Tikran, his eyes blazing. "I said, *fight me*."

Tikran met his friend's gaze, unflinching. He could see pain in Naran's golden eyes. "No. But go ahead and give me matching shiners, if it'll make you happy." He saw Naran's face flicker briefly with emotion and his shoulders sag, just a bit. Tikran said softly, "Let's go back to the palace and have a drink, just you and me."

Naran stood still for several seconds, seemingly debating, but Tikran knew he would agree. They went back to the palace and sat together on a balcony that overlooked Anzor City. Tikran had asked for all manner of beverages and small, shareable dishes, and ordered that they not be disturbed. Naran drained a full glass of xew in one swallow and sat back, frowning into the distance.

Tikran rubbed his chin. "Are you still upset about—"

"No." Naran sat forward abruptly, leaning his elbows on his knees and hanging his head. "Tik, I know we've done a good thing for both Anzor and Gohar, but it feels terrible on a personal level."

Tikran let out a laugh. "Tell me about it. I've been absolutely miserable."

"Really?"

"Yeah, jackass. I've told you as much." Tikran rolled his glass of xew between his fingers. "I'm a Manzakar, not a king. I have no idea what I'm doing, and I feel like I'm messing everything up constantly."

Naran's eyes softened. "You're not."

Tikran shrugged, desperate to refocus the conversation. "Naran, what's going on? You know you can tell me, right?"

Naran looked down at his hands. "Coxani has made it clear she won't marry me and hasn't spoken to me in days. She wants me to... I don't know. Prioritize? Which is stupid, since she is my priority. She always will be. But now I have this boy... I want to take care of him. He's my kid."

Tikran watched his friend's face carefully. "Did something happen?"

"Prem. He wants me to marry Dinara." Naran closed his eyes briefly. "He's basically threatened to withdraw his support if I don't."

Tikran's anger flared. He leaned forward. "I don't give a *fuck* what Prem does. You are in no way obligated to marry his daughter."

"Tik." Naran looked pained. "Coxani won't marry me. She doesn't even want a relationship with me. Maybe it makes sense for me to marry the mother of my son if it'll save you—us—trouble."

"No." Tikran felt sick. "This is *not* the world I want to create. I want to break down these archaic notions of aristocracy and slaves."

"It's not going to happen overnight." Naran looked away, his face creased. "And to achieve it, there has to be collateral damage."

"No." Tikran scraped his chair back. "If you want to marry Prem's daughter, then do it. But don't you dare put this on me. I'd do anything to stop you or Coxani from becoming collateral damage."

"You think I *want* to marry her?" Naran balled his hands into fists. "I can't have what I want. I'm trying to do the right thing."

Tikran was about to retort when Haydar burst onto the balcony. "Tikran. Naran," he said. "Captain Moti is here with news from northern Gohar."

Moti appeared at Haydar's side, his armor dented and dull with dirt, his cheek bruised and a thick, blood-darkened bandage stretched across his forehead. He kneeled before Tikran. "Your Highness. I'm...sorry. The Dilovari have taken Sitora."

CHAPTER 8

Controlling his Essence was getting easier.

Damir sat in front of one of the palace's many crackling fireplaces, watching the flames dance. He didn't feel as drained as he used to, even after some violent conjuring. More alarmingly, the ache in his hands while he was using his Essence was not something he could call pain anymore. It felt *good*. It was like an aggressive back rub—teetering on the cusp between pain and pleasure. The real pain came as he tried to pull back on his Essence and stop the magic. That particular pain had gotten worse.

It worried him.

Still, he felt confident he could stop his magic if needed. He hadn't lost his conscience, after all. And with any luck, he would never have to use it against human beings. Even the thought of using it against the Haldorans repelled him. The Essence was meant to create and preserve life, not destroy it. Of that, he was certain. Unfortunately, he was surrounded by people who hardly cared about the magic's true purpose. They only cared about their own power. *How typical.*

Damir called his Essence and touched the air in the room with its tendrils. This was a dangerous enchantment. Gone wrong, it could kill everyone in the room—which currently was just himself and his cat, Enlil. Yes, he'd named his cat after Enlil the Weaver, the name Lord Haydar had adopted during the rebellion. It made him smile to utter the rescued feline's name. Damir's fingers twitched, directing the magic to the fire. It was his mind that was directing it, really—but it felt more tangible to use his hands. It was something to do as the ache overcame them. That gratifying ache. His Essence now surrounded the fire, permeating the air around it. As completely as he could, Damir sucked the air out of the atmospheric bubble surrounding the flames, and with a strange sound—almost like the corking of a bottle— the fire was out.

Breathing in deeply, Damir looked at Enlil, who gazed back aloofly from where he sat curled up in an armchair, amidst Damir's books. Damir smiled. He could put out a large fire quickly. He could also suffocate pretty much anything that needed air. The thought made him shudder. Still, in a pinch...

"Master Damir," a voice said from behind him. Damir knew that voice. It belonged to Amit, one of Orxan's commanders and Damir's sometimes lover. The fact that he'd addressed Damir as "Master" indicated that this was not a personal visit.

Damir stood and turned. "Yes?"

Amit tried to keep his gaze professional but failed. Damir could see the heat in it. "His Highness wishes for your presence in the throne room."

"Thank you, Commander," Damir said coolly, sweeping past him. Damir knew that Amit intended to make a personal visit in the near future, otherwise he wouldn't have come bearing a message like a servant. He strode to the great hall and was let in by the guards. Bilguun sat with his fingers steepled against his lips, his brow furrowed. He looked at Damir.

"Master Damir," he said gravely. "Sit down, please."

Damir knew Bilguun well enough to grasp that *something bad* had happened. All his confidence threatened to abandon him as he sat, his eyes fixed on the king. "Of course, Your Highness."

Bilguun didn't turn to look at him. Instead, he gazed out the tall, lancet windows at the snow as it fell over the city of Ogedei. "I've deceived you, Damir. I hope you can forgive me."

"Of course, Your Highness," Damir answered by rote, his heart hammering in his chest. He immediately expected his worst nightmare: War with Anzor. He swallowed and promised himself he would stay cool no matter what.

Bilguun sighed, finally looking at his head mage. "I have been sending troops into Gohar despite our agreement. I understand how powerful you are, Damir. But to fight these Haldorans, we need at least two more like you. They've manipulated their magic somehow... They are getting stronger." He took a deep breath. "Unfortunately, a Dilovari squadron was spotted by the Manzakars in northern Gohar. There was...an altercation."

Damir was certain his composed demeanor melted away, revealing his dread. He said softly, "What happened?"

Bilguun stood, fixing his gaze on Damir. "My men have taken the fort at Sitora. At this point, we expect Anzor to respond with force. I need to know that you're ready."

Damir blinked several times, trying to clear his mind, trying to keep the room from tilting. His stomach lurched and he gripped the arms of his chair tightly. He'd been trying to prevent this. He'd learned to destroy with his Essence to keep this exact thing from happening.

Tikran.

"You took the fort," Damir said, his voice hollow. "You always intended to wage war against Anzor, didn't you?"

"The Haldorans have, for the moment, retreated from our border. Orxan suspects they are currently dealing with another northern kingdom and will be occupied for the foreseeable future. Now is our chance to make a move against Anzor." The king of Dilovar's face was impassive. "The Essence is a resource we will always need, Damir. Only the Gohari have it. Anzor's Manzakar king claims he will free Gohar, but the Anzori won't stand for that—Gohar is far too precious. King Tikran will certainly be overthrown."

"That doesn't make sense," Damir said. "The Anzori chose Tikran knowing he intended to free Gohar."

"The Anzori chose Tikran because he's an accomplished warrior and unschooled in politics," Bilguun countered. "They wanted a puppet who would keep Dilovar in its place."

Damir shook his head, a heaviness bearing down on him. "How can you be certain that you're right?"

Bilguun smiled dimly and turned to an attendant. "Please announce our esteemed guest."

Damir held his breath, his mind racing through the possibilities. The attendant returned, flanked by a handsome, russet-haired Anzori who wore a purple brocade jacket and walked with a cane, his uneven gait echoing through the hall.

"Hello, Doctor," Prince Vazha said with a smile, his blue eyes fixed on Damir. "It's been too long."

THE ROOM STOPPED TILTING—FOR the moment. Damir stood before Vazha, blinking in disbelief. After swallowing to wet his parched throat, Damir managed to regain enough composure to narrow his eyes disdainfully and say, "Prince Vazha. I'm deeply disappointed. You would prostrate yourself before your enemy to save your skin?"

"Damir," Bilguun muttered, his tone laden with warning.

"No, no, it's fine, Your Highness," Vazha said, his smile never faltering. "Damir is right. I am prostrating myself before you to regain my throne—which is rightfully mine by blood."

"The throne of Anzor is no longer rightfully yours," Damir snapped. "Your father failed you."

"Damir, the Freed Kingfisher's reign is unsustainable," Vazha said cautiously. "But I have a proposition that can benefit all three of us."

"Damir," Bilguun insisted, "sit down and let us hear what Prince Vazha has to say."

Damir lowered himself into a seat beside Bilguun, his icy gaze fixed on the prince, his hands trembling ever so slightly.

Vazha drew a deep breath. "Tikran had the support of the most powerful lords of Anzor against my father for reasons that had little to do with the Gohari's well-being. I expect you know this. They disagreed with my father's economic policies and feared Anzor had become too soft...too effeminate. The lords wanted their sons to learn to fight and become less reliant on the Manzakars. They thought that freeing the Gohari in Anzor from slavery would be enough for Tikran, and he would keep his mind on military pursuits and let the lords do the rest. But it's not. Tikran has become a real thorn in the aristocracy's side, insisting on reforms across the board. This push to grant Gohar its independence from Anzor is the final straw." Vazha stepped over to a pearl-inlaid back stool and sat, holding his cane between his legs. "The lords will no longer watch as Tikran directs the wealth of the kingdom toward helping slaves instead of ensuring the loyalty of the elite. But now, they face a war with Dilovar, so Tikran will remain king until that war is won. He is, after all, the best shot Anzor has at winning."

"We have yet to hear a proposition," Damir said aloofly, his arms crossed on his chest, ignoring the sinking feeling in his gut.

Vazha looked to Bilguun. "Your Highness, may we call him in?"

Bilguun waved a hand to the guards at the door. "Bring the young man to me."

A Gohari adolescent half hid behind the massive guards as he was escorted into the hall, his soft leather boots dragging against the tile with each reluctant step. He reached Vazha and stumbled forth, his eyes darting from Damir to Bilguun fearfully. Vazha murmured, "Genuflect, boy," upon which the lad immediately descended to his knee, his plaits swinging across his face as he bowed his head.

Damir couldn't help but roll his eyes. He spoke before Vazha had a chance. "Let me guess. The boy has the Essence, and you think you can dangle him before the king of Dilovar as bait."

Vazha's smile twitched. "You would be correct, Doctor." He set a firm hand on the boy's shoulder. "This is Berk. He's from the Davlat tribe. He has more powerful Essence than anyone in the southern kingdoms has ever witnessed."

Damir grit his teeth. "I'll be the judge of that."

"Stand, boy," Bilguun commanded. Berk rose unsteadily to his feet and stared at the floor.

"Tell His Highness and Master Damir what happened to your clan, Berk," Vazha said. Berk went rigid but remained quiet. He swallowed convulsively, his brow furrowing behind the locks of hair. Vazha ventured, "They were attacked by Manzakars, weren't they, Berk?"

Damir flinched. *What?* "Rogue Manzakars?"

Berk looked up then, his eyes flashing. "No. By order of the king," he said, his voice rasping with anguish. "They killed my brother. They burned down our yarms and took our food."

A surge of indignation sent Damir to his feet. "That's impossible. You must be mistaken."

Berk made a strange, strangled noise and shuddered with anger; the tremor began at his head, traveled down his body, through his feet, and sank into the floor beneath them. The earth rumbled, then the walls groaned. The intricately painted blue and white mosaic tiles of Bilguun's great hall rattled and shifted underfoot, causing Bilguun to grip the arms of his throne and Damir to stumble back into his seat. Cries went up throughout the palace and soldiers rushed to Bilguun's side, covering him with their shields. This was no naturally occurring earthquake—this was Berk's wrath.

Vazha tried to stand, clutching his cane with his gloved hands. "Berk, that's enough!"

When Berk continued to tremble, Damir pushed out of his chair, took two long strides toward the boy, and firmly grabbed him by the shoulders. "Berk," Damir said softly. "Come back before you kill people."

The boy's pupils shrank as they tried to focus on Damir. He gasped, his body falling limp in the doctor's arms. Damir caught him as the world stopped shaking abruptly. Somewhere in the palace, glass shattered as it fell. In the hush that followed, the soldiers dropped their shields and Damir exhaled, lowering Berk to the cracked, uneven tiles.

"He is very powerful," Bilguun muttered, straightening.

Damir glared at Vazha. "How did you find him?"

Vazha swiped dust from his shoulder. "After the Manzakars attacked the clan, Berk attacked the Manzakars—not consciously, I don't believe. But it was enough that my guards got wind of it. My...place of exile is not far from where it happened."

Damir almost snorted. "Place of exile? You mean your manor in eastern Gohar."

"For a prince who was meant to inherit the crown, it is a place of exile," Vazha replied, his face like stone.

As Berk's breathing seemed to steady, Damir asked gently, "What did you do, Berk?"

"I burned two of them alive," Berk whispered, his face pale. He pulled away from Damir and curled himself into as compact a ball as he could, considering he was mostly arms and legs.

Damir kept his voice steady. "With what tinder?"

"I don't know." Berk pulled himself in tighter. "It all felt like tinder to me."

Holy Cenk. Damir stood slowly and looked at Vazha, feigning indifference. "I hate to repeat myself, but we have yet to hear your proposed plan. Unless it involves using your young Gohari mage to destroy all of Ogedei?" Damir curled his fingers and the flames of the candelabra flared abruptly, casting a dangerous orange brilliance across the hall. "The boy may be powerful, but he has little control over his Essence. I, on the other hand..."

"Indeed," Bilguun muttered, his brow creased. "Prince Vazha, what are you suggesting?"

Leaning forward with both hands on his cane, Vazha said, "I will lend you Berk to train and use against Anzor. Upon Dilovar's victory, the Delger dynasty will be reinstated and we will each take half of Gohar."

Damir sneered at the prince and turned to Bilguun. "We are more powerful than Anzor now, you said so yourself. We could dictate the terms of negotiation without this nonsense."

"I'm afraid you're mistaken, Doctor," Vazha said. "Anzor has a new head mage, and reliable sources tell me she's as powerful as you are, if not more so." The prince's eyes gleamed in the firelight. "I am offering something Tikran would likely never consider, you know. And without Berk's help, Anzor and Dilovar are comparable in strength. You would lock in battle and lose innumerable troops as a war stretched out endlessly before you."

He has a new head mage. Damir dragged his mind from the news. He said, "Why would a king determined to give Gohar its independence set out to murder Gohari clans? There are inconsistencies—"

"I'm not done with my proposal, Doctor," Vazha interrupted, tilting his head. "After Dilovar wins the war, I am crowned as king, and we split Gohar evenly in half...Tikran's life is spared. He will be exiled to a place of his choosing and allowed to live in peace." He stared evenly at Damir. "Not only is this the only trajectory in which Anzor and Dilovar can maintain a peaceful relationship while both benefiting from the Essence equally, it is the only course in which the Freed Kingfisher is guaranteed to live in the aftermath."

After a long moment, Bilguun looked gravely at Damir. "I would choose half of Gohar over an endless war with Anzor. And if the Freed Kingfisher's reign is doomed, I would bargain with his successor."

Struggling to maintain his composure, Damir said, "We don't know that it's doomed."

Vazha stroked the handle of his cane thoughtfully. "Is it worth the risk, Doctor Damir?"

Damir set his jaw. Somehow the prince had unraveled him. He looked down at Berk and saw sad desperation in the boy's face. The doctor then turned his gaze to Bilguun, refusing to look at Vazha, his heart aching as though it had been pulled from his chest. "I will do whatever my king decides."

CHAPTER 9

A large, leather-bound manuscript lay open before Tanith as she sat cross-legged in the grass and peered up at the massive oak tree several paces away. Touching the tempera and ink illuminations on the parchment with her fingertip, she straightened. She wanted to try this, but a trickle of fear made her hesitate. Since she'd begun experimenting with her Essence, her hands had begun to ache. They had never ached before, when she'd grown food for herself or the nomads, or summoned groundwater to drink, or created fire for warmth or cooking. They had only ever ached like this once, and it was a memory she kept at bay. But recently they had ached when she'd raised the earth and created a great mound of crumbling rock that took the plants and bushes with it; they'd ached when she'd called lightning from the sky during a rainstorm and struck a tree. *Something about the violence of it...*

She took a deep breath and buried her fingers in the grass and against the ground, anticipating the ache before she began to call on her Essence. She felt the magic burrow into the soil and touch the roots of the oak, swirl about them and grasp them, coaxing them into movement. The earth beneath her trembled and cracked as the roots emerged, caked in dirt and slithering through the grass. They crept across and over anything in their paths, twisting around other plants and trees. The ache in her hands felt almost good now; she pressed her Essence further and the roots grew, curling, climbing, crushing.

She heard a vigorous shaking of leaves from the bushes beyond the tree and a deer leaped out from its hiding place, only to be grabbed by the reaching roots. Before she had time to even consider pulling back her Essence, the roots had enveloped the thrashing, desperate animal, tightening on it until it ceased moving. *Stop!* The ache was all-enveloping, tempting her to continue, to do more. She gritted her teeth and pulled back on her Essence with a hard yank, squeezing her eyes shut and yelling oaths at the flash of pain it caused.

When she reopened her eyes, the roots had receded back into the earth, leaving a trail of destruction in its wake. She rose unsteadily and staggered over to the deer; the tree had asphyxiated it to death. Its throat was turgid and purple, its mouth open and tongue hanging over its lips. *Oh Archil, what have I done?* The fact that she could kill wasn't new to her. She had discovered her ability to wither plants and drain water from the earth—as well as from animals and people—long ago and by accident and hadn't done it since. But this was a new horror, a new way to bring about death...

She heard hoofbeats and a woman's voice calling from a distance. She turned to see a Manzakar on her horse, approaching. "Mistress Tanith," the Manzakar said when she was close.

Tanith was tremulous and aching all over. "Yes." The woman Manzakar was stunning, with large green eyes in a heart-shaped face. "You must be Captain Coxani," she said, certain she was correct.

Coxani nodded once. "I am. Tikran needs you to join him as soon as possible."

"Yes, I can come now." She grabbed her book, mounted her horse, and followed Coxani back to the palace and past the great hall, where several members of the council discussed an attack by Bilguun's troops on a northern outpost.

"We finally have a warrior king who can lead Anzor's armies into battle and a head mage as powerful as Dilovar's," she overheard Lord Gennadius say. "If Bilguun wants a war, we'll give him a war."

War with Dilovar? Her heart raced. As a warrior, she was always ready. As a mage? No. She had just unintentionally killed a deer, for Archil's sake.

Inside Tikran's suite, she found him in a chair, one leg pulled up onto the seat, his elbow on his knee, and his fingers buried in his hair. She recognized that pose. It said, *I wish I were anywhere else.*

She sat on the couch opposite from him, taking a deep, shaky breath. "Tikran...I overheard what happened. Are you okay?"

"I'm fine." The deep line between his brows made him look anything but fine. He looked up then, his eyes softening as they met hers. "How did it go today?"

"You're asking me if I'm ready for war," Tanith said, avoiding the question. "Master Damir has more experience than I do using the Essence. He's likely far more prepared than I am."

"That's not necessarily true," Tikran said. "What he did during the battle against Delger's army was an exception. The Damir I knew loathed using his magic to destroy."

"Tikran, this magic is...unreliable," she said. She considered telling him about the deer, about the strange urge to continue destroying, then thought better of it. Who knew what he would do if he thought she was dangerous? She couldn't lose her position as his head mage. "When I do certain things that are violent or cause destruction, my hands begin to ache and I'm quickly drained of my strength."

"It was like that for Damir, too," Tikran said. "I think the two of you are more evenly matched than you know. That is, unless he's been preparing for war these past ten months." He dragged his hand through his hair. "I can't believe this is happening. I thought we'd established at least a short period of peace with Dilovar. In the back of my mind, I hoped Damir would help maintain it." The corners of his mouth drooped as he stared dully at the floor. "I'm becoming increasingly convinced he betrayed me."

"You don't know that," Tanith said. "You shouldn't let that impact your decisions."

"Nothing can impact my decision to do everything I can to prevent war," Tikran said firmly. "Not even the betrayal of...a friend."

Tanith fully suspected Damir had been a bit more than a friend. Funny, how Tikran was more Gohari than Anzori, despite his strict upbringing in Anzor. "You're a good man, Tikran."

He snorted. "Perhaps, but that doesn't make me a good king."

"You'll get there," she said. "I can see it happening."

He stood and offered her his hand. She took it and rose from the couch, feeling an unexpected rush of tenderness for the Manzakar king. She placed her hand on his face innocently, cupping his bristly jaw, intending to allay his fears with a motherly gesture. She opened her mouth to say something comforting but stopped as she registered the look in his eyes. It was a look she hadn't gotten in a long while from a man, but there was also no mistaking it. *Surely not.* How delusional was she? The young, ridiculously handsome king of Anzor couldn't possibly want *her.* Besides, she'd done nothing to encourage him...except, perhaps, what she was doing right then. She began to draw her hand back when he caught it in his, turned his head, and placed a kiss in her palm.

The feeling of his warm mouth jolted through her. She pulled her hand away, trying to coax her brain into functioning. She managed to say, "What?" *Brilliant, Tanith.*

He stepped closer, his eyes scanning her face. "I'm sorry. I don't know what compelled me to do that. But now...I really want to kiss you."

For some reason, she didn't step back. She couldn't believe what she was hearing and willed herself not to look at his lips.

Incredulous, she said, "I'm too old for you, Tikran. I'm nearly old enough to be your mother."

He rolled his eyes. "Twelve years is not old enough to be my mother."

"I said nearly," she said, her heartbeat pulsing in her ears.

He was close enough now that she had to tilt her head back to look at him. Tentatively, he placed a hand on her waist. When she didn't move away or protest, he slid his arm around her, pulling her against him. He said softly, "I certainly don't see you as a mother figure, I can tell you that much. But perhaps you still see me as the pretty child with the black curls?"

Archil, help me. No, there was no pretty child with black curls here. Everything about Tikran—from the strong arm around her, to the hard body pressed against her, to the musky scent of him— screamed *man*. She finally relaxed against him, resting her hands on his upper arms. She managed to say, "Definitely not at the moment."

He chuckled. "That's good enough for me." He ducked his head and brought his lips to hers. She was only aware of how the soft, moist heat of his mouth reached every part of her body. When she felt his lips part, she pulled back.

"This can't... What am I doing?" She could barely breathe. She'd been an adult when she approached Gamze seventeen years ago. She'd offered to watch over Tikran—who'd been a little boy of seven years old! *What am I doing?*

His arms loosened and concern wrinkled his brow. "Do you want me to back off?"

Say yes. But she couldn't. She wanted more of him. She shook her head. "No."

"Are you sure? I don't want to make you feel—"

"You don't, Tikran," she whispered, swaying toward him, dizzy with need.

"Good," he muttered as he tightened his arm around her and lowered his head again. This time, Tanith gave in to the hunger that he'd unexpectedly awakened, standing on her tiptoes and clutching him, responding to his kiss fervently. Her body vibrated at an elevated frequency, making her lightheaded. At some point she realized that the firm ridge pressing against her belly was Tikran's erection and she pulled away with a gasp, taking a step back. Bewildered, he raised his eyebrows. "What did I do?"

"No, nothing, it's..." She took a deep breath. "Tikran, it's been a long time since I've been with a man." Her cheeks burned. "A *very* long time."

"Oh," he said, a shy smile tugging at his lips. "Well. I imagine it's like riding a horse..." Tanith surprised herself by laughing out loud. He looked at her with what seemed like fascination, his eyes wide and mouth ajar. "You're unbelievably beautiful when you laugh."

He was not helping her cool off. "I'm...an acquired taste," she said, embarrassed.

His gaze was scorching. "I've acquired it."

He may as well have lit her on fire. She opened her mouth to say something—she had no idea what—when a firm knock on the door made her jump. Tikran scowled. Before opening the door, he touched her cheek, cupping her jaw as she did to him before. "Tanith, I don't care about the age difference or that you're my head mage or anything else. If, at some point, you decide you want me..." He let the words hang in the air, unspoken, and dropped his hand.

Then it was over and there were people in the room, talking about war as she stood quivering.

Nothing killed an erection faster than a room full of rich, old men —who had likely never been in a physical altercation, let alone combat—lusting for war. Tikran heaved a sigh as he sat in the great hall with the council, listening to them discuss the likelihood of war with Dilovar, how much it would cost, recruitment of militias, the supplies needed... Tikran half listened to the conversations. The other half jumped between two things—or people, as it were.

Damir and Tanith.

He was becoming increasingly convinced that Damir had betrayed him. Why else would Bilguun feel confident enough to send troops into Gohar and take an Anzori outpost? The thought hurt. Badly. Still, a tiny piece of him refused to believe that their time together had meant nothing to Damir. He'd *felt* Damir's love. Two competing beliefs waged war in Tikran's head, and he had to distract himself or go mad.

That perfect distraction was Tanith. What he'd done had surprised him almost as much as it had surprised her. It hadn't even occurred to him that he was attracted to her until they'd gone out and shot arrows together. Her skills were impressive and her joy was absolutely mesmerizing. He had the strange desire to make her permanently happy just to see that laugh, that light. Still, he wouldn't have kissed her had she not given him an opening by touching his face, real affection apparent in her eyes. And now he was having a hard time *not* thinking about her. He truly hoped she would take him up on his offer.

"...isn't that right, Your Highness?"

The entire council was staring at him. *Shit.* He looked quickly at Naran, who nodded his head subtly. Clearing his throat, Tikran said, "Yes, it is." Tikran exchanged subtle smiles with Naran. The question had been about forced conscription of able-bodied Anzori men and Tikran had apparently answered correctly. He made a mental note to revisit the issue and saw Haydar watching him, his eyes narrowed. *Oh, boy.* He had to get his act together. He blinked hard and leaned forward, trying to listen intently. He didn't have to try for long.

"Your Highness, our armies must march to Dilovar immediately," Lord Prem said, the loose skin of his neck wobbling with rage. The other lords pounded the table in assent, their faces twisted with anger.

"My lords, we will prepare for war," Tikran said, raising his voice. The men paused and looked at him. It was the first time Tikran had shown any sort of decisiveness during that meeting. He certainly wasn't afraid to speak against the council, but knowing that they saw him as somehow lesser made him suppress his desire to speak before them at all. Still, he said, "We will mobilize the available forces and reinforce the forts within Gohar. We'll also establish supplies to stage excess food and arms at those locations. Here in Anzor, we'll assemble Anzori militias and double down on training the Manzakar cadets." He drew in his breath. "I know Bilguun's head mage, Master Damir, well. I know Prince Orxan on a somewhat personal level. I intend to seek a parley. With any luck, we'll be able to negotiate something."

"The time for negotiation is long past," Gennadius insisted. "Force is the only appropriate response."

"You don't know what you're saying." Rage filled Tikran's body like an all-consuming fever. *Easy. You need their loyalty.* "Anzor and Dilovar are matched defensively. Both armies can move and entrench quickly. We would set ourselves up for eternal war over Gohar and the Gohari would ultimately pay the price."

The tip of Prem's nose reddened. "Your Highness, we must crush Bilguun entirely this time and without mercy."

"No," Tikran said again, more forcefully, still containing the anger that threatened to spill out. "War is still a last resort, and I won't even consider it until all other options have been exhausted." Consternation rumbled across the hall as Tikran stood, his pulse in his throat. The council hastily rose to their feet as he said, "This discussion has devolved into juvenile chest-pounding and I'm done listening." With that, he strode from the great hall.

His hands balled into fists, Tikran wanted nothing more than to punch something repeatedly. How had he ended up here? Why had he agreed to it? He was a soldier. He would have been happy with the role of commander-in-chief to Anzor's armies. He would have thrived, in fact, with Haydar as king. *And what about with a different king?* Tikran's pace slowed. He had no idea. He sensed that he could only follow a king with the same moral compass as himself, but how many possible options had that?

As he entered his suite, he heard Coxani's voice behind him. "Tikran, may I have a moment with you?"

He turned. "Of course. I'm just trying to get away from those—the council." He shook his head as she followed him in and shut the door. "It's as though they're playing a game of chess and not gambling with people's lives. It's infuriating."

Coxani sighed. "Thank Cenk you're king. Delger would have rushed headlong into a war without hesitation."

Tikran was pacing. "I just don't understand. Why make me king if that's clearly what they want? Did they expect I would rush headlong into war as well? Perhaps they thought that by making a young, ignorant soldier king, they'd be able to manipulate him?"

"I don't know," she replied, "but you're doing the right thing. Stand firm. No one wants an endless, costly war. They'll come around."

"Or turn against me," he muttered. "I need to prove to them that they made the right decision crowning me or everything falls apart. All our strides in Anzor and Gohar will go to waste." *And I could end up drinking poison, like Delger.*

He flopped down at his desk and looked miserably at the scrolls, codices, and ledgers that littered it. Haydar and the chancery staff would arrive shortly to write letters of pardon, record financial transactions, create charters for grants of land... He couldn't think of anything he wanted to do less. *But I must do it.* He scrubbed his face with his hands and looked at Coxani. "What did you want to talk to me about?"

She stood straight, her hands behind her back. "I agree with sending food rations to Gohar in return for military support. I think it will achieve two objectives—feeding the nomads and amassing Gohari forces. I would like to be in command of that effort."

Tikran stiffened. He wanted Coxani at his side, if only to keep her out of harm's way. At the same time, he knew she struggled with her place in court and desperately needed a purpose. He said carefully, "If you're sure that's what you want…"

"I am." The look in her eyes told him all he needed to know.

"Okay." He tried to hide his concern. "I'm going to send Captain Moti with you. He knows Gohar well and has many Gohari informants across the steppe. My sister, Bruneta, has been communicating often with me since the rebellion. She's organized something of a Gohari army, consisting of Sachin warriors. She'll be instrumental in helping you rally the nomads. I suspect the two of you will get along—she's a skilled flight archer and a force to be reckoned with."

"That doesn't guarantee we'll get along," Coxani said with a chuckle. "But I look forward to meeting her."

Tikran wasn't in the mood for banter. "I'll make sure you have everything you need in preparation for the mission." Coxani sat down in a chair across from him, indicating she wasn't about to leave. He asked, "Was there something else on your mind?"

She shrugged, studying her nails. "We just haven't had a good talk in a while, and I suspect that I've been replaced."

"Replaced?"

She looked at him, her lips pursed, before saying, "Your new head mage, Tanith. You're spending an awful lot of time with her."

He blinked. "She's my head mage. Is that so unusual?"

"Can you trust her?"

"Yes. She knew my mother. I absolutely trust her." Tikran folded his arms over his chest, frowning. "What, are you jealous or something?"

Coxani scowled. "Of course not. I'm just looking after you." She resumed examining her nails, continuing to scowl. After a moment, she said, "Maybe I am a bit jealous. It's just that we haven't really talked since she arrived."

Tikran raised his eyebrows. "Well now you know how I felt when you and Naran…became a thing."

She narrowed her eyes and slid her jaw to the side. "Three things. First, I have always made time for our friendship. Second, you gave Naran *your blessing* to pursue me, in case you've forgotten. Third, we are not a *thing*."

Tikran leaned his elbows on the desk, his head between his hands. "Coxani, are you really doing this to me now? Do I look like I need more shit to deal with?"

"Fine." Coxani stood, her nostrils flaring. "I'm leaving. Just...be careful who you trust, Tikran."

Tikran rolled his eyes. "You just don't want to see me get close to anyone, do you?"

Coxani looked at him for a long moment, a pained expression on her face. Then she said, "Suit yourself." She turned on her heels and left the room in a hurry, the doors slamming behind her.

⸻

As Coxani walked through the palace corridors to her suite, an overwhelming feeling of dread came over her. Nothing was within her control, try as she might—not Tikran, not Naran, not the fates of Anzor or Gohar. She wanted more than anything to run into Naran's arms and insist he hold her tightly. Naran's embraces were warm, safe, often stifling cocoons. At the moment, she would have welcomed even the stifling. But she couldn't do that to Naran. She had to follow through with what she'd told him she'd do, for him as much as for her.

She needed to figure out what she wanted before she hurt more people. Men, in particular. Good grief, how had she gone from a girl who lived only among women to a girl who lived only among men? All she'd ever wanted—

"Captain Coxani."

Coxani stopped and turned. Tanith had been walking behind her but stopped as well, several yards away. Anzor's new head mage wrung her hands, an uncomfortable look on her face. She said, "I hope I'm not keeping you from other obligations. If so, let me know. But I would very much like to speak with you."

It was then that Coxani realized Tanith must have been older than she looked. Something about her voice, her posture, the command of her expressions... Coxani kept her face aloof. "Of course, Mistress Tanith. How can I be of assistance?"

Tanith tilted her head. "I would appreciate some privacy, if possible."

"Certainly. How about my suite? I can dismiss the attendants," Coxani said, wondering what in the name of Cenk this woman wanted with her.

Tanith nodded. "Thank you."

Coxani led the way to her suite. Had her jealousy really gotten the best of her? She hadn't been jealous of Damir, even after she'd realized Tikran was in love with him. But the instant Tikran began spending more time with another woman, she apparently couldn't tolerate it. *Stop being such a judgmental asshole.* Besides, Tikran's relationship with Tanith wasn't romantic—the woman must have been many years older than him and seemed to be all business.

On the balcony of the suite, the two women sat down across from each other. Coxani folded her hands in her lap. "How can I help you, Mistress?"

"Please call me Tanith." The mage smiled politely. "As a newcomer, I'm a bit lost in the politics of the palace. With a war pending, I feel like I should know more about the various alliances within the court. I was hoping you could give me a summary of who's who. I would ask Tikran, but his time is limited. Besides, I'd rather a woman's assessment of things. Women tend to be more perceptive."

Coxani smiled back. "I generally agree with that, but there is one exception: Lord Haydar. He couldn't have masterminded a rebellion without his ability to read people. It's almost uncanny."

Tanith's eyes widened slightly and she leaned forward. "I wondered about him. I can see he and Tikran are very close, almost like father and son."

Coxani nodded. "Haydar bought Tikran and me as children for the express purpose of turning us into Manzakar rebels. Commander Naran as well, in fact."

"And he succeeded," Tanith said, admiration in her voice. "I know that Delger's heir, the former queen, and his sisters were exiled to eastern Gohar. The Davlat tribe was not thrilled about that, since it's their territory."

"Tikran would know if Vazha was making trouble," Coxani insisted, "and he would put a stop to it immediately."

"I don't doubt that. And what about the other lords?" Tanith asked. "Which of them is not to be trusted?"

Coxani broke down the alliances of the lords, hesitating as she spoke of Prem. She settled on, "Lord Prem is a wild card. He sided with Haydar to overthrow Delger, but his loyalty can be bought."

"Ah. I see. So definitely not trustworthy," Tanith said. After a brief pause, she said, "And what of Master Damir of Dilovar? Tikran has expressed doubts regarding his loyalties, despite what he did for the rebellion."

Coxani chewed on her lip. Tikran had told her quite a bit, it seemed. "I know Damir well. During the rebellion, he came to my aid more than once, risking much and gaining nothing from it. I, for one, trust him completely. I don't believe he would betray Tikran. I'm frustrated that Tikran himself even considers it."

Tanith continued to stroke her robe with her fingers studiously. "It seems to me that Tikran is unable to think objectively about Damir. I find that this occurs when two people are...romantically entangled, don't you?"

Coxani blinked. Tikran had apparently not shared that particular detail with Tanith. *Well, I'm not going to either.* "That's something you should probably ask Tikran."

Tanith smiled slightly. "I respect that answer." She looked out over the balcony and said, "So how will succession work now? Will it continue to be hereditary? Will Tikran begin his own dynasty?"

"That's a good question," Coxani said. "It was raised briefly in council a few times while I was there, but I don't know if a final decision was made." A strange feeling in her chest made her pause. She watched Tanith carefully. "Why do you ask?"

Tanith shrugged and waved a hand in the air. "Oh, I'm just

curious. It would be interesting if a dynasty of Manzakars ruled Anzor for generations, wouldn't it?"

"Somehow I don't think the Anzori aristocracy would tolerate that," Coxani said. "The king is usually chosen from their ranks, after all. And now they would be forced to have a series of brown kings."

Tanith chuckled. "That's fair. But still... It seems to make sense to keep succession hereditary if they want to continue having warrior kings, no? Strong warriors usually beget strong warriors, after all."

And that would mean Tikran would need a queen, wouldn't it, Tanith? Coxani didn't like the direction this conversation was taking at all. Maybe this woman had a pretty younger sister she wanted to push on Tikran. In any case, there was a glimmer of intent in the mage's eyes that left a knot in Coxani's gut. Tactfully, she changed the subject. "Tikran tells me you led warriors against Manzakars several times back in Gohar."

"I did." She smiled that infuriatingly polite smile at Coxani. "Tikran tells me you're an amazing flight archer. I would love to shoot with you sometime."

Coxani grinned. "I would love to as well. I'd thoroughly relish vanquishing your ass."

Tanith's eyes widened, then she unexpectedly threw back her head and laughed. "We could have definitely used you back in Gohar, Coxani," she said. "I'm not surprised Anzor took the best of us as slaves."

Coxani felt torn by different emotions at that moment. On the one hand, she respected Tanith's courage—it must have taken a lot for her to come to Anzor alone, unsure of what awaited her, and offer her Essential services to the king. On the other hand, the woman had a streak of ambition that worried Coxani. Tikran was not going to be a pawn in anyone's grand scheme, not if she could help it.

Shit.

This, like everything else, was going to be complicated.

CHAPTER 10

The stone of the balustrade was cool under Haydar's palms as he leaned over the balcony, gazing out into the horizon. The setting sun bathed Anzor City in soft orange and pink light, and the spires of Cenk's temples shimmered gold. He'd been sleeping poorly of late and seemed to have a constant headache, but somehow the sunset's colors soothed the throb between his temples, at least temporarily. Thoughts of war with Dilovar were ever-present, haunting his dreams. It had been his greatest fear for decades—now, in fact, for more than half his life.

Haydar sighed, closing his eyes briefly. He'd been Delger's envoy to Dilovar before becoming a durai and the king's chief advisor. Over the course of a decade, he'd made the trip several times. His relationship with Bilguun had become complicated, and he'd convinced Delger to find someone else to serve as emissary for the sake of peace. After nearly fifteen years, Haydar very much doubted his presence at the parley would benefit anyone.

He straightened away from the balustrade and folded his arms on his chest. He was determined to make leaders out of Tikran, Coxani, and Naran, even if it killed him. They'd been thrust into their roles before they were ready, something Haydar hadn't entirely anticipated. *I should have anticipated it.* Tikran had been galvanized into action even before he'd become a Manzakar, drawing the attention of the king. But what was done was done, and now Haydar's protégés, ready or not, had to take charge. Haydar wasn't getting any younger, and the fates of Anzor and Gohar were in their hands.

"Lord Haydar, you summoned me?" Lord Revaz walked out onto the balcony, led by an attendant. The Anzori lord walked with youthful vigor, his handsome face bearing a kind smile, his blue eyes bright.

"Yes, Lord Revaz, thank you for coming." Haydar dismissed the attendant and filled two goblets of wine from the decanter left on the table. He handed one to Revaz and, as their fingers brushed, felt a tingle race up his arm. Pushing his body's unexpected reaction from his mind, he held his goblet aloft. "To Anzor. May it continue its current path toward tolerance and justice."

"I'll certainly drink to that," Revaz said, taking several swallows.

Haydar looked out over Anzor City. "My lord, I have not had a chance to thank you personally for what you did to aid the rebellion. You really were the linchpin to our success."

Revaz shook his head. "I simply used my birthright to influence what I could. The real work fell to you and your Manzakars, Lord Haydar."

"That doesn't change the fact that your influence saved us all. And please," the durai said, flashing a smile, "call me Haydar. No more need for formalities between us."

Revaz smiled back. "Very well. Then I insist you call me Dejan."

Well, this will be a new experience. Haydar had never called an Anzori lord by his given name—at least, not without repercussions. He tamped down his discomfort as he said, "I suppose that's only fair...Dejan." Revaz blinked and Haydar could have sworn that the Anzori's cheeks colored a bit. Pushing the implications of a blush from his mind, Haydar continued, "King Tikran will inevitably leave Anzor to face Bilguun, and as Chief Justiciar, you will serve as regent."

Revaz was nothing if not a well-trained aristocrat and, other than a subtle lifting of his brow, showed no indication that he was surprised by Haydar's words. "You are Tikran's closest advisor and have served as regent for Delger. My title means nothing under the circumstances."

"Ah, but you're mistaken, Dejan." Haydar shook his head. "The Anzori elite need to be pacified with knowledge that one of their own is in a place of power. They are growing wary of so many dark-skinned individuals running about the palace."

"Ostensibly, then, I will be regent," Revaz said. "But it will really be you."

"It will be us both," Haydar said. "Co-regents."

"King Tikran would give me that authority?"

"Of course," Haydar answered. "Tikran and I trust you implicitly."

Again, Haydar wondered if he imagined the hint of color in Revaz's face. "You flatter me, Haydar. I am, of course, honored."

"I will ask a favor of you, however." Haydar set down his goblet. "Commander Naran needs coaching in the ways of the court. He is very much a soldier and could use your help in navigating the sometimes treacherous politics of the aristocracy."

This time, Revaz failed to hide his surprise. His eyes widened and he tilted his head. "Commander...Naran?"

Haydar stifled a smile. "Dejan, I selected Tikran, Coxani, and Naran as slaves to the king very deliberately. I hadn't anticipated things would happen so quickly, but they did. And now, those three need to learn the ways of the Anzori if they are to lead Anzor. You are the perfect teacher—not too much older than them and kin to the last Anzori king. I am hoping you can provide guidance as a peer rather than a father-figure, which is how they view me."

He could tell Revaz wanted to tug at his collar but resisted. "I can certainly try. Of the three of them, I am least acquainted with

Naran. I hope my...friendship with Coxani doesn't become a problem."

Haydar took another sip of wine before asking, "It shouldn't. Unless, of course, you have intentions with regard to Coxani?"

Revaz let out a laugh. "No one has intentions with regard to Coxani. Coxani has intentions with regard to *them*. And in my case, well...I think Coxani is still trying to find her place in this new world. My role in her life, at the moment, is inconsequential."

Haydar met Revaz's eyes. "I'm sorry."

Revaz didn't avert his gaze. "I'm not. I think she needs to focus on herself."

"I agree. Besides, I'm sure there's someone out there right for you, Dejan," Haydar said, annoyed with the way the words came out of his mouth...almost as a question.

This time, there was no mistaking the blush, and as Revaz seemed to debate on what to say next, the door opened and Tikran entered, his hands in his pockets, a mutinous flicker in his eyes until he spotted the pair on the balcony. "Am I interrupting, my lords?"

Haydar reluctantly turned away from Revaz. "No, Tikran. Come in." He thought it was endearing that Tikran still called him "my lord." The boy was king, after all. He could call anyone anything.

Revaz cleared his throat and bowed. "King Tikran, good evening. You may have Lord Haydar to yourself, as I have important matters to attend to before I can call today's work done."

"Yes, of course. Have a good evening, my lord." Tikran watched Revaz leave, then asked, "What was that about?"

Haydar drained his goblet before saying, "I've asked Revaz to teach Naran the ways of the Anzori court."

Tikran's eyebrows shot up. "Are you sure that's a good idea? You know they're both in love with Coxani. It might get...messy."

Haydar smiled. "Revaz is a good five years older than Naran and very well versed in blue-blood diplomacy and cunning. I think Naran would be wise to learn from him."

"Naran's going to have to do some growing up and fast," Tikran muttered with a chuckle.

Haydar tilted his head. "As are you. Listen, Tikran. I agree that war should only be an option should a thorough parley with Bilguun fail, but you need to keep your Anzori supporters happy at all costs. They are watching you carefully, particularly after your swift abolition of slavery. Loyalties can shift far too quickly in this political climate, and that can be catastrophic for all of us." He paused, pouring himself more wine and offering a goblet to Tikran.

The young king declined, his brow furrowed, his eyes fervid. "It's become very apparent that I was made king because they thought they could use me—ignorant, simple-minded soldier that they think I am—to their advantage."

"Except you are neither ignorant nor simple-minded," Haydar said. "I would like to make a suggestion, if I may?"

"Of course," Tikran said, his voice lacking even a hint of enthusiasm.

"Do their bidding." Haydar took a sip of wine. "They want a war with Dilovar. Tell them you will give them what they want. Right now, focus on preparations for the pending war. Revaz and I will take care of all else, quietly and in the background. If you can avoid a war with Bilguun and ensure Anzor is no worse off, then they will have nothing to complain about."

Tikran rubbed his face. "I can't envision a scenario where that would be the case, Lord Haydar. I can't let Gohar fall into Bilguun's hands. And I won't let the Anzori continue to exploit Gohar for their benefit."

"One step at a time, lad," Haydar said. "There's no reason to reveal your every intention at the moment." He paused before saying softly, "You must play the long game, as I did."

Tikran sat quietly, his eyes lighting, his expression subtly changing. Finally, he said, "Yes, you're right."

Haydar took another sip of wine. "You will also have to keep your emotions in check with Bilguun when the time comes...and particularly with Master Damir." Tikran sat up, tightened his jaw.

Haydar continued, "I know you became close with Damir during the rebellion. I understand what you must be feeling now."

Tikran shook his head. "I don't think you do. Besides, I wonder just how much he's told Bilguun."

"You believe he betrayed us, do you?" Haydar rubbed his chin. "Are you sure those aren't your emotions talking?" Haydar had long suspected Damir had feelings for Tikran—the doctor had saved Tikran's life twice and joined the rebellion without a second thought if it meant continuing to protect Tikran with use of his Essence. When Damir left to return to Dilovar, Tikran was visibly distraught for months. It was then that Haydar understood the depth of Tikran's feelings for Damir.

Tikran let out a disdainful laugh. "Emotions? What emotions? Sure, I was upset he had to leave—he was my good friend, after all. But what really upsets me is that he knows everything and now we're facing a war with Dilovar. The logical conclusion is that Damir told Bilguun what he knows, and now Bilguun thinks he can win a war against us."

Haydar nodded gravely. *He won't tell me the truth.* He was slightly hurt but reminded himself that Tikran had grown up seeing him more as a repressed Anzori than an unconstrained Gohari. He likely felt uncomfortable sharing any homosexual tendencies with his mentor, despite their closeness. Pushing his feelings aside, Haydar set a hand on Tikran's shoulder. "I suppose there's no way of knowing, but I will say that I trust Damir. Yes, even now. I don't think he betrayed you, Tikran."

Desperation flashed in Tikran's eyes, as though he wanted to believe it. But it was just a flash. "I appreciate your opinion on the matter, my lord," he said. "But I am king, as you so often remind me. I must assume the worst."

Haydar smiled sadly to himself. *Some lessons can't be taught.* He squeezed Tikran's shoulder then let his hand fall away. "Get some sleep tonight, will you? Tomorrow I expect you to train with me."

Tikran met his eyes in surprise. "Train?"

"Well, yes." Haydar stretched his shoulders. "I'm forty-six

years old and work at a desk most of the day. I need to get back into fighting form. Just in case."

A smile crept across Tikran's face. "I get to train with you? Holy Cenk. That will be amazing."

Haydar chuckled. "You'll have to go easy on me. I'm a bit rusty."

"I'm sure you'll get back into it quickly." Tikran's adoring grin was enough for Haydar's eyes to moisten with emotion. He quickly laughed and slapped the young king on the back, caving in to his Anzori acculturation when he wanted nothing more than to pull Tikran into a tight Gohari embrace.

***

COXANI WAS DONE SHOOTING. Her arrows protruded from the straw and burlap targets on the far end of the field, casting long shadows as the sun dipped closer to the horizon. She flopped down under the infamous oak and drained her flask with rapid swallows. Wiping her mouth with her sleeve, she peered out into the distance, giddy with anticipation. She'd invited both Tikran and Naran to the remote training grounds tonight. Not personally, of course. She'd had messengers do the dirty work. She was afraid they wouldn't come.

She was also afraid Tikran would bring Tanith.

If he does, I'm beating the shit out of him.

A couple nights ago, she'd awakened in a cold sweat. Things were changing quickly. Soon she would be heading into Gohar with food rations to help rally nomad support. Soon Naran would have to deal with Prem—and his beautiful daughter—without her presence. Soon all three of them would be heading to war against Dilovar. These things were out of her hands, try as she might to control them. She could control nothing, but she could remember the strength of their bonds to each other and remind Tikran and Naran of them too.

As the sun sank lower, setting the sky afire in orange and red, she began to despair. *They're both so busy. Why would they come?* She drew her knees to her chest. She would close her eyes and wait until she had to light a lantern to—

She heard hoofbeats. She raised her head to see the pair riding toward her. She grinned. *Thank Cenk.* She stayed where she was, waiting for them to approach. Both men leaped from their horses almost simultaneously.

"Coxani," Tikran called. "Everything is good, right? This isn't an emergency?"

"No, no emergency. I just wanted to..." She sighed, standing, waiting for them to get closer. "We haven't done this in forever. Just us three. Laughing, carefree. And now everything is changing so fast. *So* fast. I need the old us before everything is different. I think you do too." Their expressions went from mildly concerned to somewhat desolate. She quickly added, "I meant for this to be fun. You know? Just the three of us idiots being...us." She bent down and pulled a bottle of wine and three cups from the satchel at her feet. She beamed at them. "I brought something to...relax us."

Tikran glanced at Naran. "I'm game."

Sadness flickered briefly in Naran's face as he looked at Coxani. Then he said, "Sure. Why not?"

Coxani immediately began to feel at home. They lit a fire and sat around it, each holding a full cup of wine. Their conversation fell into an easy, teasing, sarcastic cadence, just as it had before...everything. They reminisced about training and shared stories about their time apart during the rebellion, delicately avoiding Coxani's time with Nasch. She appreciated that more than they knew. After a full cup of wine, Coxani felt bold and mischievous and decided to veer their conversation into uncharted territories. Out of nowhere, she said to Tikran, "May I ask you a personal question?"

The men exchanged looks. Tikran said, "Why does my heart drop every time you ask that?"

Naran raised an eyebrow at Tikran. "How often does she ask you that?"

Tikran sighed, avoiding the question. "Fine. Ask away, Coxani."

She pursed her lips. "Did you and Naran have a romantic relationship as cadets?"

Tikran's eyes popped in surprise, then he glared at Naran. "Did you tell her that?"

Naran pinched the bridge of his nose. "Oh, Coxani..."

She grinned. "I think it's sweet."

Tikran stifled a smile. "I don't know that I would have called it romantic *or* sweet."

Naran guffawed. "Yeah, romantic and sweet aren't really the right words. More like..."

Tikran's lips twitched. "Don't say what I think you're going to say."

"...desperate?" Naran said.

"That's one way to put it," Tikran said.

Coxani threw back her head and laughed. She wanted to wrap them both in her arms and never let go.

"Speaking of which," Tikran said, leaning toward Coxani, a naughty gleam in his eye, "If I recall, your first lover was a woman, wasn't it, Coxani?"

"Wait, what?" Naran's smile widened. "You never told me that."

Coxani waved a hand dismissively. "It's not a big deal. Tashi was the only other good archer among us. She was also pretty cute. We didn't even get along that well. But she was skilled at lovemaking."

Naran grew serious. "Hold on. *How* skilled?"

"Get over it, Naran," Tikran muttered, grinning.

Naran sat up. "Well, now *I* have questions." He narrowed his eyes at both his friends in turn. "Where did you go, Coxani, the night of Tikran's birthday celebration?"

Smiles faded. After a few seconds of tense silence, Coxani cleared her throat. *Might as well come clean now.* She made the mistake of looking at Tikran, whose eyes were like saucers. She said, "I went to Lord Revaz's house."

Naran's expression didn't change but his voice, when he spoke, was lower, softer. "Why would you go there?"

The wine was fortifying her, giving her courage she wouldn't have otherwise. She said, "Because he's my friend. I trust him."

Naran was silent for a beat, then he looked at Tikran. "Why wouldn't you have wanted me to know that?"

Tikran turned his face away from Naran. "Because you were going crazy and I didn't want you to go crazy on him."

Naran met Coxani's eyes and a shiver went through her. He said, "Nothing happened between you and Revaz, right?"

"I kissed him," she said, straightening. "It was a mistake. It was also entirely my idea. He actually tried to talk me out of it."

"Why'd you do it?" A mix of anger and pain played in his expression.

"I was drunk. I was hurt. I don't know." Coxani rubbed her temples. "It was a mistake, Naran."

Naran looked like he had more to say but couldn't decide on the words. Finally, he said, "We aren't a couple, Coxani. You can kiss whomever you want." He drank the rest of his wine with two quick swallows.

Coxani felt a strange pang at his words. No, they weren't a couple. They could both kiss whomever they liked. Silence befell the trio for several moments.

"Hey," Tikran said suddenly, "I have a question of my own, come to think of it. You both keep hinting at something...some mistake I made..." He titled his head at Coxani. "What aren't you telling me?"

Coxani's heart lodged into her throat. *Oh, no.* She asked, "What do you mean?"

Tikran leaned forward, his eyes fixed on hers. "Coxani, I'm not stupid. Please be honest. When you were sick... Was it because of me?"

Their playful bantering had taken a dire turn. Coxani drank

deeply of her wine before answering. "It was because of both of us, Tikran. Not just you."

He covered his face with his hands. "Oh, *fuck*." He leaned his arms on his knees and cracked his fingers apart to look at her. "Coxani, I'm so sorry. Why didn't you tell me?" He lifted his head, a desperate look in his eyes.

She struggled to keep her expression flat. "I found out I was pregnant just before you were burned in the Fire Game. I wasn't about to tell you. I asked for Damir's help. He gave me an elixir that ended it. It was unpleasant, but he was there to help me through it." She gave Tikran a meaningful look. "I trust him with my life."

The crickets' song and the crackling fire filled the silence that ensued. Naran sat holding his cup between his bent legs, staring into the flames, a downward twist to his lips. Tikran continued to grasp his head between his hands, a pained expression on his face. Finally, he said, "I understand why you didn't tell me. I just wish I could have been there for you."

Coxani blew out her breath in frustration. "Can we stop keeping secrets from each other? Please? None of this—our relationships, our hopes for Anzor's or Gohar's future—will work if we can't trust each other."

Both men nodded and silence befell them once again, until Tikran said softly, "Well, here's some honesty for you. I'm terrified. I've been having vivid nightmares every night. One keeps recurring; I'm fighting Manzakars in battle and I can't tell who's on my side and who's the enemy. I cut one down and, as they die, they remove their helmet. Both of you have been under that helmet at some point. So has Haydar." He looked down into his lap. "I'm terrified I'll let everyone down—Haydar, the two of you, Anzor, and Gohar. One single mistake could cost the lives of thousands, and I've been making plenty of mistakes lately."

"The only way you could let me down is by shutting me out, Tikran," Coxani said.

"You're not alone in this, brother," Naran said. "You don't have to bear this burden by yourself."

Tikran sighed. "If I mess this up, this whole being king thing, I won't be able to live with myself—if I live at all."

"Let us help you." Coxani crawled over to Tikran and draped her arms around his neck. "We want to help you."

Letting his head fall against her shoulder, Tikran gestured to her bag. "All right, then... You wouldn't happen to have another bottle of wine in there, would you? I think we can all use another round."

CHAPTER 11

They're afraid of me.

Berk avoided the wary gazes of the servants and soldiers as he followed Master Damir to his chambers. And why wouldn't they be? He was afraid—no, terrified—of himself. The attack of the Manzakars on his clan had awakened something in him that was so much bigger than the Essence he thought he had. Dilovar's head mage was the only person who didn't seem fearful of him. As Berk tried to keep up with Damir's brisk clip, his hands shook, his legs felt like jelly, and his chest constricted his lungs in that familiar way, making him gasp for breath.

Damir stopped and turned, scowling. "Are you in distress, boy? You sound like you're having trouble breathing."

Berk braced his hands on his knees, wheezing. "This happens...a lot. I was born...windless."

"Windless?" Damir scratched his chin. "That must be Gohari dialect specific. An Anzori doctor would call you asthmatic." As Berk continued to pant, Damir raised his hands, flexing his fingers just slightly. Cool air suddenly rushed through Berk's nostrils, compelling him to breathe deeply. He exhaled and Damir's fingers moved again, sending the air into Berk's lungs. After repeating this several times, Berk stopped wheezing. Damir looked satisfied. "That's better. Your lips were turning blue."

Berk stared at Damir in wonder. "How did you do that?"

"What are the mages teaching you out there in Gohar? You should know how to do this," Damir admonished, his eyebrows drawn. He turned and continued to walk, a bit slower this time.

"You'll teach me?" Berk asked, traipsing behind.

"Of course. An asthmatic with the Essence shouldn't be struggling to breathe, for Cenk's sake."

Berk latched on to the last part. "I don't worship Cenk."

Damir heaved a sigh. "It hardly matters, boy."

"Can you call me Berk, please, sir? I hate being called 'boy.'"

"I'll stop calling you 'boy' if you stop calling me 'sir.'"

"Yes, s—ah, Master Damir."

"Just Damir is fine."

Berk scratched his head. "Prince Vazha calls you 'Doctor.'"

"That's because I served as his doctor."

Damir opened the heavy wooden door to his chambers and Berk followed him in, peering up at the shelves and shelves of thick, leather-bound books that lined the walls. Berk had been overwhelmed by Ogedei, a city of massive, gray stone towers nestled in a valley of snow. He had never seen so much stone in one place. The city's inhabitants had intimidated him further with their stunning beauty—alabaster skin, glossy black hair, and lithe, elegant figures. Master Damir was clearly one of them, despite the rumor that he was half Gohari. Now, as Berk looked about the mage's chambers, he realized he almost—*almost*—felt safe there. A fire crackled in the arched fireplace; a black cat lay on the windowsill, its yellow eyes half-shut in repose; and books were everywhere—neatly color-coded on shelves, stacked haphazardly on chairs, and laying open on tables. "Did you read all of these?" He asked, his mouth ajar.

"Most of them," Damir said, shutting the door. "Some of them aren't supposed to be read, only used as reference."

"I would want to read them all," Berk said, walking toward a shelf and running his fingers along the spines of books with intricate gold lettering.

Damir tilted his head. "You like to read?"

"Yes," Berk said with a sigh. "But I haven't read much. Books aren't very important when you're starving, or sick, or...just trying to survive."

"No, I can't imagine they are." Damir almost smiled. "I suppose I'll have to teach you Erdem too, then, so you can read all of them." He folded his arms across his chest and rubbed his chin. "You must have known you had the Essence growing up. It's too powerful for you not to have known."

Berk nodded slowly, resigned. "I knew. I was scared. So I tried to hide it. And I never used it. But Beg Zolto knew from the start."

Sympathy flashed across Damir's face before he said, "Sit down, Berk."

Berk obeyed tentatively, gazing at Damir from between his plaits.

"Now, I know this will be uncomfortable for you," Damir said, "but I need you to tell me what happened the day the Manzakars attacked your clan."

Berk's chest tightened. "Why?"

Damir licked his lips. "Berk, I am not in any way diminishing what you experienced. I can't imagine how awful it must have been. But certain things don't make sense. Manzakars may have committed this atrocity, but I'm not convinced they were sent by the king of Anzor."

Drawing his legs up on the chair, Berk wrapped his arms around his knees and pressed his forehead against them. His throat began to ache and his eyes filled with tears. Through his clenched teeth, he said, "They yelled, 'In the name of the Freed Kingfisher!' Over and over again. They bore the flag of Anzor." The memory assaulted him—the Manzakars with the torches setting fire to the yarms, indifferent that a baby slept inside one of them; their horses trampling over the crops, their arrows skewering the clansmen and women at short range, propelling their bodies to the ground. He could still hear Baydor's screams, still see his brother's body in the blood-stained grass, impaled on a Manzakar's lance.

"Berk... Berk..." The voice was distant but getting closer. He became aware of Damir, who was shaking him. "Berk! You must stop!"

The cat leaped away with a scream and Berk saw the books tumble from the shelves. He gasped and regained his senses. "I'm sorry! I'm sorry! Oh, Archil..." His entire body hurt as the room stopped rocking.

"It's all right, lad," Damir murmured, his steady hands gripping Berk's shoulders. "It's all right."

As soon as the pain resided, tears began streaming from Berk's eyes against his will. "I didn't mean to destroy your books, Master Damir," he managed between sobs.

Damir shook his head, not letting go. "The books are fine, Berk. I just don't want you to destroy the entire palace and everyone in it." He quirked a smile.

Berk relaxed and let out a relieved sigh, wiping the snot from his face with the back of his hand when Damir finally released him.

"I will teach you to control your Essence so that this doesn't happen again," Damir said. "But in the meantime, do you think you can keep from retreating into that memory while I ask you some questions?"

Berk nodded furiously. "Yes. I can. I will."

Damir smiled. "Good." He paused and Berk was grateful for the few seconds to collect himself. Then he met the head mage's gaze. Damir put his hands behind his back and asked, "Was there a commander among the Manzakars? Someone who seemed to be in charge?"

Berk closed his eyes. "I don't know." He felt Damir's hand on his shoulder.

"How did Vazha find you?"

Opening his eyes, Berk said, "He and his men stopped the Manzakars from slaughtering the rest of us."

"His men fought the Manzakars?"

"No." Berk shook his head. "They just talked."

"Vazha talked them out of killing you?"

"Yes." Berk stared miserably at the floor.

Damir frowned. "What was Vazha doing there? Did he see what you did to the Manzakars?"

"I don't know. I don't *know*." Berk made a fist as another tear slipped down his cheek.

Exhaling, Damir said gently, "I'm sorry about your brother, Berk. I'm sorry about your clan. I'm truly sorry." He remained quiet for a few moments before saying, "I don't think you understand what Vazha has signed you up for."

Berk gritted his teeth and tightened his fist. "The Manzakars have killed my people for too long. We thought we'd been saved by the Freed Kingfisher, but he's no different than the rest. And even if he is, he can't seem to control his Manzakars. I want them wiped from existence, and I'm happy to help do it."

Damir blinked at him, as if digesting his words. Then the head mage leaned forward and said, "That's not what you'd be doing, Berk. Instead of helping Gohar, you'd be sealing its fate as a broken land and allowing not just one, but two kingdoms to pillage it. On top of that, you'd be replacing the only Anzori king who has ever given a shit about Gohar with one who cares only for himself."

"Prince Vazha saved my life," Berk snapped, anger twinging in his chest.

"I wonder," Damir muttered. "In any case, I suspect it's because he knew you'd be valuable to him."

What's this guy about? Berk lowered his legs to the floor. "I'm so confused. Where do your loyalties lie? With Anzor? Gohar? It sure doesn't feel like Dilovar."

"Loyalties should lie with people, not kingdoms," Damir answered. "That's your first lesson as a mage." Damir dragged a chair over to Berk and sat facing him. "Your second lesson will be to keep yourself from suffocating to death. Are you ready?"

Berk gazed suspiciously at the Dilovari, unsure of what to

think. A hundred questions flooded his mind. Still, learning not to suffocate was definitely a top priority at the moment. He nodded once. "Yes, I'm ready."

HE'S TEACHABLE. Damir walked down the corridor back to the throne room after leaving Berk in his new accommodations. The boy had planted facedown in the bed, fast asleep before Damir could close the door. Awkward, intellectually curious, emotionally fragile...Berk reminded Damir of himself at that age in many ways.

Except with the hair.

Holy Cenk, Damir was dying to tie the boy's plaits back from his face with a thick leather thong. He suspected Berk used the hair to hide—both literally and figuratively. And who could blame him? A Gohari youth on the cusp of manhood, asthmatic his whole life, witness to his clan's demise, and suddenly in possession of great power...

Damir couldn't imagine what the boy had been through. And he'd been utterly surprised when Berk had revealed he knew how to read. Of course, Damir was too diplomatic to probe. It wasn't so much an innate prejudice on Damir's part as it was genuine astonishment that a race of people struggling for survival still had the wherewithal to teach their children to read. A smile threatened to stretch across his mouth despite everything. *I will teach him to read Erdem too, if he wants.*

He entered the great hall to find Bilguun pensive, his lips pursed and eyebrows drawn tightly. Vazha was no longer there, thank Cenk, and Damir felt he could speak more freely. The head mage sat and folded his hands, waiting for his king. Bilguun's eyes darted pensively in Damir's direction.

"You have things to say, Master Damir. I can tell."

Damir restrained his expression and kept his voice even. "The boy Berk is intelligent and can be taught."

Bilguun visibly relaxed. "Good." He cleared his throat and lowered his voice. "And...?"

Damir tilted his head. "He is very young. And desperate for guidance."

Bilguun didn't move, save for his lips. "Desperate enough?"

Despite the niggling feeling in his chest, Damir nodded once and said, "Yes." And he wasn't lying. Berk was a yawning gap of need. While he might have insisted his loyalties lay with Vazha, Damir could tell that all the boy truly sought was real, genuine affection. *Give him that, and his loyalty is yours.* The realization left a pit in Damir's stomach.

"Good." Bilguun smiled broadly this time, relaxing on his throne. He gave Damir a cursory glance. "Damir, I realize you're likely upset with me, but my actions have brought us nothing but good fortune." He weaved his fingers together before him and tapped his chin with his forefingers. "We managed to capture several of the Anzori forts in northern Gohar along the Damla before King Tikran could mobilize his troops. As it stands, we can defeat Anzor, acquire half of all Gohar, and spare your precious Freed Kingfisher's life."

Damir stared straight ahead. "Why do you call him *my* precious Freed Kingfisher?"

"Because it's obvious you care for him." The king turned a stern gaze on his head mage. "I admit to having had moments of doubt regarding your fidelity to Dilovar since you returned from Anzor."

Facing Bilguun fully, Damir said, "My allegiance is strictly to you, my king. I won't deny fearing for King Tikran's life, but Prince Vazha's promise to show him mercy has resolved that particular issue, I hope. I can now focus fully on training Berk and myself in case of war."

Bilguun rumbled. "War, at this point, is a certainty, Damir."

"I know Tikran," Damir said softly. "He will attempt to negotiate."

"Unless he offers me half of Gohar, as Vazha has done, he will fail." The Dilovari king gripped the arms of his throne tightly, his face grim.

He would never agree to that. Damir was silent, dread making his mouth dry. "And what if he wins the war?"

The king smiled humorlessly. "I am counting on two things to prevent that. First, the Anzori aristocracy's divided allegiances and Anzor's resulting instability. Vazha claims to have the support of some powerful lords with hundreds of Manzakars at their disposal. And second...you."

Damir nodded slowly. "If I can train Berk quickly and effectively, he and I could do great damage to Anzor's forces."

Bilguun chuckled. "Oh, yes. Tikran's new mage will not stand a chance."

THE LOATHSOME TASK before him weighed heavily on Damir as he returned to his chambers to retire for the night. The lives of thousands were destined to end, and one young life in particular would be inevitably corrupted—all because of him. He wanted to believe that he had no choice in the matter, but it was a lie and he knew it. *I could simply refuse.* He would certainly lose his life, but Bilguun would not be equipped to wage a successful war against Anzor without Damir's assistance. Even so, Tikran's reign would still hang in the balance. With Dilovar out of the way, Vazha would likely quickly regain the throne of Anzor and Tikran would die, like Delger before him.

I would sooner murder.

He wasn't sure what that said about his character, and the ever-present fear of the Essence itself filled him with trepidation. As Damir entered his suite and shut the door, dwelling on how the Essence made him feel, the silhouette of a man wavering by firelight on the wall before him made his heart stop.

Shit.

"Hello, Doctor," Vazha said, his voice like velvet.

Damir stiffened. He kept his voice even. "I could have you thrown out, Prince Vazha," he said, not turning.

The prince chuckled as his shadow grew taller. "You wouldn't do that. I know you wouldn't. You love the Freed Kingfisher too much."

Swallowing, Damir closed his fists. "What do you want? You already have Anzor and half of Gohar within your grasp."

Vazha's shadow enveloped his, and Damir stifled the impulse to flinch when a hand dropped down on his shoulder, its fingers curling tightly. "You're right," he said. "I have everything I want within my grasp. Including you."

"I'm not yours to take," Damir replied, his tone threatening, his muscles flexing.

"Damir," Vazha said through a sigh, "Tikran could never love you the way I do." Gently, he turned Damir to face him. The prince's expression was solemn, but his eyes glowed with hunger.

Damir could easily overpower him; the prince was of the same height but slight by comparison, and with a paralyzed foot. He fought the desire to kick Vazha's feet out from under him, knock him to the ground, and set something—anything—on fire. "Very clever of you, Your Highness," Damir said, half stalling for time, half fishing for evidence of the prince's treachery. "You've convinced young Berk that you saved him. He believes he owes you his life."

Vazha smiled as he propped his cane against a chair and shed his jacket. "I *did* save him, Damir."

With his teeth clenched, Damir muttered, "Bullshit."

A slow smile crept across Vazha's face. "Your defiance makes me want you all the more, Doctor. As if that were possible. And I do admit, I wish you wanted me just as much. I think you would, if not for the Freed Kingfisher. But even so, I hold no grudge against him."

A snorting laugh escaped Damir before he could stop it. "Oh, really?"

The prince's expression grew serious. "Yes, Damir. My father was a desperate man. I shed no tears when he died—not for him, at least. I was glad his life ended. For that, perhaps, I owe Tikran thanks." He lifted a hand and slowly reached over Damir's shoulder, running his fingers through Damir's long, black strands. "But the throne of Anzor is rightfully mine, and I will get it back. Whether Tikran survives when I do..." He tentatively touched Damir's face with his fingers. The prince's voice was breathy and low. "Well. That's up to you, isn't it?"

Damir refused to show emotion. He thought of Coxani in that moment, of her stoic sufferance as Nasch's wife, and felt a sudden sense of calm. Vazha's fingers went to work on Damir's robe, unfastening its silk buttons and slipping beneath it greedily. Damir suppressed a gasp as Vazha's fingers touched his skin, resisting the urge to yank away even as every fiber of his being screamed at him to break Vazha's hand. He squared his shoulders and raised his chin, hoping his contempt was obvious. "I will do what you want, however unwillingly, so long as you spare Tikran." His expression darkened. "But heed me, Vazha. Should you harm the Freed Kingfisher, directly or otherwise, I will destroy you and everything precious to you. Is that clear?"

Vazha let out a short, uneasy laugh. "Abundantly." Then he ran his hands across Damir's shoulders, pushing the robe open, and moved closer. "You certainly know how to set the mood, don't you, Doctor?"

CHAPTER 12

Tikran stands in the steppe, fully armored, blinking in the smoke. The grass is scorched as far as the eye can see and the sky is a sooty gray. Figures approach in the distance, their armor distinct. The Manzakars seem to multiply, more of them materializing from the haze by the second. Tikran draws his saber and holds his shield before him, his heart pounding. The whites of their eyes glisten and their teeth flash in the darkness; they brandish their weapons and charge him.

Tikran doesn't think. To quickly bridge the gap between himself and the closest of them, a Manzakar wielding a battle axe, Tikran leaps forward, parrying the oncoming blow and following immediately with a strike to his attacker's neck as he passes. *One down.* Twisting to the side, he parries a slicing blade, steps forward, grabs the soldier's wrist, and chops at his head. *Two down.* As he cuts them down one after the other, the Manzakars fall limp and silent; their blood seems to float in the air.

When none are left, Tikran pants, surveying the bodies that litter the singed field. He tears his helmet from his head and looks down at the fallen soldiers in a confused fury. *Who are they?* Dread wells within him as he approaches the only one still moving. Frantic now, he kneels down and pulls off the dying Manzakar's helmet. Beneath it, Damir lies gasping, his face spattered with mud. Tikran cries out in anguish, lifting the doctor and cradling his head in his arms. Damir's eyes focus on Tikran and he opens his mouth to speak, his hand reaching for Tikran's face. Blood then spills from his lips, choking him, and as Tikran tries desperately to sit the doctor up, Damir's eyes go glassy and his chest stops heaving.

No...

No!

Tikran's body was on fire as he awoke, shouting aloud. His bedchamber came into focus, looking just as it had before he'd gone into battle. Two Manzakars rushed into his room, their swords ready. "Your Highness!"

Good grief. He couldn't even have a nightmare without the Aslans practically jumping into his bed. "No...I'm fine. It was a nightmare. I'm fine." With every muscle in his body tensed, he watched the guards leave his room. When the door shut behind them, he inhaled sharply, sweat beading his brow, the base of his neck. The nightmare receded as he clutched the sheets, blinking in the moonlight that spilled through the mullioned windows. He reached for the pitcher of water at his bedside, poured himself a full cup, and drank deeply. After setting the cup down and falling back into the pillows, he considered his dream. *Is Damir in danger?* Despite logically talking himself down, something deep within him wouldn't let the fear go. Frustrated, he chastised himself. The head mage was likely the reason Anzor was facing a war with Dilovar. *Damir's more than fine.*

...Wasn't he?

Tikran closed his eyes. He missed Damir more than anything, and he hated it. That dry wit; that deep, sexy voice; those thoughtful silver eyes; the way he moved, slinking confidently like a fox. It was driving him mad. He no longer knew what was right, what was wrong. While he desperately wanted to prevent the deaths of thousands—Anzori, Gohari, Dilovari—he had no idea how to do it. Sleep slowly overtook him, but he awoke what felt like minutes later to find that the moonlight was now sunlight.

Today was the day Coxani and Moti left for Gohar.

As he got out of bed, Tikran's anxieties over his nightmare were compounded by his trepidation over Coxani's journey into Gohar. Again, he upbraided himself for worrying about nothing. Since the rebellion, the nomads had become far more tolerant of the Manzakar presence on the steppe. They were understandably wary, but from what Naran and his other commanders had told him, the overall sentiment was improving quickly. Prince Vazha and the Delger family, after all, had been exiled to eastern Gohar and had not been harassed by the surrounding tribes at all.

Moreover, Coxani and Moti's mission was largely humanitarian. They would travel through Gohar, increasing the defensive potential of each outpost with Gohari militias in exchange for much-needed supplies and food. Tikran had sent word to Bruneta—who had, since the rebellion, become something of a Gohari "commander" and unifying force to the Sachin tribe warriors—and she'd agreed to meet his two captains in Eter to provide additional encouragement to the nomads to support Anzor's war efforts.

It'll be fine.

...Wouldn't it?

He began to dress as his attendants entered his suite, followed by Haydar and his staff. The durai had been training with him for a couple weeks now and Tikran was thoroughly impressed by how quickly his mentor had gotten back into the swing of things. Haydar may have been nearly twice his age, but he was a formidable opponent—even after nearly seven years behind a desk and almost completely off the training grounds. It was one of the few things that brought a real smile to Tikran's face these days.

"King Tikran," Haydar announced, his hands behind his back,

his expression as serious as ever, "Captains Coxani and Moti have readied their detachments for departure and await your mandate."

As the attendants attempted to help him into his boots and tie the sash around his waist, he waved them off. "Thank you, but no." Yanking on his boots and haphazardly knotting his sash, Tikran stepped forward with a sigh. "I'm ready."

Three hundred Manzakars, along with a robust retinue of support personnel—including one of the Anzori mages—awaited him at the Citadel gates in carriages and wagons. Moti approached Tikran and bowed, excitement lighting his face. "We're ready to head into Gohar at Your Highness's behest."

"Show me your supplies," Tikran said. "You've made sure to load everything we discussed?"

"Yes, my king," Moti answered, leading Tikran to the supply train. The wagons were filled with legumes, grains, preserved meats, and even livestock for the nomads. Cards of wool and bolts of linen filled a wagon, stacked atop bundles of dried medicinal herbs that were found only outside Gohar and stored in ceramic jars and earthenware pots.

Tikran nodded. "And you have blacksmiths, farriers, and armorers? Enough for your party as well as for each of the major forts?"

Moti nodded. "Yes, Your—"

"What about a doctor?" A voice barked from behind.

Tikran smiled without turning. "It's already been taken care of, Commander," he said. As Naran stopped beside him, Tikran tilted his head toward the yellow-haired Manzakar. "Surely you know I wouldn't forget that."

A woman's voice sliced through the conversation, decisive and clearly annoyed. "We don't need a doctor. The Gohari have their own healers, and we will provide them with medicine that they don't have access to."

Tikran's response died on his lips as he turned and took in the sight of Captain Coxani, the steel lamellar plates of her flight archer's cuirass gleaming, two bright green eyes flashing from beneath her domed helmet. She strode confidently over to them and set her hands firmly on her hips. Finally, he said, "The doctor isn't for the nomads. He's for you and your Manzakars."

"What are you talking about?" She shook her head in disbelief, her long dark braid swishing across her back. "We're not going into battle, boys. No one is getting an arrow through the gullet."

"You'll be getting awfully close to the Damla," Naran said gruffly. "Anything is possible."

Coxani blew out her breath. "There are doctors at each of the major outposts. If we need—"

"Coxani, please," Naran snapped, anger and fear playing on his scarred face, his eyes limpid and beseeching. "You're insisting on leading this mission despite my pleas to let Captain Tural go in your stead. Give me this small peace of mind."

Tikran lowered his gaze, letting the pair have a moment. He was worried about Coxani, no question, but he was also worried about Naran. His commander didn't have the luxury of falling apart over Coxani this time; he had to mobilize Anzor's militias, stage arms, and double down on training the Manzakars in preparation for war. *No booze and brothels this time, big guy.* Not that he believed Naran to be into brothels anymore—or much booze, for that matter. Naran had cleaned up quite a bit over the course of a year.

"Fine," Coxani said after several moments, and her voice had lost its edge. "We'll take the bloody doctor." She turned toward the waiting company and, after nodding to Moti, mounted her horse.

Tikran looked up at her, hoping he didn't appear as distraught as Naran. "Captain," he said softly, "We need you to stay in one piece, yeah?"

She rolled her eyes but still smiled. "The way you're worrying, you'd think you didn't train me yourself."

"It's not about your abilities, Coxani," Tikran said. He left the rest of the sentiment unsaid and patted the horse's neck before stepping back. "Remember to send me updates at each outpost. Do you have enough homing pigeons—"

"We have cages simply *crammed* with pigeons, Tikran," Coxani answered, offering him a crooked, affectionate smile. "Relax. I won't let you down." She shifted her gaze to Naran, who stood several feet back, his arms crossed on his chest, his face like stone. She said, "I'll see you both at Sitora in a few months."

"Captain Moti," Naran said suddenly. "Watch after her."

Tikran winced. Coxani gasped as her face went bright red. "Naran! What the fuck?" She turned to a flustered Moti and grumbled, "Let's get out of here."

As the wall that separated Anzor from Gohar came into view, Coxani's heart raced. Unlike the previous time she'd gone into Gohar—rushing to aid Tikran against Delger's Manzakar forces—this time, she would be able to savor the land of her birth.

She had no real memories of Gohar. She could remember her mother, just barely. At least, she *thought* it was her mother—a beautiful, smiling face that had Coxani's green eyes and made Coxani feel this melting warmth. The only other memory from her time in Gohar was of her aunt, her father's sister, whose face was neither smiling nor beautiful. In fact, most of Coxani's memories of Gohar were associated with Aunt Khava, who took Coxani in after her mother and father were wiped out by the red plague, and those memories were awful. The woman yelled constantly, smacking her children and Coxani at the slightest misstep. Young Coxani understood very clearly that her aunt resented her existence and likely wished the little girl had perished with the rest of her immediate family. The feeling that she was a burden persisted even after coming to Anzor, particularly when she didn't fit the mold at the girls' school.

Haydar and, eventually, Tikran, allowed her to realize that, not only was she not a burden...she was an asset.

"So, uh," Moti said, after clearing his voice repeatedly. "It's nice to meet you, Captain Coxani."

Coxani stared directly ahead. "Nice to meet you, too."

"Is it?"

Coxani frowned. "What?"

Moti shrugged, grinning sheepishly. "You said it was nice to meet me, but you haven't actually made eye contact with me."

Fair enough. Coxani looked at her co-captain earnestly. "I'm sorry."

"It's all right." Moti looked forward, raising his chin. "As usual, Commander Naran fucked up by implying that I'm his minion or something. Which I'm not. I'm not here to watch over you, Captain."

"I didn't think you were," Coxani answered. Prior to that moment, she'd had no opinion of Moti other than what Naran had told her. But his desire to stand up for himself made a difference in her mind.

"Naran and I were at Otebek together," Moti explained. "When he first arrived, he was a...mess. I tried to help. I hope I helped."

Coxani smiled. "I know you did. He told me all about it."

Moti's eyes lit up. "He did?"

"Yes." Coxani looked away. "He credits you with quite a bit."

"That's nice to hear." Moti's cheeks pinked.

Coxani looked down, frowning. "What was it like, the attack on Sitora?"

Moti stared straight ahead. "It was...brutal." He paused for a long moment. "I don't think I'll ever forget it."

Swallowing, Coxani asked, "Do you feel like you can tell me about it?"

Moti hesitated. "Maybe. But not right now."

"I understand," she said. And she did. She'd seen real battle—real death—and knew it was not something easily talked about. Cenk, she still couldn't speak of Nasch in life or death.

"So," Moti said, clearing his voice, "what was it like for you at the girls' school? Were you tormented like I was?"

Thunderstruck, Coxani turned to look at her co-captain. "What do you mean?"

Moti smiled without looking at her. "Ola was always strict, but she was kind. The other students, though...they could be real assholes."

Zarina. Coxani was quiet for a few moments, debating on her next words. "I think it's because we chose an alternate path, one that was...wrong in their eyes."

"No kidding!" Moti let out a laugh. "But you know..." He looked over at her. "Fuck them. Because we made it."

Coxani grinned back, feeling warm all over. The "cautionary tale" had not just become a Manzakar, but a rebel leader, and one that both Tikran and Naran respected.

They fell silent as they passed through the heavily guarded fortification and into Gohar. She was struck by how quickly the landscape changed from lush and green to an arid brown. How much had Gohar changed, she wondered, since Tikran had made that fateful journey into the land of their birth? She asked Moti, "Since the Essence has returned to Gohar, have the changes been noticeable?"

"Yes," Moti answered. "I mean, it's still Gohar. It'll never have forests or lakes or anything like that. But the horses have returned to the steppe. The sheep are plumper. The nomads have more to forage—strawberries, wild grapes, onions—and can grow their own food in limited quantities with the help of the mages."

Gazing across the endless stretches of long, dry grass, Coxani said, "How do you anticipate the nomads will react to us? I can't imagine they've seen this many Manzakars cross into Gohar since the rebellion."

"King Tikran sent word to his sister, whom he says has become important to the biggest tribes' warriors, particularly in central Gohar," Moti replied. "Hopefully she's notified the chiefs of our arrival and purpose." He scratched his chin. "Other than that, I can't imagine their reaction will be negative. Wary, perhaps. But Tikran *did* save them, so..."

"I know." Coxani shifted in her saddle. "I can't help but put myself in their shoes... The Manzakars were an oppressive force for over a century. Just the sight of a Manzakar's uniform must still make their hearts stop."

"Yeah," Moti muttered in agreement. "Especially after Commander Nasch's reign of terror…" Moti looked at her in alarm. "Fuck. I'm sorry, Coxani."

Coxani shook her head. "It's okay." She'd taught herself to steel herself when it came to Nasch. While she couldn't have kept him from killing innocent Gohari, she'd kept him from foiling Haydar's plans. She kept telling herself that it was the most she could have done at the time.

When the company finally came across a clan two days later, the reception was mostly warm—children cheered and ran alongside the Manzakar's horses; adolescents and adults waved and smiled, occasionally calling out, "Long live the Caged Kingfisher!" The change of Tikran's name either hadn't registered with the Gohari or they simply preferred to call him by his original moniker, since it was as the Caged Kingfisher that he'd saved Gohar. *The Freed Kingfisher hasn't proven anything yet.* Coxani made eye contact with several of the Gohari on horseback and saw many reverent, hopeful faces. But more than a few armed nomads watched warily, unsmiling, particularly the older ones. Coxani looked away. *They still don't trust us.* And why would they?

"We need to prove to them that we're worthy," she said out loud.

Moti turned toward her. "What?"

"Only the Caged Kingfisher has proven to them that he's worthy of their love," Coxani said, looking at Moti. "The Freed Kingfisher and his Manzakars still have a lot to prove."

"Yeah, I get it." Moti smiled. "Let's prove it, then."

Coxani smiled back, then halted the train. They had been given enough food, supplies, and arms for stops at the outposts along the route to Dilovar. She said to Moti, "Let's figure out how we can dole out enough food for the larger clans along the way. There must be enough."

"I'm sure there is," Moti replied, firming his jaw. "And if there isn't, I have no doubt our king will send more."

Yes. Tikran would no doubt send more. As she hopped from her horse and opened her mouth to order that sacks of grain, legumes, and dried meat be brought out, a feeling of foreboding assaulted her. *The more food Tikran sends into Gohar, the more the Anzori lords will protest.*

And the more Tikran's reign would hang in the balance.

She turned to Moti, who had dismounted and stood beside her. "We need to be prudent with our supplies," she said. "Sending back to Anzor for more isn't an option, even if it increases Gohari goodwill. Can we allocate the food we have so we don't run out?"

Moti considered. "We can try." He looked at the puzzled faces of the nomads. "But we need a strategy, otherwise we may really run out."

Coxani nodded then strode toward the nomads who stood along the road, her hand raised in greeting. "Where is your head clansman?"

Heads turned in the direction of an older man with a braided beard and a fur-lined cap. Suspicion gleamed in his eyes. He said, "I am the head clansman, Manzakar."

Coxani stepped toward him. "I'm Captain Coxani, emissary on behalf of the Freed Kingfisher, King of Anzor, and I was tasked with delivering food and supplies to the major Anzori outposts for the Gohari people. While my fellow Manzakars and I seek to ensure that everyone in Gohar has food, we want to distribute what we have equitably. How is your clan faring?"

The head clansman chuckled sardonically. "We can *always* use more food, Manzakar. Unlike some of the other clans, we have no one among us with the Essence, so for the most part, we rely on the food from Anzor or the occasional visit of the mages. It's been...inconsistent. Sometimes we have food, sometimes we don't."

Coxani chewed her lip. "Is it like that for most clans?"

The man shook his head. "I don't know. You realize Gohar is a big place with several tribes, don't you? While I might know how some fellow Sachin clans in west and central Gohar are faring, I certainly can't speak for the Davlat tribe or any of the smaller tribes in northern or southern Gohar."

She squelched the embarrassment that threatened to redden her face. *I don't know much about Gohar at all, unfortunately.* "Thank you," she said, and turned to Moti. Lowering her voice, she said, "This is a problem. We can't just breeze through Gohar and not feed the clans who are short on food."

Moti's eyes suddenly brightened. "What about the mage? Could he help?"

"Perhaps. Bring him here."

The mage, a man in his late thirties named Irek, frowned as he surveyed the several yarms clustered in the long grass. "I could grow some food now, yes... But if we happen across another clan within the next day, I won't be strong enough to do it again."

Coxani crossed her arms on her chest thoughtfully, her brow creased. "Plus, we can't afford to stop for every clan...we need to get these supplies to their destinations quickly." She sighed. "Irek, since we've stopped for this clan, can you grow some food for them? Moti, let's give them a peck of grains and legumes each."

When the company finally set off again, the cheers for the Caged Kingfisher resumed, and while the older nomads seemed somewhat less wary, ducking their heads in a sign of both respect and gratitude, an uneasy feeling settled over Coxani. *It's not enough.*

So long as the Anzori lords kept Tikran's hands tied, it would never be enough, and a distrust of Anzor—and, eventually, its new king—would simmer in Gohar.

Thankful for the heft of her armor, Coxani shivered beneath her cuirass. It was early spring but still quite cold in Gohar; with no trees or high hills to lessen its bite, the wind snapped at them freely as they rode across the plains. The garrison town of Eter, less than two days' travel away, was the halfway point on the route between Anzor and Dilovar, nestled in northernmost hills that bordered the central steppe. It was where Coxani would meet Bruneta, who was, according to Tikran, Coxani's age and a leader among the Sachin tribe's warriors. Coxani would be lying if she'd said she wasn't curious to meet Bruneta—while they'd both been involved in the fateful battle against Delger's Manzakars outside Areg, there had been no time for formal introductions before she, Tikran, and Damir had raced back to Anzor. Coxani looked forward to meeting the young woman who, as far as she could tell, had the same daring as Tikran.

Her company had passed through six garrison towns so far, three of which were larger and in need of supplies and extra troops. The nomads continued to treat them ambivalently, greeting them with cheers for the "Caged Kingfisher," but clearly suspicious glares at the Manzakars. The head clansmen and clanswomen in and around the towns received Coxani and Moti coolly, expressing appreciation for the food and, more often than not, a willingness to form militias to defend the forts in return. Yet something was nagging Coxani, a feeling that something was *off*, beyond the nomads' hesitation to embrace Tikran's reign fully.

As the company made camp for a quick rest that night, Coxani readied herself for the first watch. She strung her bow and sucked the cold night air into her lungs, feeling its tendrils tug at her unruly curls. Mounting her horse, she marveled at the endless black sky dotted with the brightest stars she had ever seen. Was this the way Tikran had felt during his many night watches on that first trip into Gohar? Had he felt as exhilarated? As terrified? As naked? She knew he must have; he'd told her as much.

"Good evening, Captain." Moti rode up beside her and, though she didn't look at him, she knew he must be smiling. Moti had an instantly likable character—he took things in stride and was both thoughtful and self-effacing. She fully understood why Naran had grown so close to the baby-faced Manzakar. *What's not to like?*

Coxani hid her smile. "Call me Coxani. We're both captains and we sound ridiculous addressing each other as 'captain.'"

Moti whistled, shaking his head. "Commander Naran would highly disapprove of such familiarity."

Coxani snapped him a look, her eyes narrowed. "I thought you said you're not his minion."

He grinned, revealing two dimples and a slight snaggletooth. It was an utterly endearing smile. "I'm not. But I'm his good friend. And I want to respect his wishes, at least regarding something as small as how to address you."

She snorted. "Respect his wishes regarding anything *not* involving me, please."

Sighing, Moti cleared his throat. "I'll try, Capt—er, Coxani."

The pair sat quietly for several minutes. The screech of a burrowing owl echoed in the silence and the long grass whispered to them, as if telling secrets long forgotten. Coxani was lulled into complacency, wondering what her parents would have been doing on a night like this. Granted, her family had been of the Davlat tribe and from farther east, but Gohar was Gohar. Would they have sat together beneath the stars, holding their baby daughter in their arms, hopeful and oblivious to what the future held? She shivered again, wrapping her arms around her waist, her mood now tinged with sadness...

With a punch in the chest so powerful she was propelled off her horse, Coxani felt the wind burst from her lungs as she hit the earth—hard. Gasping, she sat up, her chest throbbing and tightly compressed within her armor. Her vision danced as she tried to inhale.

Moti's arm was drawn, already loosing arrows from behind his shield. "Cap—Fuck! Coxani!"

Coxani covered herself with her shield, trying to draw breath despite the collapsed sensation in her chest beneath the cuirass, and yelled brokenly, hoarsely, "To arms! Manzakars to arms!" She looked down at the twisted lamellar plates of her cuirass, just below the neck. *Holy Cenk.* Just a couple inches higher, and she'd surely have...*gotten an arrow through the gullet.* The offending arrow lay in the crushed grass beside her—two feet long, with a bodkin arrowhead made of hardened steel, a shaft made of birch and fletched with eagle feathers.

Dilovar.

But how?

Holding her shield aloft, she hopped back onto her horse, still gasping. The attackers could see them on account of their campfires, but the Manzakars could see nothing in return. She, Moti, and their men relied solely on the sounds of hoofbeats approaching in various directions. She drew her bow from its holster along with five arrows, which she loosed one after the other into the blackness, toward the sound of the riders cantering around them, her mind running through the possibilities frantically. Had the Dilovari advanced this far into Gohar without Tikran's knowledge? Was Eter under Dilovari control?

Another arrow struck her helmet with a loud *ping*, this time falling harmlessly into her lap. In a split second, she glanced down: Short, light, with small fletching and a bone tip.

A Gohari arrow.

Wait...What?

Disoriented and in pain, she continued to fire her arrows in quick succession, unsure of who her target was or where they lay. The enemy arrows rained down on them in a deafening *rat-tat-tat-tat*—some the deadly Dilovari arrows, most the light Gohari ones. Metal and bone struck metal, leather, and occasionally flesh. Beside her, Moti stood his ground, loosing his arrows steadily, alongside her own.

"Moti, some of the arrows are Dilovari," Coxani cried, her breath rasping and chest aching. "Accompany Irek, have him light the grass at the base of the nearest hill. See if our men can outflank them!"

Moti nodded and immediately rushed to fetch the mage. Before he could return, a fire ignited behind her with a great *whoosh*, an enormous flame reaching upwards from the grass within the encampment. Their enemy had mages as well, it seemed—whether they were Dilovari or Gohari was still a mystery. Of course, Irek had been trained to immediately put the fires out—which meant their own as well—and the rain fell suddenly across the steppe in an unnatural cascade of water from the clouds above. Coxani grit her teeth as everything fell black again, raising her shield to the inevitable pummeling of arrows. The grass was certainly too wet to serve as tinder, and the battle would ensue in the dark. Some of the Dilovari arrows sounded distinctly different from the Gohari ones—their whistles were deeper, more menacing, and landed with more terrifying screams.

Who are we fighting?

Just as the Manzakars had readied themselves for a long skirmish in the pitch darkness, the assault stopped—for the time being. She and Moti rushed about, assessing the injuries of their men which, thankfully, weren't extensive. Coxani was suddenly extremely grateful for the doctor Tikran and Naran had insisted on sending with her, as he was kept busy attending the wounded. When an hour passed with no new attacks, she assigned rotations to the Manzakars. She also immediately sent two messenger pigeons back to Anzor. If her worst fears were true and Dilovar had indeed advanced this far into Gohar, Anzor needed to confront the enemy immediately. And if the alternative was true—that the Dilovari had managed to turn the nomads against Anzor and were arming them... Her gut tightened.

Tikran needs to get here fast.

"Coxani," Moti said, his face wet with dirty rain and sweat, his helmet tucked beneath his arm, "how badly are you hurt?"

"I'm fine," she insisted, crawling into her tent with Moti behind her. She peeled away her armor and tunic, taking stock of the mottled, scarlet bruise that stretched across her collarbone and down her chest.

Moti groaned. "Naran's going to kill me."

"Shut up," Coxani snapped in a huff. "You keep insisting you aren't Naran's minion, but you sure act like one. And it could have been much, much worse. I'll get the doctor to make a poultice for it as soon as he's done tending to the others."

Moti draped his arms over his knees and stared blankly at his hands. "What happened out there? Why would the Gohari fight us, let alone with Dilovar?"

Coxani slipped back into her tunic with a wince. "I don't know. Something must have happened. It makes no sense."

Moti stood with a puff. "Get some rest. I'll have the doctor come to you in a bit."

She nodded and pulled on a new cuirass, gritting her teeth as she did so. Lying on her bedroll, her eyelids slipped down with fatigue. As she sank into light, fragmented sleep, she thought of Naran and Tikran, and how absolutely infuriated they'd be if they knew...

She was determined to see this mission through, and the thought allowed her to sink into a deeper, albeit brief, repose.

CHAPTER 13

A great fire crackled in the middle of the valley, contained only by the small mage before it. Orange light danced in Tanith's eyes as her hands moved subtly, pulling the flames upward while keeping them from spreading to the surrounding grass, bushes, and trees. Like a snake's tongue, the fire licked into the air, higher and higher. Anzor's three other mages stood behind her, some distance away. At her signal, the mages turned and lit a semi-circle of fire around her and themselves.

Tikran sat on his horse, watching the proceedings with interest. Tanith had asked him to attend the drills in order to showcase her and her mages' abilities. While Tikran still had an innate distrust of magic, he'd incorporated some of its more reliable elements in his battle tactics. He knew Dilovar would do the same. He resisted the urge to cover his nose and mouth from the smoke, his eyes fixed on Tanith as she raised her arms over her head, swirled her hands, and looked up at the quickly amassing thunderclouds.

When the lightning flashed and thundered, Tikran looked up as well. The clouds gathered then parted in the center, just above Tanith and her fire, revealing an eerie center of blue, clear sky. The mages on the periphery then called the rain, and water fell in sheets, dousing the semi-circle of fire while Tanith's inferno continued to blaze. She smiled at him from behind the flames, her teeth flashing. Tikran couldn't help but notice how the glow of the fire accentuated the curves of her body beneath the black robe. She slowly twitched her fingers and the fire began to shrink, smaller and smaller. With a curious *thump!* the fire died completely.

"Very impressive," Tikran said as Tanith approached him, drawing her breath in unevenly. He frowned. "Are you all right?"

She nodded, finally breathing easily. "Suffocating a large fire is tricky," she said. "Because I'm so close to it when I deprive it of air, I find myself deprived of air too."

"You'll have to be careful not to render yourself unconscious mid-battle," Tikran said.

"I'm not worried," she answered with a smile. "It's just a matter of practice." She turned and looked at the smoke that rose from the burned grassland. "But now we have a way of maintaining our fires while putting out the enemy's. While I can't promise every one of our fires will remain, I can stop them from soaking the larger ones."

Tikran looked at Tanith thoughtfully. "These skills are impressive, but it's your knowledge of Gohar that will be the biggest advantage to us. While Damir's Essence may match your own in strength and his mastery of the magic may exceed yours, he doesn't know the lay of the land the way you do." He straightened. "Keep up the good work."

Tanith stepped back, casting her eyes downward. The mages stood behind her now, bowing to the king. She said, "Thank you, Your Highness."

With a despondency he didn't understand, Tikran rode back to the city and to the royal stables, where he left his horse with the grooms and strode directly to the dovecote for the second time that day. The pigeon-keeper began shaking his head as soon as he saw Tikran. "I'm sorry, Your Highness," he said somberly, "but nothing yet."

Tikran tried not to tense his jaw. "Thank you, Bekat." He headed back to the palace, his despondency transforming into trepidation. He'd been visiting the dovecote and checking for messages from Coxani or Moti because none had come in nearly a week. Coxani had promised to send a message at every other garrison town, which were no more than a couple days apart. At this point, she and her company should have been arriving at Eter any day now. *Has something happened?* He felt his stomach tighten as he turned the corner into the great hall at a brisk clip and collided with Naran.

Tikran let out a grunt as his commander grasped him by the shoulders. Naran could plow down a bevy of Manzakars without slowing his stride. "Anything?" Naran asked hurriedly, his eyes scanning Tikran's face.

"No." Tikran frowned.

Naran dropped his hands. "We need to send someone out there."

"Try not to overreact, okay?" Tikran said, fully aware of his hypocrisy.

"Tik, we should have received two messages from her since the last one," Naran said.

"Yes, I know." Tikran rubbed his chin. "Maybe she's asserting herself. You know, defying us because we're overprotective assholes."

Naran winced. "You think she'd do that to us?"

Tikran let out a slow breath. "I don't know. I wouldn't think so, but... Look, Naran, western Gohar is safe. It's been established time and again. Maybe something slowed them down, and she doesn't want to tell us about it. Cenk, maybe she decided to feed every Gohari between here and Eter."

Considering this, Naran said, "Actually, that does sound like something she'd do. Still, we should send someone out to—"

"Naran. Think about it. Sending someone after her won't guarantee we'll find her, since she may have taken an alternate route for one reason or another. Besides," Tikran said, lowering his voice, "can you imagine how angry she'd be if we sent someone to check up on her and she was fine?"

Naran's face fell. "But what if she's *not* fine?"

Tikran pursed his lips. "Let's give her a couple more days. Surely she'll send us a message once she arrives at Eter. And if she doesn't, Bruneta certainly will."

Naran scowled. "How am I supposed to get anything done in the meantime?"

Tikran offered him a small smile. "Have a drink. But just one."

"I can't," Naran said gruffly. "At least, not yet. Revaz has somehow talked me into going to a fancy dinner party at his manor this evening. If I wasn't actually beginning to like the guy, I'd break his jaw."

Tikran managed to keep his smile from widening. "Oh. That's good. Do some political maneuvering for me."

Grunting, Naran said, "Party or no, send for me the second you hear word from Coxani, ok?"

"Of course."

Tikran spent the rest of the evening reviewing war expenses with the council, his mind elsewhere, his knee bouncing with nervous energy. *But what if she's not fine?* Dragging his fingers through his hair, he squeezed his eyes shut briefly. He *had* to trust her abilities as a Manzakar and resist the urge to "rescue" her. If Naran had been the one in her shoes, Tikran would have been far from worried at this point. And while he would insist that it was because of her lack of experience in Gohar and, well, his love for her, she would see it very differently. He could hear her outrage: *It's because I'm a woman, isn't it?* He grimaced to himself. He had to get a grip.

It was well into the night by the time Tikran returned to his suite to retire, worn and anxious. *Maybe I'll have a nightcap.* Good grief, how had alcohol become a regular thing for him? The Manzakar who had sneered at his fellow soldiers for needing intoxicants to get through life? It was this whole "King of Anzor and Gohar" thing that was getting to him, there was no question.

Before the Aslans opened the doors to his suite, one of them cleared his throat and said, "Your Highness, Mistress Tanith awaits you inside."

Tikran paused at the doors. He'd made it clear that he did not "work" past a certain hour unless it was an emergency. He looked at the Aslan. "Is her matter urgent?"

The Manzakar lowered his eyes. "I don't think so." He shifted uneasily. "Her hair was down."

"Oh." *Oh.* Tikran's heart jumped. Was she finally taking him up on his offer? He considered a moment before muttering to the guard, "Maybe...don't burst into the bedroom tonight if you hear...noises, okay?"

The Aslan's lips almost twitched. "Yes, Your Highness."

Sitting on the very edge of the settee across from Tikran's bed, Tanith wrung her hands nervously. Since she and Tikran had shared that intimate moment those weeks ago, they had only discussed official matters, and always in the company of others. He'd been polite, friendly even, but brief, averting his eyes before she could discern any heat in them. In the meantime, she'd mulled over the implications of a relationship with the king, and it gave her goosebumps every time.

He's not just the king, she chastised herself. *He's Tikran.* And she was beginning to know him well. She knew in her core that she dealt with a young king who was kind, perceptive, thoughtful, and steadily coming into his own.

So what was she afraid of? She sighed in mild frustration. She was more than a decade older than him, for Cenk's sake. *And it's just been so long...* She'd been married to a man for a couple years but had never wanted any man this much. Only women had ever made her feel this way—one woman in particular, in fact. Perhaps her attraction to Tikran was a sign.

Maybe I'm meant to become more than just the head mage of Anzor.

She heard the doors open and she slowly got to her feet, her hands clasped tightly before her as Tikran entered the room, his eyes lit on her. "Good evening," he said softly, removing his turbaned cap and tossing it aside.

"Good evening, Tikran," she said, measuring her words carefully. "I don't mean to intrude on your private time. I just..."

He raised his eyebrows, waiting.

She looked down, her face hot. "I just thought you might want some company."

Tikran chuckled as he removed his sash and belt. "Some company? No. *Your* company?" He slipped from his jacket and draped it over the back of a chair. "I know I established that I wanted that. I was beginning to think you wouldn't take me up on it, to be honest."

"I'm..." Tanith released her breath. "...nervous, Tikran."

"Holy Cenk, Tanith," he muttered. "Don't be nervous. We're friends, remember? I may be attracted to you, but I want your friendship first and foremost."

She forced her shoulders to relax. "I'm glad to hear that."

He tilted his head, quirking a half-smile at her. "Let's just talk and play backgammon or something. While I can't deny that I want you, I certainly don't want you to feel pressured."

She felt both a tingle of surprise as well as a tiny release of tension. "I don't feel pressured. I wouldn't be here if I did. No one pressures me into anything."

Tikran sat on his bed and yanked off his boots and stockings. He shot her a meaningful look. "Not even the king of Anzor?"

She smiled. "Not even the king of Anzor."

He raised one eyebrow. "What about the Caged Kingfisher?"

"Not him either."

"And the Freed Kingfisher?"

"Nope."

"Good to know." He sat in his undershirt and breeches, grinning. "Well, should I bring out the dice?" She laughed and stood, then walked over and sat beside him on the bed. His gaze was molten. "By Cenk, you're incredibly sexy. It's been hard to ignore that fact these past several weeks."

She blushed. "You're just flattering me to get me in your bed."

"Strictly speaking, you're pretty much in my bed already. I just need to flatter your clothes off now."

Tanith laughed again, feeling her anxiety ease as Tikran smiled at her, touched her arm, joked with her. She could see that she was as therapeutic to him as he was to her, and it relaxed her further. Driven more by need than by courage, she finally leaned forward and kissed his mouth, gently. He remained still, his eyes closed until she pulled away. Embarrassed, she said, "Tikran, I want you. But I'm feeling terribly awkward…"

"Okay," he answered. "I'll make it easier for you." He jumped up and, in two quick movements, stripped completely naked. Then he hopped back on the bed and sat against the wall, holding out his arms. "I'm yours for the taking. You control everything."

Oh, Archil. She felt woozy, quivering and hot as she took in the sight of him. He was beautifully made, like a bronze god. And he sat there grinning at her, his eyes shining and cock standing at attention…

"I can still bring the dice out," he said.

"Don't bother," Tanith answered, her voice low and sultry to her own ears, her unease washed away by desire. Her hands finally steady, she unbuttoned her robe, tugged it off and away, then crawled onto the bed toward him.

CHAPTER 14

Coxani's bruise had become a tumescent purple and it hurt to even think about. The doctor thought she'd likely fractured her sternum and recommended frequent poulticing and rest. Coxani snorted to herself. *Rest. Ha!* She and Moti had been on high alert since the attack, alternately sleeping in brief intervals, in full armor, their horses almost always saddled.

What do you do if, say, you're sleeping when there's an attack?

You don't sleep. A Manzakar never sleeps.

Right. But seriously, what do you do?

You sleep with your breeches on.

Coxani smiled, remembering how she'd found Tikran's advice to "sleep with your jacket, boots, and sword on, and make sure your horse is always saddled" utterly impractical.

It's practical when you might have Dilovaris shooting and hacking at you at any moment.

He had been so right.

Now, as they approached Eter, Coxani's Manzakars were prepared for anything. She'd had scouts ride ahead and confirm that the outpost was still under Anzori control. The scouts reported that there was a heavy nomad presence in and around the town, but she'd expected that—Bruneta was supposed to be there with her warriors. Still, she felt apprehensive. Why were the Gohari siding with Dilovar and attacking the Manzakars? Which tribes were they from? Surely the attackers weren't among Bruneta's warriors...

A number of them sat on their horses and watched from atop the hills as Coxani's company rode into Eter. The warriors were well-armed, sporting leather cuirasses, two bows each, and painted wooden shields, their faces calm but vigilant. The company's reception was equal parts warm and aloof, with the occasional cheer for the Caged Kingfisher ringing out from groups of children. The fort's commander, a man named Mamun, approached the Manzakars as they came to a stop, a young Gohari woman walking alongside him. Coxani knew instantly the woman was Bruneta— not from the eagle feathers in her hair, or the beaded calfskin tunic, or even the gorgeous recurve bow she carried at her hip. *She has his eyes.* More than that—she had Tikran's gaze, its intensity.

Coxani and Moti dismounted and stood side by side. She heard her co-captain mutter, "Oh, wow..."

"Captains, welcome to Eter," Mamun said as he and Bruneta stopped before them. Mamun was a Manzakar-looking Manzakar if Coxani ever saw one, with his black mustache and muscular neck.

"Thank you, Commander," Coxani said, then looked at the woman and smiled. The woman bore the dark, thin tattoos of a Gohari warrior across her cheekbones and down her chin. "You must be Bruneta," Coxani said. "You look so much like Tikran it's almost startling."

Bruneta smiled back. "He's prettier than I am, by all accounts," she said.

"Oh, I disagree," Moti blurted. Coxani gave him a strange look as he went red. He cleared his throat and held his hand out to the Gohari warrior. "I'm Captain Moti."

Bruneta's smile faded as she eyed his outstretched hand,

making no move to take it. Mamun quickly swept in. "I expect your journey thus far has been smooth?"

"Actually, it hasn't." Coxani straightened, pulling the Dilovari arrow from her quiver. "I was struck by this two nights ago, just outside Robi. We were hit by both Dilovari and Gohari arrows, but we never got good looks at our attackers. They had mages with them and the skirmish took place mostly in the dark."

Mamun took the arrow from her, his brow heavily furrowed. "By Cenk! How did that get over here? We must send a message to Anzor."

"It's been done," Coxani said. She looked at Bruneta. "Is there any reason the nomads would take up arms against us?"

Bruneta frowned thoughtfully. "None of my warriors would do that, I can promise you. Their allegiance is to me and Beg Ayym, and we both fully support Tikran."

Beg Ayym, Coxani knew, was the chief of the Sachin tribe. She tilted her head. "And the other tribes?"

"I know the Davlat tribe has been more reluctant than the others to get behind Tikran," Bruneta said, setting her hands on her hips. "But there have been no sightings of Davlat warriors this far west in months, as far as I know."

"We'll send a scouting team out across the central steppe," Mamun said. "See if we can find any indication of who they are or where they went."

Coxani looked at Bruneta. "Any chance your chief might know something?"

"There's always a chance," Bruneta answered. "Beg Ayym wanted to meet you and Captain Moti, in any case. I'll take you this afternoon."

After setting up camp in Eter, Coxani and Moti walked to the fort to meet up with Bruneta. Coxani gave Moti the side-eye as they walked through the town to where the wooden fort stood, at the center square. "You think you can keep your mouth from hanging open this time?"

Moti raised his eyebrows. "What? What are you talking about?"

"Good grief, man, you were practically drooling on Bruneta's boots."

"Oh." Moti shrugged and smiled his crooked smile. "Well, she's gorgeous. I hope I didn't come across as too much of a moron."

Coxani winced. "You came across as...something."

"Whatever. Time to focus, Coxani." Moti loosened his shoulders and turned his head from side to side, as if preparing for a boxing match. "I've heard this guy, Beg Ayym, is some tough shit. He and his warriors skirmished against Manzakars in the east a few times and caused quite a bit of damage. We have to prove our worth to him."

"Prove our worth?" Coxani scratched her head. "Why?"

Moti gave her a meaningful look. "Since Tikran became king of Anzor, fresh Gohari blood has come to power. These new chieftains are young and ready to fight. I used to think it was all for the Caged Kingfisher, but now I'm beginning to wonder." He rubbed his chin. "They're angry at what's happened to them and determined to bring Gohar back."

Coxani chewed her lip. "The Sachin tribe is on our side. Bruneta said as much."

"I don't know, Coxani," Moti said, lowering his voice. "I want to believe it. But we still don't know who attacked us two nights ago. We need to go into this expecting that they're going to judge us. We need to represent Tikran in the best way possible."

Trying not to smirk, Coxani said, "Well, then, Captain, maybe don't salivate over their commander like a hopeful puppy, yeah?"

As she picked up her pace, she heard Moti mumble, "Whatever," and it made her smile. It was crystal clear how he and Naran had become close friends.

Bruneta awaited them at the fort with their horses, dressed in what Coxani guessed to be her Gohari commander's attire. She wore a red felt hat with a curved, pointed top and long sides that covered her ears. The rim and sides were intricately embroidered and beaded. Over her tunic, she donned a sheepskin vest that was tasseled with red-dyed horsehair. She looked formidable, to say the least. Leaping onto her horse, she looked back at them with a smile. "Ready?"

Moti mounted his gelding and asked, "How far are we going, ah, Miss—"

Bruneta threw back her head and laughed. "Just Bruneta, Captain. We're not in Anzor. We're not going too far, just half an hour north."

After a stretch of silence, Coxani rode up beside Bruneta. She said, "I don't know how much you know about my history with Tikran."

Bruneta didn't look at her. "I don't know anything. I've only just begun to get reacquainted with Tikran. I was four years old when he was sold."

"Right." Coxani cleared her throat, ignoring the sharp pain in her ribcage. "We were bought and sold by the same slave trader. I was younger than him and so distraught by being separated from what family I knew that I cried constantly. Tikran eventually gave me his toy rabbit to soothe me."

Smiling, Bruneta said, "Wig. Yes, he told me he gave the toy to a girl." She looked down, as if remembering some private memory. "When I was a child, the rabbit was the only thing that felt safe to me. It was Tikran's doing. He thought my sister and I would put more faith in a stuffed toy than in our brother, since he was also scared and just a little boy."

Something about Bruneta's words caught in Coxani's battered chest. "Bruneta, he's still that boy."

Bruneta looked over at her gravely. "He needs to stop that shit."

Coxani kept silent, feeling abruptly anxious for Tikran. *Yes, he does.*

After some time, Coxani noticed figures in the distance, shimmering in the daylight. As they came closer, the figures solidified and took shape—clusters of yarms dotted the stretches of long grass ahead, with nomads herding, riding, cooking, and cleaning in their midst. Sheep and goats rambled on the periphery, guided by young herders in felt hats who clicked their tongues; elderly women washed clothes and hung them to dry on a line, laughing amongst themselves; children chased one another with long sticks, pausing long enough to shout "Caged Kingfisher" in the Manzakars' direction.

Beyond the yarms, a long line of horsemen snaked along the horizon, watching them. There were hundreds of them. Her hand slipped to the grip of her saber instinctively and she heard Moti's sharp intake of breath beside her. They were two lone Manzakars, riding into the nomad heartland. *It's out of our hands.* Her fingers fell away from her sword as she exhaled slowly, mentally forcing herself to relinquish her power to the Gohari. She felt Moti stiffen at her side.

The warriors all had feathers and beads adorning their hair and tunics, with bows, arrows, and daggers hanging from their belts. They bowed their heads as their leader approached, their eyes darting surreptitiously to the Manzakars. Bruneta led Coxani and Moti to the center cluster of yarms. They were larger and elaborately painted with big cats that had long, dark hair extending from their ears. *The lynx.* Tikran had told Coxani it was the Sachin tribe's emblem. "Wait here," Bruneta said before ducking into the largest of the yarms.

"Here goes," Moti muttered under his breath, his arm brushing against Coxani's.

Bruneta re-emerged from the yarm with the chieftain of the Sachin and the Manzakars gaped. Coxani found her voice first. Showing respect in the Gohari way, she stepped forward, bowed her head once, put her hand over her heart, and said, "Beg Ayym, you honor us. Thank you for receiving us."

Beg Ayym smiled, the beads of her headdress tinkling, her rich brown eyes taking in the sight of the two soldiers. Crossing two bare, sinewy arms over her chest, she said, "Respectful Manzakars. I never thought I'd see the day."

A LARGE, hollowed-out ibex horn was passed from person to person, around no fewer than six central fires just as the sun sank beneath the horizon. When the horn reached her, Coxani received its glossy, ridged exterior within her cupped hands and bowed her head at the smiling nomad who handed it over. She had no idea what its contents held, only that she had to drink, or risk offending her hosts. Without thinking, she put her lips to the horn's edge and tilted its contents into her mouth.

Salty. Thick. *Oh, Cenk.* Was it horse's blood? *Doesn't matter. Doesn't matter. Doesn't. Fucking. Matter.* They were here to convince the Sachin to fight alongside Anzor against Dilovar, and she would drink whatever was in that horn. She swallowed, licked her lips, and handed the horn to Moti. His eyes were huge. She narrowed hers in response. He took it dutifully, not hesitating before taking a big gulp. *Good boy.* Coxani smiled to herself. Her smile faded a bit as her stomach growled in protest.

"We're pleased that you have joined us tonight in our istarek sharing ritual, Manzakars," Beg Ayym said, her dark eyes twinkling at them from across the campfires. Ayym, likely in her late twenties, was not a small woman—she was as tall as many of the men, with just as much muscle. She stretched her legs out before her now, leaning back on strong, brown arms.

"Of course, Beg," Coxani answered. "Tikran wants to make clear his commitment to Gohar's safety and protection, as well as its eventual independence."

"Is that so?" A male voice, belonging to one of the warriors, cut in.

"Sit down, Omid," Bruneta said calmly, not even bothering to look in his direction.

The young man, likely Coxani's age, paced beside the fires, his face tight with emotion. He was tattooed with lines across each cheekbone and down his chin like the rest of the warriors; he wore a calfskin tunic adorned with feathers and horsehair and carried no fewer than three daggers in his belt. "No, Bruneta. I need to understand what this Manzakar means." He looked sharply at Coxani. "The king of Anzor supports Gohar's independence, you say?"

"Careful," Moti muttered from the corner of his mouth.

"The king of Anzor," Coxani said slowly, her gaze held steady on the warrior, "is Tikran of the Caged Kingfisher. Have you forgotten?"

Omid let out a skeptical laugh. "Should that mean anything to us, Manzakar? We know what power does to people, even the most well-meaning. The Caged Kingfisher no longer exists. He has been declawed and become a puppet to Anzor's elite."

Coxani felt the heat rise into her throat. "What—"

"Careful," Moti hissed.

Coxani stood, if only to get away from Moti's hissing. She leveled a look at Omid. "Tikran risks his life as we speak to ensure Gohar goes free."

He stared aloofly at her. "Why should we believe you?"

She hesitated for just a moment. "He didn't want to be king. He wanted to fight for Gohar. He was prepared, in fact, to die for Gohar. The fact that he's king changes nothing."

"You're wrong," Omid said, shaking his head. "The fact that he's king changes everything. And the ones who put him in power know exactly that." The warrior paused, narrowing his eyes at Coxani. "So tell me, Manzakar. Why should we follow your king against Dilovar? What can he guarantee us, other than death?"

In the silence that followed, Coxani understood that she was alone. She would get no support from Bruneta or Beg Ayym. If Moti hadn't looked positively green around the gills, he might have been some help. She lifted her chin, her eyes not wavering from Omid's. "There's nothing I can say that will convince you, but I stand by what I said: Tikran will fight for Gohar's freedom if it's the last thing he does."

A small, cruel smile twisted Omid's lips. "Oh, I see... Are you his lover or something?"

"That's enough, Omid," Beg Ayym said softly, still leaning back casually on her arms, her strong legs kicked out in front of her. She let out a deep sigh. "I believe this Manzakar. While I never got the chance to meet him personally, I think Tikran has our best interests at heart. If nothing else, he's more interested in protecting us than Dilovar ever has and likely ever will. As such, we will fight alongside him."

Oh, thank Cenk! Coxani felt more relieved than victorious. She looked back at Omid. His eyes were fixed on hers, his arms crossed on his chest, his expression giving nothing away.

"Don't mind him." Bruneta stood beside her, a small smile on her face. "He's trying to mess with you. It's mental warfare."

Coxani looked at her. "He won't win."

Bruneta's grin widened. "I like you, Coxani. Tikran was right about you."

Coxani stammered, "I thought you said... What did Tikran—"

"Your co-captain looks like he's going to be sick," Bruneta interrupted, an eyebrow raised.

Oh, shit. Coxani sat back down next to Moti, where he hunched with his head hanging between his knees. "Moti, you need to get a grip," she whispered firmly as she crouched next to him. "You absolutely cannot throw up right now. It would likely be seen as a huge insult."

Moti nodded miserably. "Okay. But... I'm gonna need to throw up eventually."

Grabbing him by the shoulder and squeezing, Coxani muttered, "Just not anytime soon, soldier. Mind over matter."

"All right," Moti said weakly, as the fire closest to the pair suddenly flared, making them both flinch from the heat. Two old nomads and a young one approached the fire from the other side, their faces washed orange from the dancing flames. The elderly nomads wore elaborate collars of feathers, horsehair dyed in every color, beads, and bones. Their heads were shaved bare, regardless of whether they were male or female. They each held scapula bones out into the fire, their lips uttering a soft chant, while the younger nomad, a woman wearing a short, conical hat made of a patchwork of fabrics, owl feathers, and beaded tassels of leather, moved her slender fingers in the air, drawing the fire higher. *A Gohari mage.* Coxani leaned closer, fascinated. The nomads had already begun incorporating the Essence into their traditions, it seemed. With the flick of the mage's wrist, the fire shrank, and the older nomads turned away from the fire. They approached Beg Ayym together and showed her scorched, cracked bones.

Ayym nodded, then stood and walked over to Coxani and Moti, a strip of leather strung with small blue beads and sheep's knuckle bones in her palm. She looked from one to the other as they stood, then said, "The spirits of our ancestors have spoken through the bones. The Sachin tribe vows to follow King Tikran into war against Dilovar." She held up the string of beads and bone. "Give this to your king as a token of our commitment to him. Tell him to wear it into battle." Coxani bowed her head and held out her hand, whereupon Ayym wrapped it several times around Coxani's wrist, then tied the ends of the leather in a knot. Ayym smiled. "Now, we feast."

Coxani smiled back. She could practically hear Moti's misery as several nomads brought over a whole roasted lamb, garnished with onion bulbs and dandelion leaves, on a tray. When Ayym turned away, Coxani patted her co-captain on the back in both a gesture of comfort and warning. The pair sat once again and accepted heaping servings of lamb each. As they ate, the mood became more casual and the Gohari seemed to relax, laughing and talking amongst themselves. As Coxani pulled a chunk of meat from the bone with her fingers, Omid came and sat next to her. She paused before taking the bite but didn't look at him.

"Your king now has the Sachin's tribe allegiance, Manzakar," Omid said, leaning on his knees and staring into the fire. "But that's just half the battle. How will you get the Davlat to side with you?"

She chewed slowly and swallowed before saying, "I will ask for your tribe's help in persuading them."

"That won't work," Beg Ayym said from where she sat cross-legged, looking pensively into her bowl of lamb. "Rumor has it that the Davlat have thrown their lot in with Bilguun."

Bruneta, who sat beside Ayym, snapped her chief a look of surprise. "You didn't tell me that."

"I'm telling you now," Ayym answered, staring at Coxani. "I don't know what their reasons are, and they have been very closed off about it, avoiding the other tribes like the plague in the last few months."

Coxani's breath caught. "We were attacked two days ago, near Robi. The attackers had both Gohari and Dilovari arrows."

Ayym rubbed her chin. "Bold of them, to wander so far west. But yes, it had to be the Davlat."

"Beg Ayym," Coxani said, straightening. "Help me convince them otherwise."

Beside her, Omid threw back his head and laughed. "Are you crazy? Confronting the Davlat at this point would be completely idiotic of you, Manzakar. They would shoot you with their Dilovari arrows and be done with it."

"My mission in coming to Gohar was to secure the allegiance of the Gohari," Coxani said steadily. "The Davlat make up approximately two-fifths of the Gohari, according to Anzori estimations. Does that sound right to you, Beg?"

"Yes," Ayym answered reluctantly. "They are a larger tribe than we are."

Coxani pursed her lips, her heart racing. "I don't know what happened that made them side with Bilguun, but Tikran needs their support. I am originally from the Davlat tribe. Perhaps I can speak to their chieftain."

Omid leaned back, his hands in hair, an incredulous smile on his face. "The Manzakar is stark, raving mad, Beg."

"Beg Ayym." Bruneta stood. "I request your permission to accompany the Manzakars into eastern Gohar to negotiate with the Davlat."

"Oh, shit," Omid muttered under his breath, but Coxani heard him.

Ayym frowned, her eyes darting from Bruneta to Coxani. "We don't want to fight our own people. It would be in our best interest to try and sway the Davlat to fight alongside us, to keep the tribes united." She fixed a fierce gaze on Coxani. "But this could go very, very badly. You could inadvertently force your king into war before he's ready."

"My goal is to negotiate," Coxani answered evenly. "But either way, Tikran will be ready."

As if in response, Moti dove for the nearest bushes and retched, bringing up his dinner. Coxani resisted the urge to cover her face.

Perfect timing, Captain.

CHAPTER 15

Berk lay down on the riverbank, letting the freshly sprouted grass tickle his nose as he peered across the rolling surface of the water. Turning to his side, he dropped his hand into the gentle waves with a splash. He lifted his head to look at Damir, who crouched beside him, gazing broodingly into the river. The head mage had been distant since that first day, and Berk would have been lying if he'd said he wasn't disappointed. Oh, Damir was still kind to him, and a patient teacher. But for some reason, Berk had expected...he didn't know what.

And it angered him.

"Do you sense any tinder?" Damir asked, looking straight ahead.

"Yes," Berk answered softly.

The mage looked at him sharply then. "What?"

Berk shrugged. "Plants beneath the water. The fish."

"The *fish*?" Damir gaped at him.

"Well, not the fish, exactly," Berk amended. "Parts of the fish. Maybe it isn't the fish at all." He huffed. "I don't know."

Damir heaved a sigh. "Right. Listen, Berk. If you can avoid the fish, that would be best. But slowly—and I *do* mean slowly—begin to warm what tinder you feel."

"Yes, sir." Berk exhaled slowly and closed his eyes, reaching deliberately with his Essence like Damir had taught him. He slowly warmed the things that didn't flick quickly away from him; the water was heavy and made warming anything more laborious. He found himself getting frustrated.

"Easy," Damir murmured, resting a firm hand on Berk's shoulder. "There's no reason to feel discouraged. Steady, now."

Damir's touch was soothing, and Berk's anger dissipated some. He felt the water around his fingers grow hot, and he wiggled them, sending the heat away. It felt good—and better by the second. He continued to do this, his fingers aching pleasantly, when suddenly he heard Damir utter an oath. Berk lifted himself onto his elbow, watching in awe as the surface of the river stilled and began to bubble. What began as the soft simmering of a warm drink rapidly transformed into the aggressive boiling of a cauldron. Dead fish began to float to the surface, their bodies stiff, their scales pale and opaque.

"Holy Cenk, Berk, *stop*," Damir commanded, jumping to his feet.

Berk's hand felt like it would shatter as he tried to reel his Essence back in. "I'm...trying..." He let out a cry of agony. "It hurts!"

He felt Damir's tight grip on his shoulder. "There, now. Draw it back in. The pain will stop soon."

Berk whimpered as the tendrils of Essence retreated into his trembling hands. "I *hate* that feeling, Master Damir," he managed, trying to keep his voice from cracking.

"Every powerful mage has to contend with it," Damir said softly, patting Berk's back in encouragement. "You must learn to manage it."

But I'm more powerful than most, aren't I? Berk didn't say the words out loud, but he felt them in his bones. Could Damir truly understand his pain? Could anyone? With a wail, he yanked the last of his magic back into himself. The flash of pain blinded him briefly, then all was calm.

"Berk," Damir muttered, rubbing Berk's back gently, "it's all right. You did well."

Like the unfurling of a leaf, Berk shuddered and relaxed against Damir's hand. He opened his mouth to speak when Damir jerked away. "Come. We must head back to the palace."

Berk sat up, still shivering. "Why?"

The Manzakars came into view, their armor and domed helmets gleaming in the daylight. Berk's reaction was visceral, starting in his core and quaking outward. His vision began to shake when Damir clamped a hand on each of Berk's arms. "No, Berk. No. Do you hear me?" His voice was unyielding and as deep as Berk had ever heard it. It wasn't until he felt the skin of Damir's palm, its warmth against his own, that he stopped trembling.

The mage's gray eyes peered down at him, shimmering with sympathy. "If you learn nothing else, you must learn to prevent your emotions from controlling your Essence. Come on, lad."

At that moment, Berk would have followed Damir to the ends of the earth. "Yes, sir." As they stood and began walking toward the Manzakars, Berk asked hesitantly, "Where are we going?"

"Back to the palace," Damir said, the softness in his tone dropping away, leaving nothing but jagged edges. "Prince Vazha is here."

Berk would have felt a modicum of joy, if not for Damir's obvious dread. Who could he trust in this place? Could he trust anyone? As he followed the Dilovari mage, Berk reached for the bracelet around his wrist—a leather strip of blue beads and sheep knuckle bones—and prayed silently to the spirits of his ancestors.

Oh, Archil. Help me.

"MASTER DAMIR, why am I not surprised to see you here again today?" The fencing-master, Meyhan, laughed as Damir entered the large area beside the arena that had been cordoned off for weapons training.

Damir smiled as he went to the wall of lances, axes, maces and swords, and selected his usual saber. "You were right, Meyhan. The sport is quite addictive," Damir replied, watching the saber's blade blink in the light as he twisted the hilt in his hand. *It's also a perfect outlet for certain frustrations.*

"Indeed." Meyhan paused. "Unfortunately, I am retiring for the evening, so you will have spar with a dummy until tomorrow."

"Oh, that's fine," Damir said, looking at the hay-stuffed figures that stood halfway across the training grounds. "I just wanted to practice my attacks and get some exercise."

"Of course," the fencing-master replied as he walked toward the gates that led out of the training area. He paused then, tilting his head and looking at Damir. "Are you quite all right, Master Damir?"

Startled by the question, Damir said, "Yes, Meyhan. Perfectly."

After the gate creaked shut behind Meyhan, Damir frowned. Was he looking so pathetic these days that the fencing-master felt the need to ask him if he was all right? Yes, perhaps he'd channeled a bit too much of his frustrations into his lessons, but it couldn't be helped. The moment he held the saber in his hands, he felt power —*normal* power. Not magic. He imagined that he experienced the same sense of power Tikran did, the type of power people understood and respected, not loathed.

He approached the dummy and lunged, striking the thing in its amorphous torso. He couldn't just rely on magic. Magic, after all, was unreliable. He didn't trust it—particularly after watching Berk *boil fucking fish in a river.*

Damir subjected the dummy to the thrusts and cuts of his blade several more times, lost in thought. He'd tried to avoid allowing Berk from experimenting on living things, plants and trees aside. The dead fish had been an unexpected result of Berk's lesson with heat and water—a *very* unexpected one. The incident had, much to Damir's dismay, become a point of pride for Berk, and while it may have had nothing to do with the unintended death of Cenk knows how much aquatic life, the boy's pleasure struck fear in Damir.

Fish are not people, Damir kept reminding himself. While this should have eased his fears to an extent, Damir knew firsthand how the Essence felt when it was used to destroy life. It was a dark, tempting abyss, an overwhelming lure to continue...The Essence seeped into his bones, into his very fiber when he used it to destroy and kill. *It feels so good.* Every time Damir imagined what that kind of feeling could do to a youth like Berk, he began to feel helpless, nearly frantic. How could he keep terrible things from happening when the boy's Essence was clearly more powerful than his, and yet the boy himself was so much weaker than he was?

Swinging his saber again and again, Damir lost himself for several moments as the dummy took on the features of Prince Vazha. Damir saw nothing but the red of his rage. *Vazha Delger.* The monster had manipulated Berk's mind. He'd taken advantage of his position and seduced a traumatized teenager to do his bidding.

Revenge. I will get revenge.

"Master Damir! Master Damir!" Berk was suddenly grabbing his arm excitedly. It wasn't until Damir heard the boy's voice that he realized he'd set the straw-filled sack on fire.

And what a fire. The straw crumbled into ash instantly, consumed by the angry flames Damir had conjured unwittingly. Drawing his magic back with a painful wince, Damir dropped his saber. He moved his hands above the flaming dummy and, with a thump, the fire went out, leaving a charred pile of straw in its wake.

"Wow," Berk uttered, watching the smoke rise from the pile of burned detritus.

Taking a deep breath to steady himself, Damir said, "What are you doing here, Berk?"

The boy stepped back, swallowing. "I...followed you. I'm sorry, Master Damir. You seemed happy to be going somewhere for a change, and I wanted to see why."

Startled, Damir blinked. "What? I'm generally happy—"

"You're not, though," Berk interjected vehemently, his brown eyes large and full of...something.

Damir drew himself straight, refocusing. "I've been learning how to wield a saber. It's good physical exercise. I suppose it's brought me joy."

Berk tilted his head. "More joy than the Essence?"

Damir smiled sadly, his fingers still tingling with pain. "The Essence, lad, only brings real joy when used to reinforce life. When it's used as a weapon of war..." He trailed off.

Berk frowned. "It's brought me joy."

"That's not joy," Damir replied, trying his best not to sound concerned. The pitch of his voice became lower, heavier, as he said, "That's the feeling of raw power." When Berk peered up at him in confusion, Damir mentally shook himself, smiled, and said, "Would you care to learn the art of the blade, Master Berk?"

Berk grinned. "I would, Master Damir."

Damir nodded and stepped away, toward the rows of weapons that lined the stone wall. He chose a saber much like his own and handed it, hilt first, to Berk. "This is the Dilovari soldier's blade of choice. It's also the Manzakar's."

Berk's eyes lit up at the mention of Manzakars. He took the saber from Damir and tilted it from side to side, his eyes wide with fascination. "Will you teach me to use it?"

"Yes, on one condition." Damir leaned forward and narrowed his eyes at his charge. "Absolutely no magic."

Berk's head jerked up. "But I saw you using—"

"That was a mistake," Damir said firmly. "I made a mistake. I let my anger get the best of me." He backed away slowly, considering for a moment. Finally, he said, "We'll begin with footwork. Set the saber down for now."

"What? But I want—"

"Berk." Smiling, Damir raised his eyebrows. "Would you rather be reading? Because if so, you're welcome to go back to your books."

Berk let his sword fall to the ground with a thud. "No, Master Damir. I'd rather be with you."

Something in the boy's tone made Damir want to crumple to the floor and sob. Instead, he swallowed, smiled, and said, "Very well. First, you will learn to run as fast as you can, stop, turn, and run back."

Berk stared in disbelief. "How will I keep from getting winded without magic?"

"For that," Damir said, holding up a finger, "you may use your Essence. But only for that."

Grimacing, Berk muttered, "This still sounds awful."

Damir grinned. "Indeed. But I will do it with you. We will run one fourth the length of this furlong and back."

The boy slowly smiled, clearly sensing some friendly competition. "All right, then. Let's go."

Damir unbuttoned his robe, slipped it off, and set it aside. Then he bound his long hair in a thong. Crouching in his undershirt and breeches beside Berk, Damir winked and said, "On three. One...two..."

CHAPTER 16

"Your Highness." Bekat smiled stiffly. "My deepest apologies. But—"

"Nothing?" Tikran scrubbed his face with his hands, then dragged his fingers along his scalp. *Something's wrong.* "Are you certain?"

Bekat's face fell. "I'm so sorry, my king. But there's nothing from Captain Coxani or Captain Moti."

"What about Bruneta? Of the Sachin tribe?"

"No, Your Highness. Nothing."

"Commander Mamun of Eter?"

The pigeon keeper tilted his head. "I don't think so, but we did have a bird arrive from another part of Gohar this morning."

Tikran sucked in his breath. "Show me."

Bekat brought the bird from its cage, untied the message from the pigeon's leg, and handed the small scroll to Tikran.

Captains Coxani and Moti have arrived safely, well received by the Sachin.—Commander Mamun

Dizzy with relief, Tikran exhaled. "Thank you, Bekat."

"Your Highness..." Bekat inspected the bird in his hands, stroking the maroon and white streaks in its neck feathers, the corners of his mouth downturned.

"Yes?"

The pigeon keeper shook his head. "It's likely nothing. I just find it strange that this particular bird came from Eter. I could have sworn it was sent to one of the eastern outposts."

"You know your birds well enough to tell?"

Bekat shrugged. "I trained them, after all. Of course, I could be mistaken."

"Perhaps there was a swapping of pigeons between outposts," Tikran said, feeling doubt worm into his mind.

Bekat nodded. "Yes, it was likely a mix-up. Forgive me for wasting your time, my king."

"You were incredibly helpful, Bekat," Tikran replied. "No apology necessary."

With most of the weight lifted from his shoulders, Tikran headed straight to the hippodrome, where he knew Naran was subjecting the Manzakars and cadets to some rigorous training. All Level Three cadets would be sent to the front lines, much to Tikran's dismay. Still, the council had tried to convince him to send the Level Two cadets as well, but Tikran was having none of that idiocy. *What, send a bunch of boys out there to die? Are you crazy?* Furiously, he wondered whether the council would be as willing to sacrifice Manzakar lives once rich Anzori boys began joining their ranks.

He heard Naran's voice before he saw the commander's hulking figure standing in the middle of two concentric circles of mounted Manzakars, holding a lance in his hand as he barked orders. He saw Tikran approaching and immediately directed the lance-master to take over. The Manzakars turned, saw their king, and began dismounting.

"No, no," Tikran shook his head emphatically. "Continue with your training, I command it!" Being king was a real pain in the ass. As the lance-master nodded and called the Manzakars back to attention, Naran jogged up to him.

"Coxani?" He came to a stop before Tikran, his eyes hopeful.

"Yes." Tikran smiled. "A message from Commander Mamun arrived this morning. All is well."

"Thank Cenk." Naran let out his breath, reached out, and squeezed Tikran's shoulder. "I appreciate you, Tik." He paused, hesitating. "But you know, I still think we should send—"

"Your Highness, Lord Haydar requests your immediate presence in the great hall," an attendant said, striding toward them.

Good grief, it never ends. Tikran nodded at the servant and said to his friend, "Naran, I have to get back to the palace. I'm sure everything is fine. You need to relax, brother."

Naran scowled and turned away, and the doubt that the pigeon keeper had left in Tikran's mind suddenly grew. As Tikran entered the hall, dwelling on Bekat's words, Haydar beckoned to him. "King Tikran, Lord Ruslan requests an audience with you."

Oh, no. Tikran grimaced. "Why?"

Haydar narrowed his eyes in disapproval and put his hands behind his back. "He says it's of utmost importance to the kingdom of Anzor."

Great. "Fine, call him in." Rather than sit on the throne, which made Tikran feel ridiculously pompous, he usually chose to sit at the council's table when receiving people. The fact that the subject visiting was Ruslan, however, kept him on his feet rather than sitting at all.

Ruslan entered with a broad smile on his sun-tanned face, his long strides full of energy, trailed by two attendants carrying large sacks. The Anzori lord bowed before Tikran with a flourish. "Your Highness, King Tikran, my liege, thank you for receiving me."

Tikran was immediately annoyed. He crossed his arms on his chest and lifted an eyebrow. "Lord Haydar says you have news of utmost importance to the kingdom. I'm all ears."

Ruslan turned to his attendants and nodded. They promptly opened the sacks to reveal folded rugs, which they spread out on the floor, side by side. The wool of one was intricately woven into brightly colored medallions of red, blue, and yellow hues; another depicted suns and moons in complex geometric patterns; a third shimmered with silk thread, rendering gazelles and lions in muted shades of cream and brown. "I have been traveling through Gohar these past several weeks, and I discovered that the Gohari are skilled artisans. Look at the craftsmanship of these rugs!"

"They are indeed beautiful," Tikran murmured, crouching down to run his hands along the plush surface of one of the rugs. He fingered the carefully braided edges and soft fringe. He remembered seeing some very old, faded, or plain rugs while in Gohar, but nothing like these.

"I didn't know they were capable of such creations," Ruslan said.

Tikran tried to bite back his acerbic response but failed. "When people aren't starving and fighting for survival, they are always capable of amazing things."

Ruslan looked unfazed. "Naturally, Your Highness. And I think they should be rewarded for their productivity. This type of merchandise would sell very well in Kalevi, now that you've reinstated trade with the northern kingdoms. It would line Anzor's coffers, without a doubt."

Tikran stood slowly. "Anzor's coffers? Are you suggesting we exploit the nomads?"

Ruslan splayed a jewel-encrusted hand on his chest. "I make no such suggestion, my king. The nomads will be well paid for their work, of course. The arrangement would benefit them immensely."

"But it would benefit *you* more, wouldn't it, Lord Ruslan?" Tikran said, resisting the urge to make a fist—a fist he'd wanted to throw in Ruslan's face for months.

A slow, seemingly benign smile slid across Ruslan's face. "I am a servant of Anzor, and you are its king, Your Highness. Lest you forget."

"A brilliant idea, Lord Ruslan," Haydar interjected from his corner, approaching briskly. Tikran had nearly forgotten the durai was there, he'd been so quiet. Haydar squatted down to the rugs and ran his fingers across them. "Of unsurpassed quality! One rug must have required the fleeces of four sheep, at least, and an entire season of work."

Tikran snapped out of his furious trance then, immediately understanding what Haydar was doing. He also suddenly grasped that, whatever Ruslan was doing, he was succeeding. *Relax, you idiot.* "Come to think of it," Tikran amended, rubbing his chin, "I think this arrangement could benefit everyone equally, if done right."

Dismay flitted across Ruslan's face very briefly, his smile faltering. "I'm glad you see my side of things, King Tikran."

"Oh, absolutely." Tikran turned and grinned at the men of the council who sat about, watching. "I will most definitely consider your proposition, Lord Ruslan." He paused. "You may leave the rugs."

Ruslan frowned. "Leave the rugs, Your Highness?"

"Yes." Tikran crouched down again, stroking the rugs as though they were precious but vicious pets. "I want the entire court to appreciate your contribution to Anzor's economy."

As Ruslan left the great hall, Haydar rested a hand on Tikran's shoulder. "Laid it on a bit thick, didn't you, lad?"

Tikran smiled vaguely. "Barely veiled disdain is the only language these Anzori aristocrats understand, my lord."

Haydar's lips twitched. "Indeed, Tikran. Indeed."

***

AFTER LEAVING THE GREAT HALL, Haydar headed to Lord Revaz's office, his pulse quickening. He was immediately annoyed with himself. *Stop it. You're much too old for this silliness.* Still, as he turned the corner and heard Revaz's voice, his heart skipped a beat. As much as he hated to admit it, spending time in Revaz's company had become the indisputable highlight of Haydar's days. And luckily for him, the two men spent much of their time together since Revaz had been made chief justiciar, attending council meetings, advising Tikran on legal matters, managing the treasury...

Trying to temper his giddiness, he reminded himself that hoping for any sort of romantic reciprocity from the young, handsome lord was not just ludicrous, it was laughable. Revaz was a blue blood Anzori, likely only interested in women, and a good fifteen years younger. *Get a grip, old man.*

He raised his knuckles to rap against Revaz's door when he heard what was unquestionably Naran's baritone voice: "I didn't curse at all during the dinner, what are you talking about?"

Haydar paused, his hand poised to knock, choosing to eavesdrop for a moment.

"You let a few choice phrases slip a couple of times," Revaz replied.

"Bullshit!" Naran's voice was a growl.

"Commander," Revaz said calmly, "I distinctly remember you turning to Lord Miras and saying that I had a 'shit-eating grin' on my face."

"Well, that's not cursing!" Naran protested. "That's just foul language. And for the record, you *did* have a shit-eating grin on your face."

Haydar snickered quietly to himself before clearing his throat, rearranging his expression to be suitably solemn, and knocking. Was it Haydar's imagination, or did Revaz's face light up when he opened the door and saw Haydar there? *He's probably just glad someone interrupted his argument with Naran.* "Lord Haydar," Revaz said, opening the door wider and stepping aside. "Please come in."

Haydar moved into the study and raised his eyebrows at Naran. "I hope I'm not intruding?"

"Lord Haydar." Naran stood, a scowl on his face. "What kind of people think the word 'shit' is off-limits during a casual conversation?"

Haydar stifled a smile. "Unfortunately, most polite society disapproves of the word in any sort of conversation, particularly those that take place in the company of women."

"But there weren't any women there!"

Revaz cleared his throat. "You've forgotten about Ladies Miras and Bagrat."

Naran rolled his eyes. "They were on the other side of the room. Besides, they're ancient. I'm pretty sure they couldn't hear a—"

"Commander," Revaz cut in, an alarmed look on his face, "let's finish this discussion later, shall we? I'm sure Lord Haydar has important matters to discuss with me."

Naran had the good sense to look embarrassed. "Yes. Of course. Sorry about that, my lords."

As Revaz showed the big Manzakar out, he said, "Don't forget about the garden party tomorrow afternoon."

"*Another* one?" Naran winced, then slumped in defeat. "Fine. See you there."

As Revaz shut the door, he turned and blew out his breath. "I certainly have my work cut out for me, don't I?"

Haydar let out a low chuckle. "He'll come around. He's smart."

"Clearly, he's smart," Revaz replied, shaking his head. "He's just...very rough around the edges."

"Indeed. Growing up in the barracks will do that to you." Haydar put his hands behind his back. "I have no doubt you can handle him."

Revaz walked back to his desk. "Won't you sit, my lord?"

"Oh, I just wanted to stop by briefly before I headed out to the hippodrome," he said. "I've been training with Tikran a bit in the afternoons."

The Anzori lord smiled curiously. "I know. Naran told me and I came to watch you the other day, in fact."

Haydar's heart leaped into his throat. "Did you?"

"Yes." Revaz crossed his arms. "You were practicing mounted archery. I daresay you're as good as Tikran."

It had been a good long while since Haydar had felt *this* particular type of heat flood his face. "Once upon a time, I might have been," he replied, fighting to maintain eye contact, "but now my old body aches for days after just a couple hours of training."

A look came into Revaz's eyes, one Haydar couldn't place. The chief justiciar said, "There's nothing old about you, my lord."

Change the subject. "Well…I know you have work to get back to. I just wanted to ask you a quick question." The words tumbled out of Haydar's mouth as he shifted his weight from foot to foot.

"Of course. Ask away."

Focus. "Lord Ruslan." Haydar straightened, feeling in control again. "What do you know about his court alliances?"

"I've been wondering about him as well," Revaz replied, lowering his voice. "Unfortunately for us, he's been very good lately about keeping his thoughts to himself and his company broad. While he has often disagreed with Tikran's stance on slavery, he has lauded the king's trade and tax reforms quite openly."

"Yes." Haydar chewed on his lip. "He seems to be making frequent trips into Gohar these days, looking for ways to capitalize on Gohar's recovery."

Revaz nodded. "While he strikes me as all talk and no bite, I can certainly keep an eye on him."

"Thank you, my lord." Haydar turned and walked to the door. "I'll see you this evening, at the king's council."

"If I have time," Revaz said, "I'll stop by the hippodrome in a bit." He grinned. "Watching you and King Tikran is quite enjoyable, I must admit. Your skill with the bow is undeniably breathtaking."

Haydar wanted to claw and tear at the joy filling every part of him. "I hope you do, Lord Revaz."

CHAPTER 17

Eastern Gohar was more desert than steppe, with sparse patches of long grass that grew across its rocky, brown expanse. The warmth of spring had yet to arrive to its desolate stretches of earth, and the scattered sand dunes were tipped with a dusty white frost. Coxani tugged at the collar of her tunic, trying to cover her throat. *This is where I'm from.* How did it feel so alien to her? She thought again of Tikran and how he had called himself Gohari before King Delger, only to be scoffed at.

Manzakars lived in between worlds because they were not enough of either.

Coxani looked around her. They were two Manzakars and fifty of Bruneta's best Sachin warriors, headed into the realm of the Davlat, a tribe with which the Sachin historically had mostly cordial relations. But now that the Davlat had taken up arms with Dilovar against Anzor, it was anyone's guess how this encounter would go. Bruneta seemed confident that the Davlat would not become aggressive—the Gohari, she insisted, were at their core a peaceful people. Coxani hoped this proved true. She looked up at the cloudless sky, breathing deeply despite the sharp stab of pain in her chest. Holy Cenk, when would it heal? She needed her body's cooperation, now more than ever. It would take three days to reach Davlat territory, and she hoped she'd be healed by then.

"Coxani." Moti rode up beside her, his eyes wide and imploring. "Listen, I am so sorry about what happened..."

Coxani smiled without looking over. "How are you feeling, Captain?"

"Fine." He huffed, straightening in his saddle. "I'm so fucking embarrassed."

"Don't be." She looked at him then. "No one held it against you. In fact, they were impressed that you managed to keep it in as long as you did."

Moti frowned. "You had the same stuff I did, and you didn't puke."

"True." Coxani shrugged. "In the eyes of the Gohari, that was probably a very lucky thing." She could see the humiliation in his eyes, so she added, "Look, I've always had a tough stomach. It isn't some weakness on your part."

He rubbed his eyes. "They all likely think I'm pathetic."

"I don't."

Both Manzakars turned in surprise as Bruneta came near, smiling. She looked at Moti. "I puked the first three times I drank tumis. It's not easy on the innards."

Moti smiled. "Yeah, but you were probably, what, five years old?"

"What? No." Bruneta laughed. "I was easily thirteen."

Grinning from ear to ear, Moti shook his head. "I don't believe it."

"It's true, Manzakar," Bruneta insisted, still smiling. "Not being able to keep tumis down is no sign of weakness."

Moti's face was flushed with obvious joy as he continued to rib the Gohari commander. And Bruneta, from what Coxani could tell, seemed for all the world to be enjoying it. Coxani turned her face away to hide her own smile. *Well. What do you know?* She put some space between herself and the pair, allowing them privacy to banter without her obvious attention. Focusing on the landscape ahead, she realized that her messages had likely made it back to Anzor, and Tikran and Naran were probably hot on her company's heels by now. It gave her a sense of peace and some renewed strength...

"Manzakar."

Coxani lifted her chin. She didn't feel up to mental sparring at the moment, but she knew the voice belonged to Omid. "Nomad," she answered, her voice just as firm.

She heard him snort behind her. "What did you just call me?"

"Nomad," she said loudly. "You keep calling me Manzakar. I think it's only fair."

"I have a name," he said.

She snapped her head to look at him. "So do I."

He sighed, pulling up beside her. "Fine." He wore a long, sheepskin vest over his tunic and a fur cap over his head, covering his ears. A plait of long, black hair, beaded and feathered, fell down his broad back. Coxani had noticed that the Gohari men tended to shave their faces clean, proudly displaying their tattoos. Omid's eyes darted in her direction when he sensed her gaze. "What *is* your name?"

"Are you serious?" She shook her head in disgust. "You think of all of us as just...*Manzakar*?"

"Yes." He glared at her. "For as long as I've lived, I've watched the Manzakars slaughter my people. They have no names. Their faces are like mine, but their souls belong to Anzor."

Omid's words resonated with Coxani, and she nodded slowly. "Yes. I understand." She drew in an unsteady breath. "I'm Coxani."

"Yeah, I know," he muttered. "And I'm Omid, which you probably knew as well."

Unexpectedly, Coxani let out a laugh that made her chest hurt. "We're both being assholes for the sake of being assholes, eh?"

Omid let his head fall back as he smiled at the sky. "Sure seems like it."

After a quick look back at Bruneta and Moti, Coxani asked, "What do you know about the Davlat chief?"

Omid continued to gaze up at the sky, a small smile on his lips. "You think I'd tell you?"

Coxani sighed. "I feel like it would benefit you to tell me, since you're helping us."

"Or maybe," Omid said lazily, "I'm leading you into a trap."

"Bullshit." Coxani narrowed her eyes at him. "Your tribe has sworn to support Tikran. You would be betraying them too."

"I'll tell you the truth, then." He fixed his gaze on her. "I think this is a fool's errand. Beg Marbek is not a warrior, and he's a moron—too young, too male, too uneducated in the ways of the Gohari. He will do what he thinks will benefit him personally over what his tribe needs in a heartbeat."

Coxani stared, open-mouthed. *Did he just say..."too male"?*

Omid looked away, his mouth set. "But you think you can convince him otherwise, don't you?"

"I don't know," Coxani said. "But I mean to try."

Omid let out a laugh. "You are definitely Gohari, Manzakar Coxani."

Shaking her head and grinning, Coxani said, "Just call me Coxani. Please. Nomad Omid."

"Fair enough." Omid rumbled with laughter.

After a moment of amicable silence, Coxani shivered. "I was born out here," she said softly. "How does anything even survive in this place?"

Omid tilted his head. "You're seeing Gohar through Anzori eyes. It's a harsh place, no question, but it's so alive. You just have to be willing to look." He squinted, leaning forward, then pointed. "There, behind that rock. Two marbled polecats. See them?"

Coxani nodded excitedly as she caught sight of the weasel-like creatures with large ears and a stripe of black across the eyes. "Yes, I see them."

Shading his eyes and looking up, Omid said, "And up ahead are sand plovers. They're small but not terrible to eat, particularly if you have some onion bulbs with them." Coxani gazed up at the white underbellies of the soaring birds as he added, "Bet you anything there are a few leopards lurking around the dunes, hunting gazelles."

Omid continued to point out signs of life in the steppe to Coxani until the group stopped to make camp for the night. So far, they hadn't happened upon any clans, which Coxani found strange. Omid reassured her, "The Davlat aren't like the Sachin in this respect. They like to keep to themselves. That said, several clans likely know we're here. I imagine Beg Marbek knows as well."

Coxani and Moti watched as two yarms, large enough to house thirty people each, went up in the blink of an eye. Smoke swirled out from their felt roofs and they glowed with warmth in the cold desert night. Moti leaned toward Coxani. "Which one are we sleeping in?"

Shaking her head, Coxani said, "I have no idea. Hopefully they'll tell us."

Bruneta emerged then and walked toward them, a small, mischievous smile on her lips. "Manzakars, come sleep in my yarm tonight." The pair followed her without hesitation. Inside, they unfurled their bedrolls atop beautifully woven rugs. Bruneta kneeled beside them, then handed Moti a single bead. "Sleep well, Manzakars." She rose and retreated to her corner of the yarm.

Moti stared at the green bead in his hand in consternation. "What...?"

Coxani shrugged. "I have no idea what it means." At that moment, Omid appeared beside them, grinning at Coxani and holding a bedroll under his arm. She pointed to the bead in Moti's palm. "What does it mean?" She asked, facing Omid fully.

"Oh, ho-ho!" Omid's eyes widened as he laughed. "Who gave him that?"

Moti swallowed. "Bruneta."

"Bruneta! Wow. Well." Omid fixed his gaze on Coxani's. "It means she wants to have relations with him."

"Relations?" Coxani managed, her eyes wide.

"Yes." Omid didn't flinch as he set his hands on his hips. "To give someone a colorful bead from your hair is an invitation to have sex with you."

"Oh," Moti muttered, his face a deep shade of red.

Omid shrugged nonchalantly. "It's not like she handed him a feather. That would mean she wanted him as her partner—a very different proposition."

"Can I have a moment with Captain Moti, please?" Coxani asked, thunderstruck.

Omid smiled. "Of course." Before turning away, he slowly pulled a bead from his plait and held it out to Coxani. When she made no move to take it, her mouth open in shock, he took her hand in his and placed the bead in her palm. Then he nodded briefly and retreated.

"Well, that came out of nowhere," Moti whispered once Omid was out of earshot.

Coxani turned to look at him, unable to think straight. "This is ridiculous."

"Is it?"

"Yes!" Coxani could barely restrain her outrage. "What *is* this? Do they just want to bed Manzakars?"

"I mean," Moti managed, "I'm completely fine with that."

"Moti!"

"Coxani," Moti said softly, "what if they take our rejections as an insult?"

Coxani snorted. "Nice try. Are you serious?"

Moti smiled as he looked at the bead in his hand. He met her eyes, forcing the smile from his face. "Look, you can't accept yours, obviously. Naran would have my head. But I think I need to...probably honor mine. She's Beg Ayym's right-hand woman after all..."

Dragging a hand down her cheek, Coxani said, "I think you maybe spent a bit *too* much time with Naran." When she saw the look on his face, she growled. "Fine. Go. Be discreet, for the love of Cenk."

Moti grinned and shrugged. "I'll be honest, I don't think Cenk would approve of *any* of this. But then, he hasn't approved of either of us our whole lives, has he?"

As Moti stood and wandered into the dimness of the yarm, Coxani dropped on her bedroll, Omid's bead in her fist. She brought it close to her face, rolling it between her fingers in the firelight, watching as its glossy orange exterior gleamed. *Fucking ridiculous.* Despite her inner turmoil, the moment she closed her eyes, sleep overtook her.

Coxani awoke to find her hand before her face, just as it had been when she'd fallen asleep. Except... *Where's the bead?* She lurched up, her chest throbbing painfully. She patted her bedroll, then the ground beside it, with her palm. Finally feeling its hard, smooth surface embedded in the dirt, she exhaled. What was wrong with her? *About to face off with the chief of the Davlat tribe, who is deliberately siding with Dilovar against Tikran, and I'm looking for a stupid hair bead?*

Sticking the bead in her tunic pocket, she stretched as much as possible and groaned, looking around in the dim pre-dawn light that filtered into the yarm. Many of the warriors were already outside, readying their horses. She had no idea where Moti was and had no interest in searching for him. *He'll turn up.* Standing and staggering from the yarm as discreetly as possible, she relieved herself several paces away, behind a small patch of bridlegrass. It was unbearably cold, and Coxani wondered if any of her early childhood in this uninhabitable climate impressed upon her at all. What she wouldn't do for Anzor's crisp air and sunshine. She packed her belongings and buckled on her cuirass just as Moti and Bruneta emerged from the yarm, both smiling. Coxani focused on helping the nomads disassemble the yarms as Moti came up beside her, joining in the effort.

"Good morning," he said cheerfully. She grunted in response, not looking at him. He continued, "Bruneta told me some interesting stuff about this Beg Marbek. Apparently he recently usurped leadership of the tribe."

Coxani paused. "Why?"

"Bruneta doesn't know. She suspects it has something to do with their sudden siding with Dilovar."

Well, that's not good. Coxani squinted into the east. "We need a plan."

"We have one," Bruneta answered, striding up to them as she sheathed her bow at her hip. "Late last night a Davlat scout approached and asked our intentions. I made it clear we were there to negotiate with Beg Marbek on Anzor's behalf. So they know we're coming, and that we come in peace."

Coxani chewed the inside of her cheek. "Do they know there are Manzakars among you?"

Bruneta's eyes flickered. "No."

Coxani exhaled. "Well, that's definitely not good. What if they get violent when they realize—?"

"That's not how the Gohari work," Bruneta said impatiently. "Violence against another tribe is a very last resort."

Coxani gestured emphatically at herself and Moti. "*We* are not your tribe."

"Don't worry, Manzakar," Omid said, riding up beside them, a roguish smile on his face. "We won't let them hurt you." Several warriors mounting up behind him snickered.

Coxani's temper flared. "I'm not worried about us. I'm worried that our presence will cause your people's unnecessary deaths."

He raised an eyebrow. "Should've thought about that before you asked to come out here, no?"

Coxani turned away and took a deep breath. This Omid fellow was infuriating—but not wrong. She couldn't decide if she wanted to pummel him or take him up on his whole "bead" offer. With her lips pressed together tightly, she walked quickly to her horse and hopped on its back. "Let's get this over with," she muttered.

The sun began to rise, its heat finally seeping into her armor. She shivered, enjoying the warmth, breathing in the sharp, clean scent of the sagebrush and dry earth, when Omid rode up along-side her. She said, "So, the bead. I need to know what the implications are." She looked over at the Sachin warrior, her eyebrows drawn tightly. "If this is an elaborate explanation, wait until after we talk to Beg Marbek. I'm not dealing with it now."

Omid peered at her inquisitively. "Elaborate? It's pretty simple, Manzakar. Surely even the Anzori understand physical attraction."

Coxani cleared her throat, looking away abruptly. "So you just hand a bead to anyone you're attracted to?"

"Depends on the nature of the bead's owner, but usually, yes."

"Usually?" She stole a peek at him.

He grinned. "If someone makes us feel special, we are both of age, and we want to feel their skin against ours…"

Coxani grit her teeth, trying to mentally shut out his words. "And what if the bead is rejected?"

Omid was quiet for a few moments. Then he said, "We're human. We feel hurt. But we also understand that life is such."

Coxani looked at him then. "You don't feel anger?"

"Again, that depends on the owner of the bead," Omid answered. "I, for one, do feel anger. I just understand that my anger is natural, as is rejection."

Coxani shook her head. "This is…strange. What happens when someone offers you a bead, but then turns around and offers another bead to someone else?"

"It's perfectly acceptable. It's expected, in fact. Until someone offers you a feather—which no one does until they are absolutely certain—you should assume they will offer several people beads. I think most of the anguish disappears when you accept that a bead is just, well, a bead."

For some strange reason, Coxani felt relief. She traced the curve of Omid's token through the fabric of her pocket. "Yeah, that makes sense." She thought about it for a second, then asked, "What happens when a bead, um, accidentally becomes a baby?"

"Ah." Omid chuckled. "Well, there are ways to keep that from happening. Still, it happens. And both parties, and their clans, commit to providing for the baby."

She tried not to look shocked. "But no feather?"

"No." Omid looked at her quizzically. "A feather is a serious thing. Why would you force it between two people who don't want it?"

She swallowed. "Because of the baby?"

Omid rolled his eyes. "You Anzori. Good grief. Are you doing the baby any favors by forcing its parents together against their will?"

"I don't think so," she found herself saying. The more this crazy nomad spoke, the more doors opened in her mind. She had to stop him, if only to keep from getting overwhelmed. She had to focus on the task at hand. If she didn't handle this well, blood would be on her hands. In a voice that was foreign to her ears, she asked, "Is there a time limit?"

"On what?" Omid sounded genuinely perplexed.

Coxani closed her eyes. "The bead."

His surprised laughter almost made her smile. "No, Manzakar. Well..." He paused, waiting until she looked over. Then he raised his eyebrows suggestively. "I can always ask for it back."

"I suppose that makes sense," she said, then tilted her head. "Are you asking for it back?"

"No," he answered. "Are you rejecting it?"

Say yes. Give the bloody thing back. Coxani looked out at the horizon and said nothing, the words caught in her throat. She thought of Naran and wondered if he'd followed her suggestion to pursue Dinara. Even if he hadn't, she was convinced that he wouldn't remain without a certain type of company for long...

Omid laughed again. "Ah! You want to play games."

"No." Heat crept up the collar of her tunic. "It's just that this is all very strange to me. It's not how we do things in Anzor at all."

"I can appreciate that, Coxani," he said quietly.

The heat continued to spread through her face, frustrating her. "Well, even if it *was* how we did things in Anzor, I still wouldn't necessarily accept your fucking bead, nomad," she snapped.

He was quiet, forcing her to turn and look at him. A small smile danced on his lips. "I'm definitely not taking it back, Manzakar."

Hiding her expression as best she could and hoping her face wasn't flaming red, she rode ahead, pulling her shield in front of her. *Enough flirting!*

The next two days passed uneventfully. Each night Moti would find Bruneta in a semi-private corner of a yarm while Coxani pulled a wool blanket over her head, her fingers touching the bead in her pocket. On the final day of their journey, Coxani was jumpy with anticipation. She concentrated on the rocky ridges and mesas in the distance, scanning for any sign of horsemen. More rock than sand, the grayish-brown landscape was bleak and rugged, and offered plenty of places to hide. She turned and called to Moti. "Captain, what's the nearest Anzori outpost?"

Moti cantered over to her, reluctantly ending a conversation with Bruneta. "I'd have to look at a map."

"Then look at one."

"Okay, okay, Miss High and Mighty," he muttered as he rummaged in his satchel, finally retrieving a roll of parchment. He squinted at it for a moment then said, "Zifa. Under the command of a Manzakar named Ilyas."

"May I see the map?" Coxani said, holding out her hand. Moti dutifully passed over the parchment. She nodded. "There are three Anzori forts between Zifa and the ones Dilovar captured, at least as far as we know." She looked at Bruneta. "Is there any way of verifying that the Dilovari haven't crept further south along the river?"

The Gohari commander shook her head. "No. Only the Davlat could verify that for you. It's their territory."

A chill rushed up Coxani's spine. She caught her breath. "Bruneta, what if the Dilovari are with them?"

"No," Bruneta said, straightening, her face fierce. "It's a matter of respect between tribes. They know we're coming. They wouldn't allow the Dilovari to be there too, especially without telling us."

"Bruneta." Omid's voice was hushed and urgent. "We're talking about Marbek. Are you serious?"

"Even Marbek, massive idiot that he is, wouldn't be that disrespectful to his own people," she insisted.

Coxani stared straight ahead, feeling like her heart had stopped. A line of horsemen crested the flat-topped, rocky hills ahead, their bows, lances, and shields prominently displayed. Hundreds of them. Her eyes sought the familiar shape of the Dilovari helmet, with its broad brim and plumes of hair from the top. She had never seen one personally but knew exactly what they looked like.

"Coxani," Moti said, his voice rasping. "Holy shit."

Coxani tugged her helmet firmly over her head, unsheathed her bow, and drew five arrows in her bow hand.

Holy shit, indeed.

CHAPTER 18

Tikran's arm snaked around Tanith's waist, his hand slipping gently up her belly and to her breast, waking her. He pressed himself to her, spooning her, his chest against her back, his breath in her hair. She placed her hand on his, smiling sleepily, enjoying his body's warmth, when he slowly pushed his hips against her lower back.

Sweet Archil, the man is inexhaustible. It would be the third time that night, and this was after a long, hectic day of audiences, meetings, and hours of training in the hippodrome. Where he found the energy, she had no idea. She could barely keep up with him, even though she'd admittedly also had a long and trying day. *To be twenty-four again...*

"Tanith," he whispered, his voice heavy with a blend of desire and slumber. She responded by guiding him inside her then clasping his hand between hers as he moved rhythmically, his breath quickening. After several minutes, he shuddered and grunted something inarticulate, every muscle in his body flexing around her. As his breathing slowed and his body relaxed, he stroked her throat with his fingers once, twice, and...instantly fell back asleep.

Tanith laughed softly to herself. Very much awake and

aroused, she was certainly not falling back asleep now. As carefully as she could, she slid from underneath Tikran's limp, heavy arm and out of the bed. The sky was just beginning to lighten, a new day beginning to dawn. Tanith dressed quickly and quietly, casting an affectionate glance at the Manzakar king before leaving. He lay sprawled and tangled in the bedsheets, snoring softly, his face boyish in repose.

She avoided looking at the Aslan guards as she left the king's suite and moved swiftly through the palace corridors toward her chambers. More than anything, she wanted to bathe, wash her hair, change clothes, and—

"Mistress Tanith, good morning!"

Oh, no. Tanith turned slowly to see Lord Haydar striding toward her, a broad smile on his face and a spring in his step. "I thought for sure I was the only one awake at this hour."

"I was just..." *...headed back to my suite after having sex with the king—multiple times.* She cleared her throat. "...trying to find time to myself to study in the library, my lord."

"Of course," Haydar said congenially. He tipped his head. "You are headed in the wrong direction, however."

She clenched her teeth behind her smile. "I enjoy taking a few laps around the palace. To stretch my legs. I'm Gohari, after all. All this sitting is very foreign to me."

"I can imagine. And I certainly don't want to interrupt you during your morning exercise, but I would be most pleased if you joined me for breakfast in my suite, Mistress," he said.

Even though Haydar's expression hadn't changed a single bit, Tanith understood. *This isn't optional.* "Of course, Lord Haydar."

As she followed the king's top advisor (and, for lack of a better term, foster father), Tanith tried to tame her mane and wipe the sleep from her eyes. If only she'd had just five minutes to wash her face and braid her hair... But they were standing in Haydar's suite far too quickly, and she took a seat obligingly as the sun began to peek over the horizon, brightening the sky with a soft orange light.

He sat across from her as servants brought coffee and honey-drizzled cake on trays.

"Tell me," he said, pouring her a cup, "do the Gohari enjoy a strong coffee?"

Tanith had to admit that Haydar had a way with people—while she would have rather been doing absolutely anything else at the moment, his easy manner relaxed her. She said, "Yes, my lord. As a matter of fact, 'strong' is the only way the Gohari will take coffee."

He took a sip from his cup, smiling with his eyes. "I would imagine so, particularly if in need of energy." He set the cup down. "But with Tikran's efforts, that won't be an issue anymore."

She kept her face composed. "I hope not, my lord."

Haydar leaned back in his chair and weaved his fingers together in his lap, his dark eyes fixed on her. "You have ambitions, Mistress Tanith. I saw them from the first, I see them now. I would wonder what they are, but I think I know." Though he smiled benignly, her stomach flipped. "You spend your nights in his bedchamber—surely you didn't think that would remain secret. No, you're too smart for that." Tanith's heart beat faster, despite her confidence that she'd done nothing wrong. He brought his fingers to his lips. "Why don't you tell me what you want?"

She swallowed, straightening in her chair. "I want a free Gohar."

He raised his eyebrows in surprise. "Is that all?"

"Yes."

He frowned. "Strange, that you would go through all this...effort...for a free Gohar, when it's obvious Tikran wants the same."

"It's obvious *he* wants it, but what of the men around him?" Tanith asked, gripping the arms of her chair. "I've sat in many a meeting where he's been silenced by the council—and the Anzori aristocracy. He's utterly diplomatic, as are you, my lord, but we all know who wins in the end."

Haydar turned and looked out a window absently. After a few seconds, he said, "They won't win this time. Call it foresight, if you will. Prescience." He sat up straight and met her gaze. "You've set your sights on Queen of Anzor. You don't need to confirm this, I already know it. Perhaps you think if Anzor has a Gohari queen, it increases the likelihood that Gohar will earn its independence. Or perhaps you believe that, as queen, you will have the power to sway things in Gohar's favor." He tilted his head. "You need to understand that there is only one thing that can guarantee Gohar's independence."

She lifted her chin. "And what's that?"

"A lasting peace with Dilovar."

"We're about to go to war against Dilovar," she said.

"And Tikran will do his utmost to either prevent it or win it." He sat forward. "And when he does, he will forge an alliance with Dilovar that will unequivocally grant Gohar its independence."

She held her cup in her hands and stared into its murky, steaming contents. "An alliance? Are you suggesting that Tikran should marry Dilovari royalty?"

"Something like that," Haydar answered vaguely, looking her in the eyes again. "Listen, Tanith, what if I could promise you a free Gohar...and a position as its head mage?"

She stared. "You can't possibly be able to promise that."

Haydar lifted his chin, an enigmatic smile hovering on his lips. "I will certainly try, as will Tikran. But—and this is important— you must set aside any notions of a romantic future with him."

For some reason she couldn't have articulated right then, Tanith hesitated. Haydar was offering her something she'd had no reason to believe was possible, but it was exactly what she wanted. So what was stopping her from agreeing immediately?

Haydar's eyebrows rose in surprise, ever so slightly. "You love him."

Something about hearing the words said out loud... *Oh, Archil.* She blinked rapidly, trying to clear her mind. "You said Tikran will free Gohar and place me in a position of power if I avoid...romantic entanglements with him?"

"He must remain unattached," Haydar answered. "What you

and he do behind closed doors—and discreetly—is your own business, at least for the time being." He paused, looking down at the ground. "From what I understand, you and Beg Ayym had a long-standing love affair. Am I wrong?"

How does he know these things? Haydar must have done his research on her. Feeling suddenly naked, Tanith shook her head. "You're not wrong." She hesitated a moment before saying, "When I came to Anzor those months ago, I'd given up any thought of returning to Gohar, to my past...to Ayym. I knew I had powerful Essence and could use it to benefit Gohar in a big way. We agreed that the wisest course of action was for me to offer my Essence to the new Manzakar king, in the hopes of becoming one of Anzor's mages and helping Gohar achieve its independence. It wasn't until Tikran's interest in me became more than professional that thoughts of queenhood began to brew in my mind."

"I believe you," Haydar said. "I consider myself a pretty good judge of character, Tanith, and would not have let you get as close to Tikran as you did if I'd thought your ultimate goal wasn't aligned with ours. And now, I think, we're aligned on our path to achieve it. When all is said and done, you and Beg Ayym will be able to bring Gohar into the future, together."

She stiffened. "You make a lot of assumptions and promises, Lord Haydar."

For a fraction of a second, Haydar's mask slipped. The fierce determination in his eyes took her breath away. "I do, Mistress Tanith. But I've worked too hard, for too long, and seen too many lives lost for this to end any other way."

At that moment, Tanith knew that whispers of Enlil the Weaver should have echoed as loudly throughout Gohar as those of the Caged Kingfisher.

After leaving Haydar's chambers, Tanith wandered back to her rooms, her mind reeling. *Is any of it in the realm of possibility?* She entered her bedchamber and startled when she found Tikran standing there, half-dressed, his hair mussed, looking perplexed.

"You left without waking me," he said.

She smiled. "You were deeply asleep."

"Well, that just won't do." He walked over to her, smiling slightly. He began tugging up the hem of her robe as he kneeled before her. Reaching beneath, his hands slid up her thighs, making her gasp at his touch. He looked up at her, a roguish look on his face. "It's your turn."

Tanith closed her eyes, putting Haydar's words out of her mind for the moment. "Yes, Your Highness..."

CHAPTER 19

The Davlat warriors waited atop the mesas ahead, their feathers and fur fluttering in the wind.

"They will not attack us," Bruneta said, her eyes flashing dangerously. "They're trying to intimidate us. Marbek may be a chief now, but he's still no warrior."

Coxani swallowed. "Something tells me they know there are Manzakars among you."

"This is unbelievable," Omid muttered, his eyebrows drawn together. "Who does this asshole think he is?"

"Omid, we're here to negotiate," Bruneta snapped. "Try and remember that."

"I'm trying," he replied through his teeth. "But Marbek is really pushing it."

The wind blew, sending a whiff of sage, earth, and sweat in Coxani's direction. With one single deep breath, her mind was suddenly clear. She put away her bow and arrows, removed her helmet, then began unbuckling her cuirass.

"Coxani, what are you *doing*?" Moti hissed, his eyes wide.

As she removed the armor, she said, "Bruneta's right. We're here to negotiate." She looked at Moti. "You don't have to take off your armor, but...I want them to know I'm sincere."

"Fuck me," Moti grumbled under his breath, reaching up to tug off his helmet. "You aren't doing this alone."

Coxani looked at the Sachin commander and nodded, indicating her readiness. Was it her imagination, or did she see admiration flicker across Bruneta's face? *Tikran's face.* She turned back toward the Davlat and nudged her horse into a quicker pace. As they approached, she could see that one of the horsemen bore a headdress similar to Beg Ayym's—elaborately beaded and feathered. It had to be Marbek. She focused on him, trying to keep her body relaxed as his face came into view—young, angry, and heavily tattooed, but not in the warrior's way. She also noticed he was shorter than many of the others. At this point in her life, she'd dealt with enough men to know what triggered their insecurities, and height was one of them. She was making a snap judgment, she knew, but she had to guess how to make this Marbek fellow agree to join Tikran. If Marbek's aggressiveness was on account of some inferiority complex, then she would use it to her advantage.

When their odd party of Sachin warriors and Manzakars grew close, the individual Coxani had pegged as Marbek spoke. "Bruneta, I thought better of you than to bring Manzakars into our midst."

Bruneta straightened, gazing at the Davlat chieftain coolly. "I'll be honest, Marbek, I thought better of you than to side with the Dilovari."

Coxani's heart jumped as Marbek's scowl deepened. She had to trust Bruneta knew what she was doing. His voice was a growl. "We have good reason for our actions, Sachina."

"Sachina?" Coxani turned to Omid, whose expression was rageful.

"Female for Sachin nomad," he said, his eyes fixed on Marbek.

Obviously. She turned back to look at the Davlat chief, compelled to say something. "Beg Marbek, my name is Coxani," she said loudly, praying her voice didn't shake. "I am a Manzakar. I requested to come to you and I'm the reason Bruneta brought us here."

"Coxani, don't," she heard Moti say under his breath.

Still, she dismounted and walked toward the Davlat chief, her hands at her sides. She half expected arrows to thud into her as she walked steadily, her eyes fixed on Marbek's angry face. "Stop, Manzakar," he yelled, as his warriors drew arrows and pointed them directly at her. "Stop, or you die where you stand."

"If you shoot the Manzakar," Bruneta responded fiercely, drawing an arrow, nocking it, and anchoring it to her cheek at lightning speed, "you start a war with the Sachin." Coxani's head snapped back. Behind her, she heard fifty Sachin warriors draw their bows.

Oh, wow. Coxani wanted desperately to lock eyes with Bruneta to get confirmation that it wasn't all bullshit. But also…she hadn't meant to throw them in with her. Now, it definitely wasn't just her life that was forfeit. Her breathing was shallow when Marbek suddenly let out an angry growl. "Are we really doing this, Sachina?"

"No!" Coxani yelled at the top of her lungs, hands raised, palms open. "Beg Marbek, I come in peace. I'm unarmed. I just want to understand."

Marbek had the nerve to look annoyed. He rolled his eyes as he looked at Coxani. "Okay, Manzakar, you have my attention—for the time being. What do you want?"

"Tell me what happened. Why did you turn against the Caged Kingfisher?" She looked the chieftain directly in the eyes. "King Tikran needs your support. Without you, he likely can't win."

"Coxani!" Moti hissed. "What are you *doing?*"

She ignored her co-captain as she continued to approach the wall of Davlat warriors ever so slowly. "Beg Marbek?"

As she'd hoped, Marbek's expression softened just a bit. He was clearly somewhat appeased. Refusing to look directly at her, he answered, "One of my clans was brutally attacked by the king's Manzakars. Most of them were killed."

Coxani started forward without thinking, only to find innumerable Davlat arrows pointed at her. She stopped, her heart racing. *It's not possible.* "Are you certain they were the king's?"

Marbek smiled and nodded slowly. "Oh yes, Manzakar. They belonged to your king."

"Who commanded them?" She asked firmly. "Tell me their commander's name."

Marbek curled his lip over his teeth. "You think I know his name?"

Right. Coxani took a deep breath. "Beg Marbek, whoever they were, I promise they weren't sent by King Tikran. And if you're willing to help me, I will bring these Manzakars to justice."

"I don't need you, Manzakar," he sneered. "My tribe will bring them to justice."

You mean, with the help of the Dilovari? Coxani prudently chose not to say the words aloud. "Is there anyone with you now who survived the attack who can give me information on the attackers?"

Before Marbek could answer, a female voice yelled, "Woman Manzakar!" Coxani looked from the frustrated chieftain to a young woman who rode forward, the whites of her eyes bright in her dark face. Her beads were mostly red and black, Coxani noticed without consciously doing so. "I'm a survivor," the woman said. "I can't tell you the commander's name, but I can tell you a man was there, watching. The Manzakar commander spoke with him just before it all happened."

Coxani frowned. "Was he a Manzakar?"

"I don't know." She lifted her chin. "He bought rugs from my clan the day before."

"He bought...your rugs?"

"Yes. He had a yellow beard."

"Enough!" Marbek yelled, his face red. "That's all you get, Manzakar."

"Beg Marbek," Coxani insisted. "One more thing. Please." She looked at the woman warrior. "Do you have any idea where the Manzakars came from?"

Marbek shot the woman a dangerous look, and Coxani didn't miss it. The woman said, "No."

"Thank you," Coxani said, nodding to the woman. Then she turned to Marbek. "Thank you, Beg, for your time. Won't you reconsider—"

"No, Manzakar," Marbek answered harshly. "Now be off. So long as you and your Sachin allies are gone in the next hour, we will forget you ever came."

The two Manzakars and fifty Sachin warriors turned warily and began riding away as the Davlat remained on the hill, watching them leave.

As they rode back westward, Bruneta said, "Coxani, you know something. Tell us."

Coxani's heart had been beating rapidly against her ribcage since the encounter. She said thoughtfully, "A man with a yellow beard bought their rugs and watched the slaughter." She looked at Moti. "How many Manzakars do you know have a yellow beard *and* buy rugs from the nomads?"

"None," Moti grumbled. "Maybe you should've asked about the color of the fucker's skin."

"He has to be an Anzori," she said, turning to Bruneta. "The Gohari merchants from Anzor are only allowed to trade in slaves. Have you ever dealt with Anzori merchants who weren't slave traders?"

Bruneta shook her head. "No." She tilted her head, considering. "But there are rumors involving Anzori noblemen."

"What rumors?"

"That's right, Bruneta!" Omid said suddenly, coming up from behind. He looked from Coxani to Moti. "Your exiled prince lives in these parts. Word is that he entertains the occasional Anzori nobleman."

Coxani glanced at Bruneta for confirmation, and the Sachin commander nodded once. Coxani then looked to Moti. "We're going to visit Prince Vazha."

Moti sighed. "Yeah, of course we are. Let's get this over with."

CHAPTER 20

enk's Essence blesses mankind with life... It is light, it is water, it is food and shelter...

With his knees drawn up and a heavy tome in his lap, Berk delved into the Anzori prayers. He sat beneath the lancet window in Damir's chambers as the cat, Enlil, slept peacefully on his socked feet. Berk had already torn through all the fiction the head mage's library had to offer. While sparse, they were mostly tales of heroics, in which the warriors saved the kingdom. He loved those tales, even though he couldn't see himself in the hero. Despite his saber lessons with Damir, he would never be the sword-wielding savior, that much he knew.

But in the dry, unromantic religious texts about magic—and even the prayers of Anzor and Dilovar—he saw how he *could* become a hero. *Through the Essence, all life exists. Without the Essence, all life perishes.*

Berk knew he was getting better at controlling his Essence, and he was excited to continue practicing. *I could be the most powerful mage in the southern kingdoms—maybe even the whole Continent.*

"Berk."

He hadn't heard the door, but he looked up when he heard Damir's voice, eagerly searching the mage's face. "Yes, Master

Damir?" What he saw in Damir's face deflated him, though. *He's here again.* Berk knew Damir tried to mask his emotions around his pupil, and for the most part, he was successful. Still, Berk had come to recognize how his mentor's demeanor changed when Prince Vazha visited: Damir's tone was sharper, his grip tighter. Berk couldn't decide if they hated each other or, in the only other alternative, were having sex. *Maybe both.* While Berk himself had never personally experienced the latter, he'd been around enough Gohari teenagers to recognize its tension in the air. And the sexual tension between the two men was tangible—at least from Vazha's side.

Damir said calmly, "Prince Vazha wishes you to visit him."

"Yes, sir." Berk pulled on his boots and stood, confounded by the tug-of-war he felt between Prince Vazha and Master Damir, the two men he saw as his protectors. After all, he'd never known his own parents. They'd perished in the wave of red plague that had overtaken the Davlat tribe when he was a baby. The only family he'd ever known was his brother and great-grandfather, Beg Zolto, and only one of them was still alive.

Because of the Manzakars.

He consciously unclenched his fists and followed Damir down the long palace corridor to Vazha's guest suite. The prince turned from the window when they entered, a broad grin on his face. He leaned on his cane as he walked toward them. "Berk, my boy. I've missed you. How are you?"

Berk felt that delicious melting sensation in his chest, as if he were a lit candle. *It feels so much like love.* He approached the prince, seeking, needing... He kneeled before Vazha and bowed his head.

"Stand Berk," Vazha said, holding out his open hands. Berk stood and took the prince's hands willingly. "You may leave us, Master Damir," Vazha said softly, reaching out and stroking Berk's hair tenderly.

There was a pause. Then, "I don't think so, Your Highness."

Berk lifted his bowed head and turned, puzzled.

"I beg your pardon?" Vazha's voice was cold, his hand falling away from Berk's locks.

Damir stood near the doorway. He drew a breath and straightened. "You are welcome to spend time with the boy, but I will remain in the room."

The iciness in Vazha's tone made Berk want to step back. "What are you implying, Doctor?"

Damir didn't waver. "Berk is my ward while he is here. I've been tasked with training him to defend Dilovar. While I'm sure King Bilguun trusts you, Your Highness, I will remain in the room during Berk's visits unless the king orders me otherwise."

"Berk is *mine*," Vazha said through his teeth.

Damir's expression remained composed. "Again, until King Bilguun orders me—"

"Fine." Vazha smiled. "Play your games, Damir."

Something ominous in Vazha's expression sent chills down Berk's spine. He looked at Damir urgently but found only a tranquil indifference in the mage's pale gray eyes. "Berk," Damir said gently, "does it bother you if I stay?"

"No, Master Damir."

Leaning back against the far wall, Damir smiled faintly. "Well, then. Pretend I'm not here, Your Highness. When you're done, I will escort my young apprentice back to the library."

Turning back to face the exiled Anzori prince, Berk tried not to look concerned. He had a sinking feeling he knew what Damir was doing. While the Gohari believed that "learning love" was an important part of adolescence, adult participation was utterly taboo, often resulting in the adult's ostracism from the tribe. But surely *that* was not Vazha's intent. Damir had to be overreacting. Berk felt a spark of anger. Couldn't he enjoy a modicum of affection from anyone?

Vazha gestured toward the couch. "Come and sit, Berk. Tell me what you're learning."

Berk's excitement was tempered by the tension in the room. He sat beside the prince and said, "I can turn stone to sand."

"By touching it, you mean?"

Berk hesitated, wanting to look back at Damir but resisting. "No, sir. I don't have to touch it."

Vazha looked at Damir. "Are you saying he can turn stone to sand from a distance?"

Berk finally turned. From where he leaned against a wall in the shadows, his arms crossed and eyes luminous, Damir said, "Yes. But he must be touching something adjacent to it, something of similar composition. The day you brought him here, Berk caused something of an earthquake. He was able to do this because his feet were touching the stone floor, which in turn was on the earth. And as we know, stone is made of minerals found in the earth."

"Yes!" Berk grinned excitedly. "And the most amazing part is that I can choose *which* stone to turn to sand."

"This will allow him to be selective in his...destruction," Damir added.

Vazha smiled. "Remarkable." He squeezed Berk's shoulder. "Excellent work, my boy. Keep at it. Remember, there's no time to waste. The Freed Kingfisher's Manzakars will be marching into Gohar before we know it, and you must be ready."

Berk nodded fervently, pleased with Vazha's reaction. "Of course, Your Highness. I will be ready."

The prince let his hand drop. "I suppose that's all for now, then. You should get back to your studies. I will be back soon enough." As they stood up and walked to the door, Vazha flashed Damir that chilling smile again. "I will see you later, Doctor."

Damir was expressionless as he answered, "As you wish, Your Highness."

Berk scratched his head as he and Damir headed back to the mage's chambers. He had no idea what was going on between the two men, but it unsettled him. As he tried to put it out of his mind by thinking on his recent accomplishments, he said, "Oh. I forgot to tell the prince about how I boiled the river—and the fish in it."

Damir continued to look straight ahead, his jaw flexed. "It's probably best that he not know."

Back inside the library, Damir shut the door and said, "Berk, what exactly has Vazha promised you?"

Berk kicked off his boots and returned to his seat by the window, pulling the tome he'd been reading back into his lap. "He promised that he would get rid of the Manzakars once he was king."

"Get rid of them?" Damir tilted his head. "You mean dismantle the caste?"

"I think so," Berk replied.

"And what would replace them? Anzori soldiers?"

"I don't know. I guess so."

"Berk," Damir said, approaching, "you realize it's semantics, right? Even if there are no Manzakars, there will always be an Anzori force to keep Gohar in line. 'Getting rid' of the Manzakars won't change that."

"No," Berk said vehemently. "They won't be replaced—not the way they are now. He promised. Besides, he said he would make me his head mage, and I could make sure it never happens again."

"Head mage, eh?" Damir sighed. "And how will you ensure the Dilovari forces don't become the new Manzakars?"

Berk peered up at him. "You will make sure that never happens, won't you, Master Damir?"

Damir shook his head. "You have a lot to learn, boy."

Berk opened the book and scowled at the pages. "I'm trying." Maybe he did have a lot to learn, but he vowed to himself that someday he would become the most powerful mage on the Continent—even if it meant killing every last Manzakar himself.

CHAPTER 21

The prince's manor sat atop a mesa, a bright Anzori beacon of imported white limestone and blue tile, startling against the jagged browns and beiges of the Gohari desert. It was surrounded by battlements with two towers that cast long shadows in the early morning twilight. Coxani, Moti, Bruneta, and the fifty Sachin warriors approached slowly, holding Anzor's flag aloft.

"Manor?" Moti scoffed under his breath. "That's a bloody fortress!"

"Why do you sound surprised?" Bruneta chuckled. "The Anzori think we're savages, remember? They think that if it wasn't for the fortifications and troops, we'd tear Delger's innocent widow and children limb from limb."

"One of those grown children may not be so innocent, it seems," Coxani muttered.

"You don't think Vazha is directly involved in the slaughter of the clan, do you?" Moti asked. "What could he get out of that?"

"I admit, it doesn't seem to make much sense," Coxani agreed. "Drumming up trouble with the Gohari would only land him in hot water with Tikran, which he can't possibly want. Even if he thinks the crown of Anzor is rightfully his, how would attacking the Gohari help his cause?" She shrugged. "He probably isn't involved with what happened directly, but I bet he knows who is."

Cresting the mesa a short distance across from the entrance of the fortified wall, Coxani heard Omid say, "Something about this isn't right. It feels...off. Where are the guards?"

She held up her hand, halting them. Then she looked at Bruneta and Omid. "Stay here. Moti and I will talk to the guards and make sure they aren't hostile toward you for any reason." She nodded to Moti. "Let's go."

As the pair rode toward the gates, Moti said, "You really should be wearing your cuirass, Coxani. That thing saved your life, remember?"

Coxani shook her head, squinting at the embrasures in the battlements. "I want the Gohari warriors to trust me. I want them to see me fight with them, as one of them, without the benefits of Manzakar armor."

Groaning, Moti said, "Coxani, Naran would absolutely lose his—"

A small glint in the shadows of an embrasure set off an immediate alarm in Coxani's head. "Shields!" she shouted as she raised hers, sensing Moti's arm spring up in the nick of time. No fewer than ten arrows whistled through the air and pelted them in quick succession.

"What the fuck!" Moti yelled, turning his head to gape at Coxani as the pair drew their bows. "Why are they attacking us? Don't they see our flag? Our uniforms?"

"I don't know!" As she armed her bow, her mind reeling, a second wave of Manzakar arrows swooped down on them, striking Coxani's horse in the back leg. The animal screamed as it fell, taking Coxani with it. She twisted out from under its body and struggled to keep her shield above her, faltering as another bombardment of arrows descended, making her arm shake with effort beneath each blow. *Moti's right. Why didn't I wear my bloody cuirass?* She drew her bowstring and loosed her arrows almost blindly as she backed away, wanting desperately to yell for Moti but losing him in the eruptions of dirt, sand, and dust around her. *My horse. Those assholes shot my horse.*

The arrows—unquestionably Manzakar, and bodkins at that—plummeted down once again, drumming rapidly against her shield, grazing her shin with a streak of pain, and burrowing into the earth around her in a terrifying series of explosions. There was nowhere to take shelter within 150 yards; they were entirely vulnerable. Through the corner of her eye, she saw Moti's horse fall and Moti roll to the ground adeptly, his shield before him. She wasn't prepared. *They* weren't prepared. She continued to loose her arrows into the void, her shock transforming into dread.

They're trying to kill us.

And it looked like they were going to succeed.

"Coxani! Coxani!" A horse stomped in the dirt around her as someone dropped to her side, a handmade shield of tough animal hide held high above her. "You have to get up. We have to go." She stood on shaky, bleeding legs, recognizing Omid's voice, turning her head to see his sweat-streaked face. With her arms quaking beneath the weight of her shield and her leg burning in protest, she managed to hop on Omid's horse. She felt him climb on behind her.

"Hurry," he said between breaths. "Go. As fast you can. I'll cover us."

She wanted to give him her shield, knowing it offered better protection, but also realized it would waste precious time. They galloped away and she ducked her head instinctively at the shriek of the flying Manzakar projectiles, feeling Omid's body twist as he loosed his arrows behind them at a swift but steady pace. She pressed her legs into the horse's flanks. *Faster. Faster.* She saw the ridges of earth that would protect them, if they could just get there...

An arrow trilled close to her ear—too close, getting loud enough to make her cower—then landed with a dull, fleshy thud that reverberated throughout her body. Omid slammed against her, letting out a feral howl. She realized abruptly that the wet warmth she felt on her cheek was not her own blood, but Omid's. *No!* "Omid!"

"I'm not dead yet, Manzakar," she heard him wheeze against her ear as he struggled to keep his weight from her, his head lolling against her shoulder. She reached around and grabbed his arm, wrapping it against her waist and gripping him tightly. *Faster. Faster!*

As they finally dropped beyond a rocky ledge, Coxani pulled the horse to a lurching stop. The weight of Omid's body almost fully rested on her, and despite her shaking, she somehow managed to slip them both from the horse's back without falling over. Grabbing his arm and turning, she lowered him down to the ground, her other arm around his waist, her eyes frantically darting over him. *Oh, holy Cenk...* The arrow had hit him in the shoulder and come clean through the front side, its bodkin tip coated in his blood. Coxani stammered, "How did it not go through you and into me? You're not even wearing armor..."

He looked at her with flashing brown eyes. "You must think we're really stupid," he said, breathless. "My vest is lined and padded. It's just...they usually attack us with course-winged arrows. I didn't expect to be attacked with bodkins."

"Me neither," Coxani muttered. *They meant to pierce armor... Manzakar armor.* Omid's wound didn't seem to be bleeding, which meant the arrow was plugging it. She drew a shaky breath and tried to smile. "It's barely a scratch."

He let out something between a laugh and a cough just as Manzakar arrows whistled overhead again. Coxani kneeled over Omid as he lay on his side, raising her shield with both trembling arms. The bodkins made a deep, ominous wail just before they crashed into the ground around the huddled pair. Coxani blinked hard, unable to see anything for several seconds, her eyes watering from the sprays of dirt caused by each landing arrow. When the whirling clouds of dust began to settle, she saw that Omid's horse had been struck twice, once in the hindquarters and the other in its flank, and was writhing on the ground.

How would they get out of there? Where were the other warriors? What had happened to Moti? The direness of their situation settled over her like a shroud and, in a moment of clarity, Coxani leaned over Omid and stroked his clammy face. *This could be it. It might all be over soon.*

His eyelids fluttered open. "Oh. I don't like that look at all. Are you giving up, Manzakar?" Though his breathing was labored his and face was pale, his voice was still strong; his eyes still bright.

"Not even close, nomad." She stood, tucking as many arrows as she could hold in her bow hand. Setting her shield on the ground, she propped it up to cover Omid.

"Coxani, wait," he managed, "What are you doing?"

"I'll be back," she assured him, knowing that the chances she'd return were extremely slim. She was going to kill as many Manzakars as she could before she died, so help her. She climbed out from under the ridge and into the sunlight, her bowstring drawn tight. Indifferent to the lethal projectiles that landed all around her in blasts of earth, she loosed one arrow after another with as much precision as her shaking body and watery eyes allowed, her gaze fixed on the figures standing boldly on the wall in the distance. *You're going down, assholes.*

Nock... Draw... Anchor... Aim... Release... One down.

Nock... Draw... Anchor... Aim... Release...

It was then that she heard several ululating tongues pierce the air. She didn't dare turn around and instead continued shooting, aiming for the embrasures in the fortified wall.

Nock... Draw... Anchor... Aim... Release... Two down.

Nock... Draw... Anchor... Aim... Release... Three down.

A torrent of arrows followed her last release, their numbers casting a dim shadow as they soared toward Vazha's manor like a cloud of locusts. After two full volleys rose up from behind her and descended on the fortified wall, the assault from the castle suddenly stopped. Coxani paused, panting, finally feeling brave enough to turn. Behind her, Davlat warriors crowded the horizon, their painted shields winking in the bright sunlight, feathers fluttering in the wind, bowstrings pulled taut, hundreds of arrows pointed in the air.

Under the morning sun, Vazha's manor was idle, looking almost peaceful, as if it hadn't just initiated a brutal assault on two of its own and fifty Sachin allies. Their bowstrings drawn, the Davlat warriors waited on the mesa for the next barrage of bodkins. It never came, and Coxani rushed toward them urgently. With the help of several warriors, she got Omid out from underneath the ridge and onto a horse headed back to Beg Marbek's encampment. His face was drawn, struggling to remain conscious, and he tilted to the right, the side which was impaled by the merciless Manzakar arrow. A Davlat warrior rode pillion and held him.

"The Anzori prince seems to really want you dead, Manzakar," a gruff voice said from behind her.

She turned to face Beg Marbek, frantic. "Moti... Bruneta... I don't know where they are..."

"I'm here, Coxani." Bruneta limped out from the throng of warriors slowly, her face streaked with blood and dirt, her expression desolate.

Oh, Cenk. "Where's Moti?"

"He's alive. Headed back to the camp." Her nostrils flared with emotion briefly. "He was hit in the leg." She drew a shaky breath. "Twelve of my warriors are dead. Twelve more are injured. We've lost at least twenty horses."

Coxani closed her eyes. *No, no, no.* "Bruneta. I don't..." She looked back at the manor in a panic. "We have to get out of here before they start shooting at us again!"

"Calm down," Beg Marbek interrupted, his tone confident as he looked back at Vazha's fortress. "They wouldn't shoot at the Davlat."

Why not? The words were on Coxani's lips when Bruneta said, "Well, feel free to linger, we're getting out of here." She hopped on her horse and held her hand out to Coxani. "Come on, Manzakar. Get on."

Coxani obliged with a wince, feeling nauseous, and wrapped her arms around Tikran's sister. "Bruneta," she heard herself say, her voice trembling, "I'm so sorry. If I'd just—"

"It's not your fault, Coxani." Turning her head, Bruneta offered Coxani her sharp profile. "It's not Tikran's, either." She turned back, facing forward, her voice low. "The Anzori are trying to destroy him—and destroy you—because of what he's begun."

Coxani looked to Marbek, who rode alongside them, his face in a pensive scowl. "Why did you come to our aid?"

"My fellow Gohari were, once again, being slaughtered by Manzakars," Marbek answered without looking at her. "Trust me, I couldn't care less what happens to you or your Manzakar friend. I did it for the Sachin."

"Beg Marbek, listen to me," Coxani said, "I think the Manzakars who killed your clan were acting on behalf of the prince, not King Tikran. The fact that Vazha wanted us dead is proof that—"

"It proves nothing," Marbek cut in, "except that he disapproves of the Freed Kingfisher."

"You know, Marbek," Bruneta said, "it sounds like you're defending that piece of shit prince."

Marbek snapped a fierce look at her. "Watch your mouth, Sachina."

Bruneta curled her lip over her teeth, her eyes shimmering with angry tears. "I just watched twelve of my warriors, my friends, die because of Vazha. Don't you fucking *dare* tell me to watch my mouth, *Davlat*." When Marbek said nothing, Bruneta leaned toward him, her eyes fixed on his face. "What aren't you telling us, Marbek? Why did the prince's Manzakars stop shooting the moment you arrived?"

Marbek was silent for several seconds, frowning. Then he said, "According to the survivors of the clan that was attacked, Vazha had his men stop the king's Manzakars before they could kill everyone. The survivors believe the prince saved their lives."

Coxani was shaking her head slowly, disbelievingly. "Why would he do that?"

"Maybe because he knows the Davlat are the largest tribe in Gohar, and he wants their support," Bruneta said. "Did you promise him your support against Tikran, Marbek?"

"I promised Dilovar our support against Anzor," Marbek replied firmly. "I couldn't give a shit about the prince or his aspirations."

"Beg Marbek," Coxani said, exasperated, "Prince Vazha didn't help your clan out of the kindness of his heart. He must have wanted something from you." She stared at his austere profile. "He wanted something from you, didn't he?" Again, the Davlat chief went quiet.

Bruneta went stiff against Coxani. "What did you give him in return, Marbek?"

"I'm done with this conversation," Marbek answered brusquely. "I'm chief of the Davlat, and I will do what I think is best for my tribe. Ending the Manzakars' tyranny is what's best not just for my tribe, but for all of Gohar."

"You're fighting the wrong enemy." Bruneta's voice was rough with anger. "And your mistake will be a costly one. The price will be the peace between our tribes, the unity of the Gohari people. How many more Gohari must die, Marbek?"

"They'll die anyway, Bruneta," Marbek said. "You know this as well as I do. So if we must die, let's go down fighting the force that has oppressed us for over a century." With that, he kicked his horse into a trot and rode away from them.

When they returned to the encampment, Bruneta took Coxani to see Moti, who was lying within the largest yarm with the other injured warriors as the clan's healers tended to their wounds. Moti's face was flushed, his hair plastered to his sweaty forehead. He saw Coxani and nearly screamed in relief.

"Oh, holy fuck, am I glad to see you," he cried, his head falling back. "Bruneta came for me and I couldn't find you. I thought I'd lost you."

Coxani smiled, kneeling beside him and taking his blood-stained, dirt-encrusted hand in hers. "And Naran would have your head. I know."

Moti scowled. "He's not the only one who cares about you, asshole. I care about you."

Tears pricked Coxani's eyes. "I thought I'd lost you, too, Captain." She looked at his leg and suppressed a wince. Luckily, Moti had been wearing his heavy cavalryman's lamellar cuirass, which had blunted much of the impact. Unfortunately, the bodkin still managed to pierce through the steel plates and into Moti's thigh. Its tip, the healer explained, had hit bone, which would make extraction tricky.

"I'll be fine!" Moti insisted. "Tikran had an injury like this, remember? He was still walking around afterward. He was back in action in no time."

"He was likely *running* afterward because he was being hunted," Coxani said with a laugh. "But I think your injury is a bit worse."

"Bah." Moti rolled his eyes. "Let's get this stupid thing out of my leg and get back to Eter. Surely reinforcements are nearly there. We sent our messages to Anzor ages ago."

The messages. She needed to get back to Eter and send yet another—about Vazha. She drew her breath. "Hang in there, Moti. I'll get you some booze to drink beforehand. Surely the Gohari have something strong enough."

Moti chuckled uneasily. "*Great* idea."

She stood and turned to the healer. "Where's Omid? The warrior with an arrow through his shoulder?"

The healer motioned toward a curtained area of the yarm and replied, "He is having the arrow pushed through now."

Pushed through. Coxani closed her eyes briefly. "May I come check on him afterward?"

"Yes, of course," the healer replied, turning to tend to Moti.

Coxani emerged from the yarm to find that the bodies of the fourteen dead Sachin warriors had been laid out and prepared for the pyre. Two of the injured had died during the journey back from their wounds. Coxani watched somberly as the nomads cleaned the bodies and wrapped them in cloth. Bruneta, tears streaming freely down her cheeks, knelt beside each body and tucked a string of five white beads beneath the wrappings, against their bosoms. Then the children—some as young as three or four—wove flowers and grass into the fiber of the cloth.

"Don't the families of the dead want their bodies back?" Coxani asked a solemn Marbek, who supervised the ritual with his arms crossed on his chest.

"The families would rather see them burned as soon as possible," Marbek answered. "The Gohari believe it's the only way to ensure a clean passage back into nature. A trip back would take precious time." He looked at her briefly. "Fourteen red and fourteen black beads will be made from their ashes, and Bruneta will take them back to their families."

"Beads have a lot of meaning to you Gohari," Coxani said. "Does every bead a nomad wears have meaning?"

Marbek's eyes darted in her direction suspiciously, as if he were trying to decipher her motives. After a moment, he said, "For the most part. The families of the dead warriors will likely string their black and red beads together and wear them in their hair, or as jewelry."

"The black and red beads together mean the loss of a loved one?" Coxani asked, her breath catching. She was suddenly noticing how many red and black beads each nomad had in their plaits, looped around their necks, and tied to their wrists. *Far too many.*

Marbek nodded once. "Yes."

Reflexively, Coxani reached into the sleeve of her tunic and felt for the blue beads and sheep knuckles Beg Ayym had twined around her wrist for Tikran. She wondered at their specific meaning, but didn't dare ask Marbek. He'd likely be enraged that such a thing had been given to a Manzakar.

As she watched Bruneta and the remaining Sachin warriors

carry the shrouded bodies and set them carefully on the freshly built pyre, she wondered how many times in their young lifetimes the warriors had already performed the same ritual. She said, "Beg Marbek, I know this is too little, too late, and my words may mean nothing to you, but... I'm devastated by what the Manzakars have done to your people. I understand your distrust of Tikran, of me. But I swear to you, if I do nothing else in my life, I will fight for Gohar's freedom, even if it kills me. In my heart, it's the only cause truly worth fighting for."

Two Gohari mages chanted a prayer before the pyre, the beads of their headdresses tinkling and their hands outstretched, and with a gust of air, the pyre was engulfed in flames. Marbek said softly, "Then you should prepare to die with the rest of us, Manzakar." He turned and strode away then, leaving Coxani to stare gravely into the fire as it consumed the dead within it.

CHAPTER 22

Berk leaned forward, his eyes fixed on the smooth, flat stones sitting on the board before him, his brow creased in concentration. Damir studied the boy's face by candle-light, smiling discreetly to himself. In the time of his apprentice-ship, Berk had decidedly matured some, both emotionally and physically. For one, he'd begun tying his hair back from his face instead of letting it curtain his eyes. Finally consuming a rich diet befitting a boy his age and getting some much-needed exercise, Berk's gangly form had filled out a bit. He'd recently approached Damir rather tentatively and asked for a razor to shave the hair that had begun sprouting over his lip and on his chin.

Damir had given the boy a razor—and shown him how to use it.

Over the course of three months, Berk had acquired some nuance when speaking to others and had become much more tactful with his words, particularly with Vazha, which filled Damir with immense relief. The boy was clever and likely detected the hostility between him and the prince. As much as he loathed the thought, Damir had to admit that Berk likely sensed more than just hostility. He was a teenager, after all.

Damir's Gohari apprentice was also learning to control his

astoundingly powerful Essence. While he still grimaced from the pain of drawing his magic back in, he managed to do it more quickly. Most notably, Berk was learning to focus his Essence on discrete areas—a specific rock or tree, or a distinct portion of a river or field. He could also wield a saber without calling on his Essence to aid him, aside from helping him breathe. This, Damir knew, would be critical in preventing unnecessary destruction or death.

Despite all of Berk's progress, however, one thing plagued Damir, gnawing at his subconscious and haunting his dreams: Berk remained heavily influenced by his anger. A single spark of rage, and the Essence flowed from him in a torrential wave, albeit a mostly controlled one. When this happened, the Essence Damir sensed about them was far more sinister and, as expected, far more difficult for Berk to draw back in.

One tantrum and hundreds of people die.

"Ah!" Berk cried, his face lighting up, jerking Damir from his musings. Berk grinned wickedly at his mentor. "You're going down, Master Damir." He pushed one of his stones diagonally into an adjacent intersection on the board, behind another of his pieces.

Damir couldn't help but smile. He'd insisted they take a break from magic this particular evening—casting it, reading about it, talking about it. Bilguun was holding a banquet honoring the birth of his first grandson and Orxan's heir that evening and had insisted Berk accompany Damir. As such, mentor and apprentice were shaved, coiffed, and wearing the finest silk robes, playing a game of dhaki and awaiting a summons to the night's event. Although all Dilovar's mages wore red conical hats that folded back and covered the neck, Damir often chose not to wear his. Tonight, however, he wore his in solidarity with his young charge. As Damir contemplated his next move, the summons came in the form of a knock and a calling attendant. Together, the two mages rose and walked to the great hall.

"Master Damir," Berk said nervously, "I have no idea what to expect tonight. Will I be seated next to you?"

"Yes. And it won't be any different from when we have dinner with the king," Damir reassured him. "Well, aside from the number of attendees. I imagine all the aristocracy will be there."

Berk groaned. "I'm not…very good with people, sir. Let alone fancy people."

Damir sighed. "Just be respectful. Answer questions politely, don't share too much information. Sit straight and chew with your mouth closed."

"I never chew with my mouth open!"

"Sometimes you do. And other times you slump over your plate like a Haldoran."

"I've gotten better about that, admit it. I…" His voice trailed off as they crossed the threshold into the hall. In addition to the great braziers, several candelabra blazed throughout, illuminating the gilded, carved windows and ornamental pillars. Embellished silk banners, embroidered with flowers and mythical beasts, hung from the ceiling, fluttering ever so slightly. Dilovar's aristocracy shimmered in their brocades and fine jewels, seated around an immense table that was laden with covered dishes that steamed aromatically. Damir led Berk to where the rest of the mages sat and indicated that they should sit as well.

The first thing Damir did when he sat was look for Vazha among the guests. While the prince usually announced his visits ahead of time, Damir could never be certain when he would find himself in the unwelcome company of his rapist. Vazha, however, didn't seem to be in attendance, and a profuse, dizzying sense of relief washed over Damir. When this war was over and Damir was certain Tikran was safe, he would exact his revenge on Vazha…somehow.

After standing for King Bilguun and Prince Orxan's entrance and chanting a prayer to Cenk, the feast began in earnest. The royal family was served first as attendants rushed about, pouring enkh into every goblet. Berk leaned toward Damir and whispered, "Where's the baby?"

It took a second for Damir to understand the question. "Probably with a nursemaid or asleep, I imagine. Why?"

"Aren't people here to see the baby?"

Chuckling, Damir said, "The party is for the adults, not the baby. Besides, what's there to see? Babies all look more or less the same."

Berk shrugged. "In Gohar, we celebrate babies' births too. Everyone in the clan blesses the baby with a yellow bead that's woven into its blanket."

Damir smiled. "Sounds like a lovely tradition." He paused. "You miss Gohar, don't you?"

"Yes," Berk replied softly. "I miss Beg Zolto, my great grandfather, mostly. But I'm doing the right thing, being here." He took a sip of the enkh and frowned. "Master Damir, this tastes different than usual."

"It's likely got a higher alcohol content than usual," Damir said. "They do that for special occasions." He considered before adding, "Maybe don't drink too much."

The feast proceeded with all the pomp and circumstance expected. Dancing girls whirled beyond the table while each course of the meal was brought out in turn, culminating in a whole roasted ox. Damir talked war with the other mages, eventually noticing that Berk's incessant questions had stopped. He turned to check on his apprentice and found the boy staring at someone or something at the far end of the table. After observing for several minutes, he realized that the object of Berk's attention was Bilguun's fourteen-year-old niece, Maral. The girl was a classic Dilovari beauty, with her milky white skin, wide-set eyes, and lustrous black hair, and was rumored to have received several marriage proposals already. To Damir's surprise, however, Maral appeared to be returning Berk's attention, blushing and gazing shyly in his direction. Maybe it was the enkh, but Damir's first reaction was to grin. Then he felt a tinge of sadness—Berk would never have the opportunity to interact with the girl, as he was not an aristocrat and, even more significantly, he was Gohari.

"Master Damir," a familiar voice said from behind him.

With a deep breath and a large gulp of enkh, Damir stood and turned toward Commander Amit. "Yes, Commander?"

Amit's expression was a clear attempt at indifference. "I'm surprised you're even here, considering Prince Vazha is not in attendance."

Damir drew in his breath, praying to the gods for patience. Amit had been his occasional lover before Vazha had...interfered. Since then, Damir's desire had waned considerably—and understandably—for Amit. In truth, the thought of physical intimacy with anyone other than Tikran made Damir physically ill. His desire for Tikran, fueled by his love for the Manzakar king, was the only thing that gave him the ability to endure Vazha's assaults. "Are you here to tell me something worthwhile? Or simply to express some petty jealousy?"

It was both the right and wrong thing to say. Amit visibly clenched his teeth. "Our king would like to speak with us."

"Now?" Damir looked around. "During his grandson's banquet?"

Amit lifted his chin. "He's had quite a bit to drink, it seems. He wants to see us now."

With a glance back at Berk, who was exchanging flirtatious smiles with Maral, Damir said, "Let's make it quick, then."

The two men approached Bilguun, whose face was flushed with intoxication, a wide smile creasing his face. "Doctor Damir!" Bilguun cried cheerfully. "Has Commander Amit told you the news?"

Damir kept his expression steady. He had never seen Bilguun in this state and it put him immediately on edge. "No, Your Highness. He has not."

Bilguun leaned toward his head mage. "Something is amiss in Gohar. I suspect it has to do with Vazha's absence from this celebration tonight. My sources tell me that he has intercepted messages to Anzor and destroyed the company in charge of rein-forcing the Anzori forts in Gohar. King Tikran has no idea that any of it has happened."

Damir's mind raced. *What?* He had so many questions. Rather than ask them, he calmly said, "Yes, Your Highness?"

Bilguun clapped his hands together, rubbing them vigorously. "Now is our chance, Damir. We can capture more Anzori forts along the Damla while Tikran is none the wiser."

A pit of dread balled in Damir's stomach. "And what does this have to do with me, my king?"

Bilguun's face was lit with drunken excitement. "This is our chance to display young Berk's power, Damir. I want you and Berk to travel to the last captured garrison, Faiz, and participate in the capture of Zifa." Bilguun looked up at the silk banners absently. "I want you and Berk to strike fear in the Manzakars' hearts."

Damir's dinner threatened to come up. "Your Highness, Berk is not ready. I am willing to—"

"Master Damir, you will do as I order," Bilguun snapped. "You will journey to Gohar in the next two days with Commander Amit and allow Berk to display his strength before the Manzakars. Kill all of them, if you must." He lifted his chin proudly. "Anzor will know the true power of Dilovar when this is over, so help me, Cenk."

The rest of the banquet passed in a haze. By the time mentor and apprentice returned to Damir's chambers, Damir had drunk far more alcohol than he had in a very long time. While he certainly wasn't visibly drunk, he knew he should get to bed sooner rather than later, before he did or said anything he might regret. How was he going to ensure Berk didn't lose control of his emotions, and therefore his Essence, the moment he saw a hostile Manzakar? *He's not ready!* Damir would have to be the one to perform most of the magic, if he could help it. He was not as powerful as Berk, however, and couldn't focus his Essence the way Berk could. *Oh, Cenk.* Either way, it seemed there was going to be collateral damage...

It wasn't until the pair was back in the library that Damir realized just how drunk Berk was. "Master Damir," the boy slurred, stumbling as he kicked off his boots, his mage's hat askew on his head, "I think I'm in love."

Damir sighed. "I think you're drunk. Perhaps you should sleep here tonight, instead of wandering the palace, babbling about love." He helped Berk remove his robe and guided the boy to the couch, where Enlil lay curled, watching them suspiciously.

"No, no," Berk insisted, shaking his head. "I need to know her name."

"What would be the point?" Damir said, his tone coming out harsher than he'd intended. "You are Gohari. She is of royal Dilovari blood, and likely already betrothed to a lord's son."

Berk's face fell and Damir instantly regretted his words. After allowing Damir to coax him into drinking a cup of water, Berk curled up on the couch, a look of despair on his face as he turned his back to his mentor.

Damir took a deep breath and squeezed the boy's shoulder. "Rest. We have a busy day ahead of us." *A major understatement.* As he turned to leave, he added gently, "Her name is Maral."

But Berk was already fast asleep, purring as loudly as the cat at his feet.

CHAPTER 23

The removal of the arrow from Moti's thigh had been a complicated procedure, and the healers insisted he not move for several days. "This is ridiculous," he muttered to Coxani and Bruneta as they sat beside his pallet in the healers' yarm. "Omid had an arrow go through his shoulder and he's already moving around."

"You heard what the healer said, Moti," Coxani said as Bruneta brushed a strand of hair away from his face tenderly. "Omid was lucky. The angle of the shot prevented a lot of damage. Getting the bodkin out of your bone, unfortunately, was difficult. You need to sit still for a few days and let your body recover."

He huffed in frustration and gave the two women each an imploring look. "So you're leaving me here? A lone Manzakar among a tribe that hates Manzakars so much it's allied with our enemy? What if the Dilovari show up?"

"Marbek has given me his word that he will not betray you," Bruneta said firmly. "He may hate Manzakars, but you are the Sachin's guest and you're wounded. I'm also leaving several of my warriors with you, including Omid. They'll watch out for you."

Moti lowered his voice and said, "I don't trust this Marbek guy. He knows things he's not telling us. Who attacked the Davlat clan, and why? Why did Vazha step in? What shady deal did Marbek make with him?"

Coxani blew out her breath. "I don't trust him either, but I don't think he'd hurt you or turn you over to the Dilovari." She leaned forward. "Moti, I must get back to Eter. I have to see if there are any messages from Anzor and if reinforcements have made their way into Gohar yet. I'll have to send one about Vazha, too."

"And I have to head back to the Sachin and update Beg Ayym on what's happened," Bruneta said. "I sent a scout when we first arrived, but she needs to hear things from me." She paused, her pain clear in her voice. "I also have to give the warriors' beads to their families personally."

Moti took Bruneta's hand and squeezed it. "I get it. Just don't be gone long, please."

"A week at most," Bruneta promised. "By the time we get back, you'll be up and moving around."

Moti smiled. "Oh, don't worry. I will be."

Later, as Coxani readied her horse for the trip back to Eter, Omid approached her, his left shoulder heavily dressed and his arm in a sling, bound to his torso. "So you're off, then?"

"I'll be back." Coxani looked over at the healers' yarm. "Visit Moti on occasion, will you? He's nervous about being left here."

Omid snorted. "*I'm* nervous about being left here," he admitted, frowning. "I worry my days as an archer are over."

"That's not necessarily true," Coxani reassured him. "You just need time to heal."

"I want to be able to fight alongside you," he said. "This war won't wait for me to heal."

Coxani considered. "What weapons can you wield one-handed?"

"I can throw javelins." He flashed her a flirty grin. "Maybe you can give me some sword-fighting lessons when you get back."

She turned away, still smiling, discretely touching the small lump in her tunic pocket before mounting her horse. "All right. It's a deal."

He looked up at her, his face growing serious. "Be careful, Coxani. I don't know why that prince tried to kill you and Moti, but if there are Manzakars out there willing to carry out that order, you need to watch your back."

She nodded. "I know."

Coxani, Bruneta, and twenty of the remaining Sachin warriors set out, heading northwest toward Eter. The group was somber, riding silently throughout most of the first day. They made camp for the night, setting up a single yarm, and after eating a meal of bustard and bread around a fire, retired to the yarm to sleep.

As Coxani lay down on her bedroll, she noticed Bruneta had not come in to sleep yet. She wandered back out to find the Sachin commander still sitting by the fire, her face in her hands and her shoulders shaking. Without hesitation, Coxani kneeled and wrapped her arms around Bruneta. Squeezing tightly, Coxani whispered, "I'm so sorry, Bruneta. I'm so incredibly sorry."

Bruneta seemed startled at first, stiffening within Coxani's embrace. After a moment, she relaxed, placing a hand on Coxani's. "I don't know why I'm crying like this," she managed to say. She wiped her face and took a steady breath. "This sort of thing has happened my whole life. I've always known that the people around me, the people I love, will likely die at any moment, and brutally. I thought I was past this."

Coxani released her tight grip and leaned back to look into Bruneta's tear-stained face. "I can't imagine going through what you've gone through. But you're still human. You need to grieve."

Looking at Coxani with red-rimmed eyes, Bruneta said softly, "I think it hit me hard this time because I really wanted to believe the Manzakars were our allies."

"We *are* your allies," Coxani insisted. "What happened at Vazha's manor was..." Coxani sought the right words. "I'm convinced Moti and I were the primary targets of that attack."

Bruneta stared into the fire, tears in her eyelashes. "Gohar must be free, Coxani. Until that happens, we will continue to die at the hands of Manzakars, or the Dilovari, or whoever believes they have dominion over us."

"I agree," Coxani answered. "And Tikran agrees. It will happen, Bruneta."

Unmoving, her eyes locked on the flames, Bruneta said, "Things must not be looking good for Tikran in Anzor if the deposed king's heir feels confident he can kill Manzakars—let alone nomads—and get away with it." She turned her gaze on Coxani, then. "Am I wrong?"

Coxani pursed her lips. Of course, Bruneta was right. But hearing the words spoken aloud... "Truthfully, I don't know the extent of it. I know there were several Anzori lords who were very put out by Tikran's abolition of slavery in Anzor. When he didn't stop there and repealed a law forbidding the commingling of Anzori and Gohari bloodlines, he likely lost the support of some others."

Bruneta smiled sadly. "It will never happen, will it?"

"Don't say that." Coxani shook her head and clenched her fist. "It *will* happen. So help me, Cenk."

"You mean Archil," Bruneta said. "Cenk won't help shit."

"Yes." Coxani drew in a breath. "It will happen, Bruneta. So help me, Archil."

A small smile hovered on Bruneta's lips before she leaned forward and kissed Coxani on the mouth, gently, then more insistently. Somehow, Coxani was not surprised by the kiss. It was eerily like kissing a softer and, if she was being perfectly honest, more skilled Tikran. Just as the kiss deepened, Bruneta pulled back a fraction, gauging Coxani's reaction. Coxani realized she wanted more and held still, her eyes half-closed. The Sachin commander hesitated before saying, "You Anzori don't like sharing beads, do you?"

Coxani blinked, feeling her face grow warm. "Er... No, they... We..."

Bruneta tilted her head. "I want to give you a bead, Coxani. But I worry it will upset Moti."

Yeah, it would most likely upset Moti. Coxani sat back, tucking an errant curl behind her ear, embarrassed that she hadn't thought of Moti first. "You're right. He would...not be happy."

Bruneta smiled. "Maybe when you and he are more accepting of the Gohari ways, I will give you a bead."

I'm sure Tikran would be thrilled by that turn of events. Coxani's face went from warm to hot. She nodded and looked away, smiling, unsure of how to respond.

After several moments of amicable silence, the two women retreated to the yarm, where Bruneta laid her bedroll beside Coxani's. They fell asleep quickly, their hands clasped and fingers interlocked, exhaustion overcoming them both.

***

THEY PACKED up the yarm and resumed their three-day journey to Eter and the Sachin encampment. The first light of dawn illuminated the sky and bathed the rugged Gohari landscape in faint pastels. The stars still shone brightly in the cloudless sky and burrowing owls dove into the sparse tussocks of long grass, hunting for mice, lizards and snakes.

Coxani rode alongside Bruneta, sharing the details of her childhood in Anzor: Mago's visits and his much-anticipated date cookies; Haydar allowing her to train with a bow at an early age; the mind-numbing etiquette and elocution classes at the girls' school... When she described the choosing party, Bruneta uttered a sound of disgust and gaped at Coxani. "Holy shit! I thought the rumors I'd heard about what they did with female slaves were exaggerated. But they're actually true? So all these Anzori men, some of them much older, some of them already married, are choosing lovers from a pool of teenage Gohari girls who have no choice in the matter?"

Coxani sighed and said, "Yep."

"That's beyond repulsive," Bruneta said, shuddering. "Do

older, married Anzori women get to choose lovers from a selection of teenage Gohari boys as well?"

A laugh burst from Coxani's lips. "No, no. It doesn't work that way. Up until Tikran changed the law, any sort of relationship between an Anzori woman and a Gohari man was a punishable offense."

Bruneta scowled. "I can't decide who the Anzori hate more, the Gohari or women."

"Well, they clearly hate Gohari women most," Coxani said. "I was lucky, I think, because Lord Haydar took me under his wing. He's the reason I was able to train as a Manzakar, why I didn't have to become a courtesan...well, not initially, at least."

"Has Tikran changed the law about courtesans?"

"I know he'd planned on it," Coxani said. "He's got more pressing issues at the moment."

Bruneta looked out on the horizon in contemplation. "I'm truly proud of Tikran. I can't believe what he's been able to achieve, and in such a short time. I hope that—" Jerking on her reins and bringing her horse to a sudden halt, she stopped speaking, her eyes fixed on the distance.

Coxani scanned the steppe nervously. "What? What is it, Bruneta?"

The Sachin commander held her hand up, signaling to the other warriors. Then she said, "Smoke. Less than fifteen miles away." She pointed at a spot on the horizon where a smudge of black hovered between two mesas.

Coxani squinted. "Couldn't it be Sachin?"

"Not this far east," Bruneta answered. "This is still Davlat territory. But it wouldn't be either Sachin or Davlat, in any case."

"Why not?"

"The smoke is black," Bruneta said, looking at Coxani. "You've helped us build fires before. We use dry, seasoned wood or, more often, charcoal, because it's less wasteful. It's also lighter and easier to carry. Both burn much cleaner." She gazed again at the amorphous plumes of black smoke. "Whomever that is, they're likely burning wet wood and brush. They definitely aren't Gohari."

Coxani felt the hairs of her arms stand on end. "Maybe they're Manzakars?"

"Hopefully." Bruneta gave Coxani a meaningful look. "It's pretty far south for them to be Dilovari."

Coxani swallowed. "We have to find out."

Bruneta nodded and turned to the other warriors. "Go back to the Sachin and tell Beg Ayym that Coxani and I are doing some reconnaissance. We should be no more than a few hours behind you." Reluctantly, she pulled a pouch from her belt and handed it to one of the warriors. "These are the beads of the dead. Give them to Ayym, just in case."

Coxani sucked in her breath. *Just in case of what?* As the pair parted ways with the group, her nerves were drawn as tight as a silk bowstring. "Moti and I should have completed our mission instead of getting sidetracked by the Davlat," she mused aloud.

Shaking her head, Bruneta said, "No. I disagree. Without the Davlat, Anzor really is in trouble."

"That's what I'm afraid of. But other than their size, what advantage do they have?" Coxani asked.

"Archil was from the Davlat tribe," Bruneta answered. "I don't know if that has anything to do with it, but they have the most nomads with the Essence." She looked at Coxani earnestly. "Magic might be what saves Tikran."

Coxani mulled this over in silence as they rode at a brisk pace. *Magic.* Manzakars were taught not to put much stock in it; the Essence was volatile, imprecise, and often unpredictable. Until Damir, she hadn't believed it was worth the time or effort in battle. But when she'd seen what Damir could do... Supposedly, Tanith could do the same. Perhaps Bruneta was right. "How many nomads do the Sachin have with the Essence?"

"Five, of varying abilities and strengths."

"And the Davlat?"

Bruneta shook her head. "I don't know. But probably twice as many."

That's it? No wonder Anzor scoured Gohar for those with the Essence. "What about the other tribes?"

"If they had anyone powerful, we would know about it," Bruneta answered. "The Mehrab and Vata likely have less than five somewhat powerful mages put together."

Coxani realized abruptly that she had never heard the other tribes' names—other than the Iroda. Tikran had told her about the Iroda's destruction, and it still filled her with anger and sadness every time she thought about it. "So the Davlat have the most powerful individuals with the Essence?"

"Yes," Bruneta confirmed. "We had one who was very powerful. She now serves Tikran."

"Tanith. Of course." Coxani felt stupid for not realizing it sooner. "She is, according to Tikran, as powerful as Damir. I'm assuming you trust her?"

Bruneta shrugged. "I respect Tanith as a warrior and have no reason *not* to trust her. Beg Ayym trusts her implicitly. But she would, since they were lovers for a while. That is, until Tanith left for Anzor."

Tanith had been Ayym's lover? Coxani blinked, wondering how that information fit into what she knew about Tanith—and Ayym, for that matter. Rather than dwell on it, she filed it away and focused on the black plumes of smoke that rose higher into the horizon.

Riding at an easy trot, it took them a little over an hour to reach a series of low hills about half a mile away from where the fires were burning. After dismounting quietly and moving as close to the ground as possible, they reached the top of the tallest hill and lowered themselves to their bellies, holding their collective breaths in anticipation.

A cavalry squadron of at least two hundred Dilovari troops made camp beyond the hills, their fires like scattered candles, their soldiers' distinctive spiked, broad-brimmed helmets adorned with long plumes of hair.

Coxani's blood ran cold as she sank down and turned. "I have to get to Eter. Holy Cenk, Dilovar has managed to capture at least five more forts since I left Anzor!"

Bruneta tugged at Coxani's arm. "Let's get out of here, quick."

As they crawled as quietly as they could back to their horses, something—a strange scent, a change in air flow, grass that rustled when it shouldn't have—made Coxani abruptly hyper-vigilant. Bruneta grasped Coxani's shoulder in a vise-like grip as they both turned their heads. A Dilovari soldier crested a low hill on his horse just a few yards away, gazing in the opposite direction, a horn strung around his neck. *The lookout.* Luckily, Coxani and Bruneta's horses were tucked behind a shadowed ridge, so the soldier likely had no idea anyone was in the vicinity.

Frozen with fear and deliberating on her next actions frantically, Coxani didn't anticipate what her Gohari companion did next. With the speed and stealth of a wildcat, Bruneta rushed toward the soldier, her dagger in her hand. The Dilovari had just finished yawning when he turned in their direction. In the instant he spotted them, Bruneta leaped onto his horse behind him. Standing on the back of his saddle, she tried driving her blade into the openings between his pauldrons and cuirass. He grunted in surprise and teetered, grabbing Bruneta by the leg and dragging her off the horse and to the ground with him as he fell.

Shit! Coxani scrambled to her feet and ran to where Bruneta and the soldier rolled on the ground. The soldier's helmet had fallen off and his long, black plait flopped back and forth as he and Bruneta grappled. He was bigger than she was, much bigger, and had pinned her down. As he reached for his belt, Coxani drew her bronze-hilt dagger and, leaping into the scuffle, plunged its tip into the base of the Dilovari's skull. To her horror—or was it relief? —dark, thick blood bloomed immediately, soaking through his hair. He let out a croak and went completely limp, his armor creaking as he landed on Bruneta. *Oh... What have I done?*

Bruneta scrabbled out from under the soldier's heavy, still

body and yanked the horn from around his neck while Coxani stared, aghast, at the bloody dagger in her fist. Her eyes wide, Bruneta hissed, "What are you waiting for? Let's go!"

The pair ran with abandon to their mounts and sent them into full gallops instantly, desperate to leave the Dilovari behind them. Coxani didn't release her breath until they were a good several miles away, and even then her heart continued to pound, her hands flecked with the soldier's blood and still shaking.

The Dilovari's alliance with the Davlat had clearly emboldened them. She needed to send a message to Anzor. She needed to get the rest of the supplies to the remaining forts.

She needed Tikran and his forces in Gohar—*now*.

CHAPTER 24

reparations remain on schedule. We will continue to await your regular updates.

Standing with Commander Mamun in his office, Coxani turned to him, the scrap of parchment in her hand, her brow furrowed. "This is it? This is the only message from Anzor?"

The commander nodded. "Yes. This is it."

"It's like he's not getting my messages," she said, half to herself. Like a fist in the gut, the realization hit her. *He's not getting my messages.* It was the only explanation. She looked sharply at Mamun. "Have you sent a courier to Anzor?"

"No." He hesitated. "I didn't think—"

"No, you clearly didn't," Coxani snapped. "You knew my company was attacked by Dilovari arrows, but you did nothing when you got this reply? And now, the Dilovari have captured every Anzori fort nearly halfway down the Damla River." She could barely breathe, she was so infuriated. "Send a courier to Anzor this minute and tell him it's urgent."

Mamun straightened, his nostrils flaring indignantly. "I think you forget yourself, Captain."

Coxani was simmering with rage. Mamun was a good half foot taller than her, but that didn't stop her from attempting to bring her face as close to his as possible. "Listen to me, *Commander*. My co-captain is lying wounded in a Davlat encampment because of a Manzakar's arrow. Do you hear me? We were attacked by Prince Vazha's Manzakars. Then, just a few days ago, I stumbled across a Dilovari squadron so close to Eter they're about to crawl up your ass, and you have no *fucking idea*, do you?" She was certain she looked and sounded crazed, and it gave her a smidge of satisfaction to see a flicker of concern in his eyes. She continued, "Things are looking very, very bad for Anzor right now, so I need you to put away your ridiculously oversized ego and send a courier to Anzor *five minutes ago*. Am I clear?"

With his disdain for her written clear on his face, Mamun turned from Coxani and ordered a nearby soldier, "Call my scribe. We need a letter dictated to King Tikran immediately. Double time!"

Coxani took a deep breath. "Thank you. Now, where are my pigeons? In fact, I need my entire company ready to go. We're going to get Moti then head to the remaining forts on the Damla."

Mamun scowled. "You don't have the authority to do that."

"You're right," Coxani replied, turning on him again. It was taking every ounce of her willpower to keep from kneeing Eter's commander in the groin then smacking him upside the head. "But I'm not getting any direction from Anzor, am I? They must have no idea what's happened. And I suspect I know why. So I'm making some executive decisions."

The scribe entered Mamun's office and sat at the desk immediately, his quill poised over a sheet of parchment. The commander began, "To His Highness, King Tikran, with utmost urgency—"

Coxani cleared her throat loudly. "Not to further piss you off, Commander, but I think I should be the one to dictate the letter, since I have personal knowledge of the facts." She smiled with affected sweetness. "Don't you agree?"

Disdain transformed to contempt as Mamun's nostrils flared. "Suit yourself." With that, he turned and strode from the room, the heels of his boots hammering loudly against the wood floor.

Ignoring him, Coxani hurriedly dictated the message to Tikran and made sure the courier was on his way to Anzor within the hour. As extra assurance, she had the same message sent by two of her pigeons.

In the day that followed, she prepared her company for departure and waited just long enough for Bruneta to return from the Sachin encampment. "Bruneta," she said, already tacking her horse, "I think Vazha is somehow intercepting my messages to Tikran. He must have more allies in Anzor than I thought. This is an emergency. I'm going to get Moti and head to the Damla with these reinforcements."

Bruneta scowled. "Not without me, you're not."

Coxani shook her head. "I've endangered enough of your warriors as it is. Please. I can't—"

"What are you talking about, Manzakar?" Bruneta looked bewildered. "Your fight is our fight. We've pledged ourselves to the Freed Kingfisher. Don't be ridiculous." She then flashed a smile so like Tikran's that Coxani's breath hitched in her throat. Bruneta said, "Give me a few hours to gather my warriors and we'll leave immediately."

In silent solidarity, Coxani and Bruneta led their respective troops into eastern Gohar. Together, they had three hundred Manzakars and two hundred Sachin warriors. Bruneta had sent scouts ahead of them to Marbek so that he wouldn't be alarmed by the number of Manzakar troops encroaching on his turf.

Despite being consumed with worry, Coxani was still very cognizant of the fact that the soldiers in her company disapproved of her seizing command. They had tolerated her when Moti had been at her side; Moti may have had a controversial past, but he'd proven himself in Otebek and Sitora, and the Manzakars had accepted him as one of them, for the most part. Coxani, however, was still an unproven warrior, despite her participation in the rebellion. Her orders were met with hostile looks and scornful grumbling. She was having none of it—Tikran's reign was at risk and these overgrown children were pouting because a woman was in charge? *I need to let Bruneta handle the lot of them.* The thought made her smile, however briefly, and kept her from faltering.

When they at last breached Davlat territory on the fourth day of travel, several scouts greeted them, announcing that Marbek had been waiting for them. It had been nearly ten days since she'd seen Moti. She had so much to tell him. She hoped he would agree with the decisions she'd been forced to make, the life she'd been forced to take...

The Manzakar captain settled her troops several miles from Marbek's encampment and chose Kir, a Manzakar she trusted to keep command of the company as she, Bruneta, and the Sachin warriors finished the journey back to the Davlat camp. As they approached, the Sachin who had stayed behind rushed out to meet them. Coxani spotted Omid and almost smiled until she saw his somber expression. Immediately, a feeling of dread gripped her.

Oh, no.

Bruneta must have seen it as well, because she hopped off her horse first and strode with purpose toward him, Coxani hot on her heels. "What's happened?" Bruneta demanded.

Omid turned, indicating they should follow him as he walked briskly toward the healers' yarm. Over his shoulder, he said, "Moti's wound... It's not looking good."

Inside the yarm, Moti slept fitfully, twisting his head from side to side, a sheen of sweat covering his face and neck, his cheeks flushed with fever. The healer who tended to him, a middle-aged woman with mostly silver hair and the faded tattoos of a former warrior, carefully lifted the poultice from his leg to reveal a swollen, red gash that wept yellow pus. She said, "We've done everything, tried every remedy. We've been coating the injury in our special salves, which usually work with deep wounds." She looked up at the two exhausted warriors with sad brown eyes. "I'm sorry. We will keep trying, but..."

At that moment, Moti opened his eyes, grimaced in pain, blinked, and focused on Coxani and Bruneta. Coxani wanted to burst into tears when he smiled. "Oh, holy shit," he croaked. "Look who's finally back?"

Bruneta stepped toward him, kneeled, and took his hand in hers. Coxani saw the Sachin commander swallow nervously, her eyes glistening, before she spoke softly. "Captain Moti, you need to get better immediately. We need you."

Moti's grin widened. "Fuck yeah, you do." He brought Bruneta's hand to his lips and kissed it, closing his eyes as he held her fingers to his cheek.

I can't do this. Coxani turned and rushed out of the yarm before a sob escaped her lips. She clasped her palm to her mouth and squeezed her eyes shut as tears ran down her cheeks. She was about to sink to her knees when a strong arm looped around her waist and held her. Before she even opened her eyes, she knew it was Omid. It was his scent, the feel of him. When he spoke, his voice gentle but firm, a fraction of the tension she held in her body dissipated. "Hey. Hey. Coxani. Coxani…"

She controlled her sobs, nodding. "You can let me go. I'm fine."

His arm was still wrapped around her tightly. "But I don't want to let go."

For some reason, his words soothed her like a medicinal balm. She wanted to continue leaning against him but resisted. "I should go back to Moti."

Omid looked over his shoulder. "You should give him time with Bruneta."

Her heart ached. "Yes. Okay."

He pulled her closer to him and she didn't resist. "Come sit with me by the fire," he said. "Have some arash."

"Arash," she repeated, the ghost of her humor returning as she wiped her nose with her sleeve. "That sounds like some serious booze."

Omid's low, rumbling laugh made her feel lighter. "It's an herbal tincture with a lot of alcohol. It's some heavy stuff, but it helps with...pain. Both physical and emotional. Don't worry, I won't let you have much. Just enough to help you relax."

They sat beside a fire and Omid poured them both small cups of a brown liquid. Before handing her one, he asked, "When was the last time you ate something?"

"Sometime this afternoon," she lied. She hadn't eaten in twelve hours, at least.

"Are you hungry?"

"Not even remotely."

He frowned, then tossed half of the cup's contents in the grass. "This will be enough."

She held the cup between her fingers for several seconds before bringing it to her lips. It wasn't terrible. Perhaps even better than xew. As she let the strange flavor coat her tongue, a shadow fell over her.

"I'm sorry about Moti, Coxani." She looked up to see Beg Marbek standing beside the fire, his arms crossed, his face in that perpetual scowl. "I know my healers are doing what they can."

Was he really sorry? It was one less Manzakar for him to worry about, after all. *But he said my name.* It was the first time, she was sure. Unable to feel too much without breaking down, Coxani said, "Thank you for taking care of him. But there must be something we can do. I'm going to have the Anzori doctor examine his wound. Surely there's a remedy that hasn't been tried."

Before Marbek could answer, an old, gravelly voice carried over the fire. "Coxani? Her name is Coxani, you say?"

Marbek raised his head, his arms falling to his sides. "Yes, Beg Zolto. The Manzakar's name is Coxani."

Beyond the flames, Coxani saw the wavering, hunched form of an old man stand and hobble toward her. As he approached, she didn't need to be told that he was a highly respected elder—Marbek's behavior alone revealed it. The chieftain cleared the old man's path and laid a wool blanket across a bench for him to sit on. Coxani sat up.

"Your name is Coxani?" Beg Zolto's beady eyes were fixed on her as he used the knotted wooden staff in his hand to help him sit.

"Yes, Beg," she answered.

"You are Davlat, are you not?" The old man's wrinkled face was lit with excitement.

Confused, she said, "Yes. I was sold to Anzor when I was four years old, by my aunt, after my family died of the red plague."

For several heart-stopping moments, Beg Zolto's breath came in hitches, his eyes wide. Coxani almost panicked. *Have I killed him, too? Oh, Cenk...*

"Your aunt," he finally said. "Do you remember her name?"

"Yes." She hesitated, trying to anticipate the old man's reaction. "Her name was Khava."

After muttering under his breath, bowing his head once, and placing his hand on his heart, Zolto leaned heavily against his staff to stand. He smiled, his eyes shimmering with unshed tears. "The child lives." He looked at Marbek. "Archil's descendant lives!"

What the fuck? Coxani swayed, both the arash and the elder's words slamming into her all at once.

If anything, Marbek's scowl had become more menacing. "Impossible," he said. "The child died, her aunt said so."

"Khava must have lied," Zolto insisted, his head trembling. "She had no idea who the child was and sold her. Then, when she was told the child was Archil's descendant, she feared the consequences of her actions and lied."

Marbek blanched. "Are you telling me that Archil's blood runs through a *Manzakar*?"

Zolto laughed with abandon, a high-pitched, wheezy laugh. "Yes! Marbek, how many of our children were sold to—or taken by —Anzor? And you are truly surprised? Archil wouldn't be surprised. In fact, they would likely say it was part of their plan."

Coxani looked at the stunned faces around her, Omid's included. She stood and stammered, "I'm not... There must be a mistake, I'm just..." The crowd was growing quickly—Gohari men, women, children, warriors, all with a look of awe on their faces—

making her want to crawl under a rock. Zolto's eyes fixed on Coxani's hand and he moved toward her, grasping her wrist between his bony fingers and holding it up in the firelight. "She is chosen. Look."

Realizing the old man meant the bracelet of blue beads and sheep knuckles Ayym had given her, Coxani tried to pull away unsuccessfully. Zolto's grasp was firm. "No," she protested. "It's not even for me. The bracelet is for Tikran, from Beg Ayym."

All around her, nomads were chanting, their lips moving, their voices like wind through the steppe's dry grass. So many of them. Their eyes glistening by firelight, their dark faces hopeful, their hands over their hearts. Every single one looking at her. Even Marbek's scowl had fallen away and he stood, looking almost awestruck, his hand over his heart, his eyes fixed on her.

This is complete insanity. Feeling faint, she swayed on her feet, the faces before her blurring. Omid once again wrapped his arm around her, holding her up. She heard Bruneta's voice, slightly muffled.

"Beg Zolto, please, Coxani hasn't eaten or slept in days…"

Then everything went black.

CHAPTER 25

Naran was the life of the party.

As Tikran watched his commander-in-chief work the room—or, more accurately, hall—he couldn't help but smile. *Who would have guessed?* Naran had been the most unwilling participant when Lord Revaz had begun "training" him in the social arts of diplomacy. But just a mere couple months later, the Stalking Lion was in his element. It wasn't that Naran enjoyed it, per se. Tikran knew the big guy would have rather been doing almost anything else. But something had changed in Naran since he'd discovered he was a father, something subtle but significant.

Perhaps calling the event a "party" was something of a stretch; it was an audience with the Anzori aristocracy, something Tikran understood he had to do often to ingratiate himself with the lords who held his fate in their manicured hands.

"Would Your Highness care for some more wine?" An attendant stood beside him on the dais, a jug poised in his hand, gazing at Tikran expectantly.

"Yes, thank you," Tikran answered, holding out his goblet, enjoying his moment of respite from socializing. He sat on his throne and watched as lords and ladies dined and danced and gossiped and argued. As king, he'd decided he had the right to end a conversation politely, walk away, and be left alone for a moment. He didn't have Naran's social stamina—human interaction exhausted him.

And as king, he "interacted" almost all day.

Of course, still being the dutiful soldier at heart, he never allowed himself more than a few minutes of escape. He had a job to do, after all. Tikran spotted Tanith across the hall, where she spoke with an Anzori lord and his wife, and they made brief eye contact. He smiled and winked; her lips twitched and she quickly looked away, color in her cheeks. *She'll make me pay for that later.* The thought made him want to continue teasing her.

"Taking a much-deserved rest, Your Highness?"

Tikran looked at his mentor, hoping his annoyance was obvious. In a low voice, he answered, "Yes, Lord Haydar. I can only handle so many uneducated opinions about military strategy at a time." Haydar giggled and Tikran felt himself relax. His relationship with Haydar had changed in a way that both disconcerted and pleased him. The durai had stopped attending every one of Tikran's council meetings and audiences. He'd become more and more absent at critical times when Tikran would have sought the durai's guidance, often forcing Tikran to make decisions on the spot. Slowly, however, Tikran came to realize it meant that Haydar trusted him not to make mistakes with enormous consequences. *He trusts me not to fuck up.* Either that, or he was too tired to try and correct course. *I'm going with the former.* The latter would have been too out of character. If it was true that Haydar trusted Tikran to make crucial decisions on his own, that alone gave the Manzakar king the confidence to continue being decisive—and, he hoped, correct.

"Look at Naran," Tikran mused, fascinated. "He looks...civilized."

"Doesn't he?" Haydar leaned his arm on the throne. "He's come a long way since becoming a Manzakar."

"He sure has." Tikran tugged on his earlobe, suddenly

distracted by a thought. "I have to get back out there. But before I do..." He looked at the durai. "Do you know if we've heard from Coxani or Moti today?" He'd mentally been keeping track, and it was due time he'd heard from them. Their last couple messages had been a bit too vague and mechanical for his taste. *Coxani is always direct. Sometimes too direct.*

"I don't," Haydar answered. "I can certainly have an attendant run to the dovecote to check."

Tikran sat up, his mouth open to answer, when he spotted a lithe figure in maroon approaching the dais through the corner of his eye. To Haydar, he said softly, "Yes, please, my lord." As he faced the woman, Haydar turned and called an attendant.

"Your Highness, my deepest apologies for interrupting you during your...break," the lady said. Tikran kept his expression steady as gazed down at the bowed woman, whose golden hair glimmered in the firelight.

Is that what people were calling it? His "break"? *Good grief.* "No apology needed, my lady. Please, rise." The woman straightened, her blue eyes wide and full of...urgency? "Lady Dinara?" His eyes darted toward Naran, who was none the wiser, his back turned as he spoke to a group of durais. Lord Prem, also in attendance, faced him but seemed to be distracted by his own conversation. Tikran cleared his throat. "How may I be of assistance?"

"I'm merely here to offer a gift from my son," she said. "He is so grateful to be united with his father, Commander Naran, and he credits you." She held out a small, beautifully carved and painted box.

Taking it in his hands, Tikran knew he had no choice but to open it before an audience. He hinged the lid open and pulled out a miniature bow and arrow. He couldn't help but smile—they had clearly been crafted by a child. Still, they were a good likeness. He lifted his eyes to Dinara, smiling. "It's wonderful. I would like to thank Kadyr personally."

Dinara smiled back. "He's hopefully fast asleep tonight, Your Highness. But yes, he would be honored."

Something in the woman's smile put Tikran on edge. He stood and stepped down off the dais, offering her his arm, which she took. Her grip around his biceps was tight—and tightened further—as he walked her to her father's side. "Lord Prem, your enchanting daughter and grandson have given me a most wonderful gift." He opened the lid of the box and showed Prem and other onlookers the small bow and arrow within.

Prem chuckled. "Yes, Your Highness. What a good lad Kadyr is."

"I will cherish it, Lady Dinara," Tikran inclined his head in her direction, trying to ignore the distracted, almost frantic look in her eyes as he asked her questions about Kadyr's education. *Something's not right.* He glanced in Naran's direction and became convinced his commander was as clueless as he was. Did she have something to tell him? If she did, it was clearly something she wanted to discuss privately. Problem was, she was an Anzori lady —there *was* no privacy as far as she was concerned. Even with the king, there would always be a eunuch in attendance.

As the evening wore on, Tikran noticed that, no matter where she was, Dinara kept casting glances in his direction. *She definitely has something to tell me.* Something she didn't feel comfortable sharing in present company. Perhaps even Lord Prem's company. How could he get her alone? He couldn't think of a way that wouldn't further tarnish her reputation—not to mention his—and raise Prem's suspicions. *I'm fucking king. There must be a way.* Yet he could think of nothing.

Late that night and long after the audience had ended, Tikran lay wide awake while Tanith, curled against him, slept soundly. Careful not to wake her, Tikran climbed out of bed, pulled on his underpants, and walked over to his desk. He opened the box Dinara had given him and examined the miniatures, turning them between his fingers. What had she wanted to tell him? For surely that was it. Nothing else made sense. He would have to ask Naran about her strange behavior tomorrow. Tikran set the miniatures on the desk and looked at the open box. He lifted it, turning it over in his hands, and touched the red inner lining. The bottom of the box was hollow. Pulling his dagger from the belt that lay neatly on a chaise, he carefully sliced open the felt lining and slipped a finger inside, feeling parchment. He pulled the folded scrap from beneath the lining, his breath coming a bit quicker now. The handwriting was neat and feminine, if a bit shaky:

The messages from Gohar are being intercepted.

Intercepted? *But why?* An icy tingle rushed through his veins, numbing him, making him dizzy. As soon as he could think again, Tikran leaped into action. He hurried into the outer chamber and threw open the door. "I need Lord Haydar and Commander Naran summoned immediately," he said to the Aslans standing guard. "Hurry!"

As the Aslans ran off, Tikran walked back into his chambers and began throwing on his clothes. Closing the door to the inner bedchamber so as not to wake Tanith, Tikran lit a large candle and tried to focus his thoughts. Coxani and Moti were in danger. As much as Tikran tried to ward off the thought, it crashed into him, hard: *Are they even still alive?*

"What's happened, Tikran?" Haydar strode into the room, somehow still looking put together despite being roused from sleep just a few moments ago.

At the sound of Haydar's voice, Tikran felt a modicum of relief to his mounting panic. He held out the parchment. "Someone is intercepting—and clearly falsifying—Coxani and Moti's messages."

His brow tightly knit, Haydar examined the message. "Where did you get this?"

"It was hidden inside the box Dinara gave me," Tikran said. "Which means she must have come about that information from her father. Prem must be involved." He clenched his jaw. "We must head into Gohar immediately. We have no idea what's happened there. For all we know, Dilovar could be halfway to Anzor by now."

The two men heard Naran before they saw him. "This better

not have anything to do with Coxani," he said as he walked in, half dressed.

"Unfortunately, it does." Tikran showed his commander the message. "It was hidden in Kadyr's gift. I had a feeling all last night that Dinara was trying to tell me something."

The blood drained from Naran's face. "Oh, fuck."

"We can't summon Dinara, since we don't want Prem to know that I know," Tikran said. "We need to be very careful with how we tread here. We don't know who is betraying me."

"Tik," Naran looked bewildered. "We gotta go. Now. We're out of time."

Tikran nodded. "We send a party immediately and begin final preparations to head into Gohar. We'll tell the council that there's been intelligence that's spurred us into action. Lord Haydar, we need to find out who is intercepting the messages and why." Tikran ran his hand through his hair, a pained expression on his face.

Haydar reached out and set a firm hand on Tikran's shoulder. He murmured, "Lad. Calm yourself." He looked up, meeting Naran worried stare. "Naran. Tikran. Have faith."

Tikran nodded, collecting himself. Finally, he said, "Who other than Dilovar could possibly benefit from this?"

Haydar frowned at the ground, his handsome face creased in thought. "I don't know. But I intend to find out."

As Tanith opened her eyes, the first thing that occurred to her was that she was hungry. Starving, in fact. She smiled sleepily to herself. *As if I haven't been eating three enormous meals a day.* Rising, the second thing that occurred to her was that Tikran was not in his suite. This was not at all unusual—he was often gone when she woke. He was likely meeting with the council, listening to grievances, or overseeing preparations for war. She grabbed her robe and slipped into it, realizing suddenly that it was snug. *Very* snug.

She could barely button it. *Anzor's made me soft*, she thought with a chuckle.

While she didn't like the inconvenience of having to get new robes tailored, she did like the fact that she was no longer bone thin. Fastening her robe as best she could, she headed into the outer chamber, where breakfast had been left for her. Her cheeks burned. She'd promised Haydar to be discreet, but the entire staff apparently knew about her overnight stays with Tikran.

Well. He's the king. He can do what he wants.

Her stomach growling loudly, she approached the table with appetite. As the smell of the yogurt, eggs, olives, and fresh bread reached her nostrils, an unexpected wave of nausea overcame her. She nearly dry-heaved on the floor but managed instead to lower herself into a nearby chaise and breathe deeply. The desire to vomit retreated and doubt seeped into her mind.

No. Surely not.

In a near-panic, Tanith tried to think back on her last cycle. *Oh, Archil...* They had been very irregular during the famine. She'd gone months at a time without bleeding. But she wasn't starving anymore, was she? And while Haydar had managed to obtain an elixir for her to prevent such unfortunate accidents, she now worried he'd been too late...

Standing slowly, she ran her hand down the curve of her belly. She'd been pregnant once before, and by the time her belly had been this big, she'd been a ways along. And she, like an idiot, had just assumed she was plumping up.

No. No. This can't happen. I can't do this.

Her last pregnancy had ended in tragedy.

What was she going to tell Tikran? What was she going to tell *Haydar,* for Archil's sake? With her arms wrapped around her middle, she stood and walked back to her suite. She had no idea what to do, but she was also still head mage of Anzor. After freshening up, she headed to the great hall as usual. The place was in near-pandemonium—noblemen and durais spoke over each other while Tikran sat, a leg drawn up on his chair, looking consumed in thought. *What's happening?* Tentatively, she approached the Manzakar king. "Tikran?"

He looked up, clearly distracted. "Yes?" His eyes softened. "Tanith."

"Is something wrong?"

He lowered his leg and sat up. "Yes. We're moving into Gohar as soon as possible."

She gasped. "But why? I thought we had—"

"Our timeline has been shortened," Tikran said, and she could see the strain in his face. "I have intelligence that the Dilovari have advanced into Gohar further than we've been convinced to believe."

She held her breath. "How?"

He gave her a meaningful look. "I've been lied to. Coxani and Moti's messages have been intercepted and forged."

Coxani. "Do you think she's in danger?"

Something in Tikran's eyes made her stiffen. He said, "I hope not."

Tanith opened her mouth to speak when Lord Prem stood. "Your Highness, we as the council insist on knowing who fed you this so-called intelligence," he said firmly, his jowls trembling. "If we must go to war now, we at least deserve to know how this information was acquired."

Neither Tikran's expression nor his posture changed as he answered, "Master Damir, King Bilguun's head mage, sent me a message, if you must know." He leaned forward. "He must have risked everything to send it. He told me that the Dilovari have advanced to Eter."

A horrified silence befell the hall. Prem's face was like stone as he asked, "And where is this message, Your Highness?"

"I destroyed it," Tikran answered, meeting Prem's gaze evenly.

Tanith knew instinctively that the reason Tikran had given wasn't the real reason he knew this "intelligence." But the fact that Tikran stood by it, unwavering, before fifteen powerful Anzori lords... She felt a sudden sense of pride.

Almost immediately, voices exploded—expressing concern, urgency, dismay.

Tikran turned back to her. "I'm sorry. I should have told you right away, but I've been trying to cope with all this. And you were sleeping." He gave her a tender look. "Do you think you and your mages are ready for this war?"

Other than the fact that I think I'm at least three months pregnant...yes? Tanith somehow maintained her composure despite the hysteria that welled up in her chest. Even if Haydar had a remedy, she couldn't afford to be indisposed for several weeks. *We're going to war.* Besides, she sensed she was past the window of opportunity for that. Which meant that if she told Tikran now, he would likely try and keep her from going into Gohar with him, and that would doom Anzor—and Tikran's reign—for sure. *That simply can't happen.*

Her voice was slightly tremulous but firm as she said, "Yes, Tikran. We're ready."

"Commander Naran, please make yourself at home," Lady Prem said as she showed Naran into the inner courtyard of the lavish country estate. The lady's silk wrap fluttered behind her as she led him to a dinette beneath the shade of an oleander tree. "Dinara will be with you shortly," she assured him.

He sat, flashed a smile, and said, "Thank you, Lady Prem. You are a most gracious hostess, as always."

The older woman smiled and lowered her eyes. "You are too kind, Commander. I will see that Dinara makes haste. I know your time is limited."

Naran kept his head bowed as Lady Prem bustled off. He usually met Dinara and Kadyr together out in the vast gardens of the estate, or occasionally inside the massive house itself. But today was different. He'd requested to see Dinara alone. This was certainly a deviation from his typical visits. Ordinarily, he came to see Kadyr, often to take the boy to the hippodrome—sometimes in the company of his mother, sometimes not—so the boy could watch the Manzakars train and spend time with his father. Keeping Dinara's company was always secondary. It wasn't that he didn't enjoy her company; quite the contrary. He just hadn't wanted to mislead her into believing he wanted a romantic relationship with her.

But now things had changed. Coxani and Moti's lives were in danger. Dinara had taken a risk by revealing Prem's betrayal and had made her loyalties clear. Her actions had caused Naran to reevaluate her. Now, he found himself thankful for—and intrigued by—this high-born Anzori woman who was obviously not what she seemed. He found himself wondering what *he'd* sacrificed in all of this, while Dinara had committed herself to bearing his son and chosen to betray her father for Kadyr's sake. For Tikran's sake. *Maybe even for my sake.*

Naran scratched his jaw nervously. His entire life had been constructed around two paths: what was definitively right and what was definitively wrong. He'd often chosen the latter path, but only if he thought he could get away with it. To his good fortune, he often *had* gotten away with it. While getting away with things had been exhilarating, it hadn't filled the hole in his chest. In his life, there had been three things, or people, as it were, that had filled that hole: Tikran, Coxani, and recently, Kadyr.

He wanted to do the right thing by all three of them.

"Commander Naran. Good afternoon." Lord Prem approached, as Naran had expected he would.

Standing, the Manzakar commander bowed. "My lord. Always a pleasure."

The old Anzori lord sat without acknowledging Naran's words, gazing out into his garden without seeing it. "I must admit, it is unusual that you would call on my daughter and not my grandson, Commander." Prem looked at Naran coldly. "Particularly after King Tikran decided unanimously that we would go into Gohar several weeks early—and without providing any proper evidence of deceit."

Naran nodded slowly. "Yes, my lord. It's the reason I'm here." He took a deep breath. "I must go into Gohar soon and leave my son and his mother. There's always the chance I won't return." He met the old man's skeptical eyes. "And they are precious to me."

Prem raised his eyebrows. "What are you saying, Commander?"

Naran drew in his breath before saying, "I would like to ask for Dinara's hand in marriage. I want her to live free of the stigma of an unwed mother. I want Kadyr to live the life of a legitimate heir, not one of a bastard. I want to ensure all this happens before I leave for Gohar." Naran knew he was sacrificing his greatest desire —Coxani—to win this game. But at least he would also be doing what he could for them. All of them. Just to make sure Prem realized how serious he was, Naran pulled a jewel-encrusted gold ring from his pocket. Holding it out between his thumb and forefinger, he said, "I will cherish Dinara and Kadyr forever."

Naran could see the conflict in Prem's expression. And honestly, as a father and grandfather, how could the old man *not* feel conflict? He may have hated Tikran and everything the Manzakar king represented to the Anzori—savagery, chaos, otherness—but his own grandchild was that otherness. His own daughter had sullied herself and her father's reputation with that otherness. And if there was anything an Anzori blue blood prized above all, it was his reputation. Naran was offering Prem an escape from the judgment of his peers and in the eyes of Cenk, something the old man had wanted from the start.

Unbeknownst to Prem, Naran was also ensuring that Dinara would be able to divulge everything she knew about her father's traitorous activities privately and safely to him and Tikran, since once Naran and Dinara were married, his dominion over her as her husband would supersede her father's.

Prem refused to look Naran in the eyes. He stood, his back

turned, and said over his shoulder, "If she accepts your proposal, so do I."

I've got you now. Naran smiled congenially as he stood too. "Thank you, my lord. I can't tell you how much this means to me," he said to Prem's back as the nobleman walked away. As he waited for Dinara, Naran recalled Revaz's words and took a deep breath: "Remember that if they resort to pettiness—refusing to look you in the eyes, refusing to acknowledge your politeness—they are beneath you from the start."

"Naran?" Dinara entered the courtyard in a salmon-colored kaftan and her hair loose around her face, looking lovely. Her brow was knit in puzzlement. "Kadyr isn't here. He's—"

"I'm here to see you," Naran said. "Not Kadyr."

Dinara tilted her head. "Why?"

Here goes. "Please, Dinara. Sit."

She sat, however tentatively, a look of trepidation creeping into her eyes. "Are you all right?" She glanced over her shoulder quickly, indicating the eunuch who stood nearby.

Naran nodded then kneeled before her, looking down nervously. "Dinara, I leave for Gohar soon and I've been thinking..." Flustered, he finally looked her in the eyes. "I would be honored if you married me." He held the ring out to her with bated breath.

She looked at the ring for a long while, not speaking, not smiling, and Naran's heart began to sink. Finally, she said, "This would be a marriage of convenience, of course."

Naran hesitated. "It would be convenient, you're right. But I also see it as an opportunity to...get to know each other better." She raised her eyebrows, a small smile dancing on her lips, and Naran chuckled, surprised to feel his face go hot. "You know what I mean."

She took the ring from him and slipped it on her finger. "I accept. And I assume you'll want this done soon?"

"As soon as possible, really," he replied.

She nodded and stood, her tone serious, efficient. "I can arrange everything. Does tomorrow work for you?"

Naran blinked, startled by her lack of sentiment. "Sure."

"All right. I will send you a message with the details as soon as I can confirm them. I should begin my preparations now." With that, she promptly showed him to the door. As she saw him out, she said, "If you happen to change your mind, just let me know."

He turned and met her gaze. "That's not happening." He bowed, his awe in Dinara growing by the second. "Until tomorrow, my lady."

CHAPTER 26

Nothing was working.

Gohari healers were traveling from other clans and tribes to try their hand at treating Moti. Of course, they were also traveling to gape at Coxani, much to her dismay. Word had spread quickly: *Archil's last descendant*. Moti slept fitfully as Coxani held his hand in hers, occasionally wiping the sweat from his feverish face with a wet cloth. She refused to consider the implications of who she was; saving Moti was her priority. The nomads, their faces reverent and earnest, surrounded her in the yarm, murmuring prayers and watching as she tried to minister to Moti and shut their presence out. At the end of her rope, Coxani was about to scream for everyone to leave her alone when a familiar voice spoke.

"Hey."

She turned to see Bruneta standing beside her, her arms crossed and brow creased. The Sachin commander said softly, "Can I speak with you for a minute?"

Laying Moti's hand gently across his chest, Coxani stood and followed Bruneta out of the yarm. When they were outside, Bruneta said, "Why haven't you talked to Marbek about joining Tikran? He's waiting for *you* to ask."

"For Cenk's sake," Coxani replied. "Moti is sick. I can't think about—"

"Coxani," Bruneta said firmly. "Your refusal to confront who you are will cost us not just Moti's life, but thousands of others." She must have seen the horror on Coxani's face, because she softened her tone and stepped closer. "Listen, I know this is new to you, this whole seeing the people you love...die. I keep thinking I've gotten used to it, but the truth is, you never get used to it."

Coxani clenched her teeth. "Moti won't die, not if I can help it."

"Then use who you are to your advantage." Bruneta stepped back and spread her arms. "Use who you are to save Moti. To save Tikran. To save Gohar. But for Archil's sake, don't just hide from it."

Coxani took several deep breaths. She'd discovered her status as the Gohari prophet's progeny less than thirty-six hours ago. But of course, Bruneta was right. She didn't have the luxury of time. "Stay with Moti, please." She turned with sudden determination and headed directly to Marbek, who had just emerged from his personal yarm. The man certainly loved his finery; the Davlat chief often wore his headdress, which Coxani suspected was to make him appear taller, and donned layers of beaded bracelets and necklaces at all times.

Was it her imagination, or did he flinch when he saw her? "Beg Marbek," she said, deciding she wasn't going to mince words, "surely your allegiances have changed since discovering who I am?"

She could tell he really wanted to scowl at her. Instead, however, he said, "Naturally, we will follow you, Rasula. But first, we must conduct a rite." His eyes shifted to her face briefly, uncomfortably. "You will have to be involved."

Of course I will. Coxani paused. "What does Rasula mean?"

Marbek looked away. "Female prophet."

"I'm not—" Coxani caught herself, closing her eyes. She could deal with all that later. She had to focus. After a moment, she nodded. "Yes. All right. Let's do it."

Marbek tilted his head and put his hands behind his back. "We must also be careful. The Dilovari won't be forgiving when they find out we've changed allegiances."

"No, they won't." Coxani gazed into the distance, at the yarms and small herds of goats that dotted the landscape. She fervently hoped the courier reached Anzor soon. "I'm sorry, Beg Marbek. I've been so consumed with finding a remedy that will save Moti that I..."

The idea suddenly hit her like a lightning bolt. *Holy shit.* Could it work? She looked at Marbek with urgency. "Do you think you could play nice with the Dilovari long enough to ask for a certain doctor's help with treating Moti?"

Marbek frowned. "A Dilovari doctor?"

"Yes." Coxani swallowed. "Doctor Damir. He's my friend."

Marbek's eyes widened. "The head mage of Dilovar? Rasula, surely you aren't serious."

"Are you really going from calling me 'Manzakar' to calling me 'female prophet'? Can you please call me Coxani?" She stared at him incredulously. "And yes. I'm serious. I know he would try to come."

Marbek finally let his true colors shine through and scowled at her. "Why would he do that? Other than to try and kill you? He's your enemy, remember?"

"Damir is not my enemy," Coxani insisted, scowling back. "He's my good friend. And he loves Tikran."

Marbek said, "He's your friend, he loves Tikran, but he's King Bilguun's head mage. So whose side is he on? When he sees you, how can you be certain his reaction won't be to destroy us all?"

"It won't. I know him. He's a good person, and foremost a doctor."

"He's foremost Dilovar's weapon of war," Marbek argued. "Besides, he won't be able to make it in time to save Moti. I doubt your co-captain will linger for—"

"Beg Marbek," Coxani interrupted, "I'm out of ideas. Will you do this for me?"

Marbek sucked in his breath. "I likely have to, don't I, Rasu—Coxani?" He rubbed his face with his hands. "All right. We would have to play nice with the Dilovari until your armies arrived in any case. I will speak with my Dilovari contact and see if they will relay my request."

Dilovari contact. It was the rude awakening Coxani needed. She stepped closer to Marbek, her eyes meeting his. "Marbek, what's the nearest Anzori fort that Dilovar has captured?"

Fear flashed in the chieftain's eyes briefly, but he answered without hesitation. "Faiz."

"Holy shit!" Coxani needed to sit down. Instead, she walked in a small circle, trying not to scream. "That's really close. There's, what, only one garrison town between here and Faiz?"

Marbek nodded curtly. "Zifa."

"They've nearly taken all of eastern Gohar." She turned on Marbek again, her rage mounting. "What sort of bargain did you make with Vazha? And don't lie to me."

Again, fear crept into the Davlat chief's eyes, lingering there a bit longer this time. "I told you that the survivors of the devastated Davlat clan believed Prince Vazha saved them. It's the truth."

"And?" Coxani wanted to grab him and shake him.

"Vazha asked for one of our mages in return." The creases around Marbek's mouth revealed his feelings of guilt. "To help Dilovar against Anzor."

Coxani blinked rapidly. "He just asked for a random mage? Or your most powerful mage?"

"Our most powerful mage, presumably." Marbek added, "Mind you, none of us had any idea how powerful he was until the Manzakars killed his clan, including his brother."

"And how powerful is he?" Coxani held her breath.

"No one is sure. He had just begun his formal training as a Gohari mage when his clan was attacked. During that attack, he burned two Manzakars to death on the spot. That's all I know."

Doesn't sound so bad...? "How old is the mage?"

"Sixteen or seventeen. A sickly boy," Marbek answered. "He

could hardly walk a short distance without getting winded. But one of our elders and his great-grandfather, Beg Zolto, claims he is much more powerful than we all know."

Coxani didn't know much about the Essence, but she had a hard time believing anyone was more powerful than Damir. Surely the doctor would make certain that some wheezy teenager didn't kill people unnecessarily? "What sort of deal did Vahza make with Dilovar in exchange for the mage?"

Shaking his head, Marbek said, "You've reached the limits of my knowledge, Coxani. Although I can make a guess."

The throne of Anzor. She closed her eyes briefly. It was the only thing that made sense. How much did Damir know about it, she wondered? He knew Vazha, after all—he'd cured the prince of leprosy. She couldn't imagine Damir would side with Vazha against Tikran, but who knew what kinds of leverage Bilguun and Vazha had over him? Seeing Damir could be an opportunity to find out how Vazha was involved. At the very least, she hoped that seeing her would flood the doctor with memories of Tikran —and remind him of what they'd fought for together, not so long ago…

She opened her eyes and looked at Marbek. "I want Doctor Damir brought to Gohar. We can meet him on Davlat territory, somewhere near Faiz. The Dilovari won't know we're Manzakars if we dress as nomads. Tell them one of your…top warriors? No…mages!…was mortally wounded by a Manzakar's arrow. Someone who the Dilovari want in the fight against Anzor. Tell them whatever you must to get him here. Even if he shows up too late. I need to speak with him."

"They'll never agree. And even if they do, you're playing a dangerous game, Coxani," Marbek warned her.

"We're at war. Every game is dangerous." She turned and walked out of Marbek's yarm feeling purposeful.

So Vazha thought he could bribe Dilovar into making him king of Anzor?

Not if I have anything to do with it.

Coxani returned to Moti's bedside to find Bruneta asleep, her head resting near his chest, her face stained with tears. After making sure Moti was still breathing steadily, Coxani pulled a blanket over Bruneta's shoulders, careful not to wake her. Coxani's nose burned with the desire to cry. *Oh Archil. If you're listening...I need help.* How stupid was she, hoping for spiritual intervention?

But she was desperate.

Deciding to leave Bruneta and Moti alone, Coxani debated on where to sleep. Previously, she'd slept in the healers' tent, beside Moti. But tonight she needed a change. Knowing Bruneta was with him allowed her to step away. She wandered out of the yarm and was considering going back to her company when she heard a familiar voice.

"Hey. Coxani."

She felt relief before she even turned. "No arash tonight, Omid," she said, facing him. "I know your tricks."

"Tricks? Come on, now." He scowled, clearly worried she believed he'd tricked her.

She smiled. "I'm kidding. I'm just...so tired. And overwhelmed."

His face softened. "Yeah. I can imagine."

"Omid," Coxani said, "how did my aunt not know who I was? It makes no sense. I was her brother's child."

The Sachin warrior's eyes were lit by starlight. He looked up into the night sky as he said, "Well, I can tell you what I know. It's a story, though."

"Tell me," she said.

He lowered his eyes to her face. "In 112 of the Dark Age, when it became clear to the Gohari that the Akmaral War was inevitable and that Gohar would fall into either Anzor or Dilovar's hands, an effort was made to hide Archil's descendants." All humor left his expression. "Archil had stolen their god's magic. Whomever ended up ruling Gohar would come for Archil's descendants."

Her eyes were wide. "So what happened?"

"Names were changed, babies were shuffled between clans, and over time, as Gohar sank into famine, even the descendants themselves lost the knowledge of who they were. Nothing was written down, after all. It was all based on memories." Omid paused. "Then, about ten years ago, Several elders, Beg Zolto among them, found a series of inscribed scapulae that had been created by a deceased elder, a healer and midwife. She had tracked down the descendants by visiting clans across Gohar and pieced together what memories the nomads had until she learned the fates of Archil's bloodline. Beg Zolto continued her quest. He was seeking out your mother, Jale, when he found your aunt, who revealed that both Jale and her baby had died of the red plague. Your aunt must have told Zolto the baby's name was Coxani."

Jale. Coxani's mouth formed the consonants and vowels of her mother's name silently. Half to herself, she said, "Khava had sold me, but she was too scared to admit it to Beg Zolto."

"Apparently," Omid said softly, something akin to affection in his eyes as he looked at her.

Afraid of her emotions at that moment, Coxani turned and began walking.

"Wait," Omid said. "Where are you going?"

She breathed deeply and shrugged. "Back to my company to sleep."

"But you can sleep here."

She stopped and turned. "Where?"

"You're Archil's descendant, you can sleep anywhere you want. You could kick Marbek out of his yarm if you wanted." He grinned.

She shook her head. "I'm not doing that."

"Well, you could also...you know..." Was it her imagination, or did he blush? "You could sleep in the warriors' yarm, next to me," he said. "I've saved you a spot and even prepared it for you."

She tilted her head. "Prepared it for me?"

Looking uncomfortable, Omid said, "I know you Anzori like

privacy. I hung a curtain for you." He smiled sheepishly. "Obviously, I had help."

"Well, that sounds nice," she said, intrigued and touched by the gesture. "Okay. Lead the way."

She followed him back to the warriors' yarm where, true to his word, he had curtained off a small corner next to his bedroll. Unable to keep from smiling, she pushed the curtain aside to find a neatly made bedroll, complete with a woven Gohari blanket and feather-stuffed pillow. Feeling the tears well in her eyes not for the first time that night, she said, "Thank you, Omid."

"It's nothing." He smiled at her, seemingly pleased by her reaction. "Hopefully you get some rest."

Behind her curtain, Coxani undressed and crawled under the warm blanket. She could see Omid's silhouette as he lay on the other side of the thin fabric veil. In the dim light, she stared at his profile, at the slope of his nose and curve of his chin. After several minutes, she whispered, "Omid."

His head turned in her direction. "Yeah?"

She realized the words that were about to come out her mouth were...strange. But she desperately needed to feel his arms around her. "Can you come over to this side for a second? I need a hug."

Without much hesitation, Omid obliged, scooting underneath the curtain with his one free arm. She found herself up against him immediately in the small space, feeling his warmth and inhaling the scent of his skin. She realized abruptly that she needed more than just a simple embrace from him. *Much more.* The fact that other warriors slept or chatted softly mere feet away did nothing to temper the exigency she felt. Not even the pang of guilt she felt as Naran flitted inconveniently through her mind was enough to lessen her need for Omid.

He grunted as he leaned back against the pillow. "I can't wait for this stupid wound to heal already," he muttered. "Doing everything one-handed is a pain in the ass." He turned his head toward her, his dark eyes glistening. "I really wish I could give you a proper hug."

Coxani sat up and held the bead he had given her up between her fingers for him to see. Once she heard his sharp intake of breath, she tucked it back away in the pocket of her cast-off uniform and turned toward him. In the softest whisper she could manage, she said, "I would like to redeem my bead now. Does the offer still stand?"

His eyebrows rose and this time he definitely blushed. "Coxani, you've had a rough past few days. I think you need to sleep on everything first. I don't want you to...do something you might not otherwise do just because you need a hug."

Coxani smiled, enchanted by his response. If anything, it only made her want him right then even more. "You're right. The past few days—weeks, in fact—have been a total nightmare. But I'm a grown woman. And I want you, Omid." She licked her lips. "So does your offer still stand?"

When he couldn't seem to find the right words, he smiled coyly and gestured to the rigid tent in his breeches. "It still very much...stands."

Heat flooded her face and neck as she stifled a smile. Discreetly, she tugged off her underclothes then pulled the wool blanket over her shoulders. She lifted herself to her knees, straddled him, unlaced his breeches, and tugged them down over him. Leaning forward, she kissed him, feeling his lips part and his soft tongue meet hers. His hand cupped her face then slipped down, roaming over her breasts and hips and thighs. They both gasped in synchrony when she lowered herself onto him. Omid's chest rose and fell rapidly as she moved slowly at first, savoring the feel of him inside her, the taste of his lips, of how his fingers left a tingling trail on her skin. He began tilting his hips to meet her, compelling her to move faster, his breath hot against her mouth, his eyes half-closed. She'd lost track of time when waves of intense pleasure crashed into her.

Struggling to keep quiet, she kept moving for him. Omid gripped her thigh tightly with his free hand, his body stiffening with his release. "Coxani..." His eyes fluttered shut and his head fell back.

Bracing herself on the pillow behind Omid so as not to put pressure on his torso, Coxani panted, dropping her forehead to rest against his good shoulder.

As their breathing slowed, a pleasurable silence stretched between them. She nuzzled the crook of his neck as he caressed her back, running his fingertips along her spine. Finally, she said softly, "So...what are the chances your entire tribe is going to know what just happened between us?"

His chuckle reverberated against her. "Not just *my* tribe. And I'd say they're pretty good."

She groaned, heat prickling her cheeks. "That's so embarrassing."

He made a *tsk* sound. "We're Gohari. It's not embarrassing. It's normal and healthy." He pinched her chin between his fingers and turned her face to look at him. "It's beautiful." He smiled wickedly. "And with you, Rasula, it was downright spiritual."

"Stop it," she said, stifling her laughter as she rolled off him and curled up at his side.

Nestled against him with his arm wrapped around her, she began slipping into the depths of slumber. Just as she faded out, she could have sworn she heard him whisper, "Coxani, I would die for you..."

CHAPTER 27

The trip from Ogedei into Gohar went far more quickly than Damir remembered. It made sense, though, as the season was late spring and the snow had melted from the mountainsides. And now that Dilovar controlled most of eastern Gohar with the Davlat tribe's blessing, the Damla River was within its dominion. Dilovari ferries transported troops across the river with little fear of attack. What had taken over a month before now took two weeks, if that.

As the steppe stretched out before him, with its patches of undulating grass and rocky hills, Damir couldn't help but remember the last time he'd seen it when not just passing through. He'd been at Tikran's side, battling Delger's Manzakars. The memories—both good and bad—flooded back in an instant as he looked out at the horizon. Their time together in Gohar had been trying, to say the least, and yet he somehow thought back on it nostalgically and with some regret. All those nights they'd spent silent, inches away from each other, when they could have been wrapped in each other's arms...

When the party reached Faiz, the last Anzori outpost that Dilovar had captured, Damir clenched his teeth; it looked strikingly like Areg on the eve of battle. Its small fort was more wood than stone and the town's inhabitants had fled, abandoning their hovels for the steppe.

"It's so strange being in Gohar again," Berk muttered, reining his horse closer to Damir's. "I feel like a visitor in my own home. It's like it hasn't changed, but it has."

Pulling himself out of his reverie, Damir glanced at his charge curiously. The boy's hands trembled ever so slightly, betraying a fear the head mage hadn't anticipated. Would fighting in Gohar be an obstacle to Berk? Damir's concern for the boy battled with his frustration. He felt like more of a parent than a mentor at this point, if he was being perfectly honest. It had been that way for a while now, and he had more important things to worry about. *Like war with Anzor.* Unfortunately, the two things—war with Anzor and Berk—were inextricably linked. The boy's power was something that simply could not be ignored and could ultimately be the deciding factor in who won this bloody war.

Choosing concern over frustration, Damir reached out and took Berk's hand, holding it tightly within his. When the boy looked over, startled, Damir said evenly, "You'll be all right. I'm here." The look on Berk's face made Damir's choice utterly worth it. The boy's fingers curled around his mentor's and squeezed.

The commander of the fort was a man with a hooked nose named Harun. Amit apparently knew him, and the two soldiers attempted to verbally out-command each other for far too long. After several minutes, Damir cleared his throat and said loudly, "Begging your pardons, Commanders, but my young charge and I are exhausted from a long journey. If you wouldn't mind directing us to our rooms, we can be out of your way so that you may continue to browbeat one another in some bizarre, personal competition."

Both commanders glared at him, their nostrils flared. If Damir hadn't been the head mage of Dilovar, he was certain he'd have to pay for his insolence. Instead, Damir smiled and waited. Harun spoke first, turning away from Amit. "Master Damir. The chief of the nomads asked for your help with one of his mages. Apparently, the mage was mortally wounded and is on his deathbed."

Frowning, Damir replied, "The chief of the nomads? Commander, in case you hadn't noticed during your extensive time here in Gohar, the nomads have several chiefs. Would you care to tell me which chief you spoke to?"

Harun was growing increasingly agitated—it was obvious in the way his face went from pale to a distinct shade of pink. "The chief of the tribe that rules eastern Gohar, Master Damir."

Damir raised his eyebrows, waiting for just a beat before saying, "The Davlat?"

"Yes!" Harun nodded curtly. "The Davlat chief. Marbek is his name. A small party of nomads have brought the injured mage and set up camp ten miles west of here."

"Why don't they bring the mage to Faiz?" Amit demanded. "We shouldn't have to travel to meet a bunch of sick savages."

Damir clenched his jaw but resisted the desire to respond to Amit with some scathing remark. Had Berk understood Erdem, Damir would have certainly let Amit have it.

"They're scared of us," Harun answered. "They're accustomed to ill treatment at the hands of the Manzakars. But I think it would be wise for Master Damir to tend to the mage. According to Marbek, he's very powerful and could be an asset in the war against Anzor."

"This is ridiculous," Amit muttered. "Tell them to come here."

Damir glared at Amit. "These nomads are our allies, Commander. And if this mage is even remotely as powerful as Berk, we want him alive and well. A short trip is certainly worth the possible reward."

Amit pressed his lips into a tight line before saying, "Fine. We'll head out first thing tomorrow. You and the boy should probably get some rest."

Damir and Berk were given a small room with a window that overlooked the steppe. As Damir splashed fresh water from the basin on his face, washing away the grime from their journey, Berk sat on one of the narrow beds and asked, "Master Damir, what were you and the commanders talking about? It sounded serious."

After drying his face with the sheet that hung beside the basin, Damir said, "Chief Marbek has asked me to tend to a Davlat mage who was fatally wounded and is dying. I don't know if I'll be able to help, but I plan to try. I will meet the nomads a short distance from here tomorrow."

Berk leaped to his feet, his eyes wide. "May I come too? I might know them! Did they say what clan the mage is from?"

"No." Damir considered. "Are you certain you want to come? This could be...difficult for you to see."

"Yes, I'm certain," Berk answered without hesitation. "I miss my people. I promise I won't be in the way, Master Damir."

"All right, then." Damir sighed. "Let's get some supper and rest." He didn't see the harm in letting the boy accompany him. On the contrary, he felt it could benefit Berk to see Damir using his skills as a physician rather than his magic, for a change.

And this time, it would be in an attempt to save a life—not destroy it.

IT WAS impossible to miss the white yarms, stark amidst the sand and rock of eastern Gohar. Several mounted warriors surrounded one in the center, waiting.

"Damir," Amit said, his hand on the hilt of his sword, "rest assured, we will be watching for any hostility from the nomads."

Damir's skin prickled at Amit's familiar address. "*Master* Damir, Commander," he corrected firmly. "And I feel like I shouldn't have to remind you that these nomads are our allies." He shot Amit a withering look. "I'm here to treat one of their injured. Please try and remember that and put your fucking weapons away." He pressed his horse forward into a faster gait, trying to shed himself of Amit's presence, when he heard Berk ride up beside him, clearing his throat.

"I wish I understood Erdem," Berk said, grinning, "Because whatever you said to that commander made him *angry*."

"Commander Amit is always angry these days," Damir answered briskly. He shot a quick glance at his pupil. "Learn from him. Don't be like Amit, Berk."

Berk's smile faded as he registered the rebuke. "Yes, sir."

Damir immediately felt regret for the harshness in his tone. It couldn't be helped; he was terrified he wouldn't be able to help this sick nomad. Would the Davlat hold Dilovar in such high esteem after its celebrated head mage couldn't save one of their own?

When the warriors began to approach slowly, Damir reined his horse to a stop and dismounted, his hands at his sides. He looked to Berk, indicating the boy should do the same. Berk complied, his eyes seeking the faces of the warriors eagerly. A lean young man with a bandaged arm and shoulder, astute dark eyes, and the distinctive warrior's tattoos on his face, hopped off his horse and came toward them.

"Master Damir," the warrior said, looking at the head mage. "My name is Omid. I will take you to Behnam." His eyes shifted to Amit and his men. "They stay behind, yes?"

Damir nodded. "Yes."

"Then let's go." Omid turned and gestured with his hand.

Damir and Berk began to follow the warrior toward the yarm when Omid paused, turning to frown at Berk. "It's probably best for the boy to stay out here," he said.

"No," Berk insisted. "Please, Master Damir, let me come with you."

"This is my Gohari apprentice, Berk, and I would prefer he remain with me," Damir said.

Omid was silent for a beat, seeming to debate on what to do. Finally, he said, "All right," and continued toward the yarm.

Damir's stomach was in knots as he and Berk followed. His anxiety only doubled as he ducked into the yarm and the smell of the festering wound assaulted his nostrils. *This is bad.* Two women in traditional sheepskin vests crouched beside the sleeping mage, whose wound was covered in a thick poultice. His...*her*...face was free of facial hair and they looked either like a very young man or a woman. His eyes focused on the wound and he immediately dropped his bag to the ground, kneeling beside the mage's pallet. Damir cleaned his hands thoroughly with alcohol and carefully lifted the poultice, causing the patient to grunt and grimace. An angry, red abscess encrusted with thick yellow pus stretched across the patient's thigh, and Damir's heart sank. It was an arrow wound, of that he was certain. In the back of his mind, he wondered if it had come from a Manzakar's bow. He took the patient's wrist between his fingers. Without looking at the two women, Damir said, "Her pulse and body temperature are quite elevated. When she's awake, is she lucid?"

"He, not she," one of the women corrected. "And...barely. He has just brief moments when he recognizes us and has a somewhat coherent conversation before slipping back into delirium."

That voice. Puzzled, Damir looked up at the speaker and saw Tikran peering back at him for a split second. He sucked in his breath sharply as his body tingled, going nearly numb with surprise. *Bruneta.* A warm hand suddenly covered his, and he snapped his head around to look at the second woman. *Holy shit.* His voice came out softly, hoarsely. "What the—"

"We're so utterly grateful that you made the time to come out here, Doctor Damir," Coxani said, her green eyes imploring and earnest.

"Master Damir?" Berk had been standing at the front of the yarm timidly. He stepped forward now, concern wrinkling his brow. "Is everything all right?"

"It's fine Berk," Damir said over his shoulder, surprised to hear his voice come out steady.

"Hey, Berk," he heard the warrior, Omid, say. "Do you want to go outside for a bit with me?"

"No," Berk replied firmly. "I'm staying with Master Damir."

Damir blinked hard, trying to clear his mind. What were

Coxani and Bruneta doing here? He realized that there was no speaking freely with Berk there. He turned and looked at the boy. "Berk, go outside with Omid, please."

"But Master Damir, you—"

"Heed me, Berk," Damir said as gently as he could, considering how he felt at the moment. "I will call you back in shortly." Berk obeyed in a huff and Omid followed him. Damir began speaking before he could even think properly. "Whom am I treating?"

"Captain Moti," Coxani answered, her voice a low, hurried hush. "A Manzakar. You probably don't remember him. He came from Otebek to fight with Tikran. He and I were part of a company tasked with taking supplies to the Anzori forts in Gohar and recruiting the tribes to help Anzor fight against Dilovar."

Damir's mind raced. "I thought that company was destroyed by—"

"Vazha," Coxani said through her teeth, her cheeks flushed with anger. "That's how Moti was injured. Vazha tried to kill us."

A multitude of questions flooded Damir's mind. As he tried to articulate them, Berk burst back into the yarm angrily, Omid hot on his heels. "Master Damir," Berk cried, "I can help him!"

After a beat of startled silence, Coxani uttered under her breath, "This is the powerful Davlat mage, then?"

Damir said, "Berk, listen, the best way you can—" He stopped abruptly, looking at Moti. *Holy Cenk.* It was very possible his apprentice was right. If Berk could somehow isolate the diseased tissue from the rest of the wound... *But how?* He met Coxani's anxious gaze, then Bruneta's. "Listen. I can't do much for your friend, unfortunately. What your healers have done is as much as I'm capable of. But there might be a solution, if a risky one."

"Risky how?" Bruneta demanded.

Damir tilted his head. "My apprentice, Berk, is still learning to control his Essence. His power far surpasses mine. In theory, he could rid the wound of the festering, but he has never tried anything like this before. A worst-case scenario could be...deadly, to say the least."

The two women exchanged a look that made him hold his breath. It was clear that they both loved this Captain Moti. They nodded to each other and Coxani said, "Let's do it."

Damir closed his eyes briefly, praying that Berk would be able to see this through. He turned toward his apprentice and nodded. "Come, Berk."

Berk approached slowly, warily, his eyes darting from each of the women's faces and back again. He sat tentatively next to Damir and whispered, "Don't I need to clean my hands, Master Damir? Just like you did?"

Damir blinked. "Yes. Of course." He reached for his bag. As he soaked a clean cloth in alcohol and handed it to the boy, he muttered, "Now, Berk. We've been practicing this. You've isolated elements before, in both earth and water. Make sure you—"

"I know," Berk said with a confidence Damir had never heard from the boy. "I'm...pretty sure I know what I'm doing."

I suppose that's good enough. Damir scooted to the side, allowing Berk access to the feverish patient.

Gently, Berk set his bare hand on Moti's thigh, just beneath the wound. He glanced uneasily at the owlish faces around him. "Will this make him...feel a lot of pain?"

Damir nodded, looking at Bruneta, Coxani, and Omid, and they all knew to help hold Moti down. "It likely will, lad. But if it ultimately saves him, it's all right."

With one large, audible swallow, Berk closed his eyes. After a few seconds, Moti began twisting his head from side to side, his eyes opening briefly, blanky. "No..." he uttered. Bruneta tightened her grip on Moti's upper body and lowered her mouth to his ear, whispering softly to him as he let out a desperate cry. The wound came alive, throbbing and pulsing beneath Berk's fingers. The yellowish-green purulence around and within it began to sizzle, bubbling forth from the abscess in a slow surge and emitting a stench even fouler than before. Moti let out a blood-curdling scream as his friends doubled down on restraining him. Thanks to Damir's firm grip, Berk managed to keep his hand on Moti's trembling thigh, his Essence flowing steadily. The pus spilled and spurted out, dripping down Moti's leg and splattering to the ground in globs.

When the fluid that rushed from the wound ran a pinkish clear, Damir rested his hand on Berk's sleeve, indicating the boy should stop. Berk lifted his slightly tremulous fingers from Moti's jerking leg. Damir immediately reached for his bag and yanked out his gauze. Wetting it with alcohol, he began wiping the wound of the remaining pus. He then quickly spread his honey balm over the wound and wrapped it in clean dressing.

Moti's chest was heaving, his entire body soaked in sweat and shaking violently, as Bruneta, Coxani, and Omid held him in their firm grips. Damir reached into his bag again, grabbing his pain elixir and pouring it into a cup. He tilted it into Moti's parted lips, ensuring the contents were swallowed by tipping Moti's chin back.

"You should resist moving him until he's begun to heal," Damir insisted, looking at Coxani and Bruneta in turn. "The wound could start to fester again otherwise." He handed them a small pot of the balm and a bottle of the elixir. "Change the dressing every two days and administer just a swallow of the elixir daily."

Coxani trembled as she stood and looked at Berk. "I don't know how to thank you."

Berk shrugged and met her gaze uncomfortably. "Can you tell Beg Zolto I love him and miss him?"

She nodded. "Of course."

Damir lifted his bag to his shoulder, his mind racing. He locked eyes with Coxani, wishing he could tell her outright to stay as far away from Zifa as possible. He said, "I would insist on returning to check on your friend, but Berk and I are helping to capture Zifa in the next few days. Don't worry, you Davlat have nothing to fear—between myself and Berk, the Manzakars don't stand a chance." Coxani, Bruneta, and Omid all blanched.

"Are we about done?" Amit halted abruptly upon entering the yarm, covering his nose and mouth with his hand. "Holy Cenk, it smells like death in here."

Damir swallowed, his eyes still fixed on Coxani's face. "Take care, nomads." With his heart in his throat, he turned toward Amit. "Yes, we're done."

RIDING SWIFTLY BACK to the Davlat encampment, Coxani was shaken. What had she just witnessed? Had that awkward Gohari adolescent truly just saved Moti's life? And with magic she'd never dreamed existed. Damir's Essence was astounding, but Berk... *What damage could be done with a power like that?* She had to get her company to Zifa as soon as possible.

Omid leaned forward on his horse, peering into her face. "Coxani, look at me. The head mage doesn't know that the Davlat are on Tikran's side. You heard Bruneta—she agrees with me. We plan on fighting with you."

Coxani continued to stare forward. "Omid, you don't understand. I know Damir. He was trying to warn me." They had left Bruneta and most of the party with Moti as he healed, heeding Damir's advice not to move him. Bruneta had given Omid the command of the Sachin warriors in her absence.

"I understand," Omid replied. "But, again, he doesn't realize that the Manzakars have all of Gohar on their side. The Dilovari think they have a good portion of the nomads with them, and they don't. Coxani, are you listening to me?"

She finally snapped her head around to glare at him. "Yes, I'm listening, Omid. But are you listening to *me*? Over a year ago, we both saw what Damir could do. Today, we both saw what Berk can do. I'm trying to conceive of what they could do together, and it's terrifying. I can't send the Gohari to fight alongside the Manzakars in good conscience."

"Sweet Archil!" Omid cried, letting his head drop back. "Are you serious? You think the tribes of Gohar are weak, don't you? We have our mages now, Coxani. They have enough Essence—"

"No, they don't. Besides, Gohari mages haven't learned enough about their powers to be much of a challenge to Dilovari mages." Coxani drew a shaky breath. "The power we saw today..."

Omid shook his head. "The kid probably saved Moti. I may not know much about the Essence, but I know it's meant to create and sustain life. How can a power like that be used to kill beyond what Damir can do?"

"I don't know and I wish I didn't have to find out," Coxani answered hollowly. "What Damir can do is enough on its own to completely decimate our combined forces. The Gohari must not participate in this battle. Do you hear me, Omid?"

"So you just want us to sit by while the Manzakars try to fight Dilovar and its ridiculously powerful mages alone?"

"Yes." She glared at him. "You would have been more than happy to do so a few weeks ago."

"I didn't realize how crazy in love with you I was a few weeks ago," Omid managed, his voice thick with emotion.

Coxani's heart jumped. *Is he joking?* His gaze was intense, beseeching. The words came out of her mouth before she could stop them. "No love is worth the lives of thousands. And you don't love me—you're just infatuated with Archil's descendant."

Omid's cheeks instantly flushed red, his expression transforming into one of anger and pain. "Fuck you, Manzakar. I gave you a bead long before I knew any of that. You're not being fair."

Coxani felt tears well up in her eyes. "If I didn't care about you, I'd let you die for Anzor. So no, nomad. Fuck *you*." With that, she kicked her horse into a gallop, needing to escape—everything. The wind made the tears stream down her cheeks as she leaned forward and grasped the reins tightly in her fists.

She'd lied to Omid—she wouldn't let him die for Anzor, regardless of how she felt about him. And while she certainly had developed romantic feelings for him, was what she felt really love? Did she even know what romantic love was? She certainly felt deep affection for Naran and the cranky cadet-turned-Manzakar king who had taught her much of what was helping her survive now.

Tikran, where are you?

There was no time to dwell on love. She and her Manzakars had to fight this battle. The Gohari did not. She had no way of ensuring Omid didn't disobey her, but she had seen something stark and foreboding in Damir's face. He'd been warning her in whatever way he could. Squeezing her eyes shut, she once again prayed to the spirits of her ancestors, fully realizing it would likely do nothing. But she'd been taught to pray to *something*. Without prayer, she had nothing else to rely on other than fallible human beings...including herself.

And that was truly terrifying.

CHAPTER 28

Berk peered at his mentor curiously as they rode east and back to Faiz, the sun already dipping behind them. Damir's mind had been elsewhere since they'd left the small Davlat encampment behind. Truth be told, a sliver of suspicion had wormed its way into Berk's mind regarding the entire encounter with the injured nomad. "Master Damir, are you okay?"

Damir blinked and looked over. "Hmm? Yes, I'm fine." He sighed and one side of his mouth curled up in a half smile. "What you did back there, Berk, was astonishing."

Warmth suffused Berk's chest, neck and face, and he couldn't help but beam. "The moment I saw the wound, I knew I could do it," he said. "I can't explain how I knew. I just did."

"How did it feel?"

Berk considered, wrinkling his nose. "It felt...strange. You know how creating life is tiring but painless? This wasn't like that, exactly. It almost felt like I was destroying life, to be honest. I felt that same ache in my hands."

Damir frowned. "That *is* interesting."

The pair rode in contemplative silence for a few minutes before Berk said, "Master Damir, something felt off about those nomads.

Are you sure they were Davlat? And the mage... He looked more like a warrior than a mage."

Clearing his throat, Damir answered, "Lad, my knowledge of the Gohari is limited, unfortunately. All I know is that the request to treat the mage came from Chief Marbek himself."

"Yeah," Berk said, chewing the inside of his cheek thoughtfully.

"Listen, Berk." Damir turned an earnest gaze on his apprentice. "When we reach Zifa, I need you to follow my lead and listen to my commands. You've been practicing controlling your emotions when using your Essence, and I need you to put those skills into use one hundred percent."

"I've gotten really good at it, admit it," Berk insisted.

Damir shook his head. "You've gotten good at controlling your emotions around Vazha's Manzakars and dummies in Manzakar armor. It will be very different when Anzor's Manzakars attack us with intent to kill."

"I can do it," Berk replied stubbornly. "I'll prove it to you."

"Good." Damir let out a deep breath. "Prove it to me, then."

They reached Faiz and, as they dismounted and left their horses with the grooms, Berk sensed Damir's mood change dramatically—he became curt, his movements became rigid. *Vazha.* Berk looked about him, wondering what Damir had seen that had alerted him to the prince's presence. Damir was always vigilant when it came to Vazha, and over time, Berk had become convinced that something sinister was at play between the two men. *I just can't make sense of it.* For his part, Berk had become increasingly wary of the prince, despite Berk's desperate need for the affection and pride Vazha lavished on him.

Berk followed Damir into the fort, where Commander Harun approached them briskly. "Master Damir—"

"Prince Vazha is here," Damir interrupted. "Yes, I know. Take us to him."

Berk rushed to catch up to Damir, whose strides were long and purposeful. When they reached Harun's chambers, they found Vazha there, waiting, leaning on his cane, looking utterly put-together for someone who must have traveled through Gohar the entire day. The prince's expression struck fear in even Berk's heart. *Oh. He's angry.* Berk stopped abruptly even as Damir continued to approach.

Damir sounded furious. "Prince Vazha, why do you feel it's appropriate for you to be here on the eve of battle? Do you intend to use your superior warrior skills to help us or are you here just to harass us?"

Berk gasped. Vazha, on the other hand laughed—a cruel, gleeful laugh. "Ah, Damir. Your spirit is what I love most about you. Unfortunately, your spirit has led you astray." He looked at Berk directly. "Berk. I'm sorry, lad."

All eyes were on Berk. He swallowed. "What for, sir?" he stammered.

Vazha's eyes hardened, glittering. "Your mentor lied to you. Those supposed Davlat nomads you helped save? They were Manzakars. And Master Damir knows them."

Damir turned. "Berk, that's—"

"Do you deny it, Damir?" Vazha's voice echoed like an angry god's. "You lied to Berk so that he would help them."

Berk stared at Damir's profile, watching his mentor close his eyes briefly before turning to face his apprentice fully. "I was startled to see them there. We had no time. I—"

Berk's heart plunged to his feet. He heard himself say, "You warned them about our attack on Zifa." He felt like he might throw up. "Master Damir, why did you lie to me?"

"Because he loves King Tikran," Vazha said, a wicked smile tugging at the corners of his mouth. "Which begs the question: whose side are you on, Master Damir?"

Damir straightened his shoulders and lifted his chin, his eyes fixed on Berk's. "I'm sorry I lied to you, Berk. It was not my intention at all. When I fought alongside Tikran against Delger's Manzakars, I made good friends. And when they appeared before me unexpectedly, my instinct was to help them. Not at the expense of Dilovar, mind you. Not at anyone's expense." Damir's gray eyes were limpid as they locked with Berk's. "I simply wanted to help my friends."

He has friends he chooses over me. Berk curled his hands into fists.

"I still wonder who you favor, Master Damir," Vazha mused aloud. "Your actions call your alliance into question."

Damir's jaw flexed, his shoulders tightened. He looked like a leopard ready to pounce, like a silk bowstring pulled too taut and on the verge of snapping. Berk had never seen his mentor in such a state. The candles in the room flared with a sharp hiss and a forceful wind shook the glass in the windows with a sudden rattle. "My alliance is not—and will never be—with *the Anzori*. Just so we're clear."

Vazha smiled vaguely, leaning against his cane with both hands. "Well. I'm glad we cleared that up. It doesn't change the fact that you lied. So your words are only words, aren't they?" The prince looked at Berk. "Unlike your mentor, I won't lie to you."

Damir's explosive laughter jarred everyone in the room. "Oh, really?"

Vazha shot Damir a frigid look. "Berk will stay with me from now on."

"He will *not*," Damir spat.

"Berk," Vazha commanded. "Would you rather stay with me or the man who lied to you?"

The pain Berk felt was raw, agonizing. *Why would he lie to me?* "I'd rather stay with you, Your Highness," he said, hoping it cut Damir as deeply as Damir's betrayal had cut him.

"Berk," Damir said. "Please. You must understand why—"

"I think the boy has heard enough," Vazha snapped, wrapping his arm around Berk's shoulders.

"Vazha, if you touch him," Damir said, "I will—"

"You'll do what, Master Damir?" Vazha raised a casual eyebrow at the head mage. When Damir said nothing, Vahza steered Berk to the fort's guest room. Berk hyperventilated as the door shut behind him and the prince. He controlled his asthma with his Essence just as Damir had taught him, feeling his knees go weak.

"There now, Berk," Vazha said gently. "You're safe now, lad. Breathe easy."

Tears flooded Berk's eyes and ran down his face. "I don't understand why—"

"He's a treacherous man, Berk," Vazha said with a sad shake of his head. "He'll only ever look out for himself. I don't think he's truly capable of loving anyone but himself."

Berk was racked with sobs when Vazha wrapped his arms around Berk's shoulders, pressing the boy to him. Berk hugged back desperately, feeling his cries die within the prince's tight embrace. "There, Berk. You're safe. You're safe now. Sit." Berk obediently sat on the bed, wiping the snot and tears from his face with his sleeve. "Rest," Vazha said. "I need to speak with the commanders now. I will be back later."

When the door closed behind him, Berk kicked off his boots and shucked off his jacket. Curling up beneath the threadbare blanket on the bed, he squeezed his eyes shut and tried not to start crying again. Manzakars had slaughtered his clan, murdered his brother. The very Manzakar he'd helped might have been among them. *Why, Master Damir? Why?* He let his eyelids droop, his hands clasped tightly. Before he knew it, he was fast asleep.

The door opened and shut with a groan, waking him. His eyes opened, adjusting to the darkness of the room. He saw a shadowy figure with a cane shed his jacket and lowered itself onto the bed beside him. Vazha lay down facing Berk, his eyes luminescent. "Berk. Are you all right?"

"Yes," Berk said, looking inquisitively at the man he now considered his sole protector and friend. Behind Vazha, the glass of the windows bowed under the force of a vicious wind storm. "What's happening?" Berk asked uneasily.

Vazha chuckled. "I imagine a certain head mage is throwing a tantrum."

"Oh," Berk uttered, concerned and confused. "Is he in trouble for helping the Manzakars?"

"I doubt it," Vazha replied with a snort. "He's the head mage of

Dilovar. It will take a bit more than helping a sick Manzakar to bring him down."

Berk frowned, feeling conflicted. Despite Damir's treachery, Berk didn't want to see his mentor hurt.

"You're going to be an incredibly powerful mage. Much more powerful than Damir. I can't wait to call you *my* head mage," Vazha said softly, reaching out and stroking Berk's hair. Just a few short weeks ago, Berk would have leaned into every word, every touch. But something about this entire situation felt off. It felt *wrong*. The windows vibrated against the gusts of wind. Disoriented, Berk tried shutting out the noise by closing his eyes. He mumbled, "I think I'd like to sleep now, Your Highness, if that's all right?"

Vazha replied, "Of course, Berk."

Tentatively, Berk turned his back to the prince, his nerves humming. As he tried to calm himself by breathing in measured paces, Vazha said, "Maybe someday you'll love me the way I love you."

Berk blinked in the darkness, realizing there was no way he'd be able to sleep.

CHAPTER 29

If Berk slept, it was in fragments, and only when he was overcome by somnolence. Otherwise he remained wide awake, hyper aware of the man who slept beside him. Pain battled with rage inside him—he wanted love and guidance so badly and had truly thought he'd found it in not just one, but two, men. *I was so wrong.* One had betrayed him and the other...the other apparently wanted something entirely different, something that filled Berk with dismay.

He yearned to unleash his Essence in wild streams of fury and anguish, shattering, pulverizing, and incinerating everything around him.

When dawn broke, he felt a rush of relief. Careful not to wake Vazha, he crept from the bed and snuck from the room. He could hear men's voices shouting orders, the clatter of weapons and armor, the hoofbeats of warhorses. He reached the spiked, wooden battlements of the fort and looked over the sad little town of Faiz. Hundreds of Dilovari warriors prepared for battle below, their lamellar armor adorned with bones and feathers, broad-brimmed helmets with long plumes of horsehair flowing in the wind. Berk caught his breath. *They look unstoppable.*

"I suppose I can't sway you away from Vazha's side, can I?"

Damir stood several feet away, his arms crossed, dark circles under his eyes.

Berk stepped back. Had his mentor slept at all? "You lied to me."

Damir sighed. "I told you why. I wasn't trying to trick you, Berk."

"But you did, anyway. You—"

"He *did* trick you," Vazha said, his voice ringing out from behind Damir. He emerged from the darkness of the covered walkway, his cane making a staccato sound against the wood. Damir didn't bother to look behind him, his eyes on Berk. Vazha stroked Damir's hair as he walked past, smiling smugly. Berk could tell Damir wanted to snap Vazha in half but resisted. *Why? Why is he resisting?* The only thing that made sense was that Vazha was speaking the truth. Damir really was a traitor. *Vazha is right.*

Berk's Essence throbbed, heating his blood.

Even Vazha walked a wide circle around him. "Come, Berk. I can feel your ire. Zifa and its Manzakars await."

"Berk." Damir stepped forward, his gray eyes like beams of light even in the brightest daylight. "You know me. You know—"

"That's enough, Doctor," Vazha commanded, taking ahold of Berk's arm as Commander Amit shouted for his troops' attention. Berk went along with Vazha, willing himself not to look back at Damir. They headed down to the armory, where Berk was dressed in a lighter lamellar cuirass and iron helmet. After mounting his horse, which was likewise outfitted in armor with a spiked chamfron on the front of its head, Berk peered down at himself in amazement. A flutter of excitement tickled his stomach despite his dark mood.

"I will stay beside Berk during the siege," he heard Amit say to Vazha. "I'll make sure no harm comes to him."

"Damir will make sure no harm comes to him as well," Vazha replied. He glanced over at Damir, who was likewise being outfitted for battle. "Won't you, Doctor?"

Damir answered without hesitation, "Of course I will."

Berk resisted the warmth that tried to rise within him. *He lied to me. I hate him. I hate him.* He turned away and cantered up beside Amit, his eyes fixed on the endless steppe beyond Faiz. He *needed* to release the Essence boiling within him...soon.

Amit quirked an eyebrow at Berk and smiled uneasily. "Let's go, then."

Damir rode ahead of Berk, occasionally glancing back and attempting to meet his apprentice's eyes. Berk would immediately look away, frowning, his Essence simmering beneath his skin, hot and alive. He brooded the entire ride, even as they passed several small Davlat encampments. It should have brought him some excitement or joy, but he felt nothing but pain and a deep ambivalence. For all he knew, the nomads were just Manzakars in disguise, he thought sardonically.

They reached Zifa after two days of travel. As the town came into view, its thatch-roofed homes abandoned and its fort eerily quiet, Commander Harun yelled from the forefront, "Shields!" Amit steered his horse against Berk's and lifted his iron shield over both their heads. Berk heard the deep, hostile whistles of the Manzakar arrows just before they pelted the squadron in rapid crashes, making his ears ring. Fear sprouted in his gut and memories of his clan's destruction flooded back, paralyzing him. The shouts of soldiers blended with the clanging of armor as another volley of arrows descended on the squadron, soaring down on them from the fort.

Where was Damir? In that very moment, Berk wanted nothing more than to be beside his mentor, his fear overtaking his feelings of betrayal. But he couldn't see anything beyond Amit's shield or the shields of the other soldiers. The squadron continued to move forward, loosing their arrows in response. When firepots began soaring into their midst, igniting fires where they landed, Berk sensed Damir's Essence flood the spaces between the men, suffocating the flames before they could cause much damage. The pummeling of arrows and firepots continued as the Dilovari pressed on to the fort, and all the while Berk's hands shook as they gripped the reins, his heart racing.

A soldier appeared beside Amit, his face streaked with sweat beneath the brim of his helmet. "Commander Harun says to bring the boy to the front lines."

Amit nodded and looked at Berk. "It's time to work your magic, boy," he said gruffly. "Let's go." He grabbed Berk's reins while still holding his shield aloft and began maneuvering them both between the mounted horsemen to the front. The arrows continued to drum down on them; Berk continued to cower with each clash of iron against iron.

By the time they reached the front, Berk was desperately using his Essence to push air into his lungs. *I can't do this.* Whatever rage and pain he'd felt earlier had seemingly vanished in a flood of terror, and now his magic was barely helping him breathe. From around Amit's shield, Berk saw the fort looming before them, the archers on the battlements, loosing their arrows in steady showers. The Dilovari had propped several tall ladders against the timber walls and were ascending, moving quickly across the rungs, one after another. Harun emerged at Berk's side and shouted, "Let's have it, then! Light the archers on fire. Do something!"

Berk trembled uncontrollably. "I can't."

"What do you mean, you *can't?*"

He shook his head frantically. "I can't!"

Harun and Amit stared at each other over Berk's head. Through his teeth, Harun growled, "Get Damir over here! He must convince the boy to perform." As Amit reined his horse around, holding his shield over his back, Harun roared in frustration. "Time is wasting, boy! You're going to get us all killed!"

Flinching at the sound of the commander's outraged bark, Berk's voice shook with every quake of his body. "I can't," he wheezed. "I can't." *I can barely breathe.*

"Berk. Deep breaths, lad." Damir was at his side, shielding them both, his voice surprisingly calm and filling Berk with a steadiness he hadn't thought possible. "Let me help you," Damir said. Nodding just slightly, Berk closed his eyes briefly and focused on breathing. "Now, listen." Damir's deep voice was an anchor amongst the whistling, rattling, and crashing. "Reach out your hand, behind the shield, toward the battlements, and focus your Essence on one archer at a time—"

Several cries rang out from the back, and Berk turned when a horse pushed up against his roughly. Arrows flew in from all directions, striking the soldier beside him in the neck. As the man fell from his horse, his blood spraying Berk's cuirass, Damir's shield swooped over to cover Berk, and just in the nick of time. The bodkins struck the dome of iron with a deep clang and Damir's arm shook from the blow. Between breaths, he said, "Berk, listen. You need to focus your—"

A wave of movement forced them forward, toward the fort. As more arrows drove down on them, the confusion and panic Berk sensed from the soldiers around him made his chest tighten with terror. He heard a soldier shout from the back, "We've been surrounded! The Manzakars are attacking our flanks!"

Berk spun back around to see the soldiers on the ladders get picked off, one by one. No fewer than five Manzakar arrows, expertly aimed at armpits, legs, and faces, drove into each Dilovari, one after the other. They plummeted to the ground with a scream, sometimes taking the men below them as well.

Holy Cenk. How had the Manzakars been able to so easily sneak up on them? *The Gohari.* They really were Manzakars in disguise.

Coxani's plan would have made Tikran proud, she just knew it.

Her Gohari scouts had confirmed that the Dilovari forces didn't have reserves—because why would they? They had two very powerful mages who guaranteed a victory, as well as the mistaken assumption that they had the local tribe's support. Coxani had used the Davlat encampments around Zifa to hide her Manzakars, and as the Dilovari had begun engaging the fort's defense, she'd gotten her forces into three formations, encircling them and trapping them against the fort.

Now, her troops surrounded the Dilovari squadron. The cavalry, led by a seasoned Manzakar named Reza, charged their flanks, while she and her flight archers galloped up, loosed a bombardment of arrows into the line formations of Dilovari horsemen, then wheeled away, retreating behind the rocky hills nearby before riding in again. Reining around from atop a small mesa and holding her breath, Coxani watched the deadly tide of Manzakar cavaliers plow through the enemy's flanks in a great cloud of dirt. The guttural shouts of the men and the clatter of weapons filled the air thunderously. At the fort, the enemy plummeted from their ladders steadily, one after the other, shot by multiple arrows before they were able to scale the walls.

Despite the clear signs of a pending victory, Coxani refused to feel any relief—the mages were still at large, and this battle was far from over. Ordering her archers to continue the assault, she rode in again, this time intent on finding the mages—one in particular. While she had commanded that they both be taken alive, she knew deep down that her orders were futile. *They'll kill us all before we can even come close.*

No. The Damir she remembered wouldn't.

But would Berk?

Where are you, Berk? She was going to stop him. She *had* to stop him.

CHAPTER 30

Berk's fury rushed back as the realization hit him: He truly didn't know who was friend and who was foe anymore.

I can't even trust my own people.

It was then that his Essence uncoiled within him, seeping into his blood and flooding his veins with a shock of sensation. The magic had never felt like this before—so all-encompassing, so all-consuming. It was as though a different being had possessed his body, holding sway over his thoughts and feelings. Instead of fear, at that very moment, Berk felt a terrifying power. It filled him, roiling, demanding to be obeyed. He pushed Damir's shield to the side and focused on the embrasures in the fort's battlements. He barely needed to move his hands when one after the other, the archers on the walls who attempted to loose arrows ignited in sudden, almost explosive flames. They fell screaming while Berk intensified the fire, determined to leave nothing but a pile of ash. He heard Damir's voice but not words. It didn't matter—he knew what he would do next.

More. His Essence was a tempest within him. Dropping from his horse and squatting to the ground, he yelled at the men around him, "Get behind me! Behind me!" He'd done this with Damir a multitude of times. Laying his splayed hands in the sandy soil, he pivoted his attention to a tower that was partially constructed of stone and was undoubtedly filled with men. The tremor began in his palms, traveling through the earth and toward the fort, leaving a great fracture in its wake. As it reached the tower, each stone row in the tower's base crumbled to dust, one after another, racing upward as the tower began to collapse. It fell with a boom, shaking the ground. For good measure, Berk then wiggled his fingers and torched the wooden structure that had sat at the top with a sudden gust of fire. The soldiers trapped within were like ghostly apparitions, shimmering within the flames.

He ached to set the entire bloody fort on fire, his hands now cramping with need, but was restrained by the Dilovari soldiers that now clambered up ladders and over the wall with little resistance. Damir was again beside him, crouched, holding his shield over them. "Focus, Berk. Target the other towers as well, now..."

But killing Anzori soldiers who defended from the fort wasn't enough, and Berk turned his attention to the Manzakars that attacked the flanks. He had something special planned for them. *More... More.* He stood and, with a shocking nonchalance, strode between the horsemen and to the rear, stopping only when he reached the melee, where the Manzakars attacked. One Manzakar turned his horse toward Berk and drew his saber. In response, Berk raised both his hands, moving his fingers slightly, enjoying that gratifying release. The flames erupted from the neck of the Manzakar's cuirass, cooking the soldier's face beneath his helmet as he flailed, leaping from his horse. Berk turned to the others, who likewise were attempting to close in on him. He lit them on fire in turn at first, then in twos, and threes...fifteen of them burned, then twenty, forty, sixty... Soon, no fewer than two hundred Manzakars burned in agony while the Dilovari moved in confusion, attempting to finish off their blazing opponents with their swords and lances.

You're going down, Manzakars.

THE MANZAKARS LIT up like torches before Coxani's eyes and she reared back. *Holy shit!* Berk was close, and he was using whatever he could find as tinder. She quickly shoved her tunic's collar beneath her cuirass and tucked her hair under her helmet. She attempted to warn the men around her to do the same...too late. She drew her bowstring taut even as her fellow Manzakars thrashed desperately around her, their cries shrill and piercing, their fires casting ominous orange light over the melee.

I have to stop him.

Determined, she rode into the midst of the chaos, smoke burning her eyes, loosing her arrows point-blank into Dilovari faces, necks, legs... One of them hacked at her with his sword, striking her torso and nearly unsaddling her. Luckily, she'd begun wearing her cuirass again, and while she was certain her ribs were bruised, she was still in one piece. Her attacker fell without a scream, taken down by an arrow to the throat. She continued to seek out Damir's apprentice, her arrows flying, trying desperately to shut out the screams of her men and the unnatural, enduring heat of the fires that burned them.

Above the din of the men's cries, she heard the familiar, high-pitched ululating of the Gohari. *No!* She wasn't the only one to turn and see no fewer than two hundred nomad warriors, several of them wearing Manzakar armor, ride toward them with intent, their arrows singing through the air and striking in rapid succession. *Omid.* She was afraid he'd disregard her orders. And now, she didn't have the luxury to care. She spun back around, determined to find the young mage. Finding—and killing—Berk was the only hope they had.

Where are you, Berk?

She moved her horse with her thighs, urging it from a walk to a trot, avoiding the fallen soldiers. Her eyes fell to a crouched Dilovari soldier within her periphery. He was much smaller than the others, almost lost in his armor. He looked up, his young face as if in a trance, not seeing her. He was looking beyond her, at the fallen

Manzakars she'd left behind. She speedily drew her bowstring tightly, pointing her arrow at the boy's face.

Now. Shoot. She hesitated, her arms shaking. *Fucking shoot!*

A loud thunderclap startled her as she released. The rain surged down as the arrow flew from her bow and struck the mud beyond Berk with a dull, wet thud.

THE GREAT GUSH of rain Berk had called took the burning Manzakars down with it. Still crouched against the ground, the delicious pulsing in his hands crept up his arms and across his shoulders. He peered at the fallen, struggling Manzakars—one was wailing and scalded in the face, another gripped his leg in agony, all of them wet—and dipped his fingers into rivulets of rain that were rushing across the dry earth. While he had no idea what the exact effects his actions would have, he somehow understood it would kill his subjects quickly. *I can feel it.* His Essence flowed from him and into the runoff, slithering quickly across the space that separated him from the injured men. Within seconds of the magic reaching them, the Manzakars flushed bright red in splotches, their exposed skin swelling and purpling as if in one enormous bruise. Their screams, like nothing Berk had ever heard before, rang out over the clatter of weapons and armor, and even some of the men fighting in the melee were compelled to watch, horror-stricken. Blood—thin enough to be water—began spilling from the Manzakars' noses, mouths, eyes, and ears as they shuddered convulsively, their screams drowned and choked, their skin morphing from purple to black.

That sinister, pleasurable ache consumed Berk now; his entire body relished the feeling of the Essence as it surged through him. Berk locked eyes with a dying Manzakar for a split second. The man's face was reminiscent of his uncle Emin's, and he watched as it became a dark, swollen purple, blood dribbling from lips that moved in a silent plea.

What have I done?

The thought slammed into him, as though it had burst through a blocked door. With his panic came a slight loss of control, and the Essence spread wider, reaching any injured soldier whose blood touched both his wound and the wet ground. All around him, soldiers writhed and shrieked luridly as they bruised from the inside, hemorrhaged, and died grotesquely, their charred-black bodies contorted in pools of blood.

Oh Archil, what have I done?

BLINKING RAPIDLY and swiping the rain from her eyes, Coxani wanted to clamp her hands over her ears to keep from hearing the anguished, haunting moans that surrounded her. The fallen Manzakars around her reddened, darkened to a deep purple, then went black. As they convulsed violently, blood spurted from every orifice like red water from a fountain. She was so transfixed by the sight of men she knew go from human to anything but that she almost forgot why she was there. *Reza. Afsan. Danis.* She watched these men—her comrades—swell and shrivel, their blood-soaked bodies like toys to Berk's magic.

The water. Berk was somehow using it to kill the fallen men.

"Coxani!" Omid approached on horseback, slashing at a Dilovari infantryman with his borrowed Manzakar saber and felling the soldier with a single, unschooled swipe. He tried to reach her when an arrow struck his horse and he tumbled down, landing in a patch of rain-drenched grass with a grunt.

No! Coxani leaped from her mount and ran toward Omid's fallen form, her shield raised behind her. "Get up! Get up, Omid, for the love of—"

He'd fallen on his left side, and his bandaged shoulder was soaked and coated with mud. A faint stain of blood, just barely pink, showed through his dressing, and Coxani began screaming as she grabbed him and tried to pull him up. "Please, Omid, get up! Get up!"

He made a strange, choked sound, his furrowed brow going clear as his hand wrapped around hers tightly. He looked her in the eyes, his lips moving as if to say something, when his skin began to bruise. Her frantic yanks slowly stopped as she realized it—whatever *it* was—had already begun. *No! No! No!* She let out a desperate wail and slammed her fist into the earth repeatedly, refusing to believe she could do nothing.

His face was a mask of pain as his skin changed shades, purpling rapidly. *I can't. I can't watch.* And yet, she kept her hand wrapped around his, her eyes on his face, determined that he would not feel abandoned at that moment. She uttered frantically, "I love you, Omid. I love you," as he gasped, shaking vigorously. Even when his blood spurted out onto her, she refused to move, clutching his hand in hers. Her eyes glazed over as if to protect her from the sight of his death, her vision blurring even as she kept her gaze on his face. When he finally stopped moving, when she felt the warmth leave his fingers, she forced herself to pull her hand from his grasp.

As if in a nightmare, she stood and turned back toward Berk, who was standing now, his eyes wide and face drained of color. She wanted to crumple over Omid's body and wail. But she had to do this, and do it now. She wasn't hesitating this time.

Nock... Draw... Anchor... Aim...

A shimmering form flew into her line of sight and smashed into the boy, tossing him a good distance. She refocused, her fingers itching to release her arrow. But the enraged face before her was Damir's, and his rage was directed at the young mage who lay in the mud. *Get out of the way, Damir. I will shoot you.* Her arms shook as she watched Damir loom over Berk until the boy began shuddering uncontrollably. She felt something dark, something potent, swirl past her and back toward his trembling form with urgency, as if called by some higher force, leaving her chilled. The boy finally lay unconscious, his magic dissipated from the air.

Still shaking, she lowered her bow. Damir then fell to his knees before the blackened, twisted bodies of the Manzakars, covering his face. She turned away slowly, walking trance-like back to where Omid lay next to the fallen Manzakar standard, and dropped to her knees as well. His blackened expression was eerily peaceful, as if he hadn't died in the most painful, gruesome way possible. *He's gone.* She was too shocked to cry. She heard the rattling of armor close behind her and Damir's voice in the distance, sounding more strained than she'd ever heard it.

"Commander Harun, leave her! Where is your humanity? Don't you see what's been done to her men?"

There was some muttered deliberation, then she heard the man behind her speak in heavily accented Perchuhi. "Manzakar. You may come back and retrieve the bodies of your dead. You have two days, or we will burn them ourselves."

She must have nodded. As they retreated, a cry so anguished rang out that she didn't realize it came from her lips. *Why? Why him?*

The rain began to fall again as the wind whipped about her. She didn't have to look to know it came from Damir—his pain, his rage.

"Rasula." Gohari hands clasped her shoulders. "We'll take him back to the camp. Come. Please."

Tears flooded her eyes as she allowed the nomads to coax her from Omid's side. She cast a final look back at where his body was being gathered up by the warriors, feeling as though her heart had been ripped from her chest.

It's because of me.

CHAPTER 31

Tikran's spirits lifted as he and his forces of three thousand troops, half of which were Manzakars, ventured into Gohar. He rode beside Naran and behind his Aslans in full armor, looking about him at the numerous herds of wild saiga antelope, the vast stretches of long, almost green grass, and feeling his heart grow hopeful. "Gohar is coming back to life," he said, his voice tinged with emotion. "Do you see it, Naran?"

Naran smiled. "I see it, Freed Kingfisher. It's about time."

Tikran turned and looked at Tanith, where she rode with the other mages. "Tanith. Doesn't it look better than a year ago?"

She smiled affectionately at him. "Yes. This is your doing, Tikran, no question."

He raised an eyebrow at her. "Are you blowing smoke up my ass?"

She stifled her smile. "There are definitely times I've thought about it. And even though I'm riding behind you, now is not that time."

Naran said, "It definitely sounds like she's blowing smoke up your ass." He cleared his throat and looked over meaningfully. "You know this is your doing, Tik. You don't need us to tell you."

Tikran drew a deep breath. "I do need to hear it, though. I feel like I've been in a box, making changes that sound good on paper while I sit around in a palace, stuffing my face with good food and unable to actually *do* anything myself. I just had to trust they were getting done somehow."

"Yeah," Naran mumbled. "I understand."

Tikran looked at his friend now, keenly aware of how the Stalking Lion had changed. *Did he just say, "I understand?"* Since when was that Naran's response to any of Tikran's anxieties? And Naran *had* changed, more than he'd initially thought. Shocking both him and Haydar, Naran had married Dinara in a very brief ceremony, allowing her to share her father's duplicity with them. While Tikran still didn't know which other Anzori lords supported his removal, he had his suspicions. Dinara had revealed that, in addition to Prem, she believed at least two other lords conspired with him. Tikran fully suspected they intended to give the throne to Vazha, returning the crown to the Delger dynasty. All this, because of Tikran's "extreme" policies. Tikran wanted to grimace every time he thought about it. *Allowing the Gohari to be free, within and without Anzor. Yes, "extreme" indeed.*

Clearing his throat, Tikran looked at his commander-in-chief from the corner of his eye. He suspected that Coxani's rejection, which must have been unequivocal, had been the reason for Naran's transformation. There was simply no other way Naran would have married Dinara otherwise...

Coxani. He didn't know if she was still alive, but something deep within him believed it. Maybe that "something" was simply trying to prevent him from losing his mind—because without Coxani, he surely would—so that he could continue fighting for what was right. He swallowed. *No. No.* He refused to accept that. She was alive, he knew it. He felt it. Tikran certainly had no magical abilities, but he had a deep connection to the girl with the ear-piercing scream and fiery green eyes. She was alive. He felt it in his very being.

He'd tried to broach the subject with Naran, only to have the yellow-haired Manzakar cut him off. As if even speaking about Coxani was too painful. So Tikran had stopped trying, and each of them suffered quietly and alone at the thought of what she might be experiencing.

"Caged Kingfisher! Caged Kingfisher!"

The voices of children roused Tikran from his thoughts and he looked around at the young Gohari nomads running along either side of the road. *Caged Kingfisher?* Surely the Gohari knew of his name change? For some reason, a heaviness settled in Tikran's chest. Were they still calling him "Caged" for a reason?

As they reached the garrison town of Ukin in western Gohar, Tikran noticed the numerous nomad encampments that surrounded it. Coxani had clearly made it this far, at least. They stopped and dismounted, seeing the fort's commander standing at the town's gates. As Tikran began to approach, he spotted Gohari warriors atop the mesas overlooking the fort, their bows and arrows at their hips, their feathers and horsehair fluttering in the breeze. He said to Naran, "Go and greet the commander. I'll be right back."

"Where are you going?" Naran said, shaking his head. "You can't just wander off, Your Highness."

Tikran huffed in frustration. He glared at his Aslans, who were at his heels. "Can you guys please let me talk to the warriors without breathing down my neck? Try and remember that I was an Aslan once as well, and I know how to take care of myself." When they glanced warily at each other, Tikran stared directly at their commander, Jan, and added, "That's an order, by the way."

Although Jan's eyes were playfully defiant, the Aslan answered, "Yes, Your Highness."

The warriors seemed surprised and a touch wary that Tikran would approach them, their eyes darting over him furtively. The apparent leader of the group, a woman with riotous black curls around a dark, tattooed face, dismounted and greeted him. "Greetings, Manzakar. We are here to show fealty to your king, the Freed Kingfisher."

Tikran raised his eyebrows. "Oh. Yes. Well, uh, I *am* the Freed Kingfisher."

Her eyes widened and she stepped forward, then bowed her head once and placed her hand over her heart. "King Tikran. I'm sorry. I didn't realize—"

"Don't apologize," Tikran said quickly. "I look like just another Manzakar. I guess I'm breaking tradition with the Anzori kings of old in that respect." He smiled. "And you are...?"

"I'm Puabi," she answered, gesturing to the warriors that surrounded her. "I am in command of half the Sachin clans' warriors, under Bruneta."

"Where is Bruneta?" Tikran asked.

"Last we heard, she was with a company of Manzakars in eastern Gohar, trying to convince the Davlat to side with you," Puabi said.

His heart dropped to his feet. "The Davlat... What do you mean?"

Puabi exchanged puzzled glances with another warrior. "The rumor was that the Davlat had decided to take up arms with Dilovar against you. Bruneta went with the Manzakars to try and convince Chief Marbek to fight with you."

"And?" Tikran held his breath.

She shook her head. "I don't know what's come of it. I was tasked with overseeing western Gohar. Beg Ayym will likely have more information, though." She tilted her head at him. "Do you really not know any of this?"

"No," he said, tightening his jaw. "I don't." From his communications with Bruneta in the past, Tikran knew that Ayym had set up a large encampment near Eter, which was still at least a week's worth of travel away. "What do you know about Dilovar? How far into Gohar have they come?"

Puabi said, "I can't be certain, but we think they've advanced about three garrison towns east of Eter and gone as far south as Faiz."

Holy shit. The Dilovari had taken much of eastern Gohar, and almost all the Damla River. "Is there anything else you can tell me?"

Again, Puabi exchanged looks with her fellow warriors. She hesitated before saying, "There was a confrontation in eastern Gohar, between the two captains of your Manzakar company, who were accompanied by our Sachin warriors, and your exiled prince. He attacked them." She licked her lips, meeting his eyes uneasily. "Fourteen of our warriors died. One of the Manzakars was wounded."

Tikran's hand curled convulsively around the hilt of his saber, his pulse suddenly racing. "You said Bruneta is still with them?"

"I haven't been back to Beg Ayym's encampment in about a week, King Tikran," Puabi said apologetically. "But last I was there, Bruneta returned for just a day before heading back to Davlat territory with two hundred of our warriors."

"How long ago was this?"

"About two weeks ago," Puabi answered.

"And you're certain the Manzakars survived?" he asked, trying not to let his emotions show in his voice.

Puabi looked at him shrewdly. He could tell she missed nothing. "So far as Bruneta wasn't lying—and Bruneta is almost completely incapable of lying—I am certain."

Like sister, like brother. He closed his eyes briefly, feeling a modicum of relief, then reopened them to see several concerned warriors staring at him. He willed the frown from his face and said, "Captain Puabi. Join me and my Manzakars for supper. It would be an honor to have you dine with us."

Puabi nodded, offering him a genuine smile. "We would be honored, Beg Tikran," she said.

Despite his current state of anxiety, he couldn't help but smile back. *She called me Beg.* He said, "Please invite the clans in the area while we finish setting up camp. We'll eat before sundown."

The Sachin rode off to fetch their clansmen while Tikran headed down to the garrison town, where Naran had ordered camp be made around its walls. Ukin's fort commander greeted Tikran with all the obsequiousness he hated, and he found himself being short with the fellow. He said impatiently, "I need a message sent back to Anzor immediately. I want to write it myself."

The young commander nodded. "Of course, Your Highness." He granted Tikran the privacy of his office in the fort, where Tikran scribbled a succinct note to Haydar:

Vazha.

Haydar would implicitly understand and investigate it, if he hadn't already. Tikran was confident that the message would reach Haydar, since they'd conducted a stringent vetting and tagging of royal messenger pigeons in the wake of Prem's deception. If Vazha had the support of a couple Anzori lords in addition to Prem, then he was likely feeling bold. But even so, attacking his Manzakars was a stupid move...unless the prince had something else up his sleeve. After ensuring the bird was on its way, Tikran turned to the fort's commander, intent on making the man squirm. "Do you know how far into Gohar the Dilovari have gotten?"

"The last I heard was that they were a quarter down the Damla River, Your Highness," the commander said, clearly taking himself very seriously.

"A quarter down the Damla, eh?" Tikran felt a rage building inside him. "Commander, do you bother to speak to the nomads who travel through and around your town?"

The commander's eyes darted about nervously. "Eh, no, I have enough Anzori scouts who can tell me—"

"Let me get this straight," Tikran said, his voice low. "The Gohari have spent centuries on this land. They know it like the backs of their hands. They've become a part of it. But instead of speaking to the nomads—many of whom are warriors and watching over this very fort, attempting to protect it—you rely on Anzori scouts instead?"

"But Your Highness," the young commander blurted, "we have little reason to trust these—"

Naran's harsh laughter suddenly rang out. "My man," he said, his voice suddenly fierce, "I'd shut my mouth right about now if I were you. You're about to get yourself on the king's—and his commander-in-chief's—bad sides *real* fast."

"Not to mention, his head mage's," Tikran heard Tanith say calmly from behind him.

A warmth enveloped Tikran, filling him with a strength he needed at that very moment. He glared sternly at the commander and said, "I've invited several of the surrounding clans to dine with me. I want you to make them feel welcome while Naran and I inspect the troops. Mistress Tanith will keep an eye on you. We'll be back in time for supper."

TIKRAN TRIED to visit every one of his Anzori lords' squadrons, words of encouragement on his lips. Naran helped immensely; the soldiers loved the big guy. Tikran knew his own efforts made a difference. Still, he had limits, and Naran made up for them.

He spent extra time with Prem's men, trying to make eye contact with each of them. *Say something that makes you human with every interaction*, Haydar had said. Tikran had thought on this during many sleepless nights. Now, he looked at their anxious, wary faces and, as though he was speaking to Tanith, or Naran, or Coxani, said, "I've been in battle—one I thought I'd lost before it even started." He met as many watchful eyes as he could. "I'm not Delger. I won't send you to fight for me while I sit safely in my castle. I'm fighting with you, every step of the way. We Manzakars are one."

He cringed inwardly. *We Manzakars are one? Good grief, Tikran.*

To his surprise, he saw their faces soften almost imperceptibly. Even the squadron commander, a man no doubt hand-picked by Prem, seemed a tiny bit affected by his words.

As they walked back to the fort, Naran muttered, "We Manza-kars are one? Really?"

"Shut up," Tikran muttered back. "You try and be king for a day, asshole."

Naran laughed from deep in his chest and said, "No, thank you. Watching you makes me want to stay as far away from that job as I can."

Tikran opened his mouth to fire back a witty reply when he saw the crowd within the town's gates. He had asked the warriors to invite all the nearby clans to dine with him and, to his surprise, they all came. Over a hundred nomads stood within Ukin's square, awaiting him, some sitting around several cooking fires. They bowed their heads and touched their hearts as he greeted him, and his throat closed with emotion as he reciprocated the gesture. He wasn't sure if it was the appropriate response, but he was deter-mined to show them that he honored each of them as they honored him.

Where had all this goodwill come from? Had Coxani and Moti done this? There was no other explanation. He hadn't stepped foot in Gohar since before becoming king, and he knew the nomads had become more ambivalent in their sentiments toward him over the course of his reign. Had he actually received Coxani's messages, he would have known that he'd fallen out of favor with the largest tribe—and the one whose lands were closest to Dilovar.

"She must have fed every one of them," Naran muttered, his eyes shining.

Tikran agreed. But she must have done more than just that. *What did you do, Coxani?* Visions of her loosing her arrows against Vazha's men made him both proud and fearful. *Please be okay, Dolphin. Without you, all is lost.*

As everyone ate around the fires, Tikran walked about, greeting all the head clansmen and elders, smiling and waving at the chil-dren. He even tossed back some Gohari beverage that he could have *sworn* was horse's blood and laughed with the warriors. Several of the young men and women handed him a bead from their hair, and soon he had quite the collection of beads tucked in his pockets. While he had no idea what they meant, he felt the gesture must have indicated approval of him in some way and he accepted them with the utmost gratitude.

Finally deciding he was hungry as well, he sat between Puabi and a clan elder on a bench near the largest campfire. As bowls full of lamb and vegetable stew were set before him by Gohari hands, Tikran felt a deep shame. He deserved the food no more than anyone else. And yet, he was treated like a god by people who, until recently, were starving. "No," he heard himself say, "one bowl is more than enough. Give the rest to an uncle, a cousin, a sister, a mother. Don't give it to me. I will be fed and fed well, whether I like it or not."

Puabi glanced over at him as she ate, a contemplative look on her face. "You're a lot like Bruneta."

He turned toward her. "Well, she is my sister."

"I know." She set her bowl down. "But it's more than a physical likeness. Your hearts beat to the same rhythm."

He looked at her inquisitively. "And what rhythm is that?"

"Archil's rhythm," she answered.

His eyebrows rose playfully. "Did Archil have rhythm? I had no idea."

Puabi let out a laugh. "I have no idea if they were a dancer, if that's what you're suggesting." She became earnest. "I mean a rhythm of the heart. They made it their mission to help those in need, even at their own expense."

Tikran's smile faded. "I am honored to be compared to them, then."

She had a look in her eyes that made him wonder what she was thinking; there was something in it that nearly made him squirm. Puabi then unwove a purple bead from her curls and held it out to him, placing it in the palm he slowly offered her. She lowered her lashes briefly, some color in her cheeks, before saying, "Your Manzakar captains," she added. "The ones with Bruneta. They, also, have Archil's rhythm."

Before Tikran could answer or ask what the beads were about, his fingers curling around the one she had given him, the elder on his other side spoke. "King Tikran, I am Beg Amina. We are blessed to have you here, fighting for our people."

Turning to look at the bald, doe-eyed woman who sat shrouded in a fringed cloak, Tikran said, "I am the one who is blessed to be fighting for your people, Beg Amina."

The elder smiled at him from within her cloak, almost timidly. "The ones you sent before you. They did good. They made the Sachin believe in the Freed Kingfisher." She considered, looking about her. "Most of them don't call you the 'Freed Kingfisher' yet. But they will. Once they've seen you fight for them as the king of Anzor."

Tikran swallowed. "I will do my best, Beg."

"I know you will." She smiled, her old eyes focusing on something beyond Tikran. "It's good to see Tanith again. Our clans often traveled together when she was growing up."

It hadn't even occurred to Tikran that Tanith was returning to her tribe for the first time in many months, and as head mage of Anzor, no less. He quickly glanced back at her, where she chatted with several warriors, her face animated in a way he'd only seen privately. He said, "I can tell she's happy to be back."

"Like most Gohari, she's had a hard life," Amina said. "I think her relationship with Ayym is what gave her the strength to keep fighting."

Tikran blinked. "Relationship with Beg Ayym?"

The elder giggled softly. "Indeed! A great love affair, the two of them."

Oh. Well, that's...unexpected. He cleared his throat and changed the direction of the conversation. "She told me she commanded warriors," he said. "I've seen her shoot, she's exceptional."

"Yes, a most skilled warrior. She was always very brave," Amina said. "I'm not surprised that she chose to come back and fight alongside you, even in her condition."

He looked at the elder quizzically. "Condition?"

Amina frowned at him. "Do you not see?" Tikran stared blankly, and she hesitated before saying, "She is with child, King Tikran."

The old woman may as well have smacked Tikran upside the head—hard. He stared, mouth agape for a second, then let out an uneasy laugh. "What? No. I think you're mistaken, Beg... She's just been...eating really well."

"I have served as midwife a multitude of times in my life. I know a pregnant woman when I see one." The elder peered at him, her clear brown eyes missing nothing.

He again looked at Tanith, his entire body tingling with shock. Was it possible? He'd noticed that she'd filled out, and her new curves aroused him as much—if not more—than before. He'd simply assumed it was because she was eating properly for the first time in her life. But now that he thought about it, she'd been unusually bashful with him recently, insisting on darkness and hiding under blankets during moments of intimacy... Weight gain would certainly not cause her to behave that way. In fact, the Gohari celebrated plumpness, for obvious reasons.

Amina rested her hand on his and smiled kindly. "You have no need to worry, Freed Kingfisher."

He squelched his rising panic and tried to smile back. "Ah...I think I very much do, Beg."

She sighed deeply. "The baby is yours, then?"

Fuck. This is humiliating. "Yes." Heat crept up his neck and to his ears. "I had no idea..."

The elder's wide eyes glistened at him. "Pregnancy has never stopped a Gohari warrior. And Tanith's Essence is very powerful. All is as it should be."

He turned his hand under hers so that their palms met and squeezed her fingers gently. "Thank you, Beg Amina." He changed the subject again, asking her about Gohari rugs, the herds of horses that had returned to the steppe, how often it rained these days...anything to distract himself from the fact that, not only had he managed to get yet *another* woman pregnant, but she, like

Coxani, had chosen to hide it from him. And now, he'd unwittingly brought her and her unborn child with him *to war*.

BY THE TIME the nomads left, Tikran was seething.

Angry energy bubbled within him, his body aching for violent movement. He was mad at himself, mad at Tanith, mad at the entire situation. As night fell, he discussed the next day's plans with his commanders and headed straight to the modest training grounds within the fort's walls. Nodding briskly to the soldiers who greeted him, Tikran shed his jacket, drew his saber, and immediately began hacking furiously at a straw-filled dummy. When it was nothing but a pile of shredded straw, cloth, and splintered wood, he moved to the next one. After thoroughly demolishing no fewer than five of them, he calmly snatched up his jacket and walked out, muttering, "Sorry about the dummies," to the stunned spectators. "I'll have my men clean up the mess."

He headed back to his tent, where he unbuckled and dropped his sword belt, yanked off his boots, and fell to his bedroll with a groan of exhaustion. He'd be able to deal with everything better after a solid few hours of—

Light filtered into his tent as someone entered, slipping past the flaps noiselessly. He didn't have to look to know it was Tanith, since no one else would be able to get past his Aslans without so much as a conversation. He rolled to his side and away from her as she lay down behind him and began kneading his shoulders and back with her strong hands. *Fuck, that feels good.* Fighting against his body's desire to melt beneath her touch, he braced himself and said, "What do you want, Tanith?"

Her hand slid sensuously down between his shoulder blades and around his waist, settling on his crotch. "You, Your Highness," she said, her voice sultrier than he'd ever heard it.

Returning to Gohar had definitely had an effect on her. If only she hadn't kept secrets from him, he'd be absolutely thrilled by her current mood. *But she did keep secrets from me…important ones.* He pushed her hand away and turned to face her, his ire rushing back. His voice was gruffer than he intended. "Do you have something to tell me?"

Her eyes went wide with surprise, her hands suspended in midair. "Tell you?"

He flashed her a dangerous look and sat up. "Yes." He looked pointedly at her belly.

She pushed herself up slowly, her lips pursed anxiously. After a moment, she said, "I couldn't tell you. You wouldn't have let me come."

His anger swelled. "I would have liked to have had a choice in the matter. But now you're here, about to go head-to-head with the most powerful mage on the Continent—with a baby in your belly." He raked his hands through his hair. "What were you thinking?"

Her brow furrowed. "You don't know that he's more powerful than I am. And having a baby in my belly makes me no less powerful."

"Holy shit, Tanith." Tikran stared at her in disbelief. "Are you making this a competition? This is war. And you're pregnant!"

Tanith froze for a moment, studying his face. "You're worried about the baby, aren't you?"

"I'm worried about *you*," he snapped.

She looked at him as if seeing him for the first time. "Is the Freed Kingfisher feeling…paternal?"

Tikran closed his eyes. "Every life lost on that battlefield against Delger haunts me, Tanith. I look at the men around me now and know many of them won't make it back. They will haunt me too." He opened his eyes. "Please don't make me feel guilty for worrying that I've put just one more life in danger."

She lifted her chin coolly. "I won't. But you can't make me feel guilty for doing what I had to do. Without me, likely twice as many lives would be lost in your name." Her pale blue eyes were like steel. "Your army needs me, Tikran. I had to ensure I'd be at your side to prevent as much of it as I can."

Her words gave him pause. Of course, he'd long known his army was doomed without her. Still, a part of him refused to be mollified. His rage simmered in his gut, spurning reason. He didn't understand why until the words tumbled out of his mouth: "And Ayym? Your 'great love affair'? How does she play into all of this?"

Tanith visibly paled, her eyes wide. "Who told you—"

"An old lady sitting next to me at dinner!" Tikran leaped to his feet. "So I've spent the whole night agonizing over the fact that you hid your pregnancy from me and wondering if you're just...*using* me."

Tanith stood, wringing her hands. "Using you? Tikran—"

"Maybe I misjudged you," he said, his voice low. "I was blinded by the fact that you knew my mother, that you tried to help her." His breath came quickly. "I failed to see your ambition, didn't I? Did you come to Anzor intending to seduce me?"

Her hands were at her side now, clenched into fists. "I did nothing to seduce you, and you know it. In fact, *you* seduced *me*."

She's not wrong. "I don't know what to believe anymore," he said, suddenly feeling more sad than angry. "I will tell you that, king or not, I have no intention to marry. So if you thought getting pregnant would earn you the queenship of Anzor..."

Tanith's face reddened. "I swear to you, Tikran, I didn't intend to get pregnant. And I did not go to Anzor intending to seduce you, far from it." She swallowed. "I admit that I was determined to become one of your mages. Ayym and I wanted to see Gohar achieve independence, and we believed I could facilitate that in some way. I knew I was older than you and thought I could serve as a positive influence. I figured my relationship to your mother would help. But my attraction to you...caught me completely off guard." Her eyes were beseeching. "And I certainly didn't plan on falling in love with you. But it happened nonetheless."

Tikran realized he was holding his breath. While he hesitated to trust her, something in him sensed she spoke truthfully. His voice was husky. "I need time to digest all of this. Alone."

She nodded slowly, her expression falling. Before walking out of the tent, her hand poised at the flap, she said, "Regardless of what happens between us, we ultimately want the same thing. I will do everything in my power to help you win this war, Freed Kingfisher."

After she left, Tikran lay back down on his bedroll, feeling drained and bewildered, wondering what sorts of nightmares awaited him tonight. Despite his inner turmoil, he was asleep within minutes.

CHAPTER 32

eg Zolto sits before the fire, his arms outstretched, the edge of the scapula he holds in his hands shimmering in the flames. He looks up, sees Berk, and smiles, motioning to him. "Come, great-grandson. Come read the bones with me."

Berk smiles and hurries over, sitting beside the elder excitedly. "Beg Zolto, I have so much to tell you! You were right about my Essence. I'm more powerful than anyone could have ever guessed."

Zolto nods and continues to smile as he twists the scapula from side to side. "And you will save Gohar with your great power, Berk. I know you will."

Berk sits beside the elder, scooting close. "Beg Zolto, I missed you so much."

Zolto continues to smile and nod, glancing at Berk with his dark, penetrating eyes. "I missed you too, boy. But I knew you were saving Gohar."

Berk sits up. "I was."

"Tell me." Zolto's gaze returns to the scapula between his hands. "How have you saved Gohar?"

Berk's nostrils flare, anger spiking within him. "I killed Manza-kars. So many of them."

Beg Zolto doesn't look at him. Still twisting the bone in the fire, he says, "Was killing the Manzakars as satisfying as you'd hoped?"

"I can't remember," Berk says, frowning.

In the distance, armored men approach on foot, emerging from a dense fog and trudging slowly. Hundreds of them. Berk stands as he's able to make out the dented, damaged Manzakar armor. The limping, wounded men have blackened faces and blood trickling from their eyes, noses, and mouths; from beneath their tunics and their clasped arms.

No. I must stop them. He glances at Zolto and says, "Stand back, Beg."

Zolto merely stares, his lips moving wordlessly, as Berk releases his Essence. It seeps into the Manzakars' wounds as a cacophony of pain echoes in the air. They vanish before his eyes, transformed from ghostly apparitions to nothing but fog. Berk turns, a victorious smile on his lips, to find the old man peering at him in consternation, still holding the scapula to the fire. Zolto speaks in that gravelly voice of his. "You are the hero who kills the Manzakars. Is it everything you wanted?"

Before Berk can answer, the flames enveloping the bone darken to a deep purple-black, dissolving it to ash within the elder's grasp. As the cinders trickle between Zolto's gnarled fingers, his hands flush bright red, swelling and darkening...

Berk screams in terror, trying to draw back his Essence, but to no avail. The magic, pervasive and deliberate, creeps through Zolto's arms and to his shoulders, snaking down his torso and up his throat in a wave of swelling, purpling skin. As Zolto crumples to the ground, his eyes wide with shock in a bruised face, blood flowing from his nose and mouth, he manages to utter between gurgling chokes, "Betrayal..."

BERK FELT the bed shaking before he heard himself screaming. "No! No! Beg Zolto, No!"

A pair of hands grasped him by the shoulders and he heard Vazha say, "Berk, wake up. You're having a nightmare."

Sitting up abruptly, Berk realized he couldn't breathe. More than that, he couldn't stop his heart's frantic pounding. Unable to make sense of what was happening to him, his attempts to use his Essence to draw air into his lungs failed. *I think I'm dying.* Sweat beaded from every pore and his stomach threatened to expel its contents as he tried to stand, stumbling frantically toward the door. "Damir," he managed between gasps. "I need Damir."

"Berk," Vazha said fiercely, standing. "I forbid you from going to Damir. Do you hear me? I *forbid* you."

Berk's vision blurred as he swayed, convinced he would disintegrate on the spot if he didn't move. *Fuck you, Vazha.* Berk flung the door open and stumbled down the corridor, somehow remembering which room was Damir's. With the floor trembling beneath his feet, Berk made it to Damir's door and threw it open. "Damir," he uttered in the dark, nearly falling on his face. "I'm dying. I need help!"

Damir sprang from his bed, blinking, finally focusing on Berk. Without hesitation, he strode forward and wrapped an arm around Berk's waist. The head mage guided him to the bed and commanded he lie down. Berk obeyed, gasping wildly, his vision shimmering. Calmly, Damir sat beside him and placed a palm on Berk's chest as the other hand moved, suspended, pushing air into his lungs. The hand on Berk's chest grew icy cold and the sensation jarred Berk, grounding him. As Damir moved his frigid hand to Berk's neck and forehead in turn, the nausea began to abate and his vision returned.

Berk's breathing slowed and the floorboards stopped creaking balefully. Damir asked softly, "How do you feel now?"

Berk nodded slightly, realizing both his hands were wrapped around Damir's. He released his grip, swallowing. "How did you stop me from dying?"

Damir shook his head and pulled his hand away. "You weren't dying. You were having a panic attack."

"A what?"

Tilting his head curiously, Damir asked, "Did you have a nightmare?"

"Yes." Berk closed his eyes, grimacing. "It was awful. I don't want to think about it."

"That's likely what triggered it, then."

"I've never had a panic attack before, I don't think," Berk said.

Damir looked away uncomfortably. "War will do that to you."

Berk heard Damir's unspoken words: *Especially what happened at Zifa.* The young mage had no recollection of what he'd done during the battle beyond setting the archers atop the fort's walls on fire. Everything that happened after was a blank. His memory resumed when he found himself lying on a pallet back in the fort, men shouting and scrambling around him. He'd seen the twisted, ghastly bodies lying in the field from a distance and was unable to believe he had committed such a horrific atrocity. Vazha had lavished him with praise and, while the commanders had thanked him for handing them a victory, they were clearly afraid of him...maybe even repulsed by him. As for Damir, Berk hadn't spoken to his mentor at all since the battle—until now. Berk sat up, desperate to avoid the subject of Zifa. "Do you have panic attacks?"

Damir stood. "Yes. More often than I care to admit."

Looking toward the door, a feeling of dread rushed through Berk. While Vazha had been keeping his hands to himself, Berk sensed the prince's mounting impatience. Every night brought fear, leaving Berk wide awake until he was certain Vazha slept. And now that Berk had blatantly disobeyed him... "Master Damir," Berk blurted, "may I sleep with you tonight? I don't want to go back..."

Drawing in a slow, deep breath, Damir answered softly, "Yes, Berk. Of course."

Obviously, this was not Damir's suite in Ogedei's palace. This was an Anzori fort in eastern Gohar, and the room was small, with a single bed. And Berk was fully aware that he was sleeping in very close quarters with yet another grown man. But this man... This man, he realized, he trusted implicitly. Yes, Damir had lied to him about the Manzakars. But for some reason, Berk still turned to him before anyone else, intuiting that Damir wouldn't abuse or take advantage of him. *Even after everything I've done.*

As Berk curled up against Damir desperately, his torso pressed against his mentor's arm, he knew he was safe. He knew it in his heart.

Tʜᴇ ʙᴏʏ ᴡᴀs ᴄᴏɪʟᴇᴅ ᴛɪɢʜᴛʟʏ against him, hot, sticky skin against his.

Damir resisted the urge to squirm away from his sweaty, traumatized apprentice. *Don't be an asshole. The boy needs you.* He turned to face Berk and called his Essence again, placing slightly chilled fingers against the boy's chest. Berk let out a sigh of relief and his eyelids drooped.

"Sleep, lad," Damir murmured softly. "You're safe now."

Berk finally let out a gentle, rhythmic snore, and Damir released his breath. After the events of Zifa, Berk apparently hadn't been able to recall much of what had transpired on the battlefield, which had shaken Damir to no end. Was this a protective mechanism of the boy's brain, or an effect of the Essence? If the latter, then there was likely no hope of preventing Berk from repeating the devastation he'd wreaked on Coxani's Manzakars.

Oh, Cenk. Coxani. The Manzakars. The images were permanently seared into his mind—the men falling, screaming, going from vigorous soldiers to blackened husks, drained of blood... Damir wrapped his arms around himself, shivering. Every time he closed his eyes, he saw Tikran, his angry, flashing eyes, his strong body wounded and falling... *No. No. Stop!* Damir nearly gasped, willfully jerking away from his rampant thoughts.

Stop. Breathe.

Feeling once again present and in control, Damir exhaled slowly.

Berk. You were thinking about Berk.

Damir blinked, refocusing.

Now, Berk was having nightmares and panic attacks, which Damir saw as a good sign. Relatively speaking, of course. Nightmares and panic attacks, on their own, were never a good thing. But when it came to Berk, they could be what swayed him from Vazha's side. And Damir was certain—Berk was no Vazha. The boy had a conscience and a desire to do good. *If he can remember the horror, then he'll be less likely to do it again.*

At least, that's what Damir desperately hoped.

Ever so carefully, he turned away from the young mage, wishing the bed was bigger. Curled into a small corner of the mattress to avoid Berk's hormonal, impossible heat, Damir lay awake most of the night, planning. Sleep, after all, held no escape for him. It only held nightmares.

Berk had left Vazha and come to the head mage in his time of need. *He must still trust me.* Damir had to find a way to convince the boy to remain under his tutelage and learn to control his Essence—before it was too late. But that only solved a fraction of Damir's dilemma. The larger problem remained: Even with Berk's cooperation, how in Cenk's name was Damir going to teach Berk to control something so unbelievably powerful?

When morning broke, Damir opened his eyes as if he'd slept only momentarily. He was still in the exact same position, teetering on the edge of the mattress, as Berk lay sprawled spread-eagle across the bed, breathing noisily. After finishing his morning toilette, Damir hurried down to the kitchen to grab some freshly baked bread, yogurt, and a jug of orange juice, then headed back to his room. Berk was awake, perched on the edge of the bed, grasping his head between his hands and moaning.

"I have the worst headache. What keeps *happening* to me?" he whined, shoving his hair from his eyes. "Why can't I just be like other normal—"

"There's no point in agonizing over something you can't change," Damir cut in firmly, handing Berk a full glass of juice. When Berk didn't move, Damir nudged him with his leg. "Drink and eat. You're no use to Dilovar or Gohar—or yourself—without sustenance."

Berk guzzled the orange juice then stared at the empty glass in contemplation as he turned it between his hands. When he finally looked at Damir again, the expression on the young mage's face was far beyond his sixteen years; there was a cynical twist to his mouth, a defeated glaze over his dark eyes. "Commander Amit told me I killed several Gohari warriors at Zifa. I killed them the same way I must have killed those Manzakars, using their blood to burst them from the inside." He grimaced. "Holy shit! Master Damir, I'm a monster."

The words struck Damir at his core. He'd spent his entire childhood and adolescence, as well as part of his adulthood, shrouded in despair, believing his very spirit was tainted. A part of him still believed it, deep down. *I'm a monster.* He sat beside Berk and was quiet for several moments, leaning his elbows on his knees. Finally, he said, "While my Essence isn't nearly as powerful as yours, I've done far more damage with it. The hundreds of lives I've intentionally taken, for better or worse, plague my nightmares." He tilted his head to look at his apprentice. "Very few people, if any, can relate to that feeling, the certainty that, when you were created, something must have gone wrong. You and I can, though. They call it a blessing, but we both know it often feels much more like a curse."

Berk nodded. "Yes. That's exactly how it feels." He peered at his mentor. "How do you keep it from driving you mad? Or from...letting it take over?"

Damir smiled without humor. "I would argue those things are one and the same. And...it's not easy. I came up with my own code of honor. I decided what I was willing to kill for, and the manner with which I would limit myself to causing death."

Berk's eyes were wide. "What are you willing to kill for?"

Damir's shoulders tensed. "To defend myself and those I love against harm. To protect the innocent. To fight for the greater good."

After a stretch of silence, Berk spoke. "You forgot something," he said, his face tight. "You forgot revenge."

Revenge.

Damir closed his eyes briefly. "I didn't forget." Reopening them, he said, "Revenge is a slippery slope, Berk. Using the Essence to kill, in any case, is dangerous for the both of us—what begins as painful becomes pleasurable, and the magic calls to us, tempting us to do more. In your case, I think it may be even more dire. At Zifa, the magic seemed to possess you." He locked eyes with Berk. "When you're no longer in control of your body or mind, when you've relinquished yourself to the magic out of spite and with malicious intent...that's when you truly become a monster."

The boy's jaw flexed. "I did what I did...because I had to."

Damir refused to relent. "Why? Why did you have to?"

Berk stood abruptly, fists clenched. "The day our clan was attacked by the Manzakars. By Anzor's king." He scowled at Damir. "My great-grandfather, Beg Zolto, read the bones. He said only one word: 'Betrayal.'"

Damir waited. When Berk added nothing more, clearly expecting a response, Damir said, "Is that it?"

"Master Damir," Berk said through his teeth, "are you serious? The Manzakars betrayed us. *King Tikran* betrayed us. He murdered my clan!"

Damir processed this quietly. After a moment, he said, "So let me be sure I understand. Your great-grandfather, the elder Beg Zolto, read the bones the day a squadron of Manzakars attacked your clan. The only thing he shared from his divination was a single word—betrayal." He looked at Berk. "Am I correct thus far?"

Berk rolled his eyes. "Yes."

"So you assumed," Damir continued, standing, "that King Tikran betrayed Gohar—specifically your clan—because they were attacked by Manzakars."

"Yes!" Berk's face was a peculiar shade of red.

Damir raised his hands. "I'm merely getting the facts straight. I want to understand, lad. That's all."

Berk breathed deeply before saying more calmly, "Yes."

"All right." Damir stood with his legs apart, his hands behind his back, his fingers twitching out of sight. "Has it ever occurred to you, Berk, that Zolto's utterance could have been referring to several other things?"

"Like what?" Berk asked gruffly.

Damir looked absently out one of the narrow lancet windows. "He could have been referencing the fact that several of Tikran's Anzori lords betrayed him."

Berk frowned. "How could you know that?"

Damir turned a pair of penetrating gray eyes on his apprentice. "That Vazha thinks he can win back the throne of Anzor is all the proof any of us need." He stepped closer, refusing to break eye contact. "But there are other possibilities. What if Zolto foresaw the Davlat tribe's betrayal of King Tikran? Or the Dilovari's betrayal of the truce with Anzor? All of these things directly impact the Gohari's right to exist, its right to freedom. All of these things are betrayals. How do you know Zolto didn't see these things, Berk?"

Berk had paled enough that Damir wondered if he should ease off his verbal assault. But the boy stood tall and unwavering, meeting Damir's gaze. There was a sudden strain in Berk's face, around his eyes and mouth. "I don't think Beg Zolto meant any of that, Master Damir."

"And why not? Tell me—"

A firm knock at the door stopped Damir mid-sentence. *Shit!* That was poor timing. Damir spun around and threw open the door, determined to tell whoever was on the other side to—

Vazha leaned casually against his cane, his eyes hooded with feigned disinterest. He smiled slightly at Damir. "Good morning, Doctor. I'm here to fetch my charge, if you don't mind." His smile broadened. "Or even if you do."

Of course.

"Prince Vazha," Damir said, his voice coming out steadier than he felt. He paused before turning back to look at Berk. "Perhaps you should ask my apprentice if he wishes to come with you? It's only appropriate for the young man to make his own decisions."

Vazha chuckled. "Everything is always a competition to you, Doctor." He pushed past the entrance and toward Berk, who still bore that strange expression, looking eerily beyond his years. "My boy, Berk," Vazha said. "Come, now. Your place is by my side. Together we will rid this world of King Tikran and his Manzakars." He shot a look at Damir over his shoulder. "By now you must realize that Master Damir is in love with the king of Anzor. It's why he defends him, why he is unable to fully fight for Dilovar." He smiled. "Isn't it, Damir?"

Refusing to be baited, Damir said, "I've been fighting for Dilovar with every ounce of my being since your worthless father was deposed, Your Highness." He smiled back. "So I would say you are incorrect."

Vazha snapped his head to look at Berk. "Well? Who will it be, boy?"

A tingle ran up Damir's spine as he realized Berk wasn't panicking. No, far from it. Berk was the picture of tranquility as he looked from Damir to Vazha. Finally, he said, "I will come with you, Your Highness."

No! Damir clenched his jaw.

Vazha grinned. "Good boy, Berk. Let's go and—"

"On the condition that I be able to continue my apprenticeship with Master Damir," Berk said firmly.

His smile fading, Vazha straightened, holding his cane between both hands, and said, "I can't imagine why you would want to do that. There can't possibly be anything he can teach you."

"But that's not true," Berk replied. "Master Damir has been teaching me how to control my Essence, how to be more exact with it. I need him to help me." He tilted his head, looking once again like the lost, desperate Gohari boy Damir had first seen the day Vazha had brought him to Bilguun's palace. "Please, Prince Vazha?"

Vazha refused to look at either of them, high color in his cheeks. "Two hours a day, after supper. That's it." He shot Damir a look. "That's all you get. Understood?"

"He's also been teaching me how to fight with a saber," Berk added. "It's such good exercise. Can we make it three hours, sir?"

Vazha let out a laugh. "Oh, really? Has the doctor learned how to wield a sword? How cute." He grinned insolently at Damir. "Fine. Three hours, because I care for my young mage's physical health as well."

"Thank you, sir," Berk said, sounding utterly sincere as he walked past Damir.

Vazha's cool blue eyes fixed on Damir's face. "Should I remind you of what's at stake if Dilovar loses this war, Doctor?"

"There's no need," Damir replied, mirroring the prince's aloof expression. "I'm King Bilguun's most loyal servant, in case you've forgotten."

"Oh, I haven't forgotten," Vazha said as he turned and began to follow Berk from the room. "Make sure you don't forget either."

As they left, a pit of fear balled in Damir's chest. What was Berk thinking? The boy certainly didn't enjoy the prince's company, that much was clear. Was he that afraid of Vazha? If so, what had Vazha done to him? The prince hadn't summoned Damir to his bed since arriving in Gohar, and the notion made Damir instantly queasy. *I swear, if he's molesting that boy...*

Damir's Essence gushed through his veins with a suddenness that blinded him for a split second. His hands ached with need as the magic pushed against him, seeking escape.

Berk's words rushed back: *You forgot revenge.*

Leaning against the wall, Damir breathed steadily and regained control with calming thoughts—the way the steppe's long grass rolled like golden waves in the ocean; sleeping beside

Enlil as the cat purred rhythmically; the smell of parchment that had been freshly inked. When the desire to destroy everything in sight finally abated, he ate the breakfast he had brought for Berk and headed down to the training grounds, where he waited for Commander Amit to finish inspecting his troops before approaching.

"Has there been any correspondence from Dilovar?" he asked.

Amit flashed a cocky smile. "Indeed! Our king is thrilled with the events of Zifa. We will all be rewarded in time, no doubt."

"No doubt," Damir echoed, a desperate sadness settling over him. War was bringing out the worst in those around him—their savagery, their desire to win at all costs—and he was frustrated with himself for expecting it to be different. He realized how unique his experience with Tikran had been, how vastly different the Manzakar-turned-king was from most men.

I always knew it. From the moment I laid eyes on him.

"What else may I do for you, Master Damir?" Amit lifted his chin, his gaze chilly.

Damir composed himself, ensuring his gaze was even chillier. "I will need two sabers this afternoon, for myself and my apprentice."

Amit chuckled. "Why don't you just stick to your magic, Damir? You're no warrior."

Damir's Essence flickered, making his hands twitch. "How many wars have you helped win, Commander? I forget..." He tapped his chin. "Oh, yes, that's right. None. You didn't even really do shit at Zifa, did you? Berk did pretty much everything." Damir smiled complacently at Amit's enraged scowl. "Anyway, about those sabers. Don't make me ask twice."

Amit's face changed color—a shade between purple and red. *I'm exceedingly good at making enemies.* He smiled, remembering Tikran's reaction to those words...what felt like forever ago.

Gratefully, that was the last Damir had to say to Amit at that moment. The commander obliged, a scowl on his face, and had his soldiers provide Damir with two sabers, helmets, and cuirasses, and several dummies. Finally alone, Damir set the second weapon aside, slipped into the armor, and, gripped the saber between his hands, fixing his gaze on a dummy.

No magic.

After the fifth swing, visions of Vazha flooded his mind and the burlap on the dummy began to singe and flames quickly crawled up the straw.

Shit! Damir relaxed his grip, closed his eyes, and sucked in his breath.

The fire expired with a fizz.

No magic!

Once again, Damir focused on the straw man's blank face, tightening his hold on the saber's hilt. *I can kill you without magic, Vazha, you piece of filth.* His Essence remained surprisingly quiet. He immediately began swinging at his target. With several swift thrusts and parries, the dummy was promptly a pile of refuse at his feet.

Stunned, Damir waited, panting.

Nothing.

He turned, somewhat tentatively, to the next dummy, almost feeling sorry for the awkward tilt of its stuffed head.

No magic. I can do this.

He hacked diagonally from the left, then from the right, then again. He continued until there was nothing left before him but shredded detritus. His hands tingled with suppressed need.

Holy Cenk! Had he really done it? Had he really expressed human rage without interference from his magic?

"Master Damir?"

Damir turned to see Berk watching him, a lopsided, quizzical smile on his face. "I've been looking for you. Can we train now?"

Standing straight, Damir let the sword relax in his hands. He blew an errant strand of hair from his eyes and said, "Yes."

Berk tilted his head. "Are you all right?"

Better than I've been in a long time. "Yes." Damir snatched up the second helmet and tossed it toward Berk. "Are you ready?"

Berk caught the helmet, teetering back. He frowned anxiously. "I think so?"

"Put on the cuirass and grab your weapon." Damir grinned. "Except for breathing, no magic. You hear me, Berk? *No magic.*"

Berk's expression became pained and he swallowed hard. "Yes, sir. I'll try."

CHAPTER 33

Tikran was a sullen bundle of nerves for the entire week of travel to Eter. He'd spoken to Tanith only in her official capacity as his head mage, avoiding any personal interactions. *I'm not ready.* He needed to focus on finding out exactly which Anzori forts had been taken by Dilovar and deciding what his next move would be. While he understood why Tanith had hidden her pregnancy from him, he was afraid for her and for the baby. And because he couldn't do anything about it—Tanith was essential to conquering the armies of Dilovar and its powerful head mage—his fear translated into anger...and guilt.

I should talk to her. I should comfort her. He ground his teeth together. Every time he thought he'd summoned the strength to approach her, he froze. He was too afraid of unraveling. *I'm the king of Anzor, headed to war against Dilovar.* This was, without question, no time to fall to pieces. Tanith, for her part, seemed unruffled, granting him the space he clearly needed. He found himself feeling grateful for her maturity and poise, which she maintained even in a time that must have been terrifying for her. *I will make it up to her. I promise.*

As the long train of troops, wagons, and carriages snaked through the endless steppe, Tikran watched a beautiful falcon dive headlong into grass with a screech. It emerged with a wiggling snake in its claws and soared away, disappearing into the sun. He tightened his grip on the reins, watching absently. Were the Davlat still on Bilguun's side? Were Coxani and Moti all right? One of them was injured. The Sachin warriors had reassured him that, even if Beg Marbek had chosen to remain allied with Dilovar, Coxani and Moti would be safe, if only out of respect for the Sachin. But doubt wormed its way into Tikran's mind. If the Davlat were in direct contact with the Dilovari, what would keep a malcontent warrior from turning the Manzakars in?

Dust rose in the distance, in the shrub-dotted valley between two rocky hills, and Tikran squinted. A rider, Gohari by the look of him, approached at a gallop, choosing to ride in the grass rather than use the paved Anzori road. Several Aslans blocked his path as he got closer, stopping him. After a brief discourse, they let him through and he trotted toward Tikran, breathless. "King Tikran. I was afraid I wouldn't make it in time. Beg Ayym is expecting you. She asks that you stop at her encampment before reaching Eter."

"Before?" Naran said aloud, echoing Tikran's thoughts. The commander-in-chief looked at his king. "That's not good." His brow furrowed. "I'm coming with you."

"No," Tikran said firmly. "You need to get this army to Eter."

"Then *I'm* going with you." Tikran heard Tanith's voice float over the jangle of harnesses. *Of course, she wants to go. She wants to see Ayym.* He swallowed his pride. Having her along was a wise move, either way. "All right." He looked at the Gohari scout. "How far up is the Sachin encampment?"

"Just a few miles," the nomad answered.

Tikran, Tanith, and only ten of Tikran's fifty Aslans (at Tikran's adamant insistence) parted ways with the Anzori forces and followed the Gohari northeastward for forty minutes, until they peaked a series of mesas to see Ayym's Sachin encampment sprawling beneath them. The white yarms alternated with camp-fires in concentric circles, encompassing Ayym's yarm at the center. A line of warriors awaited them as they descended, Ayym among them. The Sachin chieftain was, without question, a sight to behold. She wore a felt hat from which colorful beaded fringes hung, a sheepskin vest decorated with red-dyed horsehair, and breeches that were woven with intricate, geometric patterns. Her bare arms were brown and muscular, and her face was both masculine and feminine all at once, bearing an angular jaw, full mouth, and penetrating black eyes. He could, begrudgingly, understand how Tanith found Ayym attractive. *She's stunning.* The chief watched him with interest, her eyes not moving from his face.

The Manzakars stopped some fifteen feet away and Tikran dismounted, gesturing to his Aslans to remain where they were. Ayym dismounted as well and the pair stepped forward, facing each other. She was as tall—if not even a bit taller—than he was. As Ayym began bowing her head and touching her heart, Tikran immediately followed. She looked at him, laughter in her eyes. "Welcome, King Tikran. We are honored by your presence."

"I am honored by your commitment to fight by my side," Tikran answered, offering her a smile.

Ayym grinned back and narrowed her eyes. After a moment, she said, "They said you were instantly likable. I see now what they meant." She tilted her head, her headdress tinkling softly. "You have this boyish charm about you. It isn't cocky. It's careful, intelligent, confident, but still...vaguely child-like."

Tikran blinked, surprised. "I'm an open book, Beg Ayym," he replied.

She rubbed her chin. "I think you're craftier than you let on. But I like your duality." She dropped her hands to her sides and smiled coolly at Tanith. "Tanith. Good to see you. I see Anzor has been treating you well."

Tikran stifled a wince. Neither Tanith's voice nor her expression gave anything away. "It has, Beg Ayym."

Ayym turned. "Come. Join us for supper. We have much to discuss."

Tikran didn't look at Tanith as they followed Ayym through the wall of warriors and between the yarms, where nomads had gathered to gape at him, bowing their heads and touching their chests, their lips moving in some quiet, reverent greeting as he passed them. His throat tightened with emotion. Then he remembered Ayym's words. *Boyish charm...isn't cocky...still vaguely child-like.* He swallowed and straightened, trying to shake off whatever "child-like" aura Ayym was talking about. *I'm a warrior-king, for Cenk's sake.*

They sat about a great fire—Ayym and her top warriors, Tikran and his—as an ibex horn filled with a dark liquid was passed from mouth to mouth. Tikran took his turn without hesitation, as did his Aslans. *Definitely horse's blood...mixed with sheep's milk?* The aftertaste coated his tongue as he wondered if Coxani and Moti had endured the same ritual.

Coxani.

He looked at Ayym anxiously. "Your courier seemed to have an urgent message from you."

She met his gaze. "Yes. Let me first say that both your Manzakar captains, Coxani and Moti, are safe."

Tikran wanted to drop his head between his knees and gasp in relief. Instead, he closed his eyes tightly, took a deep breath, and opened them again to look at Ayym. She watched him with sympathy.

"Bruneta knew you'd be worried sick," Ayym said. "She asked me to tell you as soon as you arrived."

He swallowed. "Where is Bruneta?"

"She came here briefly then returned to Marbek's territory to be with your Manzakars," Ayym said.

Stiffening, Tikran said, "I'm sorry, Beg."

"The Dilovari have a Gohari boy with incredibly strong Essence," Ayym continued steadily, her expression firm. "Marbek, the idiot, gave him to your exiled prince, thinking the prince's men had helped save a clan from you."

"From me?" Tikran leaned in closer. "What—"

"Manzakars attacked a Davlat clan—the boy's clan—and the

Anzori prince apparently stopped them all from being killed," Ayym said, her face and voice still composed, despite her words.

"Wait. Wait." Tikran buried his fingers in his hair as he stared into the fire. "Manzakars attacked a Davlat clan. Prince Vazha stopped the attack. Marbek then gave Vazha a powerful Gohari mage...who now belongs to the Dilovari?"

Ayym nodded solemnly. "Yes."

"Why would the prince give the mage to Dilovar?" Tanith asked, frowning.

Tikran continued to stare at the dancing flames. "To defeat Anzor," he said flatly. "To defeat *me*. I already know that several Anzori lords are plotting to have me overthrown. It's likely that they support Vazha's claim to the throne. If I lose this war, I will be deposed and Vazha intends to replace me." He sat up and looked at Ayym, angry heat prickling his neck. "The order to attack the boy's clan did not come from me."

"We know," Ayym answered. "Every Gohari accepts this now. But they wouldn't have, if not for your captains. They heard what happened and, with Bruneta's warriors, headed to eastern Gohar to speak to Marbek, then Prince Vazha."

"And Vazha attacked them," Tikran said hollowly.

"Marbek came to help them, and because he was allied with the Dilovari, Vazha stopped his attack. Captain Moti was wounded, and Bruneta lost thirteen of her warriors."

"*Was* allied?" Tikran echoed. "Are you saying Marbek is no longer allied with Dilovar?"

"Not anymore," Ayym confirmed. "Your Coxani single-handedly changed that."

Of course she did. Tikran nearly let a laugh escape. "How?"

Ayym clearly debated on how to convey the next piece of information, pursing her lips, the beads of her headdress chiming softly. "Coxani is Archil's descendant."

Tanith gasped. Thunderstruck, Tikran didn't speak for several seconds. *What the fuck?* Finally, he managed, "I'm sorry, she's *who*?"

"She is Archil's only living descendant," Ayym said more firmly. "One of the Davlat elders made the connection. Marbek finally listened and abandoned the Dilovari for your cause."

Holy shit. He felt like a little boy, listening to his mother tell tales of fire-breathing dragons. He collected his thoughts. "This is good news. We—"

"King Tikran, there's more you need to know." A deep furrow appeared between Ayym's brows. Tikran held his breath as she said, "The young Gohari mage was brought to Gohar to capture the garrison town of Zifa. About a week ago, he completely crushed Coxani's forces, including many Gohari warriors who fought alongside her. I'm told his strength is insurmountable, like nothing any of our elders have ever even heard of. He used his magic to burst their innards, then drained them of their blood, their...*essence.* From what Bruneta told me, what remained were blackened husks, littering the battlefield."

"Sweet Archil," Tanith muttered, her face pale.

Tikran felt as though his heart had stopped. "But Coxani—"

"Coxani was untouched," Ayym confirmed. Her eyes grew sad. "Well, her body was untouched. Bruneta says her spirit suffers."

He couldn't decide if he wanted to jump up in outrage or curl up into a ball. Where had Damir been in all of this? Had he helped the boy? Had he *trained* the boy? Bile rose in his throat. He looked at Tanith. "We have no chance against something like that. Not one, but *two* powerful mages, one of which can...drain people of blood?"

Tanith's brow wrinkled in concentration. "I just need to understand how the boy did it. We could maybe prevent the circumstances that allowed him to do what he did."

Tikran battled the dread that welled up in chest. He needed to focus on what his next move would be and not let despair overtake him. It was probably safe to assume that the young mage was still in eastern Gohar, likely at Faiz or Zifa. *And there's only one of him.* He looked at Ayym, a question he'd been meaning to ask returning to the forefront of his mind. "Why did you stop us before we arrived at Eter?"

Ayym drank deeply of the ibex horn concoction before wiping her mouth and saying, "Coxani doesn't trust Eter's commander. Told us not to, either."

And what Archil's descendant says, goes... Tikran smiled grimly. "Smart move, Beg Ayym."

THE LONG GRASS rippled as Tikran galloped at full speed. He flipped an arrow from his quiver, nocked it, and pulled the silk bowstring taut to his cheekbone. As his horse became airborne, he loosed his arrow—then another, and another, and another—watching their dust as they struck the three running antelopes directly behind their front legs. As the animals tumbled in clouds of dirt, the herd leaped over them and swerved to the left. He heard Ayym trill at her warriors as he turned with the tide of running beasts, their tan pelts shimmering in the sunlight, and watched as Tanith loosed her arrows gracefully, taking down three more.

The nomads penned the herd against a long ridge of rocky, brown hills, and now the antelopes dropped in quick succession under the assault of the flying arrows. Ayym shouted harshly, and the shooting abruptly stopped. The nomads then parted, allowing the remaining animals to escape. The antelopes bounced lithely through the opening in the wall of human predators, flickering and vanishing in the grass.

Tikran tucked his bow back in its sheath, breathing deeply of the clean Gohari air, feeling more alive than he'd felt in weeks. He hopped from his horse and approached a felled antelope, reaching down to pull the arrows from its body, when Tanith stopped him.

Her hand rested on his sleeve as she said, "We must thank its spirit first, Tikran."

He realized abruptly that he remembered seeing his parents do this—had likely done it himself. How different it was, hunting with the Gohari, he marveled. The Anzori would have shot all the antelopes with relish, as if they were entitled to the animals' lives. "Yes, of course." He kneeled in the grass and rested one hand on his heart, the other on the animal's head. "Thank you," he murmured. He was startled when the rest of the words rushed to his lips: "Thank you for your life, being of this land, we honor you in death."

Tanith smiled her approval and helped him free the arrows of its carcass. He glanced at her quickly, almost shyly. Her belly had appeared to swell larger overnight, but it didn't seem to hinder her fluid movements on horseback or with a bow. "Pregnancy hasn't really slowed you down, has it?"

She brushed a strand of hair from her eye. "I told you it wouldn't."

He shook his head as he lifted the dead beast and carried it to his horse. "Not slowing down and battling two extremely dangerous mages are very different things." He dropped it on the back of his saddle and looked at her. "I feel so irresponsible—"

"It took two of us for this to happen," Tanith stated matter-of-factly. "It was irresponsible of the both of us. Frankly, in the back of my mind I believed I was either too malnourished or too old to get pregnant, and both notions were foolish." She sighed. "Please forgive me for keeping it from you."

He softened. "Only if you forgive me for getting so angry. You're right, after all—Anzor needs you to win this war, now more than ever." He hesitated, wanting to tell her that he missed her, but before he could say the words, Ayym joined them, an antelope in her arms. She cradled it as though it were merely sleeping, like a treasured pet.

"Thank you for joining us on this hunt, King Tikran," she said with a grin. "It's as though Gohar has offered up its bounty in honor of your presence."

"I only did what any decent Anzori king would do and allowed the Essence back into Gohar, where it belongs," Tikran answered.

Ayym's smile became mischievous. "There's that boyish charm

again." She glanced quickly at Tanith, then back at Tikran. "You two seem to suit each other."

No, we're not going there. Tikran cleared his throat. "Beg Ayym, we need to talk through our military strategy against Dilovar. I would like my senior commanders to come here from Eter to discuss, since we suspect that Commander Mamoun is aligned with my enemies."

Ayym's eyes brightened. "Yes. Have them come. It's tradition to have a feast after a successful hunt. We can eat well and talk war— two of my favorite activities."

"They sure are," Tanith murmured with a lopsided smile and shake of the head.

"Great," Tikran said quickly, sensing the clear attraction between the two women. "I'll send one of my Aslans immediately to fetch them."

By the time Commanders Naran, Tural, Shamil, and Faris arrived, the sun had set. Ayym's encampment was glowing by firelight and bustling with activity as the antelopes were roasted over large fires. Groups of chatting nomads washed and peeled carrots, onions, and various roots to make stew; warriors laid colorfully woven rugs all around the center of the encampment; children dressed in beaded tassels and eagle feathers laughed as they tossed sheep knucklebones within a circle, trying to hit a central piece.

Naran grinned at Tikran after greeting Beg Ayym. "Just in time for the party, eh? I wish I'd been able to join you on that hunt."

Tikran smiled distractedly, wondering how Naran would handle the news about Coxani. He instructed his commanders to sit with him and Ayym as they began to relay all that had transpired in Gohar since Coxani and Moti had arrived. Their eyes widened in shock at the revelation that Coxani was Archil's last descendant and had swayed the Davlat to their side, and they paled in horror at the news of Vazha and Berk. By the time the Anzori king and Gohari chief had finished telling them about the devastation at Zifa, the Manzakar commanders sat in stunned silence, unsure of what to say.

"Well," Naran finally said, his voice strained, "I'm ready for whatever strong booze you have on hand, Beg Ayym."

The men muttered their agreement and Ayym signaled to the nomads behind her. "We prepared a large amount of gol for this very purpose," she said.

"Gol?" Naran whispered to Tikran.

"I think it's fermented mare's milk mixed with its blood," Tikran answered with a smile. "You've got this."

Rather than a single ibex horn, however, each man received a full horn of his own. Ayym grinned at them, holding hers high. "Cheers, Manzakars. To victory or death!"

Naran drained his horn without hesitation, then wiped his mouth. "Beg Ayym, you've got my kind of grit. I like it."

Ayym smiled. "For the first time in the history of the Continent, Gohar has Anzor's armies on its side." She looked at Tikran. "I'm assuming you will head southeast to meet your captains and stop the advance of Dilovar's forces?"

Tikran leaned on his knees, his eyes on Ayym's face. "Not exactly."

"What do you mean, not exactly?" Naran's voice was soft but threatening. "Coxani—"

"Dilovar is fully expecting us to head in her direction," Tikran said firmly. "Beg Ayym, how are the Dilovari getting reinforcements?"

"My scouts tell me they're transporting most supplies and troops across the Damla," she answered.

Tikran pulled a map from his satchel and unfolded it on the rug. He pointed to Diyar, an Anzori fort that sat further north, at a bend along the Damla. "If I remember correctly, Diyar sits at a good elevation and offers the best view of the river. I'm guessing that the Dilovari aren't crossing the widest part of the Damla, which means Diyar is the perfect vantage point." He looked at Naran. "We recapture Diyar and cut off their reinforcements. The mages are likely still in the south, so we won't have to contend with them yet."

Naran scowled, his arms crossed on his chest. He looked at Ayym. "Do the Dilovari know that the Davlat have abandoned them?"

"I highly doubt it," Ayym said. "Marbek may be an idiot, but he's not *that* stupid."

"And even if he is, Coxani is not," Tikran added. "She would encourage him to keep up the ruse and feed the Dilovari bad information."

"But what if she needs us?" Naran grumbled.

"She has Bruneta and a good faction of my warriors," Ayym replied. "Not to mention, likely the fervent support and protection of the entire Davlat tribe. Being Archil's descendant is no small thing to us Gohari."

"It's a good plan, King Tikran," Tural said. "We'll likely be able to recapture a few forts along the Damla before the Dilovari figure out what's going on."

Tikran looked at Naran. "What do you think?"

Naran grunted his approval reluctantly. "Yeah, it's a good plan."

"Beg Ayym, can you send a messenger to Marbek's camp to relay our plans to Coxani?" Tikran asked.

Ayym nodded, looking satisfied. "Yes. And now that we are in agreement, it's time to eat!"

They moved back to the central fire to feast. Ayym had their horns refilled with the potent gol while antelope meat was cut and passed from person to person until everyone had a sizable portion. The Gohari mages, wearing their conical, patchwork hats of dangling beads, flared the fires in synchrony. The elders, their bald heads shining in the firelight, raised their linked hands and thanked the spirits of Gohar for providing such abundance. What followed was serious business for the Gohari: eating. Tikran couldn't help but smile at the joy and gratitude of the nomads as they savored their food, their faces flushed and eyes bright. Eventually, one of the nomads brought out a lute while another tucked a drum beneath her arm. The music was rousing and cheerful, and children danced around the musicians, laughing.

"What a difference from the last time we were in Gohar," Naran mused aloud, his face rosy from the copious amounts of gol he was consuming. Tikran guessed his friend must have been on his fifth horn. Before Tikran could answer, Naran's eyes bulged and he suddenly blurted, "Holy shit! Is Tanith *pregnant?*"

Tikran felt all surrounding eyes on him as heat crept up his neck. Luckily, Tanith was on the other side of the fire and closer to the musicians, so she was blissfully unaware of Naran's outburst. Tikran hissed, "Naran, could you lower your voice, please?"

Naran's jaw dropped open. "The baby is yours, isn't it?"

Tikran had half a mind to punch his commander-in-chief in the mouth to stop his blabbing. "Naran, shut your—"

"Let me get this straight," Naran interrupted. "You got your head mage pregnant? Before a *war?*" He burst out laughing. "Holy shit! Who can't keep it in his breeches now, smart guy?"

"Tanith can handle herself, pregnant or not," Ayym said as she approached, grinning widely. She sat down smoothly, her legs crossed, her horn full to the brim with gol.

Oh, great. The last thing Tikran wanted was to discuss Tanith's pregnancy with Naran and Ayym, of all people. His ears burned as he said, "I know she can." Desperate to change the subject, Tikran buried his hands in his pockets and brought out the beads, dumping two handfuls on the rug in front of him. "Beg Ayym, can you tell me why people keep giving me these?"

To Tikran's utter bemusement, Ayym threw back her head and laughed heartily, her gol sloshing out into her lap. "Oh, Archil! Tanith!" she cried, making Anzor's head mage look in their direction. "Looks like you have quite a bit of competition!"

Tanith stood and walked over, her eyebrows raised.

Ayym was still laughing. "Please tell the king of Anzor why he's been given all these beads, will you?"

Tanith's eyes widened and she giggled. "Well, Tikran…a single, colorful bead from one's hair is an invitation to have sex."

Oh. Tikran was certain that he went completely red. His mind flitted back over all their faces…young, old, women, men… *And I thought it was a respect thing. Good grief.*

"Just try not to get any more women pregnant, will ya?" Naran nudged Tikran roughly with his elbow and guffawed.

Tikran shrugged sheepishly and drained his horn with two swift swallows, deciding that being the butt of a joke was a small price to pay for a moment of laughter. He had no idea, after all, when the opportunity would arise again.

CHAPTER 34

The twelve Davlat mages surrounded Coxani at the top of the mesa, their beaded hats jingling as they chanted their spells quietly. Beside her, a fire blazed in explosive puffs, its flames reaching upward with each incantation. As the fire calmed, one of the mages approached, a horse's scapula in her hands. Without looking up, the beaded tassels obscuring her eyes, the mage held the fan-shaped bone out to Coxani.

Dressed in a long, green Gohari tunic that bore an intricate horn motif, Coxani took the bone and bowed her head. The beads made from Omid's ashes—as well as a few from the other warriors who died at Zifa—weighed down her curls and swayed with her every movement. She stepped forward and the mages parted, granting her access to the fire. Sighing deeply, she held the bone out into the flames. *Let's get this over with.* Coxani twisted the scapula from side to side, watching its edges blacken, her fingers nearly scalding from the intense heat. She blinked when a crack appeared beneath the charred edge, slowly creeping down and to the left. Coxani stood stock still, indifferent to the heat and mesmerized by the hesitant descent of the crack, when a hand patted her shoulder.

"That's good, Rasula. Pull it from the fire," a calm voice said in her ear.

Withdrawing the bone from the flames, Coxani turned and showed it to the elders, who now walked within the circle of mages, looking like owls with their dark eyes and feathered collars. They each reached out and traced the crack in turn, whispering to each other excitedly, seeing things Coxani could hardly guess. Their interpretations, however, must have pleased them, because they smiled, bowed, and touched their chests over their hearts in deference.

When they finally took the scapula from her hands, Coxani nearly slumped with relief. She had no idea what the bone had revealed, but if she was being completely honest, she hardly cared. She just wanted this to be over.

One of the mages held the fractured, singed bone high over her head, turning toward the crowd. An immense roar echoed over the crackling fire. She gazed out over an endless sea of faces that peered up from the base of the rocky hill, hearing hundreds of voices chant "Rasula."

One of the elders placed a hand on her arm and said, "The Gohari will follow you to the ends of the earth."

They've lost their minds. Panic tightened her chest and her legs twitched with the sudden urge to run away. Surely the ceremony was nearly over.

Marbek approached, a bracelet not unlike the one she wore for Tikran, between his fingers. "Give me your wrist, Rasula," he said. She obeyed and he wrapped the long leather string of blue beads and sheep knuckle bones around her wrist, just above Tikran's. "This binds the Davlat to you. You, Rasula, are a true warrior and Archil's last living descendant."

The elders huddled around her, their faces and hands lifted to the sky, and uttered a prayer. *May the spirits of our ancestors guide us...exist in the earth, the grass, the animals...align us with all living things...* Coxani felt like weeping. Did the Gohari feel the spirits around them? If so, why couldn't she feel them? If she was so special, why couldn't she feel her mother, her father, Mago, or Omid? Had they abandoned her? Was it because she was a fraud? Coxani pressed her trembling lips together. She was not one with all living things, nor was she with the dead. She merely existed— in pain. And yet, these people practically worshipped her.

No. Make them stop.

When the prayer was over and the rite clearly finished, she quickly made her way back down the hill, ignoring the sound of her name on so many lips, and headed toward the field beside the encampment where the warriors' horses grazed. Yanking her tunic up, she hopped on her roan gelding's back and coaxed it into a gallop desperately.

The weight of Gohar's expectations bore down on her, and she wanted to run and hide. With the wind in her face and the feel of her horse's sleek muscles moving beneath her, she could finally breathe. As she rode through the plains, her eyes on the endless horizon, Omid's last moments appeared before her eyes yet again, his blackened skin, shocked eyes, parted lips. She let out an agonized cry and pulled her gelding to a sudden stop, sliding from its back and crumpled to the ground.

The long grass tickled her face as she sobbed. *I can't do this!* "Coxani!"

She would have been furious that someone had followed her if she hadn't recognized Moti's voice. Wiping her tears, she waited for her Manzakar co-captain to find her huddled in the grass beside her horse, which he did quickly. After slowly slipping from his mount, he grunted as he sat next to her, his healing leg stretched out in front of him.

"Hey," he said casually, as though he'd been looking for company and accidentally happened upon her. "You okay?"

"No," she replied, surprised her voice didn't crack. "I'm defi-nitely not okay." She grimaced. "They said the Gohari would follow me to the ends of the earth. They're crazy."

Moti leaned back on his elbows. "Why are they crazy?"

"Are you serious?" She glared at him. "They're putting all their faith in me just because I happen to be related to someone who, by the way, caused all kinds of issues for the Gohari over two hundred years ago." She shook her head. "Not to mention, I just led more than three hundred warriors—both Manzakar and Gohari—to their horrible, gruesome deaths."

"That wasn't your fault," Moti said firmly.

"Moti," Coxani cried, "I saw what that boy could do. Damir warned me. I still let it happen."

He sat up. "Dilovar let it happen. Not you. You couldn't have done a single thing to stop it. You did what any of us—even Tikran —would have done."

She gazed down sadly at the two bracelets on her wrist. "Then I'm just unlucky. Everyone should stay away from me."

"Unlucky, eh?" Moti scratched his jaw. "The warriors who survived Zifa saw you stand amidst the dying, untouched by that kid's magic." He looked at her. "They think you've been blessed by divine powers."

"What? No." Her eyes were wide. "That was just..."

"Luck?" Moti ventured, raising an eyebrow. "Look, Coxani, I'm not religious." He raised a hand as if she were about to protest. "I know, I know, you're shocked. But hear me out. That kid—the same one that murdered our fellow Manzakars, the same one who killed Omid—saved my life. And I'm not pointing this out because it's *my* life. What I'm trying to say is...he's just a kid. He's not evil. Someone with that kind of power certainly has the potential to become evil. But he's not there, I don't think. Not yet."

"So what?" Coxani lifted her chin. "What would you do, in my place?"

Moti flashed that enchanting, crooked smile. "I'd figure out his weaknesses. He's from the Davlat, after all. I'm sure they know everything about him."

As Coxani contemplated Moti's words, she heard hoofbeats and her name. She sighed. "Why can't everyone just—"

"It's Bruneta," Moti said, struggling to stand. Coxani wrapped her arm around Moti and helped him get upright in time for

Bruneta to hop from her horse. She approached them with long strides, her eyes bright.

"A scout from Ayym's camp arrived with a message from Tikran," Bruneta said, breathless. "He made it to Eter."

Tikran! Coxani's heart leaped. He'd finally arrived. "What does he say?"

"He's heading to Diyar," Bruneta said. "He's hoping to cut off the Dilovari's reinforcements. He wants us to help the Davlat keep Dilovar off his scent for as long as we can." Bruneta smiled, holding out a small scrap of parchment to Coxani. "And this is for you."

Taking the note from Bruneta, Coxani unfolded it slowly, her breath bated. Tikran's small, messy script was smudged but legible: *Miss you terribly. Stay strong.*

Her throat closed for a moment, tears pricking her eyes. Without looking at Moti or Bruneta, she mounted her horse, the note gripped tightly in her fist. Gazing out over the steppe, she became aware of the sounds and smells around her—the cry of an eagle as it soared overhead, the chirp of the crickets nestled within the grass, the smell of the earth after several days without rain. She suddenly felt calm, an unexpected spring of courage welling within her.

Half to herself, she said, "Well, then. Let's do this."

***

WITH A NEAR-TOOTHLESS GRIN, Beg Zolto ushered Coxani into his small yarm, prodding her to sit amidst a pile of woven pillows as he brewed tea over a small central fire. The tea, called galak, was made with sheep's milk and tail fat, and it emanated a sweet, earthy aroma that filled the dwelling. As the elder crouched before the kettle, stirring the tea with a long spoon, he said, "I wondered what took you so long to come visit me."

Coxani resisted the urge to fold over herself defensively. Instead, she centered herself, pulling the truth from a deep wound.

She replied, "I've been overwhelmed, Beg. Overwhelmed and afraid."

Zolto nodded slowly as he filled a bowl with the fragrant, milky tea and passed it to her. His eyes were a luminous black within folds of wrinkled skin. "I know. It's been a lot for you, hasn't it?" He served himself and sat beside her with an ease she did not expect from someone his age, tucking his legs beneath him without sloshing his tea. Holding the bowl to his lips, he blew on the steaming liquid while peering at her. After taking a careful slurp, he set the bowl down on the rug in front of him. "You have questions for me, Rasula. Ask them."

Coxani took a sip of tea before saying, "Your great-grandson. Berk. You heard what he did to my Manzakars and several of the Sachin warriors at Zifa?"

"Yes." Sadness was etched on the old man's face. "A terrible tragedy." He paused, folding his hands in his lap, over his tunic of rough wool.

Coxani leaned toward the elder. "Beg Zolto, I don't want any harm to come to Berk. He's just a boy and he saved Moti's life. But your great-grandson is extremely dangerous. If he isn't stopped, he could destroy Tikran's army, and that would doom Gohar to another occupying force, one likely just as bad as Delger's Anzor."

Zolto remained calm. "You say nothing I don't already know, Rasula."

Relieved by his reaction, Coxani sat back, cupping the hot bowl of tea in her hands. "I don't know if there's anything I can really do to stop him, but I'd like to try. Can you tell me about him?"

Zolto gazed absently at the small, dwindling fire. "Berk was born early. So early we were certain he would die. He was the smallest, sickliest baby I had ever seen. But even with scant milk to feed him, he survived, to everyone's surprise. I then read the bones and discovered he had the Essence, but no one believed me. This scrawny little baby, no bigger than a rat? Even if it was true, it hardly seemed to matter—we Gohari had little use for the magic, since those who had it didn't even know how to summon it. It was better to forget he had it. The Manzakars, after all, would seek him out if they knew."

He brought the bowl steadily to his mouth again, sipped, and swallowed before continuing. "It was easy to forget. Berk grew to be an equally sickly child—he was born windless. He struggled to breathe even after the slightest activity. I was stunned when, at around ten years old, he came to me crying, afraid. He knew he had the Essence, he said. He was afraid the Manzakars would come for him. I became afraid too. For him to know he had it, the Essence had to be powerful in him. Luckily, he managed to escape detection for sixteen years."

Beg Zolto smiled. "But then the Caged Kingfisher changed everything. Berk had nothing to fear anymore. He could learn to use his Essence for Gohar. And he had just begun his training, when the Manzakars attacked our clan."

Leaning forward again, Coxani said, "They were not Tikran's Manzakars, Beg."

He patted her hand. "I know, Rasula. I know."

"Do you know who led them? One of the survivors said something about a man with a yellow beard who bought your rugs."

"Yes," Zolto confirmed. "He had come a month earlier and bought several rugs. The man was certainly Anzori. He paid us in food and livestock and promised to return. And he did return, this time with a squadron of Manzakars. He was not a Manzakar, but he seemed to oversee the attack. The commander answered to him."

Coxani was on edge. Even if the rug-loving visitor was Anzori, it still could have been any of the fair-haired, bearded lords. "There must be something else you can tell me about him."

"Yes. There is something else." Zolto frowned down into his lap, patting away at something only he saw. "Us elders are not immune to self-doubt, you know. And my eyesight isn't as good as it used to be. So forgive me for not trusting my eyes."

"Of course, Beg."

He looked up at her almost apologetically. "We all saw the

Anzori speak to the prince after he stopped the assault. But, to me, there was a brief moment when they seemed...friendly. Smiling. Even as my clan died before their eyes. Even as Berk screamed in agony, curled over his brother's mangled body."

Coxani wasn't breathing. She sucked in her breath suddenly, sharply. "Prince Vazha coordinated the attack on your clan."

Zolto looked away. "When the prince made it seem like he'd stopped the slaughter, there was nothing I could do to keep Berk from going with him. I tried, Rasula, I tried."

"Why didn't you tell Marbek—"

"I was overwhelmed," Zolto cut in, his voice loud and firm. "I was overwhelmed and afraid." His eye twitched. "Like you."

Coxani's brow cleared. She couldn't tell if the beg was being honest or trying to convey a lesson. Most likely, it was both. She said, "Would Berk follow the last descendant of Archil to the ends of the earth?"

Zolto lifted his cooled bowl of tea to his lips. Before drinking, he said, "The Berk I knew? Yes. Without question."

She considered this. "Do you have any descriptions of Archil? What they looked like, maybe what they wore?"

Zolto nodded and, with a satisfied *hmph*, rose slowly to his feet. He hobbled over to the far end of the yarm and unfolded a bundle of sheepskin that sat on top of what looked like an overturned wicker basket. Taking one of the horses' scapulae wrapped within the sheepskin, he shuffled back over to her. "This is the only drawing we have of Archil, but they are described the same way every time."

Coxani took the bone, curious. The etching was carefully done, depicting a tall figure draped in a loose robe with wide sleeves. A rope belt was tied about their slender waist and what looked like a spiked diadem was on their head. "Are they wearing a crown?" she asked.

Zolto chuckled. "It is very unlikely that Archil wore a crown during their lifetime. They were humble and refused to be venerated in any way. But human memory is weak and prone to fancy.

We like to believe Archil wore a crown that represented those who died on their account." Zolto's gnarled finger ran along each spike of the diadem. "Each prong held the beads of those lives lost."

Coxani looked at the elder, an idea slowly forming in her mind. "Do all Gohari recognize this image?"

"Oh, yes." Zolto took another sip of tea. "Most every Gohari has seen this drawing or heard the description at least once, somewhere."

After he'd set down his bowl, Coxani reached over and grabbed his hand, squeezing it. "Thank you, Beg Zolto. I promise you that I will do what I can to bring Berk back."

A strange expression passed over Volto's face as he replied, "He will not come back. But he can be saved. And you are not the only one who believes it, Rasula. The Dilovari mage believes it as well."

She swallowed. Memories of Damir on his knees, his fingers grasping his scalp as he slumped over the desiccated bodies of the Manzakars and Gohari warriors, ran through her mind. "Yes, Beg. I think you're right."

As Coxani left the elder's yarm, she wrapped her arms around her waist and shivered, despite the early summer heat. A young boy herded sheep in the distance, a mangy dog at his side. He saw her and stopped, placed his hand over his heart, and bowed his head while his dog barked after the sheep. Reciprocating the gesture, Coxani closed her eyes.

She had to send an urgent reply to Tikran.

She had a plan and no time to waste.

CHAPTER 35

Diyar sat atop a mesa, overlooking the Damla river. Unlike the other forts in Gohar, those along the Damla had been built mostly with stone imported from Anzor since, across the river, Dilovari forts of imposing masonry towered over the water, their tapered crowns lit with glowing fires.

Damir isn't far from here. The thought inexplicably sent a tremor of excitement through Tikran. Somehow, the gray-eyed mage still held sway over him, and it frustrated Tikran to no end. His heart refused to listen to reason. It didn't seem to matter how often he reminded himself that Damir had likely betrayed his trust, that Damir had probably helped Berk destroy Coxani's squadron...

He looked again at the fort, forcing his mind to return to the task at hand. Glancing back at the seemingly endless sea of blinking gilded helmets, Tikran met Naran's eyes. He raised a hand, palm up. *Ready?* Naran grinned in response, his teeth flashing white in his dark face. Tikran knew that cocky look so well. It said, *Piece of cake.* He remembered Naran's words the day before: "They're going to lose control of their bowels when they see three thousand Anzori troops and Gohari warriors headed straight for them."

Tikran turned back, smiling anxiously. He hoped Naran was

right. If Coxani had gotten his message, this whole takeover would be easy, with minimal loss of life. They had moved quickly from Eter, sparing as little time as possible for rest and repairs. Tikran knew the element of surprise was critical in this instance, and even though he trusted the Gohari implicitly, he worried that Dilovar had gotten word of his approach somehow. He looked at Tanith then, seeking reassurance that she, too, was ready for possible battle. She met his eyes coolly, a small, self-assured smile on her lips, her expression reminding him enough of Damir that he almost startled. He smiled back at her, feeling the strange desire to blow her a kiss.

He faced forward once again, his eyes focused on the keep up ahead. His commander-in-chief and head mage seemed confident that this re-capturing of Diyar would take little effort. So why was he fearful? His nightmares crept into his consciousness. He still had little faith in magic—while Anzor's mages, Tanith included, had made it appear tame and easily manipulated, it had been used to drain life in the grisliest way. Damir had implied, at least once, that he was afraid of himself. Could he and Tanith truly control their magic? Tikran filled his lungs with air and let it seep slowly from his nostrils. While he knew Damir and his young apprentice must still be a ways from Diyar, the thought of facing them both terrified him—and not because Tikran was afraid of dying. *Coxani. Naran. Tanith. The baby...*

His fingers went slightly numb around the reins.

My baby.

He blinked hard. It didn't matter whose baby it was. He had a responsibility to prevent the loss of any life he could for a war he engaged in. He drew his sword, raising it high for all his commanders to see. His commanders knew he wanted this over quickly and as noiselessly as possible. Truth was, he wanted the entire war over as quickly and noiselessly as possible. *Fat chance of that.*

By the time they were within shooting range of Diyar, Tikran knew the fort was theirs. The damage it had sustained from Dilovar's attack was still apparent in its crumbled embrasures, its half-rebuilt gate. His Manzakar archers loosed arrows over its battlements, waiting for a response. When none came, Tikran's eyes fixed on the orange Dilovari flag that flapped urgently in the wind, high above the south tower. He raised his saber once again; once again, Manzakar arrows soared through the air, landing within the fort's walls. Steadily, the Dilovari flag descended. Closing his eyes briefly, Tikran let out the breath he didn't realize he was holding. *Thank Cenk.* He opened his eyes. *No. Not Cenk.* Who could he thank now?

"Thank Archil!" Tanith cried, relief plain on her face.

Yes. Thank Archil.

Ayym, who rode at Tikran's side, cupped her hand around her mouth and let out a high-pitched trill of victory. The Sachin warriors behind her responded in kind.

A horse bumped into Tikran's as a hand slapped him hard on the back. "Told you, Freed Kingfisher!" Now beside him, Naran laughed. "They saw us coming and shat themselves."

Mildly annoyed with Naran's bravado, Tikran nodded. "This was the easy part. It only gets harder."

Having disarmed the two hundred Dilovari troops and secured control of the fort, Tikran stood on the battlements with Tanith, Naran, and Tural, looking over the Damla. He'd been right—they had the perfect view of the river and would be able to spot Dilovari ferries or barges for miles in either direction.

Tikran chewed the inside of his cheek. "This will keep them from crossing the river successfully. Once Bilguun gets wind of where we are, he and the rest of his army will be forced to use the Damla Bridge, to the north. That should give us enough time to make our way down south and stop the mage."

Naran cleared his throat. "There are two mages, Tik." His expression was grim. "And we know they're together."

Tikran stiffened. "They're both powerful. I want them alive, if possible."

Naran met his gaze. "And if it's not possible?"

"Then they die," Tikran snapped, feeling a sharp pang in his chest at the words. Why did he still care so much about Damir? Why wouldn't his heart listen to reason? *He's the enemy!*

"King Tikran," Ayym announced, walking toward him and interrupting his spiraling thoughts. "My scout has returned with a message from Coxani." She stopped, folding her arms across her chest. "She says to head off Bilguun. She can handle Berk."

"What?" Naran shook his head. "How is she going to do that? She's crazy. We can't—"

"She also sent this." Ayym cut Naran off, holding out a small piece of folded parchment.

Tikran took the scrap. Her handwriting was large and clean: *I got this. Don't fuck up. Miss you too.* He smiled despite everything. Of course, she would respond like this.

"What are you smiling about, Tik?" Naran asked, his brow furrowed. "Surely she doesn't think—"

"Naran," Tikran said testily, "why can't you believe that Coxani can handle this herself? Hasn't she proven herself time and time again?" He hated to admit it, but despite his words, he felt exactly the way Naran did. Tikran's anger was misdirected, and he knew it: He was angry with himself. "Neither of us can begin to imagine what she must have experienced at Zifa. And yet, she's still taking charge. She's made of much tougher stuff than we give her credit for." He took a deep breath. "I know we both care about her deeply. I know we both feel..."

"Don't say paternal," Naran muttered, his face twisted in disgust.

"I was definitely *not* going to say that," Tikran answered, feeling disgusted himself. "She's younger. She's a woman. She was my pupil. But now she's a warrior in her own right. We need to get over this shit."

Naran's face fell. "Yeah, I know. But if anything happens to her—"

"If anything happens to her," Tikran said, "you and I are both in big trouble." Tikran reached out and grabbed Naran's hand in a tender gesture that was completely out of character. Somehow, however, it felt natural. "We've got to let her go." He smiled wistfully. "After all, she let us go some time ago."

Pain flashed in Naran's eyes but he squeezed Tikran's hand back. "Yeah. You're right."

They both looked up to see Ayym and Tanith watching, their eyes shimmering with emotion. Quickly, both men released the other's hand. Naran chuckled uncomfortably.

Ayym sighed and rolled her eyes. As she turned and walked away, she muttered, "Men, I swear..."

LATE THAT NIGHT, Tikran sat in the commander's suite, rummaging through an untidy pile of documents by candlelight. Sleep eluded him—a common occurrence, these nights—and he refused to lay awake and ruminate. The Dilovari commander who had resided in the suite before him hadn't been there for long but had still managed to make quite a mess. Empty bottles of enkh were strewn about and food-encrusted bowls were stacked on the desk. The place reeked of moldy bread and booze.

Tikran sighed, moving the bowls to the floor and wiping his hands on his breeches. With Coxani and the Davlat handling Berk and the smaller Dilovari units in the south, Tikran and his army could head north toward the Damla Bridge. It was the only way Bilguun could get his forces across the river safely, now that Tikran effectively controlled it. He grimaced as he rifled through the crumpled sheets of parchment. The text was in Erdem and he had learned just enough to identify key words and names. From what he could tell, there were no official correspondences from Bilguun among the documents, but he would have to make sure. First thing in the morning, he would have Cavid, one of Anzor's mages who was fluent in Erdem, translate the content for him. *Maybe I should wake him now.* Tikran was toying with the idea when there was a soft rap at his door.

"Come in," Tikran said, expecting one of the Aslans.

Instead, Tanith walked in slowly, her face luminous, her voice gentle. "Am I disturbing you?"

"No. Of course not." He dropped the documents back on the desk and turned to face her. "You're up late." Holy Cenk, had her belly gotten even bigger over the course of just a few days, or was he imagining things? Without her armor, Tanith was all sweeping curves, all breasts and belly and muscle. The sight of her was both alarming and arousing at the same time. His body and mind battled as he struggled to process what he was seeing.

Tanith fought a smile. "You've always been an open book, Tikran."

He relaxed his face, trying to rein in his expression. "Oh, yeah? And what does that book tell you?"

She sighed, running a hand over her swollen abdomen. "You don't know how to feel about...this."

He sat on the small, rickety bed and patted the mattress beside him. She nodded and obliged quietly, folding her hands in her lap. He said, "I guess this baby is coming, whether we like it or not, huh?"

"It certainly looks that way," she said. "And...I'm terrified. Not of fighting a war while pregnant," she quickly added, glancing at him sharply. "I'm perfectly capable of it."

He tilted his head to look at her. "Then what is it?"

She bunched the fabric of her tunic between her fists. "I told you that my last pregnancy ended tragically. I worry it will happen again."

Tikran took her hand in his. "The last time you were pregnant, you were starving and living a very difficult life. The chances of it happening twice, I imagine, are low."

"Tikran, what if it was my Essence that killed her?" Tanith asked, a hint of panic in her voice. "This magic, the things it can do..."

Tikran frowned. "You really think that's possible?"

"I don't know. I *do* know that I'm capable of doing terrible things." She met his eyes. "Like Damir. Like Berk. We have all killed things, intentionally and unintentionally, with the Essence. And to make matters worse, we have been training to destroy, to kill, and the magic..." She trailed off.

Tikran waited a breathless moment. "The magic *what*, Tanith?"

She looked back down. "The magic makes us feel good, compelling us to continue destroying. It's like a drug. I have had to force myself to stop on several occasions, and it's painful. I imagine Damir has experienced the same. For someone as powerful as Berk, I can't imagine what drawing back the Essence must feel like." She looked at him again, her eyes limpid. "I was afraid to tell you this sooner. I discovered it recently and have been practicing to control it. I know I can control it. I'm certain Damir can as well. But then we learned about Berk..." She pursed her lips. "The Essence has a dark side, Tikran. A very dark side."

Drawing in his breath, Tikran said, "And you think the Essence is the reason you lost the first baby?"

She nodded. "And could lose this one, as well."

He squeezed her hand. "There's no real reason to believe that. But I understand your fear." The truth was, Tikran was more concerned about the fact that Berk was wildly powerful, very young, and—according to Tanith—prone to being overtaken by his own magic.

Tanith gasped, drawing her hand away suddenly.

His eyes wide, Tikran asked, "What? What's wrong?"

She let out a quiet laugh. "Nothing. It's just...that I'm being elbowed in the ribs." She smiled slightly at him. "Would you like to feel the baby kick?"

"Feel it...kick?" His eyebrows were practically at his hairline. In response, Tanith took his hand and laid it palm down on her belly. Almost immediately, he felt a sharp jab, then a smooth rolling beneath his fingers. "Holy shit," he muttered. "There really *is* a baby inside you." He smiled at her. "And it's very much alive."

Her smile faded. "For now."

"I understand your fear," Tikran said, following the small being's movements with tentative fingers, "but you have help this time. And your first experience may truly have been because of circumstance."

She shrugged. "Perhaps."

Tikran continued to skim his hand gently over the slope of Tanith's belly, fascinated. If all went well, he would be a father soon. He expected the usual dismay to set in at the thought—he and the baby's mother were about to engage in what could be a lengthy, costly war—but, this time, it didn't. Instead, he felt a growing wonder and...a tiny hint of joy. He realized Tanith was watching him curiously, a small smile on her lips.

She said, "I think you'll adapt well to being a father."

"I don't know about that." He felt like he should move his hand away but was completely intrigued by the small being that seemed to intentionally punch at his fingers with its bony parts. He said, "I feel like a child myself, more often than not."

Tanith laughed quietly. "Don't we all?" Then she grew solemn, and said, "Tikran...if we win this war, I want to request a favor of you."

"If we win this war, there's likely nothing I wouldn't grant you," he replied with a chuckle. "What is it?"

Sucking in her breath, she met his eyes evenly. "I want to return to Gohar. I want to become Gohar's first head mage."

He moved his hand away, studying her face. "And the baby...?"

Tanith seemed completely unconcerned. "The baby will have two kingdoms to call home."

Frowning, he sought the right words. "How would that even work?"

"What do you mean?" She seemed genuinely puzzled. "The child—assuming it lives—will spend half its time with me, and half its time with you."

Tikran looked down into his lap, feeling vulnerable. "You have no problem leaving me, then?"

"You have not given me a feather, which would bind us together as partners," Tanith said gently. "In fact, you've made it clear no feather is forthcoming. And while I love you, Tikran of the

Freed Kingfisher, I'm also relieved. I am Gohari, and I belong to Gohar. You are the king of Anzor." She smiled, running her fingertips along his arm, making the hairs on his skin rise.

"Who will be my head mage?" He tried not to sound like a dejected child.

She smiled, her eyes moist. "Anyone your heart desires, Your Highness."

"What if my heart desires you?"

She looked away. "I think it desires someone else more."

He swallowed. *She's not wrong.* Still, he had no idea how that could ever become his reality. *Damir? My head mage?* It seemed like a faraway dream. Good grief, they were about to face off with Damir and his exceptionally talented pupil in a deadly war. Even if Anzor emerged victorious, how could he ever trust the former mage of his enemy?

A deep sadness tried to settle over him, but he shook it off. Hesitating, he said, "Will you stay with me tonight?" He quickly added, "I just want to hold you."

Reaching out and stroking his face with her hand, she said, "Yes, I'll stay with you. And I won't break if you do more than hold me, you know. Neither will the baby." She looked down, her eyelashes sweeping down against her cheeks in a way that was intimately familiar.

He laughed uneasily. "I don't know if that would be appropriate considering..."

Tanith raised an eyebrow. "We are bringing a child into this world together. I don't think there's anything inappropriate in enjoying each other as we sit on the edge of the unknown."

Everything Tanith was saying about intimate relationships between men and women was contrary to what he'd learned while growing up in Anzor. And yet, despite his discomfort and wounded ego, it all seemed perfectly sensible—and at the moment, convenient. He gathered her in his arms and pulled her against him. Nuzzling her hair, he said, "Well...I suppose we'll see."

CHAPTER 36

I bequeath one-third of my lands and tenements to Tikran of the Freed Kingfisher; one-third to Coxani of the Leaping Dolphin; and one-third to Naran of the Stalking Lion...

Haydar heard a soft rap at the door as he re-read the words slowly, careful not to smudge the ink. "Come in," he said absently.

"My lord, Chief Justiciar Revaz is here," his butler announced after opening the door.

"Yes, good. Thank you, Dihya." Haydar nodded, forcing his eyes away from the document to look at her. "Please see him into the courtyard and offer him refreshments. I will be with him momentarily."

After Dihya left, Haydar sprinkled salt on the drying ink and stood. He waited several seconds, folded the parchment into thirds, and tucked it carefully in his pocket. Taking a deep breath, Haydar left his office and strode across the house, to the inner courtyard.

Revaz paced back and forth across the garden and past the fountain, his hands behind his back. When he heard Haydar enter, he spun on his heels, his vivid blue eyes lit and piercing. His hands fell to his sides. "Haydar. We need to talk. I'm having major reservations about this plan of yours to visit Vazha."

"My lord, please sit," Haydar insisted, gesturing to the table and pearl-inlaid chairs beneath the orange tree.

Revaz remained standing, his hands curling into loose fists. "Are you going to keep up formalities all night? Because I refuse to—"

"Dejan," Haydar said firmly. "Please, I implore you to sit."

Reluctantly, Revaz sat, folding his arms across his chest. Haydar sat as well and poured them each a small glass of xew. "I'm not interested in drinking," Revaz said adamantly.

"Well," Haydar replied, lifting his glass, "I am. And I'm pouring you a glass just in case you change your mind." He then tipped the full glass of milky liquid into his mouth and swallowed.

Revaz abruptly sat forward, leaning across the table. "Haydar. Listen. I don't trust Vazha as far as I can throw him. If what you suspect is true and he has, in fact, struck some sort of bargain with Dilovar, then he is a dangerous traitor who will stop at nothing to regain the throne—even the destruction of Anzor's armies."

"We've already discussed this at length, Dejan." Haydar poured himself another glass of xew from the long-necked blue bottle. "There are only so many ways to ensure the Anzori continue to support Tikran, and dealing with Vazha is the best way."

"Then let me come with you." Revaz was hovering over his seat. "That way he stays on his best behavior."

"You are needed here while I'm in Gohar," Haydar said, his tone leaving no room for negotiation. "Someone needs to run Anzor."

"Lords Bagrat and Gennadius can do it."

Haydar frowned. "That isn't wise. We still don't know which of the Anzori lords, other than Prem, were involved in intercepting messages from Gohar and are embroiled in Vazha's plan. No, as Tikran's most trusted Anzori advisor, you must remain here and make certain nothing goes awry while I'm gone." He toyed with his full glass of xew in contemplation. "Besides, I've known Vazha his whole life. I think I can make him see reason."

Revaz sat back with a huff. "I don't know him well at all, but as a child, he struck me as a wormy piece of shit. He loved to throw tantrums when he didn't get his way. Considering everything that's on the line for him, he could become aggressive."

Haydar sighed. "I know, Dejan. Which is why I've agreed to stop in Areg and take several of their Manzakars with me, and Lord Ruslan himself will be accompanying me. Besides, it does Vazha no favors to become violent if he wants to be king. The prince will have but two choices: renounce his claim to the throne and kneel before the Freed Kingfisher in complete obeisance, or face imprisonment and probable execution."

A long pause ensued. When Revaz finally spoke, his voice was soft and low. "Haydar. You need to come back, do you hear me?"

A lump quickly formed in the durai's throat. While he'd anticipated a certain amount of resistance to his visiting Vazha from Revaz, he hadn't expected such vehemence. Working alongside Revaz in Tikran's absence had been both exciting and devastating, as Haydar's respect for—and attraction to—Revaz had grown. It had become increasingly difficult to keep his feelings shuttered away. A part of him suddenly dared to hope that the golden-haired aristocrat might return the feelings that Haydar had tried to keep concealed. *Don't be an imbecile.* In a voice that was foreign to his ears, Haydar asked, "Why?"

Color suffused Revaz's cheeks as he blinked, paused as if looking for the right words. "We've become partners, you and I," he said, looking away. "We work beautifully together. And I consider you a dear friend."

Even as his heart sank, Haydar smiled. *It's for the best.* "We do work well together. But you are easy to work with, my lord." He took a large swallow from his glass, closing his eyes as the liquor slipped down his throat with a hot tingle. Finally feeling more relaxed, he pulled the folded, sealed document from his pocket and set it on the table.

Revaz frowned, nonplussed. "What's this?"

"While I have a plan," Haydar said evenly, "I need to be

prepared for any unintended contingencies, you understand. To that end, if something should happen to me..." He shrugged.

Staring at the document with a look of loathing, Revaz stiffened. "Yes. Of course." After a long silence, he snatched it up and tucked it into the inner pocket of his jacket. Then, to Haydar's astonishment, he leaned forward and, reaching across the table, covered Haydar's hand with his. Revaz's hand was warm and trembling as he said, "I hadn't planned on saying this, but I also hadn't truly considered you might not return until..." He touched his chest with his other hand, where the will resided. "Life is simply too short, and we never know when it could end." Meeting Haydar's gaze, Revaz's eyes were like shimmering blue pools. "I *need* you to come back, Haydar."

Although joy permeated his body with a jolt of warmth, Haydar also felt simultaneously devastated. *Reject him. Now.* He slowly pulled his hand free and stood. As he opened his mouth to say something—anything—to deter Revaz from continuing with any more declarations, he found that he couldn't speak. *I need this. I need him.*

Revaz stood as well, stepped up to him, and ran his fingers lightly along Haydar's bearded cheek, sending sparks through Haydar's body. The blue-eyed lord's voice was almost a whisper. "I need you, Lightning Arrow."

Stunned, Haydar watched as Revaz tilted his head, his eyes lidded and lips slightly parted. His mouth met Haydar's softly at first, then insistently. Haydar found himself leaning down to meet the kiss ardently. He was melting, sinking. It felt like an eternity since he'd been intimate with anyone, let alone someone who attracted him as powerfully as Revaz. His arms wrapped around Revaz's waist, pulling him closer. Suddenly their bodies were pressed together and their heat melded, smoldered.

Dihya. The household. Cenk, man, control yourself!

Wrenching himself away from Revaz, Haydar stepped back and dropped his hands to his sides. The two men gazed at each other, stricken, desperate. Haydar managed to mutter, "Are you certain you—"

"I've never been more certain of anything." Revaz's cheeks and lips were flushed, his eyes bright. "As if what just happened isn't proof enough."

His head spinning, Haydar said, "But I thought... You seemed to be courting Coxani..."

Revaz's blush deepened. "I've realized certain things about myself since then. Things that, in hindsight, make perfect sense."

Too elated or shocked to speak, Haydar sought for the right words desperately—a very unusual exercise for him. Finally drawing in a ragged breath, the durai said, "I am heading to my country manor tonight to prepare for my departure to Gohar. Your presence would be... I mean to say that—"

"I will be there." Revaz smiled shyly.

"Well. Then. I'll see you out." Haydar turned and led the way from the courtyard to the front entrance, then opened the door. Before an audience of servants and passers-by on the street, he gave Revaz as cool a look as he could muster, considering how rattled and exuberant he felt.

Revaz straightened, looking nothing short of the upper-crust Anzori lord as he adjusted his turbaned cap on his head. He said smoothly, "Have a good afternoon, Lord Haydar."

Haydar couldn't find his tongue to utter pleasantries, since very specific words played in his head:

I can't wait to hold you, Dejan.

CHAPTER 37

Damir abruptly remembered summer in Gohar.

He had just successfully fractured a designated stretch of earth, and he was drenched in sweat. The crack was six feet wide and several yards long, a jagged slit of rocks and uprooted tufts of grass, its depths descending into darkness. Damir unbuttoned and peeled off his robe, which had clearly been made for the brisk, cool summers of Dilovar, and, stumbling to his horse, draped it across the saddle. What he really wanted to do was call the rain. Still winded, his undershirt soaked and clinging to him, he squinted up at the scant, wispy clouds in the sky. *That would feel amazing.*

From the opposite end of Damir's creation and across the dry, mostly grassless field, Berk began to approach, skirting the uneven drops in the earth carefully. "Master Damir, are you all right?"

Damir nodded, swiping at the rivulets of perspiration that trickled down his forehead. "Yes," he said. "It's just bloody hot."

The only sweat accumulating on Berk was from being a greasy-skinned teenager and would have been there in any case. Berk shrugged. "I don't know. I like the heat. Besides, it's not so bad."

Damir let out a laugh. "You grew up in this. Of course you don't think it's bad." He pulled the flask that hung from his horse's saddle and drank from it in several thirsty swallows.

Berk smiled complacently, looking out over Damir's handiwork. "You did good, by the way. You kept everything tight."

"Well, thank you, Berk," Damir answered, fighting a smile. "I believe I kept the destruction within the lines...?"

"Mostly," Berk replied. He shot Damir a quick, sly look. "It was a good effort."

"Well," Damir said, now fully smiling, "aren't we smug?" He nudged Berk with his elbow in an uncharacteristically playful gesture. "Don't forget, though. Being powerful means—"

"I know, I know," Berk interrupted, a pained expression on his face. "It means I have to be even more careful."

"Yes." Damir straightened. "No emotional outbursts. You must always be in control. Otherwise..."

Berk looked away. "Otherwise innocent people die."

Damir shaded his eyes against the relentless Gohari sun, analyzing his work. "What most people wouldn't do to have your power," he muttered. "You have the entire fate of the southern kingdoms, of perhaps even the entire Continent, in your hands. Do you realize this?"

Berk looked at him then, a look in the boy's eyes that Damir couldn't quite place. Berk said, "It means a lot to me that you haven't lost faith in me. Even after what I did."

Squeezing Berk's shoulder, Damir said, "I know what it's like to feel like a monster, to know you didn't want something to happen. To know it was still all your fault."

Berk opened his mouth to say something, a troubled look on his face, when they heard hoofbeats behind them. The two mages turned to see Vazha and his Manzakars riding toward them, slowing to a stop as they came close. Vazha slipped from his horse, his cane in his hand. He moved toward them at a good clip, with the vigor of a healthy man robbed of a single physical faculty.

Damir's fingernails dug into the flesh of his palms. *He wouldn't even be alive, if not for me.* He forced his hands to unclench, his face to relax. "Prince Vazha," he said, "to what do we owe the pleasure?"

The prince gave Damir an icy look, then smiled at Berk. "News has arrived that the Freed Kingfisher is in eastern Gohar."

Holy Cenk. He's here. Damir was careful to keep his face blank and his body language unaffected, since he knew the prince watched his every move deliberately, missing nothing.

"He thought he was being especially clever, re-capturing the garrison town of Diyar and cutting off reinforcements from crossing the river." Vazha smirked. "Except now, he's effectively surrounded himself—Bilguun is well on his way across the Damla Bridge to the north, and there are two powerful mages to the south."

Damir's expression remained flat. "I suppose we will head north, then, to meet Anzor's armies." He cocked his head. "Will Your Highness be accompanying us, by chance?" He knew fully well that the prince had no desire to sully his hands with battle.

"Unfortunately, I must return to my manor and miss out on all the excitement," Vazha replied with a sniff and looked at Berk. "But next we meet, Dilovar will have won this war, the Manzakars' reign of terror in Gohar will be ended, and you will become Anzor's next head mage."

Berk swallowed. "Yes, sir."

Before turning to leave, Vazha said to Damir, "I know you'll ensure Dilovar wins easily and quickly, Doctor. It would be a shame if the Freed Kingfisher paid for Anzor's victory with his life."

"The quicker and easier, the better, Prince Vazha," Damir replied blithely.

Vazha's lips curled as he turned. "Indeed."

The two mages watched the prince and his Manzakars ride away until they were a cloud of glistering dust. Then Berk said, "Master Damir...may I ask you something personal?"

"You may," Damir answered. "I can't promise I'll answer, though."

Berk toed the loose, crumbly earth beneath his foot. "Are you really in love with King Tikran?"

"I want him to live. Do you understand, Berk?" Damir said firmly. "I've stressed the importance of being as careful and calculated as possible in our attacks on the enemy, and it's of the utmost importance that nothing happens to him."

Berk raised an eyebrow. "So you *do* love him."

Yes. And I will love him until the day I die. Damir shook his head, that familiar ache assaulting his chest. "In the grand scheme of things, it doesn't matter. I am Dilovar's head mage." He turned toward his horse. "Let's get back to the fort. I'm sure the commanders are eager to begin the journey north."

CHAPTER 38

Bilguun's army of approximately four thousand troops sprawled in the distance, just at the entrance of the Damla Bridge. From the top of a low mesa some five miles away, the enemy was a dark sea of scintillating iron, starch white tents, and the occasional fluttered orange of Dilovar's flag.

"Four thousand," Naran muttered under his breath. "Well, fuck."

Tikran dismounted and said, "That's what the Davlat scouts estimated. And it looks about right." He helped his men unload the heavier cargo with Naran at his side. "They have more troops and the benefit of direct reinforcements from Dilovar, thanks to the bridge."

Naran heaved a barrel from the wagon. He grunted, setting it down on the ground before saying, "Sounds like Bilguun's got the advantage at the moment, Tik."

Tikran rubbed his cheek with the back of his hand. "Perhaps. But don't forget—other than the skirmishes with the Haldorans at their northern border, the Dilovari haven't fought a real war for over a hundred years. We have."

"*You* have." Naran snorted. "I haven't fought shit."

That's right. The big guy had never experienced this, had he?

This was his first real war. Tikran debated on how to handle this information: Should he tease his friend relentlessly or reassure him? *You're a king about to go to war. Thousands of lives will be lost. This is no time for jokes.* The mischievous thoughts disappeared instantly, consumed by his sobering reality. After a moment, he said, "There's no preparing for something like this. But when the time comes, I have no doubt you'll follow through."

Naran raised an eyebrow. "Who are you and what have you done with Tikran?"

Tikran let out a laugh. "I've wondered the same about you at least a hundred times in the last few months."

"Really?" Naran looked genuinely pleased.

"Yeah," Tikran replied. His smile faded as he stared off in the direction of Dilovar's encampment and his thoughts returned to Bilguun. "I want to parley with him. If there's a way to stop this ridiculous slaughter, I will do almost anything."

"That can be arranged," Ayym said, interrupting a somewhat private conversation with a dashing smile. She hopped off her horse and sauntered over. "Allow my warriors to deliver the message to the king of Dilovar. They'll be seen as less threatening than if you were to send Manzakars."

"Thank you, Beg Ayym." Tikran couldn't help but like the Sachin chieftain. If Tanith was determined to stay in Gohar, he couldn't think of anyone he trusted more with her—and the baby's—well-being. While he still struggled with pangs of jealousy when he saw the two women together, he had so much more occupying his mind that any form of support was welcome. And he felt, deep down, that Ayym genuinely sought to support him.

The Anzori forces quickly and efficiently set up camp while Tikran and his commanders helped. They pitched tents and lit cooking fires, unpacked and stored food and supplies, and built latrines on the encampment's fringes. As soon as he could, Tikran dictated a message to Bilguun, requesting a parley that evening. As far as Tikran was concerned, the sooner it happened, the better.

He handed the folded parchment, sealed with his mark, to a

warrior with a multitude of black and red beads in his hair and a confident, even gaze. "Be sure they see you come in peace. Hold that white flag high, now."

The warrior smiled. "Don't worry, King Tikran. I will."

Tikran watched as he rode down the side of the mesa and toward the enemy's camp. Naran came to stand beside him and asked, "What are the chances Bilguun agrees to back off?"

"Slim to none." Tikran shook his head. "He's feeling tough right now, what with that powerful kid mage at his disposal. And there's no question he wants at least part of Gohar." He sighed. "I'm still going to try and talk sense into him."

The Sachin messenger returned quickly, informing Tikran of the Dilovari king's willingness to parley that day. As the sun ducked in the west, Tikran, Naran, and a handful of Aslans mounted their horses to meet Bilguun halfway for the parley. They had barely ridden for thirty minutes when, across the broad field of long, sighing grass, Tikran could see the shimmering forms of Bilguun and his men approach. They cast long, waving shadows on the steppe, their heavy lamellar cuirasses and broad-brimmed helmets catching the light.

Each side halted when they were about twenty yards away. Tikran and Bilguun both dismounted and walked toward one another, stopping at a safe distance—close enough for conversation, but not within sword-striking range. The grass swished against their legs in the breeze as a crested lark sang cheerfully, flying overhead. Tikran could see Bilguun assess him from beneath the brim of his helmet, his eyes darting coolly over him. "Freed Kingfisher," the Dilovari king said, "how far you've come. I'm told you were present the night Delger requested my royal physician's assistance to help cure the prince. You were but a mere soldier then. And now, you stand before me as king of Anzor."

"Your royal physician," Tikran answered, "who was also your head mage." He smiled. "That detail must have slipped your mind, King Bilguun." It felt surreal, standing before Bilguun without Damir there. Inconveniently, he felt his chest tighten.

Bilguun didn't flinch. "You seem to forget that he helped you defeat Delger."

"I haven't forgotten," Tikran said. "Although I hardly believe that was your intention in sending him."

"That doesn't matter now." Bilguun straightened, tilting his head back to peer down his nose at Tikran. "What do you have to say?"

Letting his hands hang open at his sides, Tikran said, "I'm trying to understand why you would risk thousands of Dilovari lives for a handful of reluctant mages."

Bilguun rumbled with hostile laughter. "Is that all you think I'd get? A handful?"

"Two handfuls, then. Maybe three." Tikran frowned. "You witnessed what Delger had to contend with—a region of angry, rebellious natives. It did not end well for him."

"It did not end well for him," Bilguun snapped, "because of the Manzakars. Because of *you*." A smug look settled on his face. "I have no Manzakars who will turn on me."

"That's awfully short-sighted of you, King Bilguun," Tikran said softly. "Clearly, you haven't seen what's happening here in Gohar. You haven't seen the Gohari themselves rise up. You will face the same strife as Delger, and it will cripple you."

"Delger mismanaged Gohar. I would do it differently. I would make sure the Gohari saw me as their guiding hand. They would see me not as an oppressor, starving and beating them into submission, but as a benefactor, providing them with what they need."

Tikran struggled to keep the scowl from his face. "You don't think that's what Delger thought he was doing? You're telling me you'd be no different." He took a deep breath, trying to temper himself. "And what will you do when the Haldorans return to your northern border? Do you think you have the military capacity to handle both Haldor and Gohar?"

Bilguun glared at the Manzakar king. "Perhaps you should stop lecturing me and worry for yourself, Freed Kingfisher." He folded his hands in front of him. "Unless you give me half of Gohar, this war will happen, and you will lose—in more ways than one."

Tikran shook his head slowly. "I promised Gohar its independence, not another overlord, and certainly not two. Gohar will be free, if I have anything to do with it."

Bilguun shrugged. "Then the blood of thousands is on your hands, King Tikran. Not mine." He turned his head to look at his men. "We're done here."

His nostrils flaring with barely tamped down anger, Tikran said, "King Bilguun. You're making a terrible mistake, trusting a man as duplicitous as Vazha. Even if you were to win this war—which you won't—this scheme will not end well for Dilovar."

The Dilovari king, who had already begun walking back to his horse, looked over his shoulder. "I appreciate your concern, Freed Kingfisher," he said acerbically. "But *you* are the one making the mistake."

Tikran turned then, striding back to his horse. As he hopped in the saddle, Naran muttered, "It went that well, huh?"

"Vazha must have promised him half of Gohar in return for the throne of Anzor," Tikran said, wheeling his horse around. "Bilguun will accept nothing less."

Naran tugged on his reins, making his mount snort and turn as well. "All right, then." He pursed his lips grimly. "War it is."

THE WIDE, flat-topped hill stood not more than a mile away from Bilguun's camp, its craggy face bathed in morning sunshine. Tikran said, "There. That's where we'd see movement across the bridge."

Naran crossed his arms, standing beside his friend on the edge of the Anzori encampment, gazing out at the landscape. The mesa was definitely the best vantage point for scouts to monitor Dilovar's activity. "You don't think Bilguun has already noticed it?"

"Of course he's noticed it."

"Well, then, which poor bastards are you sending out there?" Naran squinted at the hill. "They'll be spotted in no time."

Tikran turned toward Naran, an eyebrow raised. "I'm not sending anyone. I'm going myself."

Laughing, Naran said, "Whoa, there, Your Highness. You're far too valuable to be gallivanting in Dilovari territory without your entire army with you."

"I have to go with my men," Tikran insisted. "It's dangerous."

"It sure is dangerous," Naran agreed, "which is why *I* am going with them."

"What? No."

"Tikran." Naran's voice deepened, his head lifted a fraction higher. "Let me do this."

"I can send Tural," Tikran said. "He's been through this kind of thing and —"

"No," Naran said firmly. "Let me do this."

Tikran hesitated. "You know you have nothing to prove, right? I know what you're capable of. I don't need you to risk your life to prove it."

"Brother," Naran answered with a chuckle, "we're at war. We're all going to risk our lives. Let me go. Please."

Tikran looked aside, hesitating for several seconds. Finally, he waved his hand. "Fine. Don't get yourself killed."

As Naran walked away, he smiled to himself. He knew Tikran so well. *He's trying not to get emotional on me.* He had to admit, however, he was impressed that Tikran had agreed—his friend had always needed to be in control, to be the actor, to be the winner. Perhaps the Caged Kingfisher had truly been freed. The thought made Naran almost wistful.

Of course, Tikran showed up not an hour later as Naran was readying his detachment of fifty Manzakars to head out. The Manzakar king strode into the makeshift stalls they'd constructed for their horses, his face tight with apprehension. Naran looked over at him, stifling a smile. "Your Highness. To what do we owe this honor?"

"Shut up," Tikran said, annoyance and concern fighting in his expression. "I'm just making sure you're prepared."

Naran neared his friend, resting a hand on Tikran's shoulder and speaking softly into his ear. "I got this, boss. Let go."

After a pause, Tikran stepped aside, leveling a cool but strained look at his commander-in-chief. "Good luck out there, Commander."

Naran flashed a cocky grin, thrusting his chest out with a bravado he didn't completely feel. "Luck? Look at me. I don't need luck, Your Highness."

Tikran rolled his eyes and watched as the Manzakars mounted their horses and left the camp, a look of trepidation on his face.

As quickly as possible, Naran's detachment rode out to the mesa, approaching it from between a series of low hills to the west in the hopes of remaining inconspicuous. Leaving their horses below, the Manzakars climbed to the top of the mesa, crouching at its top and gazing over the massive Dilovari encampment. The enemy had constructed field fortifications, including horse traps—logs with projecting spikes—all around its perimeter and at the mouth of the bridge.

"Looks like they've been busy," Naran said to Ivad, a junior commander, as he shaded his eyes.

"Commander," Ivad said, a tone of urgency in his voice, "I could be mistaken, but I think I see activity on the far side of the bridge."

Naran squinted. Tikran had been right—they could see directly across the two-mile-long bridge to the other side. And Ivad, unfortunately, was also right: Naran could see a wave of movement the width of the bridge, iron sparkling in the light.

Oh, shit.

He spun around, in the middle of barking an order at his men, when a screaming bodkin punched the lamellar plates of his shoulder armor with enough force to send all six-foot-four of him to the ground. Even as he hit the earth, one hand grabbed for his bow while the others snatched up a handful of arrows. The bodkin hadn't been a direct enough hit to pierce his armor, and if he was injured, he couldn't tell—his body flooded with adrenaline and he felt no pain. He saw the Dilovari soldiers rise to the top of the hill, tens of them, bows and sabers drawn. *They've been waiting for us.* Just as one of the Dilovari ran at him, sword swinging in his direction, Naran released two arrows at once. With a suddenness that jarred even him, the soldier vanished in a cloud of dust, his boots in the air.

Before Naran could get back on his feet, a saber flashed above his head. He knew he had no time to do anything but *roll*. He flung himself to the side, coming to his feet and drawing his sword as quickly as he could. He raised it in the nick of time. The sound of crashing metal echoed in his ears rhythmically as the Dilovari soldier hacked at him, his arms straining against the beats. The man's face was a blur of desperation and rage past their crossed swords, all bared teeth and trickling sweat. Luckily, Naran had spent a lifetime preparing for...well, *something* like this. His size also played in his favor, and he kicked the enemy's legs out from under him with the force of at least two angry mules. As the Dilovari collapsed on top of him, Naran drove his sword into the gap of his opponent's armor, just at the armpit. The soldier became dead weight, bearing down on him, screaming in pain, his blood showering them both.

Naran shoved the dying man off him, jerking his sword free. "Ivad! Ivad!" He yelled his junior commander's name frantically as he leaped over a precipitous edge of the mesa, no fewer than ten Dilovari at his heels, arrows singing so closely past his head that he felt the air around his ears displace with bursts of wind. The ground slipped and crumbled beneath him, and he was surprised to find he'd landed on his feet. He heard the shrieks of his men, and, from the corner of his eye, saw the bodies of Manzakars crumpled at the bottom of the hill.

He spun around, loosing as many arrows in succession as he could with his bow, all while holding his sword, its blade over his shoulder, its hilt gripped by whatever fingers weren't pulling and releasing his bowstring. It was then that he spotted a larger squad of Dilovari swiftly approaching from the east, their lances raised. His blood ran cold.

Time to go.

He let out the low, long whistle of retreat as he leaped on his horse, tossing his shield over the back of his head for protection. Ivad and what Manzakars were left were quick to obey, and the entire detachment was galloping off in a cloud of dirt, bodkins whizzing and landing all around and among them. As the wind and dirt lashed Naran's face and sweat stung his eyes, he heard one of his men scream from behind, likely pierced by one of the deadly arrows.

It wasn't until they had reached a safe distance that Naran's shoulder suddenly throbbed and he realized he was shaking from head to foot. *Fuck! What just happened?* The fact that he'd nearly died sank in, and he finally understood Tikran's resistance to his commanding this particular mission. As his breathing slowed, he thought to turn and say something to his men but couldn't find his nerve or his voice.

Naran had finally gotten a taste of war, and it hadn't gone the way he'd imagined at all.

***

"Your Highness, Commander Naran has returned!"

Tikran turned from his fencing exercises to face the soldier, panting, and sheathed his sword, his heart racing even faster. *Already?* "Something happened," he muttered.

It wasn't a question, but as he began to rush from the training grounds, he heard the soldier say, "Barely half of them have returned."

Tikran broke into a run to meet Naran and what was left of his detachment as they entered the encampment, dread filling his chest. More than a few of the returning Manzakars had arrows protruding from their cuirasses, several of them losing blood and barely managing to stay upright in their saddles. "Get the doctors," Tikran shouted behind him as he reached Naran, who looked battered and shaken, but otherwise unharmed. His left shoulder sagged, the armor that covered it blackened and dented.

Oh, thank fucking Cenk. Or whoever.

Tikran felt weak in the knees as he gauged Naran's expression. "Hey." He grabbed Naran's hand. He wanted to ask what happened but held his tongue. "Are you okay?" He felt Naran's fingers tremble through the glove.

"No," Naran answered huskily. Lifting his eyes to look at Tikran, he said, "I lost half my detachment. I should have known they'd be waiting for us."

Tikran tightened his grip on his friend's hand briefly before letting go. "Get a doctor to look at your shoulder. I need you back in peak condition as soon as possible."

Naran slid from his saddle with a wince. "Tik." His eyes were wide in a blood- and mud- splattered face. "There's more of them coming. Over the bridge. I couldn't tell how many, but..." He exhaled. "...a lot."

Oh, shit.

"King Tikran." Tanith stood several paces away with several of his concerned commanders, her arms crossed over her ridiculously pregnant belly. "I can help." She stepped forward. "Let me head upstream. I can stop them from coming over the bridge."

Tikran stared at her. *Are you insane? You're weeks away from popping out a baby!* But it was their only choice. They had to stop reinforcements from getting over the bridge. He breathed steadily and replied, "That could work."

Tanith nodded. "Tural can take me. We need to leave now."

"Yes," Tikran replied, looking at Tural. "Commander, take Mistress Tanith up the river as quickly as possible. Make sure it's not within scouting distance of the Dilovari."

"Yes, Your Highness," Tural answered immediately, already gesturing to his men.

Tikran spun around, forcing himself to focus. He blinked at the faces watching him intently, including Naran's. He said, "We're going to form up lines. We want the Dilovari to believe we're readying for battle to distract from Mistress Tanith. Understood?"

His men roared with approval, their faces blazing. Naran nodded, his face creased with determination beneath the blood and dirt. "Yes, Your Highness," he said with a growl. "Let's get those fuckers."

CHAPTER 39

The sun bore down on the Dilovari squadron from a cloudless sky, bright and unrelenting. The landscape remained bleak and rocky, punctuated with low hills and patches of grass and shrubs. Damir had exchanged his heavy mage's robe for a light tunic, but even so, sweat soaked the cotton beneath his cuirass. He stole a look at Berk, who seemed unfazed by the merciless heat. If it wasn't for his Essence, Damir would have serious doubts about his Gohari ancestry. It didn't help that the thought of seeing Tikran again would have made him sweat either way—even from a distance, and on opposing sides of what would be a vicious war.

Damir glanced at Berk again. The boy understood the importance of sparing Tikran's life, and Damir had faith that Berk would do what he could to ensure it. Still, all it took was a well-aimed arrow or a calculated swipe of a saber to end the king of Anzor's life... *No. Stop.* He refused to let his thoughts wander in that direction. Even if Tikran hated him—which Damir suspected he did—he would do anything to protect the Freed Kingfisher from harm.

Shifting in his saddle and wincing at the dampness of his breeches, Damir wondered if he had enough water with him to pour some of it on his head. As he reached for his flask, a cry and a quick whistle sounded. Puzzled, Damir half turned when Commander Amit yelled, "Shields!"

Manzakars! Damir raised his shield in a hurry. The arrows pelted it within seconds, a sudden roar of rapid strikes. The commanders had been confident their journey would be uneventful until they approached Diyar—most of the Anzori units had moved north to aid Tikran against Bilguun, and the nomads in the area were allies. *So who's attacking us?* As the arrows continued to fall, Damir attempted to see beyond the crush of Dilovari cavalrymen around him and Berk, to no avail.

Berk cried, "Master Damir, who are they?"

Damir shook his head. "I have no idea." It was then that an arrow embedded itself in the rear skirt of his saddle, making him flinch. It was a lighter arrow with small fletching...a Gohari arrow. *It can't be...*

"Commander," one of the soldiers shouted, shaking his head vigorously, "there are too many of them!"

Amit roared from the back, panic clear in his voice. "Fuck! What are they *doing*?"

To Damir's dismay, there were apparently enough of them—whomever they were—for Amit to order the Dilovari standard be lowered. Within minutes, the shower of arrows stopped and the cavalry loosened their formation enough for Damir to peer between them. What he saw took his breath away: hundreds upon hundreds of Gohari warriors blanketed the horizon, stretching north and south endlessly, their colorful wooden shields unmistakable.

"Sweet Archil!" Berk's face was bloodless, slack-jawed. "Davlat!"

Before Damir could speak, Amit had grabbed Berk's reins and begun leading him toward the nomads. "Come on, kid," he said. "Your people have apparently forgotten who they're fighting for." He jerked his head at Damir. "If they persist, I want you to do some magical convincing, eh? Come on!"

The three men rode out toward the nomads at a quick trot.

Damir immediately sought Coxani among the dark-skinned, tattooed warriors that watched them stonily. *She must be here.* The Davlat chieftain rode forward to greet them, looking fearsome in his beaded and feathered headdress.

"Marbek!" Amit shouted when they were just a few yards away. "What is the meaning of this?"

The line of warriors parted behind Marbek, their heads bowed and hands on their chests, making way for a mounted figure who wore a crown on their head, the tall prongs adorned with beads and gleaming in the sunlight. As they approached, Damir stifled a gasp. *Coxani.* She wore a long robe with wide sleeves that was tied at the waist and had a haughty, other-worldly expression. *What is she up to?* Beside him, Berk blinked in shock. Slowly, the boy bowed his head and placed a hand over his heart. His eyes still rolled upward, fixed on Coxani in disbelief.

Marbek crossed his arms on his chest. "Berk," he said. "Archil's descendant lives. Your own Beg Zolto discovered her, living among the Manzakars. She is the Rasula, and she is a sign we must fight with the Freed Kingfisher."

"What *is* this bullshit?" Amit spat.

Coxani drew her bow and several arrows from her quiver, looking as regal and dangerous as ever. Her voice, when she spoke, was deep and imposing. "Hand over the mages and your weapons, Commander, and we'll spare your squadron." When Amit hesitated, She pulled her bowstring taut and aimed her first arrow at him. "Don't make me ask again."

Damir moved first, taking Berk's reins from Amit's hand. The boy seemed to have recovered from his initial stupor and was leaning forward curiously. Amit grumbled a curse and turned. As the mages approached Coxani, several warriors passed them, following Amit back to his squadron.

Coxani lowered her bow and faced the two mages. "Surprise," she said dryly. She looked at Berk. "Beg Zolto can't wait to tell you everything. Let's head back to the camp." Berk nodded wordlessly.

She then turned to Damir. "Come, Master Damir. We have a lot to discuss."

***

DAMIR LOOKED around him in amazement as he followed Coxani to one of the central yarms. The nomads had set up camp in the blink of an eye, their yarms fully constructed and campfires lit before he had adjusted to the fact that he'd just been taken prisoner by Coxani, who was, apparently, Archil's last descendant. *What just happened?* His mind reeling, he ducked past the felt flap and into the yarm, half expecting to see Tikran there. *Why not?* Coxani had shown up leading the Davlat, who were presumed to be allied with Dilovar, wearing a spiked crown like a goddess. What could possibly be more outrageous? He faced Coxani. "Er, Rasula, is it?"

Coxani removed the crown. "It means 'prophet.'" She shrugged. "Ridiculous, isn't it?"

Damir considered, his hands behind his back. "If the Gohari believe it, there must be truth to it."

The corner of her mouth quirked. "Even if it's true, what does it matter? Of course, I'll still use it to make sure Berk doesn't destroy Tikran's armies." She looked at Damir, her expression earnest. "I don't believe you were complicit in Berk's actions at Zifa. Tell me I'm right."

"I was not complicit in the...last part, no," Damir replied, a ripple of nausea making him stiffen.

"I didn't think so." Stepping closer, she said, "I pulled this trick believing you would help Tikran win. Will you?"

Oh, no. Damir looked away, his heart rate accelerating. "Coxani..." Why was this so difficult? He hadn't anticipated ending up face-to-face with her, having to answer this very question. He licked his lips. "Listen. Tikran must concede to Bilguun."

She recoiled. "What?"

He swallowed. "His reign is doomed, Coxani. Vazha has conspired with Anzor's elite to see it end. The only way to ensure

Tikran lives is for Vazha to regain the throne of Anzor. We made a deal. I would ensure Dilovar won the war, and Tikran would live."

Coxani glared in outrage. "Vazha? Did he tell you Tikran's reign is doomed?"

Damir nodded. "Yes."

"And you believe that deceitful piece of shit?" Coxani was snarling now. "Damir, what's wrong with you? How could you take the word of that snake?"

Damir said softly, "But what if he's right?"

He saw her expression flicker, her fear exposed for a split second. She quickly composed herself. "Even if he is," she said, lowering her voice, "are you even thinking about what Tikran would want? He wants a free Gohar, even if it means sacrificing his life. That's what he's always wanted."

"What *I* want is Tikran—alive." Damir met her eyes. "At least this arrangement offers the possibility that Tikran will be exiled rather than executed." He knew he was being selfish, but it couldn't be helped. "I'm sorry, Coxani. I refuse to forfeit Tikran's life for the scant possibility of a free Gohar."

Coxani stepped back, her face a mask of horror. "You will fight against Anzor, then?"

"No. No." Damir drew in his breath. "If Berk and I abstain from battle, Tikran surely has a chance to win. I hear he has a powerful mage...?"

Looking defeated, Coxani slumped. "You're making a mistake, Damir."

"We will not fight." Damir's voice was firm. "But I can promise you, Coxani, that I will protect Tikran with every ounce of Essence that I have."

Coxani's large green eyes reflected a mixture of outrage and sadness. "So you'll break his heart to protect his body?" She turned away. "That's not love, Damir."

As she led him from the yarm and back to Berk, Damir felt his knees quake, threatening to collapse beneath him.

He was making the right choice.

He *had* to be making the right choice.

EVERYTHING FELT DIFFERENT TO BERK. Foreign, even.

Beg Zolto's yarm, which had been home to Berk since he was small, felt like it didn't quite...*fit* anymore. Like a tunic or pair of boots he'd outgrown. As Berk embraced his great-grandfather, he expected the old man's familiar scent to envelope him and reduce him to tears. To his surprise, Berk found himself nearly unaffected, his eyes dry. Zolto smiled, his eyes crinkled with affection as he looked Berk over carefully.

"You've changed," the elder said quietly, touching the collar of Berk's robe, his coiffed, tied-back hair. "You are Dilovari now, eh?"

Berk shrugged uncomfortably. "Not really. Not yet."

Zolto chuckled. "But you are no longer a child. You turned seventeen a month ago. Had you been here, we would have honored the end of your childhood."

"Oh, yeah," Berk said, with a smile. "I forgot all about my birthday." *I don't feel like an adult, though.* He sat beside the old man, chewing the inside of his cheek pensively. After a moment, he asked, "Is the Manzakar really the Rasula, Beg Zolto?"

"She is," Zolto confirmed, his hands folded in his lap. "A miracle that she came back, when we all thought she was dead. A sign, Berk."

Berk stared at nothing, his brow furrowed. "But she's a Manzakar."

"The Manzakars are Gohari, boy," Zolto said with a chuckle.

"No, Beg." Berk shook his head slowly. "They're Anzori, above all. Master Damir told me how they all get brainwashed over there."

"Well," Zolto replied, straightening. "Not all of them are brainwashed. If they were, this war would not be happening. King Tikran would give half of Gohar to Dilovar and be done with it."

"Unless he wants it all to himself," Berk muttered.

"Berk!" Zolto turned toward the boy, scowling. "What have they told you over there in Dilovar? More troubling, why have you believed it?"

Berk felt a sudden pang of guilt. "I'm sorry, Beg." Despite his remorse, he curled his hands into tight fists. "I'm just still *so angry*."

Zolto was quiet for a long while, working his mostly toothless gums. Then he said, "You were always angry. You need to let the anger go, Berk."

Berk nodded, avoiding the elder's gaze. "Yes, Beg. I'm sorry."

Zolto smiled and patted Berk's shoulder. "Would you like some galak? I'll make it extra sweet, just how you like it."

The tension didn't leave Berk's body. Still, he smiled back and replied, "Yes, Beg. That would be nice."

CHAPTER 40

It had been more than a decade since Haydar had been back in the land of his birth. Even so, he'd immediately noticed the change: While Gohar remained a land of semi-desert plains, it thrummed with life. Now, two weeks into his journey to Vazha's manor, Haydar watched in awe as the grass swayed and shivered with concealed activity. A marbled polecat, its white-tipped ears emerging from behind the long blades of grass, watched the travelers curiously; two marmots rushed past, their brown bodies dragging a ripple through the underbrush. The sky was no less busy—falcons soared high above, watching for their next meal, and the air resonated with the chirps of sand plovers. As the landscape became more barren, Haydar could sense the presence of large, feline predators slinking between the craggy hills, wary and watchful.

"I must admit," Lord Ruslan said as he rode alongside Haydar, "the place has grown on me. It's certainly rugged, no question, and not for the faint of heart, but it has such...promise." He dabbed at the beads of sweat that formed on his brow with a silk handkerchief, his gemstone rings glittering in the sunlight. "Obviously, Delger got it all wrong. But with the right oversight, I truly believe Gohar could thrive as an Anzori colony."

Haydar wanted to sigh. He'd ventured into Gohar with Lord Ruslan and his small squad of fifty Manzakars as "protection." Haydar knew the man was the furthest thing from it. "I doubt King Tikran would agree with you, my lord."

Ruslan made a *tsk* sound and shook his head, a hint of admonition in his voice. "It's a real shame, in my opinion."

The durai didn't look at his Anzori travel companion. The blood in his veins suddenly felt icy cold despite the heat. Haydar knew he was headed into the lion's den with one of Vazha's spies —he'd been watching Ruslan's movements carefully for some time now. While he hadn't definitively linked Ruslan to Prem, he knew the robust, tanned lord often visited Vazha during his trips through Gohar, presumably accompanying the soldiers as they took supplies from Anzor to the manor. Haydar was certain Ruslan had ordered his household of Manzakars to do the prince's bidding, whatever that may be.

An eagle screeched as it dove into the grass several yards away and Haydar watched in contemplation as the bird rose into the sky once again, a marmot in its clutches. At the moment, he felt more like the marmot than the eagle, but he knew he'd done as much preparation for this moment as was humanly possible. He had no doubt Dinara and Lord Bagrat had followed his request and were already disseminating the news of his death throughout Anzor City. Couriers were likewise on their way to every major Anzori fort in Gohar, bearing the same message. He knew in his gut that it would make an impact on the Anzori elite—while they may prefer an Anzori as king, they certainly weren't about to replace Tikran with a murderer. And if Tikran won the war, perhaps they wouldn't replace him at all.

He needed all of Anzor to know what Vazha was. All of Anzor...and every Dilovari who thought it was a good idea to negotiate with him.

Haydar felt an ache in his chest at the thought of Revaz hearing the news for the first time, then reading the letter Haydar had left him. He hadn't told Revaz about his suspicions regarding Ruslan, and he had moreover lied to him about taking extra Manzakars from Areg for protection. *I'm so sorry, Dejan.* The durai struggled to keep his pain from showing on his face. Had he been a bigger man, he would have rejected the young lord's proclamations, would have denied feeling the same and sent Revaz on his way. *But I'm not a bigger man.* No, he'd desperately needed every blissful second he'd spent with Revaz, basking in something that felt acutely like love for an entire night. Had he more time, it might very well have become love…

Haydar drew a long, quiet breath and looked out in the distance. Shimmering in the heat, Vazha's manor slowly came into view, rising over the horizon in brilliant white. *It's almost time, now.* He felt a strange flood of calm at the thought, followed by a fixed determination.

"A shame, isn't it?" Ruslan sighed deeply. "Keeping those beautiful girls and their lovely mother trapped out here, away from proper society?"

"Tikran granted the Delger women permission to visit Anzor for two months every year, Lord Ruslan," Haydar replied. "This is far more than any king has done for a political exile's family."

"I understand, but the princesses are coming of age, you know. They're missing opportunities to mingle with the aristocracy because of their father's misstep."

Misstep, eh? Haydar had the strange urge to burst out laughing. *I mustn't let the moment get to me.* Instead, he nodded gravely and said, "I will bring it to King Tikran's attention. I'm certain he would want them to have the same opportunities as other young Anzori ladies."

Ruslan seemed to approve of this response and kept quiet until they approached the manor, their Anzori flag held high. The guards opened the gates and the men dismounted, giving their horses to the waiting grooms. Haydar looked around at the small but running fountain in the front and well-kept stables. *So this is how the exiled live, eh?* He'd seen the expenses many times in the financial records, but for some reason, he'd never quite imagined it so opulent—at least, not in contrast to the way the Gohari lived. Of course, it was mostly his doing. He'd ensured the former queen, the prince, and the princesses were thoroughly provided for, with Tikran's full approval.

The great blue doors to the manor were opened by Gohari servants who had been former slaves. Haydar looked at the young men and women as they kept their eyes downcast and wished he could tell them, "You're in Gohar! Run back to your people!" Of course, he knew it would be futile. Gohar was no home to them.

"Lord Haydar."

The durai turned to see the former queen Adiyiku descend the wide central staircase. His chest tightened at the sight of her. "Queen Adiyiku," Haydar said, bowing. "I was under the mistaken impression you were safely in Anzor during this time of upheaval."

To his dismay, Adiyiku had aged considerably since Delger's execution. The lines around her eyes and mouth had deepened, and her expression was even more sorrowful than before. He knew for a fact that Delger had been a terrible husband and father, and he'd hoped being free of him would have given Adiyiku and her daughters some respite.

She looked uneasy. "My daughters are safe in Anzor. I chose to stay with my son." Turning to Ruslan, she said, "My lord, Prince Vazha has requested your presence in his study. He told me to tell you as soon as you arrived. It has something to do with the supplies you promised to bring."

"Of course, my queen."

As Ruslan disappeared down the corridor, Adiyiku grasped Haydar's hands tightly and stepped closer, searching his face almost frantically. She whispered, "You shouldn't be here, Haydar. He's gone mad. He—"

The prince's cane struck the limestone in an even cadence with the heels of his boots, echoing through the hall. Haydar felt Adiyiku's hands tremble as he released them. He looked up to see Vazha and Ruslan coming toward them and said steadily, "Prince Vazha. It's been a short while. How are you?"

The prince smiled coolly. Patting the former queen on the back as he stood before Haydar, he said, "I apologize for my mother, Lord Haydar. She's been quite unwell since my father died. She's become something of a conspiracy theorist, convinced everyone is out to get her. Isn't that right, Mother?" Vazha kept his eyes on Haydar as he waited for her answer.

Adiyiku bowed her head, gazing at the floor. "Yes, Lord Haydar, it's true. Since Orwen died, I haven't been the same."

Haydar watched her carefully as he said, "I'm terribly sorry to hear that. Have none of the doctors in Anzor been able to help?"

"It's an illness of the mind," Vazha said. "There is nothing to be done, unfortunately." He gripped his mother around the shoulders. "Would you excuse us, my lord? I'd like to see my mother back to her bed."

"Of course." Haydar watched Vazha usher his mother back up the stairs and to her chambers, dread creeping up his spine. *He's no different than his father, is he?* Even though the prince had been a victim to his father's abuse himself, he'd grown up to be exactly the same way. Clenching his jaw, Haydar berated himself internally. How had he not anticipated this? As Delger's advisor, he'd done everything he could to shield the royal family from Delger's abuses. He should have known to protect Adiyiku and the princesses from Vazha, as well. *An unforgivable mistake.*

The quick click of Vazha's cane suddenly sounded far more ominous. The prince descended the stairs once again, a disingenuous smile on his face. "My apologies for the interruption, my lords. May I invite you both into the grand salon?"

Haydar cleared his throat. "If at all possible, Prince Vazha, I would like to have a private word with you."

Vazha's smile became sincere—and just askew enough to be chilling. "It would be my pleasure." He looked at Ruslan. "Make yourself comfortable, my lord. Invite your commander inside. I will have refreshments brought out."

Ruslan inclined his head graciously. "Thank you, Your Highness."

"Won't you join me in my office, Lord Haydar?" The prince turned and led Haydar down a long corridor that ended at large double doors of imported Anzori oak. The deep boom of the doors closing shut behind them echoed in Haydar's chest. Vazha walked over to where a decanter and two small, enameled glasses sat on a sideboard. "Some xew, Haydar?"

Absolutely. "Yes, thank you."

Vazha handed Haydar a glass and lifted his. "To your health, my lord."

Haydar took the glass and said softly, "That's a disingenuous toast, coming from you. But I'll still drink to it." He drained his glass, savoring the heat on his tongue.

Vazha also emptied his glass, then said, "Why have you come here, Haydar?"

The durai walked toward a tall window that looked out on the garden. It was a Gohari garden, if there ever was such a thing—mostly blue sage and bull thistle, splashes of blue amidst the brown. He said, "Not long ago, it was brought to King Tikran's attention that a certain Anzori lord sought to have him overthrown. The new king, you see, has upended social and political norms in Anzor by freeing the Gohari and granting them basic human rights." He paused, waiting for Vazha to respond.

The prince's face was like stone. "I'm not sure if you expect sympathy, but you'll get none. And I'm not entirely sure what this has to do with me."

Haydar walked over to the sideboard and poured himself more xew. After tossing back yet another glass, he said, "Strangely enough, all of this newfound knowledge coincided with Dilovar's very clear acts of war, and, more interestingly, intercepted messages between King Tikran and his commanders in Gohar." It may have taken two shots, but the xew was finally working. Haydar leaned against the cabinet as he poured himself a generous third glass. Setting the decanter down, he looked at Vazha, the pretense of puzzlement on his face. "Of course, at that point, both

Tikran and I were both very intrigued. How could an Anzori lord benefit from Anzor's defeat against Dilovar?"

The prince hadn't moved a fraction—no twitch of the facial muscles, no movement that would indicate surprise or fear or discomfort. He watched Haydar with cool disinterest. "Why don't you get to the point, old man?" he said, sounding bored.

Haydar didn't hesitate. "You've made some deal with Bilguun. I don't know what you gave him in return, but he agreed to make you king of Anzor if he could have some part of Gohar, didn't he?"

Vazha smiled. "You know Bilguun well, don't you? Very well, in fact. If I remember correctly, my father became convinced that the two of you were fucking."

Unflinching, Haydar smiled back. "I'm surprised you'd take your father's word on anything. He was a brutal, desperate man, wasn't he, Vazha?"

The wall came down then, crashing around Haydar almost audibly. Vazha's cool demeanor vanished, incinerated by the heat of his fury. "And you did *nothing*, you piece of shit." He walked toward the durai with nearly no assistance from his cane, his face crimson, his nostrils flaring. "You watched him force me to play soldier. You said nothing when he sent me to that outpost in the middle of Gohar, to make a 'man' out of me. You just sat by and let him do it. You just sat by and let me catch leprosy from those filthy, diseased savages."

The alcohol had lowered Haydar's defenses, and he felt a flicker of regret. Memories flashed through his mind—six-year-old Vazha sobbing as Delger called him "a fucking embarrassment," among other hateful things, stopping only when Haydar stepped in. The prince, around ten years old, trying to hold in tears as his father struck him repeatedly with a small whip. Haydar, again, stopping the abuse with diplomacy—*my enduring gift.*

But could he have done more?

Haydar spoke carefully now. "At the time, I believed it was good for you to see what your father was doing to the people of

Gohar," he said, trying to keep the emotion from his voice. "I thought it might change you for the better. It was a mistake."

"Oh." The prince let out a crazed laugh, tossing his head back. "It definitely changed me, Haydar, you fucking monster." He tapped his foot with his cane. "It changed me forever."

Let the diplomacy go. For Tikran. For Coxani. For Naran. He breathed deeply. *For Gohar.* Haydar pitched back his final glass of xew, closing his eyes as he swallowed. Then he straightened, fixing his gaze on Vazha's. "If you were a fraction of the person Tikran is, you'd have seen the suffering all around you and felt anger at what your father was doing to these people—human beings, who are, at their core, no different than you. But instead, you saw only your-self. *Your* suffering, *your* pain."

He came closer to Vazha, standing a mere foot away, ignoring the hairs that rose on the back of his neck as he saw the prince's hand move subtly from the corner of his eye. *It's up his sleeve.* Vazha's chest rose and fell rapidly, his lips curling over his teeth and his eyes bulging, veined and moist with rage. There was no doubt in Haydar's mind now—the time had come. Even as his heart raced, he delivered the final blow with passion: "Your father was right about you."

Vazha let out a strangled howl and lurched forward. Haydar felt the sharp pinch over his heart as Vazha slammed into him, nearly toppling them both over. Shoving the prince away, the durai glanced down to see a small, delicately crafted bronze handle protruding from his chest. He looked at Vazha, his lips twitching into something of a smile. "You just lost, Your Highness." With a calm detachment, Haydar grabbed the handle and yanked.

He was blinded as pain tore through him. The blade clattered against the stone, spraying the marbled white with a dark red. Haydar stumbled back, resting against the sideboard. In agony, he crossed his arm over his chest, trying to stop the blood from leaving his body. It soaked through his sleeve, thick and weighty. Vazha stared in disbelief, perhaps even in horror, and leaned heavily on his cane as he backed away, toward the door. Ruslan was suddenly in the room, his commander behind him. They all blurred before Haydar's eyes as pain consumed him. For a split second, he was back in the northern steppe, helping his sister herd sheep, holding a lamb in his arms and nuzzling its warm, soft wool.

Breathing suddenly became difficult as blood filled his lungs, bringing him back to the present. He was slumped against the cabinet, his cheek pressed against the smooth wood, the pain easing inauspiciously. His glass, emptied but minutes ago, sat beside his head. Before his vision faded, he saw that it was painted with a blue and yellow, long-billed bird in the swirls and slashes that were unique to Gohar.

Blood bubbled in his throat.

Long live the Freed Kingfisher.

CHAPTER 41

The Damla was darker here, in the cool north of Gohar.

As Tanith dismounted and walked through the grass to the banks of the river, she watched the murky waves swell gently, flowing southward. The stone bridge that linked Dilovar to Gohar stretched over the river in pointed arches, its mixture of white stone and red lumber distinct on the horizon. She caught the occasional twinkle of movement on its surface—no doubt from the Dilovari soldiers who were currently crossing it.

"Mistress Tanith," Commander Tural said, slipping from his saddle and coming to stand beside her. His voice was soothing. "Let me know how I can assist."

"Thank you, Commander. I think I just need to be sure no one sees us." She smiled up at him. "Otherwise, I've got this."

He nodded, smiling back at her as he stepped away. "My men and I won't fail you."

Turning, Tanith breathed evenly. She walked down to the bank, her boots sinking into the soft, silty soil at the water's edge. She crouched and tottered back, nearly landing on her backside. *This belly!* As if in response to both her thought and action, the being inside her revolted, its little parts thumping angrily against her. *Ouch. Okay, okay.* More carefully this time, she kneeled, letting her robe sink into the sandy mud. *Are you happy now? My robe is filthy.* The being remained still, apparently appeased by her sacrifice. Tanith rolled her eyes then dropped her hands into the murky shallows of the river.

This would take every ounce of her Essence, and she would likely need a couple days to recover from it. While she still worried that using her magic was negatively impacting her pregnancy, she had to help Tikran win this war. If a thousand more Dilovari crossed Damla Bridge, Tikran's armies would be in dire straits.

She stroked the water as it rushed between her fingers, coaxing it gently. Tendrils of magic pressed against the current, weaving across the river, resisting then releasing. *Back and forth. Back and forth.* The birds had stopped singing, sensing the disturbance. The waves were great swells now, drenching her with each surge even as she moved back. The silver scales of fish flashed in the waves, tails flitting and breaking the surface. The river gasped desperately, rhythmically, and Tanith's hands shook from the pain. Still, she pressed on, building a terrific momentum.

Inhaling deeply, Tanith pulled at her Essence, watching as the current flowed swiftly upriver, exposing the muddy banks to the south by a good six feet. The magic felt good now, tantalizing her. *Here goes.* With a hissing exhale, she shoved the water forward, her Essence tumbling forth into the river.

The force of the waves as they heaved downstream threw her back, the roar deafening her. She hit the ground hard and the air was knocked from her lungs. Water poured over her as she struggled to sit up, to breathe. When the assault ceased, she wheezed, gulping at the air. *The baby!*

"Mistress Tanith!" Tural was at her side, lifting her in his arms. "Are you all right?"

She could breathe again, somewhat. Frantic, she rested a tremulous hand on her belly. The small, cantankerous being within punched her in the kidneys repeatedly. *Thanks Archil.* "Yes," she answered, panting.

"Mistress," Tural muttered, his eyes wide and fixed on the horizon, where, like a fist, the fifty-foot swell rushed toward the bridge, spanning the entire width of the river. As water struck stone and the enormous wave broke in an explosion of frothy white, she heard a great *crack!* The water rushed over the bridge, and it groaned balefully as it crumbled from the pressure. When the water finally receded, she could see that enormous chunks of the bridge were missing, hopefully rendering it uncrossable. The river roiled angrily, no doubt swallowing timber and wagons and horses and men.

"You did it," Tural said in shock.

Tanith sat up slowly. The bridge was badly damaged, the river's horizon cluttered with its remains. As if it meant to torment her with every life she'd just destroyed, the magic throbbed painfully in her hands. She grimaced, her fingers cramping.

"Come on, let's get you back," Tural said firmly, draping a sheet around her shoulders and helping her up and to her horse.

She cast a look back at the river as they rode away, at its now smooth, rolling surface, and shuddered.

They rode as swiftly as possible back south. After hours of travel, she saw Gohari warriors surveying them from the tops of small hills in the distance and knew, without a doubt, Ayym rode among them. She'd likely been watching anxiously for Tanith's return. With what energy Tanith had left, she let out a piercing, playful whistle. The Manzakars who accompanied her looking around in confusion as the Sachin warriors whistled back. She could hear the laughter in those whistles, and it made her smile.

Tanith saw Tikran's army then, standing in formation north of the encampment, and her breath caught. The Manzakars had always been a terrifying and awesome sight to her, but she had never seen so many of them prepared for pitched battle, their lines of heavy cavalry looking like fierce, mounted gods. When they were close, she spotted Tikran galloping toward them. His eyes were on her as he reached them and reined his horse to a stop beside her.

"The scouts arrived an hour ago," he said as he grabbed her

reins, his face exuberant. "You did it, Tanith. Bilguun's camp is in a state of disarray over the destruction of the bridge. They had just begun to form lines when it happened." He peered inquisitively at her. "Are you all right?"

She shrugged. "Tired and dying to get out of these damp clothes."

He nodded, then looked at her belly. "And...?"

She chuckled. "As vigorous as its father."

Tikran smiled, his cheeks pink, his eyes darting around uncomfortably. "Let's get you back to the camp so you can change and rest."

Later that evening, after she'd changed clothes and taken a short nap, she emerged from her tent, her stomach growling. Tikran, Naran, Ayym, and the Manzakar commanders conversed around several fires, eating lentil soup. Tikran and Ayym sat on opposite sides of one particular fire and, upon seeing her, stood simultaneously.

She stopped, hesitating. *Oh, Archil...this is so awkward.*

The two leaders exchanged uncomfortable looks.

Ayym grinned good-humoredly. "Of course, Tanith should sit with her employer and the father of her child."

Tikran shook his head, his neck and ears reddening. "Don't do that, Ayym." He looked at Tanith and smiled uneasily. "Don't you feel loved?"

Tanith went over to the kettle that hung over the campfire and ladled the soup into one of the bowls stacked beside it. She replied, "Something like that." With a full, steaming bowl in her hands, she made her way to Naran and sat beside him. The big Manzakar rumbled with laughter, raising his eyebrows at both Tikran and Ayym. "Take *that*, you two," he said.

Ayym laughed and as Tikran opened his mouth to reply, a sudden commotion on the far side of the encampment made him turn. A Manzakar strode over, breathless, and kneeled briefly before Tikran.

"What's going on?" Tikran asked.

The soldier rose. "I come from Diyar, Your Highness," he said hurriedly. "A thousand Dilovari warriors, led by Prince Orxan, have managed to cross the river in barges and are headed south."

Tanith watched the young king stiffen and knew he immediately thought of Coxani.

He spun toward her, Ayym, and his commanders. His eyes blazed. "There's been a change of plans."

TIKRAN STANDS IN THE STEPPE, fully armored, blinking in the smoke. The grass is scorched as far as the eye can see and the sky is a sooty gray.

Oh, no. This fucking dream again.

Figures approach in the distance, their armor distinct. The Dilovari seem to multiply, more of them materializing from the haze by the second. Tikran draws his saber and holds his shield before him, his heart pounding, even though he already knows what will happen. The whites of their eyes glisten and their teeth flash in the darkness; they brandish their weapons and charge him.

He bridges the gap between himself and the closest of them, a Dilovari wielding a mace. Tikran leaps forward, ducking as the spiked weapon whizzes through the air and following immediately with a strike to his attacker's exposed neck. *One down.* Twisting to the side, he parries a slicing blade, steps forward, grabs the soldier's wrist, and chops at his head. *Two down.* As he cuts them down one after the other, the enemy soldiers fall limp and silent; their blood seems to float in the air.

When none are left, Tikran pants, surveying the bodies that litter the singed field.

Who will it be this time?

Of course, he suspects he knows.

Coxani.

He tears his helmet from his head and looks down at the fallen soldiers. Dread wells within him as he approaches the only one still moving. He kneels down and pulls off the dying Dilovari's helmet. Beneath it, Haydar lies gasping, his face spattered with mud. Tikran cradles his mentor's head in his arms in consternation. *What? Why you? Why now?* Haydar's eyes focus on Tikran and he opens his mouth to speak, his hand reaching for Tikran's face. Blood then spills from his lips, choking him, and as Tikran tries desperately to sit the durai up, Haydar's eyes go glassy and his chest stops heaving.

No...

CHAPTER 42

The messenger arrived on the cusp of dawn.

Closely packed yarms weaved between the hills, housing a thousand Davlat and five hundred Sachin warriors. The scattered tents of two hundred Manzakars dotted the encampment's periphery.

Most everyone still slept, save for the warriors and soldiers on watch—and Coxani. She'd begun rising before the sun, brewing herself some strong coffee, and finding a low hill to watch the sky slowly brighten and sit in quiet contemplation. The desert air was crisp and she shivered as she sipped from her cup, listening to the steppe buzz and the breeze sigh. She was wondering if her status as Rasula was powerful enough to make Berk defy Damir and fight for Tikran, when she heard the hoofbeats approaching from the low hills in the west.

She set down her cup and quickly pulled her bow from its sheath. Three Gohari warriors on watch duty cantered out to meet the lone rider, and the sky was illuminated just enough for her to see that he was a Manzakar bearing the flag of Anzor. Coffee forgotten, Coxani ran down the hill and across the stretch of patchy grass to meet him. *Maybe it's a message from Tikran.*

The Manzakar's face was grim beneath his helmet as he dismounted and faced her. "Captain Coxani," he said, "I come bearing shocking news. Lord Haydar has been murdered by Prince Vazha Delger."

Coxani was quiet for too long, unable to process what she'd just heard. Time seemed to stop as she watched the man's lips move, hearing nothing but the beat of her heart. *Haydar? Dead? Impossible.* Realizing that the Manzakar awaited some sort of reaction from her, she managed, "How would... It makes no sense..."

"Lord Haydar paid the prince a visit at his manor," the soldier said, grief plain in his eyes. "All of Anzor likely knows, by now. And a messenger is headed to King Tikran as well." He reached into his saddlebag and produced a letter that was sealed with Haydar's emblem—an arrow in the shape of a lightning bolt. "This is for you."

She swayed on her feet, feeling dizzy. *He planned this.* Because of course he'd planned it. She saw her hand take the letter, heard her voice make some sort of reply.

"Rasula," one of the warriors said, "are you all right?"

She nodded. "I forgot my coffee," she said numbly, then turned and began walking back to the hill. The sky was a soft orange now, the air just a bit warmer. She reached her spot at the top and sat once again. She paid no attention to the now-cold cup of coffee at her side as she broke the seal of the letter, her hands trembling. The sight of Haydar's careful, swirling script was almost enough to break her.

> *Coxani,*
>
> *By the time you read this, Vazha will have taken violent action against me. All the Anzori elite will likewise know of it, and his prospects for replacing Tikran as king of Anzor will be dashed. Tikran's allies helped me ensure everything was set, guaranteeing the news would spread quickly and resoundingly. Anyone who negotiated with Vazha will question his sanity and, hopefully, see*

what a treacherous, vile man he is. Use this to your advantage in every and any way you can.

You need to know how incredibly proud I am of the person you have become. I am in awe of your strength, your courage, your resilience. I knew you could rise to become an awe-inspiring Manzakar, and you've proven me right in every way. I believe that however you may suffer, you will never lose your capacity to love or to see through others' eyes. From the moment I carried you in my arms when you were but four years old, I knew I would call you my daughter.

I love you dearly, Coxani. Never forget.

Haydar

Although tears streamed down her cheeks, that agonizing implosion she'd experienced after Omid's death didn't happen. She simply couldn't let it happen. *Not yet.* Instead, she carefully folded the letter, tucked it into her pocket, and stood. She would mourn him properly one day soon. But not yet. Now, they had to finish what Haydar started.

You will not have died in vain, my lord.

She rushed back to camp, relieved to see the warriors roused and beginning to pack up their yarms. She walked directly into the yarm that Damir shared with Berk, not surprised to find Dilovar's head mage awake and dressing while Berk slept face down, snoring.

Damir blinked as Coxani threw open the flaps and the bright outside light hit his gray eyes. His voice, when he spoke, dripped with sarcasm. "Good morning to you, too, Coxani."

"Haydar's dead." She was going to hit Damir with this news as hard as she could.

His eyes widened, his fingers fumbled at the buttons of his shirt. "Dead? What? How?"

"Vazha." Everything she'd pushed down at hearing about Haydar's death struggled to clamber out of her. *No! Not now.* She resisted. "Haydar went to Vazha's manor." Before Damir could speak, she thrust Haydar's letter at him.

Damir took the letter and unfolded it, swallowing almost audibly. Berk stirred, mumbling in his sleep. As the doctor finished perusing the page, he spoke half to himself, his voice rough with emotion: "Haydar, you magnificent bastard."

Coxani desperately tried to keep her voice even. "I'll ask you again, Damir. Will you fight for Tikran?"

He looked up then, meeting Coxani's eyes. She knew his answer before he spoke. "Yes."

"And Berk? You'll convince him to fight for Tikran?"

"No. No." Damir looked cautiously at the sleeping teenager and grabbed Coxani's hand. After leading her outside the yarm, he said firmly, "I don't want him fighting for anyone."

"But Damir—"

"Coxani, listen to me." Damir licked his lips. "The boy is volatile. Even if I tell him to fight for Tikran, the sight of a Manzakar—killing, no less—could still completely destabilize him. He needs to stay out of this war. And I believe that between my mentoring and your...being a prophet, we can keep him from acting out." Damir drew a shaky breath. "Besides, Tikran's powerful mage and I should be able to help Tikran defeat Bilguun without Berk's assistance."

She stiffened. "You don't think Berk would repeat what he did at Zifa, do you?"

"I've expressly forbidden him from it," Damir said passionately. "The whole thing terrified him as well, and I'm hoping he's learned to control his Essence enough to prevent something like that from ever happening again." He exhaled. "But there are no guarantees, which is why I think it's imperative for him to stay away from the battlefield."

Coxani nodded. "All right. I trust you to handle him. Let's get packed up."

Damir handed her Haydar's letter and gave her a tender look. "I'm sorry about Haydar, Coxani. He clearly loved you very much."

She pressed her lips together to keep them from trembling, then replied, "We must see this through, Damir. For him."

"Yes." His lips quirked sadly. "For Enlil the Weaver."

THE EMOTIONS that overtook Damir as he reentered the yarm were more powerful than even his Essence. He braced himself on his knees, shaking, his body flooded with a tingling, ringing relief. He was free of Vazha, once and for all. As a prisoner of war, he was also, at least momentarily, free of Bilguun.

He could fight for the Freed Kingfisher with everything that he had.

There's hope yet.

"Master Damir?" Berk was awake now, gazing bleary-eyed at his mentor. "Is something wrong?"

Damir stood upright, trying to calm himself. *No. Everything is right, for a change.* He cleared his throat, speaking with as much authority as he could muster. "Berk, it has come to our attention that Prince Vazha has murdered King Tikran's most trusted advisor in cold blood."

The sleep vanished from Berk's face as his mouth fell open. "But...that means..." He sought the words, unable to find them. "What *does* it mean?"

Damir turned to the boy mage, his voice thick with passion. "It means that Vazha is no longer a contender for the throne of Anzor. It means we are no longer bound to him. Whatever threats or promises he's made are void." Was it his imagination, or did disappointment flicker briefly across Berk's face?

Berk averted his eyes as his fingers worried a loose thread in his undershirt. "You plan on fighting for King Tikran, don't you?"

"Yes." Damir finished dressing quickly.

"Will you expect me to, as well?"

"No." Damir paused, looking at the boy. "I don't want you

fighting at all, Berk. I want you to keep your Essence very still during this entire ordeal. Do you understand?"

Berk scratched his head. "Won't Rasula want me to fight for Anzor?"

"She agrees that you should stay out of it."

"Master Damir." Berk stood, his brows drawn. "It's because you don't trust me, isn't it?"

Damir let out a deep sigh. "It's not about trust, Berk. This isn't a game. This is *war*. Remember how Zifa made you feel, how those deaths haunt you?"

"I'm much better at controlling my Essence now, though," Berk insisted.

"Your participation is not essential for Tikran to win, so you will sit this out." Damir was firm. "To go against my order is to go against Rasula's order as well. Do you understand?"

Berk nodded slowly. "Yes."

"Good." Damir crouched, rolling his bed into a bundle and tying it. "Get dressed. We're leaving as soon as possible."

As the two Dilovari mages tacked their horses in preparation for departure, a young Manzakar approached them, his stride confident, his mouth stretched into a broad smile. "Hey, uh," he said, "Master Damir. Master Berk."

Berk startled at the address and Damir said, "Yes?"

The Manzakar rubbed his neck, his eyes darting about. "I wanted to thank you both for...well, you know." He indicated his thigh, then made a grotesque popping sound.

He lives. Damir couldn't help but smile as Berk stammered, "Oh...I didn't...I mean, I'm glad it all worked out."

"It did." The Manzakar grinned. "I'm Moti, by the way." He looked from Damir to Berk. "I owe you both my life. If either of you ever need help, know that I'm your guy." He chuckled uneasily and added, "Assuming, of course, that you aren't slaughtering a bunch of Manzakars and actively trying to kill me."

"Thank you, Commander Moti," Damir replied, trying to sound appropriately solemn.

Moti let out a laugh. "Nah. Just Captain. My preference. Although, if we win this thing, they'll probably insist on promoting me to commander." He made a face then turned and walked away, practically swaggering.

Berk glowed with pride. Damir turned back to his horse, hiding his smile. *Saving life is much more satisfying than taking one, eh, Berk?*

Even with seventeen-hundred warriors and Manzakars combined, they were on the move by mid-morning. Damir marveled at how easily the Gohari packed up—and how quickly the Manzakars had adapted to doing the same. The sun rose in the sky, beating down on the long column of warriors as midday struck. And yet, Damir didn't feel the heat as intensely as before. He gazed up at the blue sky, a smile on his face as sweat ran from his temples. At that moment, nothing could bring him down.

Several shrill, staccato whistles filled the air as a line of Gohari galloped toward the procession from the west, their shields flashing. *Well, shit.* Damir didn't need to be told what the whistles meant before reaching for his shield. That's what he got for feeling a shred of optimism, wasn't it?

From somewhere in the back, Coxani yelled, "Shields!"

Raising his own over his head, Damir heard the deep, forbidding song of the Dilovari bodkins just before they struck the metal and flesh around him with devastating force. He moved against Berk, grabbing the horse's bridle as soon as he was close enough.

Berk shrank behind his shield, gasping. "They wouldn't kill us, would they?"

"Not intentionally," Damir replied, keeping a firm grip on Berk's reins. "If anything, they'd want us alive." *But I'm not letting them take us.* He turned a fierce look on the boy. "No magic, Berk. Do you understand? Let me handle things."

Berk hesitated, a petulant twist to his lips. "Yes, sir."

The Manzakars encircled the two mages, their shields held high. Damir attempted to peek past them, between the tightly knit barrier of horses and ironclad men but could see none of the attackers. Only the falling bodkins—which pummeled them at random intervals—and the cacophony of rattling, clanging, and shouting indicated a battle had commenced. He couldn't imagine there were very many Dilovari, and certainly not enough to defeat a force of seventeen hundred. Most of Bilguun's forces, after all, were in the north, facing off with the armies of Anzor...

Several minutes into the assault, Coxani shoved through the protective wall of Manzakars, her horse stomping, her teeth bared and brow furrowed, blood oozing from a gash on her cheek. She held her bow and five arrows in her bow hand as she grabbed Damir's arm. "Damir, we need you. There are at least a thousand of them, and the Gohari aren't equipped to battle heavy cavalry. What's more, the river has inexplicably risen overnight and its banks are a mere half mile away. They're pinning us in. At this rate, you and Berk will end up back in their hands."

A thousand! More troops must have crossed the river to evade Tikran's forces. Damir looked at Berk. "Stay here. The Manzakars will make sure nothing happens to you."

Berk frowned, his lips moving with questions that Damir had no time to answer. Coxani ordered the Manzakars: "Do not, under any circumstances, let the Dilovari get to this mage! Understood?"

The Manzakars shouted their assent. Damir heaved his shield higher and followed Coxani as they maneuvered their way to the Manzakars at the forefront. His heart sank when he saw the wall of Dilovar marching toward them, the long tails of horsehair flowing from their broad-brimmed helmets. Their armor was heavier, their shields larger than those of the Manzakars. Still, Damir had no doubt he could stop them. The intimidating sight wasn't what gave him pause; his Essence began brewing in his veins the moment he saw them. No, what suddenly ate at him was that these men thought they could trust him, and he was betraying them.

From this moment on, I am a traitor.

The thought disconcerted him, but he still kneeled with certainty.

I'm sorry.

He closed his eyes, shutting out the faces of the soldiers he was about to kill. As his fingers burrowed in the dirt and he prepared to release his Essence, Coxani clamped a hand on his shoulder.

"Damir. Wait." She squinted, panting. "They've stopped."

Keeping his hand in the earth, Damir asked, "Why?"

A Gohari warrior's whistle, of a different pitch this time, pierced the air in three short notes. Coxani closed her eyes and let her breath slowly seep from between dry, pale lips. Her voice was nearly a sob. "Tikran has arrived."

CHAPTER 43

When the Sachin scout galloped out from a valley between two distant mesas, a shrill whistle on her lips, Tikran felt a multitude of emotions. Her signal indicated they were mere miles from Orxan's forces. *It's time.* He wiped the sweat from his eyes as his mind raced through his battle plans. Two hundred of Ayym's warriors had remained behind and hidden in the hills, waiting for Bilguun's army to follow, and had harassed them mercilessly the entire march south. He knew Bilguun was no more than a couple hours behind them, if that, but hopefully that would be enough time to surprise Orxan's forces and gain the advantage. He'd tried to anticipate everything, knowing that nothing was really within his control.

If that boy mage pulls that trick again...

Tanith had surmised that Berk had used the pooling rainwater to enter the fallen Manzakar's wounds with his Essence. If there was rain and blood—which there surely would be—the boy could annihilate hundreds of soldiers and warriors at a time.

Damir. Why aren't you stopping him?

A strange excitement brewed beneath the pain, frustrating Tikran to no end. He would be in the same vicinity as the doctor again, and his heart hitched at the thought, despite everything.

Attempting to refocus his thoughts, Tikran looked at Naran and Tanith, both of whom rode alongside him. *What if something happens to them?* Naran looked more apprehensive than Tikran had ever seen him; Tanith, he could tell, was still exhausted from destroying Damla Bridge, despite her protestations to the contrary.

And Coxani? And Damir?

Clenching his jaw, Tikran tightened his grip on the reins. He hated that he was afraid. He was afraid of losing his friends and even his enemies. He was afraid of watching them die, unable to help them. He was afraid of losing this war, of what would happen to Gohar if he did. The weight of the world bore down on him, heavier now than it had ever been—and just hours before battle.

Get a grip!

As he chastised himself internally, he heard a voice shouting and one of his Aslans addressed him. "King Tikran, a courier has just arrived from Eter, bearing an urgent message from Anzor."

Tikran pulled on his reins and came to a stop. The strangest feeling swept through him then, as if some part of him already knew how this story ended and was gently coaxing the rest of him into acceptance. "Bring him to me," he said.

The messenger, a Manzakar whose face was worn and filthy, rode up, his mount moving restlessly. "King Tikran. I come bearing terrible news."

Haydar. The soldier spoke and Tikran watched his lips move, saw his gloved hand hold out a letter. Tikran took it, his thumb tracing the edges of the jagged arrow pressed in red wax. Naran was beside him, saying something angrily.

The courier said, "I have a letter for Commander Naran as well." As he passed it over, his eyes crinkled with sadness. "I'm so sorry, Your Highness. I know you're about to confront the Dilovari, but Lord Haydar insisted I relay the message to you before then, at all costs. He also asked that I tell you...to read the letter immediately."

Tikran muttered, "I understand. Thank you."

Naran's face was ashen, his yellow eyes wide. "He can't be dead. He *can't* be dead. He must be fucking with us."

Slowly, Tikran broke the seal of his letter and began to read.

> *Tikran,*
>
> *I'll try to make this short, since I imagine you have much on your hands at the moment. Vazha is no longer a threat to you. He made a deal with Bilguun involving the exchange of a traumatized Gohari boy with incredible Essence for the throne of Anzor and half of Gohar. I also believe he trapped Damir in going along with his plan, using your life as leverage. Rest assured that by the time you read this, Vazha will have already been apprehended by the Manzakars from Areg, whom I prepared for this very scenario.*
>
> *I know you must feel like the world is crashing down around you right now. But I've watched you go from slave, to soldier, to rebel, to leader, to king. In you, I've always seen a braver, stronger, more righteous version of myself. You, Tikran, are not just Gohar's champion, but Anzor's. Someday, all of Anzor will realize this.*
>
> *A father couldn't be prouder of his children than I am of you, Coxani, and Naran. Even if you lose this war, even if you lose all the wars, nothing can possibly change that. And nothing should ever keep you from fighting for what you believe is just.*
>
> *There's so much more I want to say. But we both need to go. It's time for action.*
>
> *I love you dearly, my boy. Never forget.*
>
> *Haydar*

Tikran turned the letter over, wanting—no, *needing*—more. Realizing there was none, he folded the letter carefully, pressing the seal with his thumb. *You planned everything, didn't you? Every last...fucking...thing.* A pain like no other racked his body, nearly crippling him.

Then that familiar fire ignited deep in Tikran's chest, roused from a too-long dormancy. All the events that had led him to this moment rushed back to him—his first campaign, the starving nomads, the murdered Gohari raiders, Mago's death, his friends' sacrifices. The pain and apprehension of earlier were gone, replaced by a razor-sharp focus, a certain madness...

The colors around him, drab and anemic seconds before, were now vivid, from the small patches of blue sage that speckled the steppe, to the silvery shimmer of the grass as it swayed in the breeze. The heft of his armor pressed his silk tunic against his chest, both wet with his sweat. The song of a sand plover trilled over the soft nickers of the mounts, and he tasted dust and a hint of saltiness on his lips.

He looked over at Naran. The big Manzakar held his opened letter in his hand, his eyes bright with a blend of pain and rage, fixed on the horizon. "Commander Naran," Tikran said, his voice husky. "Let's finish this."

Naran nodded and said softly, "For the Weaver."

Looking at Tanith, Tikran asked, "Ready?"

Her eyes were large with something like awe as she returned his gaze. "Yes, King Tikran." She then said to her mages, "It's time."

"Beg Ayym," Tikran said, turning in his saddle to face the Sachin chief. "Let the hunt begin."

AYYM FLASHED Tikran a cocky grin and a thumbs-up as she cantered out of formation with the four other mages and whistled to her warriors. Along with several Manzakar light cavalry units, the warriors headed southwest, intent on beginning the assault on the Dilovari by showering their ranks with arrows and javelins. The mages would ride up and down the enemy's lines, igniting fires to thin their ranks further and cause confusion.

When the great cloud of battle was visible to the naked eye, Tikran rode quickly to the front of his army, wheeled around, and drew his saber. He'd given his men a solemn, admittedly half-hearted speech the night before, and there were but moments to improve on it now. His eyes scanned the Manzakars before him, most of whom had been bought by Haydar personally. He shouted, "Manzakars! Lord Haydar is dead!" Tikran felt his anguish and fury gush forth, rasping his voice as a murmur of dismay rippled through the troops. "Delger's son, Vazha, murdered him in an attempt to replace me as king. My brothers, our fight did not end with the rebellion, and it will not end with this war. Lord Haydar sacrificed his life for this cause, to see the Gohari free, in both Anzor and Gohar. As we fight today, remember what we fight for, and remember Haydar." A single, errant tear rushed down Tikran's cheek. "He will not have given his life in vain."

Lances pounded the earth fervently, flushing birds from shrubs and sending rodents into hiding. Raising his sword, Tikran let out his battle cry. *For Haydar!*

The responding Manzakar roar echoed in his ears, their impassioned, tear-streaked faces as they thrust their fists and weapons in the air a thing of terrible beauty. *I hope you hear that in the afterlife, my lord. I hope you know how loved you are.* Reining his horse back around, he dropped back, signaling to Naran and Tural. Naran's unit would strike one flank and Tural's the other. As the heavy cavalry units delivered the final blow to the rear and, assuming all went well, Tikran's forces would turn and, in a defensive formation, prepare for Bilguun's arrival.

Tanith, for her part, was prepared to counteract whatever magical attacks Damir might perform and offer her own Essential aid if they found themselves in dire straits.

The one element Tikran could not anticipate, of course, was Berk.

Coxani had said she would "handle him." Tikran had no idea how she intended to do that, but there was nothing he could do to adequately prepare for what the boy mage might attempt, other than try to kill him outright. And while his commanders had disagreed with his order to only kill the mages if they cast magic destructive to their forces, Tikran had been adamant.

Now, black smoke rose over the melee as Tikran's forces approached. The sky suddenly darkened and rain fell, progressing quickly to a downpour before easing. The mages, apparently, were already hard at work. Tikran could tell that Orxan hadn't anticipated Anzor's quick advance—his forces were not positioned to defend against the flank.

Dilovari light archers galloped past their front lines, their bodkins replacing the rain as they fell from the sky. It was too little, too late. Anzor's heavy cavalry advanced at a trot, remaining silent, armed with their lances, their warhorses pounding the now-wet field. The clouds parted and the battlefield was illuminated again, enveloped in dust and smoke. Both Naran and Tural let out battle cries nearly simultaneously, and the Manzakar cavalry charged. With their lances leveled, they swarmed the Dilovari flanks with crushing force. The impact shook the earth as lances cracked and splintered against armor. The cries of men mingled with the screams of their horses as they fell and were trampled; formations broke and swords were drawn. As the men engaged in close-quarters combat, sabers and maces swinging, the occasional fire ignited, only to be quickly smothered by bouts of rain. The clouds soared in and out overhead with each casting of magic, and eerie, brief episodes of dimness fell across the melee. Tanith rode up beside Tikran, a note of concern in her voice as she blinked the rain from her eyes. "Why aren't Damir or Berk doing anything?"

He was wondering the same thing. Thus far, the magic involved had been performed by clearly less powerful mages from both sides, who were lighting fires and bringing rain. "I don't know." *Maybe Coxani really did handle it.* Part of him dared to hope.

"Your Highness!" A Manzakar light archer approached at a gallop, his face slick with sweat. "Bilguun's forces are less than five miles away."

Tikran signaled to his commanders and reached over to squeeze Tanith's hand. "I'm definitely going to need your help now."

From beneath her helmet, her pale blue eyes glowed. "I'm ready."

He still doesn't trust me.

Anger flared in Berk's gut; his Essence stirred in his blood.

I'm the most powerful mage here and I'm still being treated like a child.

Lowering his shield a fraction, Berk assessed the landscape as best he could from within the barricade of mounted Manzakars. The Dilovari arrows still fell, albeit infrequently, and the sounds of the melee had died down. Smoke filled the air, which smelled of burnt flesh and feces—both horse and human. He hadn't detected the use of Damir's Essence, only that of the minor mages on both sides. Clearing his throat, Berk said loudly, "Excuse me, Manzakars?"

One of them turned in his saddle to look at Berk, his hand on the hilt of his saber. Although the soldier scowled, a hint of fear in his eyes betrayed him. "What is it?"

Berk tried to sound forceful. "I want to join Master Damir."

The Manzakar shook his head, his voice gruff. "You're not going anywhere. Strict orders." The other Manzakars who surrounded him looked over their shoulders at him, their weapons in hand, their eyes darting as if to avoid eye contact with him.

They're afraid of me. Berk's horse snorted and stomped its feet, seeming to detect Berk's rising anger. Had these men been given the order to kill him if he disobeyed—by the Rasula, no less? Berk clenched his teeth, his fury giving the magic free rein as it swept through his veins, coaxing him. Despite Damir's constant training, the head mage still believed Berk couldn't control his Essence, that he was unreliable and volatile.

I'll show him. I'll show everybody.

Fixing his eyes on the commanding Manzakar's back, Berk noted where fabric peeked out from beneath his armor. He scanned the other men, confirming that they, too, had clothing exposed in the same general areas. He closed his eyes, tempering his Essence. *I don't want to kill them. I just want them out of my way. I can do this.* Without setting down his shield or even lifting his hand, Berk took a deep breath and moved his fingers. The fires that ignited on the first Manzakar exploded into existence at the backs of his arms and lower legs. Before the men could grasp what was happening, Berk had ignited fires on them, too, in rapid succession. They screamed; their horses panicked. Despite being engulfed in flames, the commanding Manzakar drew his sword, his eyes trained on Berk. Kicking his mount into action, Berk plowed through a gap between the fiery Manzakars, his shield protecting him against the burning heat. Once he was through and fleeing away, he moved his fingers again, calling the rain in a torrential downpour.

Free of his human prison and now soaking wet, Berk lowered his shield and looked around, unsure of where to go. A melee of cavalrymen still clashed in the mud, their lances and battle axes flying. The Manzakars were now extinguished and two of them were in pursuit of him, their armor blackened and faces contorted with rage and pain. Before either Manzakar could reach him, however, bodkins and javelins flew, striking one Manzakar in the armpit and impaling the other through the neck. They crumpled on top of one another like rag dolls and lay in the mud, perfectly still.

Berk continued forward, shaking, hiding behind his shield, intent on simply getting far away from the fighting. His horse stumbled over the bodies that littered the field, contorted in unnatural positions, splattered with blood and mud. Berk felt his stomach churn at the sight and smell of the dead. They stank of excrement and green flies already buzzed about them greedily. Trying to keep his stomach from expelling its contents, Berk coaxed his horse to move faster—away from the battlefield.

He looked out into the distance, desperate for clean air. At the foot of the hills a short distance away, Berk spotted an enormous Dilovari, watching and shouting orders. *Orxan!* Berk tried to breathe steadily as he reined his horse to a stop once again. *I have to do this. I have to.*

Summoning up all his courage, he quickly slipped from his horse and knelt beside the body of a fallen Dilovari soldier. Berk held his breath and, avoiding the dead man's open-eyed, vacant stare, pulled the standard from his grasp with a desperate wrench. He stumbled back, nearly falling on top of another distended, fly-infested body. Grasping the standard in both hands and breathing steadily through his mouth, he turned back toward his mount. The orange of the flag was mostly obscured by mud, but it would have to do. Berk clambered back onto his horse and galloped toward Orxan, his shield on his left arm and the standard held high.

Bows were armed, bodkins pointed directly at Berk as he approached, slowing to a trot abruptly. "Don't shoot! It's me, Berk!"

Orxan rode forward then, pushing his men's bows away as he passed them. As he reached Berk, he said, "Holy Cenk! How did you get away?"

Berk shrugged, using his Essence to fill his lungs steadily. "I set a bunch of them on fire."

Orxan grabbed Berk by the arm and pulled him from the saddle with a hard yank. Berk stifled a cry, landing on his feet and facing Orxan in terror. The Dilovari prince almost smiled, his heavy brow clearing. His voice boomed. "Where's Damir?"

"He's still a prisoner." Berk hesitated for just a moment before deciding on his next words. His voice shook with fear. "They're making him fight for King Tikran. They threatened to kill him—and me—if he didn't. They didn't trust me to fight, they told me to stay out of it."

Orxan nodded grimly. "Well, we have you now, and you *will* fight." He lifted Berk by the collar of his cuirass with one hand and dropped the boy mage back in his saddle with a plop. With a fierce growl, Orxan said, "Bilguun arrives soon. Let's get you to him."

CHAPTER 44

What remained of Orxan's forces retreated quickly into the hills, less than an hour before Bilguun's arrival. All Anzori standards still stood, waving in the smoke. Tikran rode swiftly toward the battlefield, his mouth dry as he navigated between the metal-clad bodies that lay twisted in the churned earth. His men searched the dead and injured, most of whom were Dilovari.

"Look who I found, picking fights with the enemy?"

Tikran swiveled in his saddle at Naran's voice, blinking in the sooty air. His commander-in-chief grinned, his teeth white in a grimy face. Beside him, Coxani slipped off her mount and yanked off her helmet. Leaping off his horse, Tikran opened his arms in time for the lamellar of their cuirasses to clash in a violent hug. *Thank Archil.* He felt an overwhelming relief, nearly gasping aloud.

She pulled away and stepped back, surveying both him and Naran, her cheek caked with blood, looking the same and yet, entirely different. Her big green eyes still blazed with passion, but now had a hardened focus he'd never seen before. "I've never been happier to see anyone," she said. Her voice was deeper than he remembered, as if she'd deliberately adopted a more commanding tone. "You received letters too, I assume?" she asked. Tikran closed his fist, his mouth refusing to form the words. Naran said nothing and looked away. She nodded once, then hopped back on her horse. "Let's win this."

Tikran licked his parched lips. "The mages..."

Coxani smiled curiously, gesturing over her shoulder. "You aren't paying careful attention, are you, Your Highness?"

Blinking again, Tikran focused on one of the men on horseback behind her wearing a Manzakar's helmet and a Dilovari cuirass. The pale gray eyes were bloodshot from the smoke but still unmistakable. Shock jolted Tikran as Damir rode forward slowly. The two men locked eyes, not speaking. Time stopped; for a moment, Tikran's resentment, anguish, and suspicion were smothered in a fog of disbelief. Was this a dream? Every dream he'd had of Damir since seeing him last had been an awful nightmare, rife with betrayal and death.

The doctor's lips moved tentatively at first, as if he couldn't find his voice, his expression mirroring Tikran's. Finally, he said, "I've ordered Berk to abstain from fighting. I think between myself and your head mage, we can win this."

We. Tikran swallowed, again making a fist. *It's really him. This is no dream.* His extremities tingled. As the fog lifted, emotions that Tikran had kept carefully at bay for more than a year suddenly rocked him, threatening to overtake him. How many nights had he lain awake, cursing Damir's name? And now the doctor was here, just a few feet away, and every inch of distance was suddenly unbearable. *Fuck! Get a grip!* Tikran finally spoke, annoyed at how he sounded like he was choking on his words. "Are you doing this of your own free will?"

Damir kept his silver gaze on Tikran. That deep, irreverent voice hadn't changed, although it sounded congested with unspoken sentiment. "One hundred percent, Manzakar."

He's fighting with us...with me. Relief washed over Tikran like much-needed rain on the steppe. He wanted to fall to his knees and weep, to grab Damir and collapse into him, to run his fingers along the contours of Damir's face and inhale his scent. *Enough!*

Focus. Tikran took two slow, full breaths before asking, "Where is Berk now?"

"He's safe," Coxani said. "I have him protected by an entire squad of Manzakars."

"He should be kept away from battle," Damir said. "It's best that he stays where he is. He's promised me not to get involved."

Tikran nodded, dragging his eyes away from Damir's face and reining his horse around. "Commander Naran, let's line up in a hurry. Bilguun's vanguard will be making an appearance any minute now." As Naran saluted and cantered off, Tikran turned to Coxani. "Will you take command of the flight archers? Ayym and Bruneta will follow your lead."

"Yes," Coxani answered, vaulting back on her horse and pulling on her helmet. "What's the plan?"

Tikran looked to the north. "We're going to play the Gohari warrior's game," he said. "I doubt Bilguun will put his infantry on the front lines after what we did to Orxan's troops. We're going to meet them right away. His heavy cavalry will charge and our center line will fall back, hopefully luring them in. Then our flanks will close in on them. They have more troops than us, but Damir and Tanith will do what needs to be done to make sure Bilguun doesn't get the upper hand."

Coxani nodded as she wheeled around, whistling to the warriors.

Tikran gestured to Damir, avoiding his gaze. "Come with me." Questions, accusations, pleas, and proclamations all sprang to Tikran's lips, longing to be spoken. Still, he resisted. *Now is not the time. You need to focus.* The pair rode in tense silence to where the Anzori forces were forming lines and Tanith awaited Tikran's return. "Tanith, this is Damir," Tikran said by way of introduction, still not looking at the doctor. "He's fighting with us of his own accord. The boy mage, Berk, will not fight."

Her mouth opened in surprise. "That's...immense," she said. "Tikran, by Archil, this could mean victory for Anzor!"

"That's the plan," Damir said, a troubled look on his face. "Mistress Tanith, a pleasure to meet you."

"Likewise," she replied with a small smile. "I've heard much about you."

Damir raised an eyebrow, shooting Tikran a brief glance. "Oh, yes? All good things, I imagine."

Damir's biting wit filled Tikran with an unexpected warmth. *He hasn't changed.* Tikran cleared his throat, trying to ignore the two head mages' conversation and the fact that Damir's frown had undoubtedly been from seeing Tanith's swollen belly. Tikran nudged his gelding forward, scanning the distant hills. Naran and Tural both signaled—his army was ready.

Several minutes before Dilovar's forces could be seen, thousands of hoof beats rolled like endless thunder, growing louder. A haze rose on the horizon, dusty and pale, glinting with iron, steel, and lacquered leather. It stretched across the steppe endlessly, and Tikran experienced a spell of dizziness. *I've lived this moment before.* Orange banners hovered over the haze, fluttering in the wind, and through the clouds of dust the Dilovari cavalry emerged, line upon line, pouring across the steppe.

He breathed deeply.

I won that battle, and I will win this one too.

NARAN'S rugged battle-cry galvanized the men forward in a clattering lurch.

The Manzakar ranks rode with effortless grace, their weathered faces pensive and alert, their lamellar plates clinking. The air was thick with dust and heavy with the silence of impending bloodshed. Tikran rubbed his gelding's glossy neck with his gloved hand, his eyes raking over the dark river of Dilovari troops as they came closer. They were, without question, as terrifying now as they were the first time Tikran laid eyes on them—their sunburned faces were fierce and expressionless beneath their brimmed iron helmets, long tails of horsehair flowing behind them. Sabers and maces and bows were slung at their hips, and their quivers bristled with arrows. They held their large, oval iron shields on their arms and their twelve-foot-long lances in their hands, at the ready.

At Tikran's signal, Naran and Tural's light cavalry detachments fanned out across the steppe from both flanks, wheeling left and right. Joining Coxani and the Gohari warriors' light archers, they began showering the Dilovari with arrows. The light cavalry rode up and down the enemy's front lines, raining arrows and javelins down on them. The Dilovari returned the volleys almost instantly, and shields were raised to a Manzakar cry, blotting out the sun. The missiles sang their deadly song before bombarding Tikran's forces, blasting into them with teeth-chattering force.

Tikran was relieved to see that both Tanith and Damir had been through enough battles to know when and how to wield their shields. He began pacing his horse back and forth, restlessly watching from elevated ground as the Dilovari cavalry charged. His heart pounded even as his focus remained steady.

Just as anticipated.

And just as anticipated, Tikran's center line fell back, retreating from the wall of crushing, piercing enemy cavalry. But as his light cavalry tried to wrap around Bilguun's flanks, more of their troops appeared on the horizon, stretching further east and west and using the hills to their advantage. They swept down from the mesas, clashing with the Gohari warriors and Anzor's light archers, razing them to the ground with horrific ease.

Tikran's horse shook its mane and grunted, stomping and churning the grass beneath its hooves into dust. *Time for magic.* He rode swiftly back to Damir and Tanith. "The hills. Can you stop Bilguun's light cavalry?"

The two mages exchanged knowing looks, then nodded at Tikran. Tanith said, "I'll head west, Damir will head east."

Tikran watched, mildly bewildered, as the mages galloped in opposite directions at breakneck speed. *Wait!* He shouted to his

Aslans. "Two of you go with Mistress Tanith, two of you with Master Damir. Now!" He continued to pace back and forth, waiting for the Aslans to reach the mages. Then his gaze swept across his lines, watching as the Dilovari heavy cavalry tore through his ranks. Bodkins swooped down, shattering against armor and shields, driving into men and horses with lurid screams. Tikran pulled his bow from his hip along with a handful of arrows and, in measured, rapid succession, released them into the air. He knew exactly where they would land—just beyond the fray, behind the front lines. They punched into Dilovari horsemen, boring through armor and eviscerating flesh with an eruption of blood.

He opened his mouth to shout orders when the ground beneath his horse's hooves rumbled, causing disarray in the melee before him. *Yes.* He looked to the west first, almost shouting with relief as Tanith's Essence rolled with practiced efficiency under the hills, crumbling them in an avalanche. As the rocks and dirt collapsed, Dilovari soldiers disappeared beneath the rolling earth, arms and legs sinking slowly beneath the waves. Tikran turned to the east then, only to see the same event—Damir's magic stirred the soil angrily, and it rose up like an open palm, taking a hundred Dilovari with it, the hungry earth's growl echoing in the air.

Yes! Shouting for his heavy cavalry to charge, Tikran felt a rush of euphoria. *We can win this.* It was then that he saw the Dilovari infantry crest the horizon—hundreds upon hundreds of troops. The Dilovari's momentum had slowed, however, on account of the two mages' magical destruction, giving Tikran time to plan his next steps. As the mages returned, both panting, sweat beading their brows, Tikran looked to Damir, an apologetic look on his face.

"I need more from you." He nodded toward the north, where a sea of enemy soldiers rushed toward them. Damir opened his mouth to speak, only to be interrupted by Tanith.

"I'm not spent either, Your Highness," she said firmly. "I can help too." She looked at Damir. "What do you have in mind?"

Damir nodded once, his face earnest. "Since we can't be there ourselves to touch the earth, we'll have to touch the air. Can you create wind funnels, Mistress Tanith?"

"I can." She peered up into the blue, mostly cloudless sky. "There's just enough moisture. Let's do it. East and west like before?"

"Can you *please* do it from here?" Tikran blurted, scowling. "I can't be worrying about you two while trying to command a bloody army."

Damir smiled. "We can. It won't be as powerful, but powerful enough to keep them from advancing."

Tikran let out his breath. "That's more than enough."

Looking at Tanith, Damir said, "Same as before. Yours from the west, mine from the east." She nodded and the two mages dismounted and raised their hands in unison, both their faces upturned to the sky. Tikran's Aslans hovered around them protectively, their shields at the ready.

Clouds gathered swiftly overhead, moving as if alive, shutting out the sun. As they darkened to blue-black hues, lightning illuminated the battlefield and thunder rumbled soon after. A wind rushed across the steppe, making Tikran's skin pebble beneath his armor. Above, the clouds churned and swirled ominously, faster and faster, until they began reaching for the earth with two ghost-like protrusions. Large raindrops pelted the men in the field, but they never stopped fighting, indifferent to all but surviving the cuts and thrusts of the enemy. The eerie protrusions danced to the ground, making it shudder as they landed. Twisting with a terrible fury, the pair of wind funnels raced across Bilguun's infantry, devouring their numbers, flinging men and metal like projectiles through the air. A Dilovari was thrown high in the air, landing amidst the melee with a crash; debris rained down on them along with a flurry of arrows. The funnels roared hungrily, deafeningly, their paths slowly converging.

"That's enough!" Tikran shouted over the wind and crackling destruction. He flinched as the rain drove down on him like needles. "Damir, Tanith! Stop!"

The mages' faces were strained, their fingers curled as if cramped. They gasped and cried out in turn, as if in terrible pain. Tikran looked back at the sky, where the funnels hastened, vanishing into the storm clouds as if they had never existed. Tikran felt dizzy as he slid from his saddle, rushing to the mages. Damir braced himself on his knees while Tanith swayed on her feet, looking faint.

Tikran quickly scooped her in his arms. "Take them to safety," he ordered his Aslans. "I want them away from the fighting."

"No," Damir said with a puff, pulling himself upright. "I'm staying with you."

Something about the way he said it made Tikran's heart jump. Tanith looked up at him, her face wan. "I won't fight you this time. But I want to stay close in case you need me."

"Yes, all right." Tikran stroked her face affectionately and helped her onto her horse. "Get her somewhere safe and stay with her," he said to two Aslans. As they rode off, he turned back to the battlefield, surveying the damage that the mages' creations had wrought. A long gash in the steppe marked their paths, littered with bodies and debris.

Tikran's stomach twisted even as his heart lurched. The Dilovari troops fell back abruptly, widening the gap between the two armies. He spotted Naran and Tural behind the heavy cavalry, ready to charge, cries of victory on their lips.

Tikran suddenly felt real hope.

BERK SHIVERED SLIGHTLY beneath his armor as the raindrops fell, razor-sharp, and the wind whipped about him. Orxan was beside him, grasping the reins of Berk's horse tightly. From the top of a low hill, he could see the damage left behind by the whirling clouds. Bodies strewn about like the toys of a petulant child, sinking in the mud. *So many dead.* Berk swallowed. *So many more to die.*

"All right, Berk," Orxan said, his voice sounding not unlike the thunder. "It's now or never."

Berk glanced at the prince. "You promise my conditions will be met?"

"On my honor." Orxan's thick eyebrows were drawn tight. "I am a man of my word, boy."

Berk nodded. He slipped from his saddle and stepped forward, looking out over Anzor's army. With a deep inhale, he crouched to the ground and touched it tentatively. He knew he didn't have to touch it—he could do what he needed to do regardless. But thanks to Damir, he'd learned that touching it with his fingers gave him more control, allowing him to be more precise with his magic.

As the clouds parted and the winds died down, Tikran's heavy cavalry charged. The Manzakars at the forefront glittered in the emerging light, their faces fierce and their lances leveled. Berk's Essence surged through his body, pulsing with hatred, fear, and envy.

Gritting his teeth, Berk drove his fingers into earth.

THE MANZAKAR heavy cavalry was a synchronized, disciplined tide as it rushed forward in a great cloud of dust. Tikran's eyes followed Naran at the back and on the left, then Tural on the right. He felt a sense of pride as he watched, gripping his reins tightly in anticipation. Part of him wished he was down there with them, his lance braced in his right hand, his shield in his left. While the horrors of being in the midst of battle lingered, the desire to fight alongside his men was more powerful at that moment. *We Manzakars are one.*

Damir rode up beside him abruptly, his face lined with concern beneath his helmet. "Tikran, something's wrong. I need to check on Berk. I feel powerful Essence in the air, coming from Bilguun's army."

"What?" Tikran snapped his head to look at Damir. "Coxani said Berk was—"

He heard the cracking before he felt the tremors. It echoed across the steppe as the shaking began. The horses spooked and stomped back, their eyes wide and nostrils flared. The earth rumbled and shook beneath them, drowning out the shouts of the men. Just beyond the cavalry charge, the earth split open like a hungry mouth. With a deep, guttural roar, it yawned open, swallowed rocks and grass in a broad, jagged swath across the steppe. Before Tikran could react, the front of the cavalry formation suddenly dropped out of sight, followed by the horsemen behind them, and the horsemen behind them... Men and horses spilled into the abyss in a horrific landslide, unable to stop. Horses tried to bolt, men collapsed, trying to grab at something, anything.

"Retreat! Retreat!" His voice was lost in the din. The world rattled so vigorously that Tikran only saw blurred, shattered movements. In spite of it, he could see it was too late. As the last of Tikran's heavy cavalry—one thousand Manzakars—vanished beyond the void, the earth groaned balefully once again, bucking and shuddering as the chasm closed.

Then, the ground was still.

Pressing his thighs against his frantic horse, Tikran spun around in a panic. *Naran!* He shouted as he kicked into a gallop, maneuvering between the debris, soldiers, and bodies, finally reaching the rugged scar that seamed the earth. Leaping from his mount, Tikran heard himself screaming. *No!* He fell to his knees on the jagged mound and began scraping at the dirt desperately. He was vaguely aware that Coxani had fallen beside him, screaming as well, scrabbling frantically. His world still shook, his vision blurred. He didn't care that he was king. He didn't care that he'd just lost a very decisive battle. He didn't care what Dilovar's army was doing. None of it mattered in that instant. The only thing that mattered was Naran.

When the soil began to rush away from his fingers, he finally looked up. Damir kneeled beside the sutured ground, his hands knuckles-deep in the soil. It rolled smoothly away, as if the magic was peeling it in layers. Slowly, arms and legs and heads began to emerge, some moving, some perfectly still, their lances and helmets protruding from the ground.

The Gohari warriors and Anzori light cavalry helped pull men, horses, and bodies from dirt as Tikran looked about, his heart in his throat. The earth retreated in waves, slowly exposing heaps of bodies. He dropped down and crawled, wiping dirt from faces, pulling on arms and hands that gasped or moved, helping whomever he could. As he perused the destruction, his sense of despair mounting, he spotted a half-buried shield bearing the emblem of a stalking lion. *Please still be alive!* As Tikran dug bare-handed, pulling the shield free, he felt Damir's Essence strip the earth away. Tikran inhaled dirt, felt its grit in his mouth and eyes, but continued to dig until Naran's face emerged, sculpted in soil. With an enormous gasp, the big Manzakar sat up, dirt collapsing from him in an avalanche.

Tikran fell back, nearly blacking out from relief. Coxani was sobbing, grabbing Naran fiercely by the shoulders. He blinked at them from a dirt-encrusted face, soil crumbling from his eyelashes, and said hoarsely, "I really thought...I died this time."

Tikran clasped Naran in a tight embrace, indifferent to the dirt that spilled into his tunic, eyes, and mouth. *Oh, thank Archil!* He sobbed and held Naran at arm's length. "Are you hurt?"

Naran still breathed heavily, wincing. "I think I broke a few bones."

"Let's get you out of here," Tikran said, standing on shaky legs and regaining control of his emotions as his men carried what survivors remained back to the camp. What had just happened? Had the majority of his army really just been buried alive? All his commanders except Naran were gone, including Tural. *Tural.* They had to keep digging, keep searching. Only twenty-two men emerged from the earth as they dug, broken but still breathing. He wanted to start sobbing again but resisted. *It's over.* "Lower the banners!" he shouted, his voice cracking, the words like a stake through his heart.

Damir was slumped and pale, his magic barely a trickle now. Tikran crouched beside him and grabbed his hand. "Damir, it's over."

The doctor's face was twisted in agony as he said, "This is my fault. I should have never let Berk out of my sight."

Tikran squeezed his hand tightly. "It's not your fault. We—"

"Tikran." Coxani spoke urgently from behind him. "We have company."

Tikran looked up to see Dilovar's army surrounding them, waiting for a single errant move—horsemen with lances poised, archers with bowstrings taut, infantrymen with swords and axes drawn.

Oh, shit. He stood slowly, releasing Damir's hand, his desire to sob vanishing. The line of troops parted then, and Bilguun's commanders, with Orxan at the forefront, approached slowly on horseback, silent and forbidding. Tikran nodded wearily at the prince, removed the weapons from his belt, and mounted his horse. He was, without question, in a state of shock. The horrific, sudden deaths of his men echoed in his head. His chest ached under the unbearable weight of Anzor's loss, and yet, he held his head high. Something within him refused to concede defeat.

No.

It couldn't end like this.

CHAPTER 45

The sun had begun to sink beyond the horizon, marking the end of the longest day of Tikran's life. *And it's not even close to over.* Across the muddy, ravaged field, the birds chirped and the sky dimmed to a soft orange, as if none of it had happened—not the terrible wind funnels, not the rattling, devouring earth, not the thousands of deaths. Nature returned to normal, ever resilient.

As Tikran prepared to meet the Dilovari, Coxani, Ayym, and Bruneta swiftly rode up beside him, their weapons left behind. They were battered and exhausted, filthy and bloodied. And yet, they kept their backs straight, their faces fierce. Tikran felt a wave of pride beneath the despair. Damir grabbed a horse and joined them, his hands trembling with fatigue but his expression earnest. Tikran felt another tiny glimmer of warmth beneath the numbness.

The two parties stopped a couple meters away from each other, and Orxan squinted up at the cloudless sky for a long moment. Finally, he said, "Your Manzakars fought bravely, Freed Kingfisher." He hesitated, as if choosing his words carefully, his heavy brow creased. "I can't help but wonder who would have won without this...magic nonsense." He cleared his throat, then said, "Even though you stand before me as Dilovar's vanquished enemy, I respect you as a king and a warrior. I believe you are trustworthy, and will continue to treat you as such, despite your defeat." He gestured at Damir. "Come, Master Damir. You are no longer a prisoner of Anzor."

Damir frowned, hesitating, and Tikran resisted the urge to scream. *What is he doing? Admitting he's a traitor?* To Tikran's utter relief, the doctor composed his face and rode to Orxan's side. Damir then turned and locked gazes with Tikran, his gray eyes full of anguish. Orxan smiled with satisfaction. He said to Tikran, "King Bilguun is waiting to discuss the terms of your defeat."

Terms of my defeat. The words made Tikran sick to his stomach. *All those lives, lost...Gohar's freedom, lost...* As evenly as he could, he replied, "Lead the way, Prince Orxan."

They had begun to cross over the site of Tikran's defeat—the massive grave of at least a thousand Manzakars—when Tikran heard hoofbeats and shouting behind him.

"King Tikran! Your Highness!"

Tikran turned to see Moti on horseback, cantering toward them, his cheeks flushed. The captain reined his horse to a stop, his eyes darting to the Dilovari nervously. "Uh, I realize this is a bad time, Your Highness, but...it's Tanith." He licked his lips nervously. "The baby is coming." Smiling apologetically, Moti added, "Now."

Tikran's heart dropped to his feet. He was certain Tanith had told him that the baby wasn't due for another month or so.

Oh, fuck.

"I'm heading back," Ayym said firmly, already kicking her horse into a gallop. Bruneta shot Tikran a wide-eyed look before following.

Orxan hmphed in mild amusement. "Let the women take care of women's troubles." He began to turn toward the Dilovari camp. "Are you ready, Freed Kingfisher?"

"No." Tikran's voice was firm, his pulse racing. "The baby is mine, Orxan. And it's...early. I need to be there."

Orxan's eyebrows shot up. "By Cenk! I have four bastard children. Two were early. I wasn't at a single one of their births. In fact, I still don't know one of them, and he's close to three years old."

Good for you. Tikran answered, "I will be back as soon as it's over. I will have an envoy send a message to King Bilguun himself."

"Prince Orxan," Coxani said, her voice so commanding that Tikran almost did a double take, "I will stay with you, as assurance." She glanced at Tikran coolly. "He'll be back."

The Dilovari prince considered, stroking his clean-shaven jaw. "All right, Freed Kingfisher. Tend to your child's birth. Those things are never quick, in my experience, so meet me here at dawn tomorrow."

His eyes darting nervously at Coxani, Tikran said, "Do I have your word that you will treat Coxani honorably, Prince Orxan?"

"You do," Orxan rumbled, crossing his arms. "I saw her on the battlefield. I have respect for her as a warrior."

Tikran had always felt Orxan was principled, even as an enemy. Tikran nodded then paused, meeting Orxan's steady gaze. "May I borrow Doctor Damir?"

Damir visibly started. "*Me?*"

"Yes." Tikran's horse shook its mane restlessly. "This birth is likely to be complicated. A skilled doctor—one with the Essence, no less—would be very appreciated."

A wide, mischievous grin split Orxan's face as he saw Damir's horrified expression. "I don't see why not. Go on, Doctor Damir. I trust King Tikran to bring you back with him."

Tikran gave Coxani a long look before turning. Her lips nearly curved in a smile. "Good luck," she said.

As he and Damir rode back to the Anzori camp, Damir said, "Orxan is an honorable man. Nothing will happen to Coxani."

"I suspected as much." Tikran cleared his throat and asked uneasily, "Were you putting on a show back there? So that Orxan would let you come with me?"

Damir winced. "Not exactly."

Tikran slowed his horse to a walk and stared at Damir. "You've never delivered a baby before, have you?"

"No," Damir answered, not meeting Tikran's gaze. "That's what midwives are for."

It suddenly occurred to Tikran that Damir could quite possibly be the worst person for the job. He hesitated, wondering how to phrase his next question. "Do you even know how women's bodies... I mean, below the waist...?"

Damir flashed Tikran a waspish look. "I know how women's reproductive organs work. I'm a doctor, for Cenk's sake." He sniffed, looking away uncomfortably. "And I've seen...diagrams."

Oh...shit. Tikran rubbed his face. "Damir, her last pregnancy ended in stillbirth. She's afraid her Essence caused the baby's death."

Damir nodded, offering what Tikran assumed was supposed to be a reassuring smile, but came across as utterly anxious. "I will do my best."

* * *

THEY ARRIVED at the king's tent and dismounted briskly, pushing the flaps aside to enter at the same time. Tanith sat up, propped by pillows, her face flushed and glistening with sweat, her lips pursed in pain. Tikran kneeled beside her and grabbed her hand.

She squeezed his filthy palm in hers, letting out her breath. "I'm so sorry, Tikran. I—"

"Don't worry about anything right now," he said gently. "Just focus on getting through this."

"King Tikran," Damir said, his voice firm as he removed his robe and pulled a bottle of alcohol from his doctor's bag. "I will need you to, at a minimum, wash your hands if you are to stay and assist." He looked at Ayym. "You as well."

Tanith frowned and tried to sit up straighter. "Master Damir, have you ever delivered a baby?"

Damir again avoided eye contact, rolling up the sleeves of his undershirt and washing his hands and arms in the water-filled basin. "Not exactly. But I have assisted in delivering a bovine calf before." He flashed her a pained, apologetic smile.

Oh, good grief. Tikran cringed, even though he had no doubt that Damir was trying to be reassuring.

Letting her head fall back, Tanith muttered, "Oh, Archil."

Ayym scowled. "If I thought I could get back in time, I'd fetch a midwife from my clan. None of my warriors are midwives, unfortunately."

"I completely understand your trepidation," Damir said, "but I *am* a doctor. I promise to do everything I can to ensure this birth is successful." Something seemed to shift in him then—he straightened, tightened his jaw. Addressing Ayym and Tikran, he said, "Make sure no one else comes into the tent, please. Neither Mistress Tanith nor I need an audience. Also, bring me several clean sheets. Refill that basin with clean water and have a second brought in, if possible."

As the king and beg returned from doing Damir's bidding, Tanith let out a shout, making Tikran jump. She grimaced with pain, gripping his hand so tightly it nearly went numb. He looked at Damir in alarm. "Are you going to do something, or what?"

Damir shot Tikran an icy glare as he kneeled before Tanith and tentatively lifted the blanket that was draped over her lap. He said gently, "I apologize for the impropriety, Mistress Tanith."

As soon as the contraction was over, Tanith gasped and gave Damir an icy look of her own. "Impropriety? Please. I couldn't care less about that. Just help me get this baby out!"

"Right." Damir swallowed then pushed the blanket to her knees. His eyes widened and he grew somewhat pale. "Holy Cenk, the baby is already crowning."

Tikran moved to see when Tanith's grip on him tightened like a vise. "No, you stay here," she said, her voice a growl. "One man between my legs is more than enough, thank you very much!"

Ayym, who held Tanith's other hand, let out a hoot of laughter as Tikran sat back meekly, feeling thoroughly chastised.

Blinking rapidly, Damir looked at Tanith, his cheeks suddenly pink with excitement. "A few good pushes, and the head will be free, Tanith."

Tikran watched Damir's face for a moment, his mouth ajar. The doctor was doing much better than Tikran had anticipated. *Seems to be taking to it, in fact.* Relieved, he turned his focus to Tanith, clasping her hand within both of his. He spoke to her softly as she grunted in pain, her eyes squeezed shut: "You've destroyed a bridge, crumbled hills, and created a terrible wind funnel, all while very, very pregnant. You can do this, love."

Something about what he said made her eyes open, and her lips almost curved into a smile. Then, she pushed with a roar.

Damir gasped and stiffened, his eyes wide. He stood then, holding a small, slimy, bloody creature in his hands. He said softly but passionately, "Hize! It's a girl!" Looking frantically from Tikran to Ayym, he commanded, "Someone help me!"

Tikran looked desperately at Ayym, only to find her cowering back and shaking her head. "This is all you, Da," she insisted, pointing at him.

Fuck! Tikran released Tanith's hand and stood, stepping forward. "What do I do? How—"

"Did you wash your *fucking* hands?" Damir snarled, his face fierce.

"Yes, of course!" Tikran was furious.

"Grab a sheet and wrap the baby in it. Get all the vernix out of its mouth and nose so it can breathe. Turn it upside-down and smack it, if you must." Damir was panting. "I need to take care of Tanith."

Smack it? Is he kidding? Holding the tiny being between his hands as if it were made of glass, Tikran watched Damir sever the umbilical cord, then began wiping its face as the doctor had instructed, petrified by its silence. Tanith stared at the bundle, her face creased with fear, her chest rising and falling rapidly. She asked, "Is she alive?"

Tikran continued to clean the waxy goo from the baby's nostrils and mouth in a mounting panic, terrified to learn the answer, when it suddenly balled its tiny hands into fists, scrunched up its face, and let out a lusty, angry wail. Tikran shook with relief and exhaled a laugh, peering down in fascination at this feisty, raging little human. "Yes," he answered. "She's very much alive." He quickly walked over to Tanith and laid the baby in her arms. It screamed mightily, its little face now beet red from exertion.

Tanith chuckled, the tension leaving her face. She looked at Damir, who carefully covered her legs with the blanket. "What did you call the baby? When you held it for the first time?"

Damir washed his hands, taking a moment to understand the question. Then he smiled and said, "I didn't call her anything. In Erdem, 'hize' means 'miracle.'"

Tanith looked down at the baby's wrinkled face. "Master Damir has named you...Hize."

Coxani was surrounded by the enemy. Their heavy scale and lamellar pauldrons glinted in the evening twilight, and the long plumes of hair adorning their helmets swayed along their backs. No one spoke; they approached the Dilovari camp in silence, their faces like stone.

She'd relinquished herself at will to help Tikran. It hadn't even occurred to her not to, even though the fact that Tanith was pregnant with his child had, admittedly, caught her off guard. *I knew she was up to something.* But if Coxani was being perfectly honest with herself, she liked the fact that Tikran didn't seem to have a physical "type." He was clearly attracted to who people were, as opposed to what they looked like.

Helping him had never been a hard decision, and she knew it would never be one.

Now, as Coxani rode amidst the Dilovari warriors, she tried not to revisit the horrors of the battle. Naran was, thanks Archil, on the mend. Unfortunately, it was still *her* fault Anzor had lost the war.

She clenched her fists. If only she'd kept a closer eye on Berk. *If only I'd done away with him when I had the chance.* She'd really believed being the Rasula had helped sway him, and she'd been fatally wrong.

She realized suddenly that they were entering the Dilovari camp and braced herself, prepared to see the skulls of Manzakars on spikes, their rotting bodies displayed for the feasting of crows. Instead, she saw a camp not unlike Anzor's—tents of leather and felted wool were pitched around cooking fires; goats roamed freely as farriers and armorers forged horseshoes and weapons; soldiers laughed as they prepared their meals and drank their grog. Stopping their revelry to show their prince the proper respect, they bowed their heads, lifting them quickly after he'd passed to peer at Coxani in fascination and loathing.

She heard it on their lips, as if they spoke of a mythical beast: *Manzakar.*

Tears sprang to her eyes and she willed them back. *We might well be mythical beasts now.*

They stopped and dismounted, and Coxani held her breath anxiously. While Orxan had promised Tikran nothing would happen to her, she was still a lone, weaponless Manzakar in the enemy's camp. *And a woman.* She knew Tikran's thoughts on Orxan—a worthy opponent, he'd said. Of course, Tikran would have never agreed to leave her with someone who wasn't honorable.

Still...

Orxan barked orders at his men in Erdem and they scattered to do his bidding. Then he turned and approached her, his lumbering form nothing short of intimidating. Coxani stood straight, meeting his gaze unflinchingly. He smiled; it was a friendly, guileless smile. Combined with what Tikran had told her, she immediately understood certain things about the prince: *Good-humored. Probably not manipulative.* She didn't smile back. Instead, she said, "I would like to wash up and have a private place to sleep."

The big Dilovari tilted his head. "Is that all? No food? You must be starving. I know I am."

Coxani hadn't realized she was hungry at all until that moment. She shrugged. "I suppose some food would be nice as well."

He smiled again. "Excellent. You will dine with me in my tent. But first, let me take you to yours. My men are preparing it now."

Dine with him? Coxani blinked in puzzlement. They were enemies who had just fought a brutal war and she was here as collateral. This couldn't be a friendly dinner date.

To Coxani's surprise, her tent was furnished with a bedroll, blankets, pillows, a large waterskin, and a basin. It was as though she were a guest, not the vanquished enemy. Orxan set his hands on his hips. "Do you need anything else?" Miffed, she shook her head, and he said, "One of my attendants will come fetch you in thirty minutes to sup with me." With that, he turned and ducked out of her tent, leaving her alone.

She washed her hands and face, wondering what Orxan wanted—for surely, he wanted something. As promised, an attendant arrived thirty minutes later and led her to the prince's tent. It was larger than most, but still austere, lacking in creature comforts and very much like Tikran's "royal" tent. A rug with cushions had been laid out, and dishes of roasted goat meat and fried potatoes lay in the center. Coxani's stomach grumbled at the smell of the food.

Orxan had cleaned up some, from what she could tell, and gestured to her. "Come. Sit. Please. I'm dying of hunger."

She complied, and as soon as Orxan was seated, he began eating. She followed his lead and the pair ate in silence. She could hear the laughter of the men outside and the distant playing of a stringed instrument. *Just yesterday, we were trying to kill each other.* As she'd loosed her arrows in a fury on the battlefield, she hadn't thought of them as human, and she was certain the reverse was true as well. But they *were* human, eating and laughing and trying to heal from the scars of war just the same.

Orxan set his plate down with a belch, clearly sated, and leaned his large frame back in the cushions with his cup in his hand, surveying her with interest. After a moment, he said, "So, you are Archil's descendant, eh?"

Coxani swallowed the last of her meal and set her plate down as well. "Berk told you that, did he?"

"Yes." Orxan took a gulp from his cup. "He said it makes you a Gohari prophet."

"That's what I'm told," Coxani answered. "Little good it's done me, though." Her throat caught on the last couple words, and she sucked in her breath. *You can't fucking cry right now!*

Orxan knit his brows, his expression one Coxani couldn't place. *Is that sympathy? Surely not.* He spoke slowly, as if choosing his Perchuhi words carefully. "Berk is...ambitious. But not without a soul. He agreed to fight only if certain conditions were met, and one of those conditions was for Tikran's life to be spared."

Coxani stared. "Really?"

"Really. The boy clearly cares for Damir." Orxan drained his cup and sat up. "Tomorrow will be a difficult day for King Tikran. Bilguun is not someone I would call merciful. The Freed Kingfisher is lucky to be loved as he is." They stood and Orxan said, "I'm going to sleep. My attendant will take you back to your tent."

The dinner was apparently over. As Coxani left, she paused, looked back, and said, "Prince Orxan, Gohar deserves its freedom."

The big Dilovari grunted and turned. "Good night, Manzakar."

CHAPTER 46

Tikran lay on a bedroll beside Tanith, hyperaware of the baby's every whimper, every grunt as it slept at its mother's breast. Perhaps he dozed in brief snatches; he wasn't certain. The vision of his cavalry tumbling into that black, gaping maw repeated endlessly in his head, snapping him awake every time he began to feel himself slip into slumber.

When Damir entered the tent to check on Tanith, Tikran sat up, recognizing that dawn was less than an hour away. He rose quietly, locking eyes with Damir, dying to say a million things. They would have to say goodbye once again, and Tikran wasn't sure he could bear it. He opened his mouth to whisper—what, he hardly knew—when the baby squalled and Tanith awoke. She sat up, rubbing her eyes.

Softly, Tikran said, "I'm meeting with Bilguun this morning." *To discuss the terms of my defeat.* He couldn't bring himself to say the words aloud. "Hopefully, I'll be back."

Blinking at Tikran, she replied, "I'm coming with you."

Tikran frowned at her. "What? No, Tanith, you need to rest."

Ayym entered the tent at that moment, and Tanith instructed her, "Take Hize to Saysa while I'm gone." She handed the baby to

Ayym while she tugged up her undershirt and pulled on her robe. "Saysa is a warrior and a mother. She'll know what to do."

As Ayym left again, holding the baby awkwardly in her arms, Damir hesitated. "Mistress Tanith, although you seem to be healing well, riding astride is ill-advised so soon after childbirth."

Tanith smiled complacently, standing as she buttoned her robe. "After my last pregnancy, I was not only riding astride the next day, but shooting Manzakars. Regardless, I will ride pillion behind Tikran this time. Does that meet your approval, Doctor?"

Damir's eyebrows rose in amusement. "There's no stopping you when you set your mind to something, is there?"

"No, there isn't," Tikran muttered, answering for Tanith as he scrubbed his face with his palms. "I don't know why you want to be there. It's going to be awful."

"I stand by you, Tikran," Tanith said. "The tribes of Gohar stand by you. This is a loss for all of us, and it's not just your fault."

"In fact, it's all mine," Damir said softly.

"No." Tikran shook his head. "You both have made your point. Let's get this over with and get Coxani back."

As he tacked his horse, the sky began to illuminate, bathing the battlefield in a hint of pinkish light. That rugged seam snaked across the battered earth, still gleaming with half-buried lances, shields, and helmets. Swallowing down his nausea, Tikran helped Tanith onto the back of his horse and climbed on in front of her. Damir, Ayym, and Bruneta joined them and they rode across the battlefield, where Orxan, his commanders, and Coxani awaited them.

Tikran's party stopped before the Dilovari and Orxan smiled. "I suppose I'll trade you a Manzakar for a mage," he said.

Coxani looked Tikran directly in the eyes and he exhaled slowly in relief. *She's all right.* As Coxani and Damir traded places, Tikran tried to keep his expression blank. *How am I going to endure losing him again?* Avoiding Damir's gaze diligently, Tikran said, "Lead the way to King Bilguun."

The soldiers stopped to gape as Tikran and his party followed

Orxan into the Dilovari camp. Amidst the felt and leather tents sat an ornate command pavilion with carved wood doors and orange banners streaming from its poles. Unlike Tikran, Bilguun was clearly a king first, and a soldier second. They dismounted and walked into the enormous tent. Inside, Bilguun sat in a cushioned throne, a goblet in his hand, surrounded by his elite guards. A young man, only just more than a boy, stood quietly in the shadows wearing a Dilovari mage's robe, his hands behind his back, his dark eyes watchful.

This must be Berk. Tikran fixed a long, pensive look on the young Gohari mage, causing him to redden and look away nervously.

"King Tikran," Bilguun said, his expression indecipherable. "Would you care to sit?"

"No, thank you," Tikran answered. "I will stand with my warriors."

Shrugging with seeming indifference, Bilguun took a sip from his cup and said, "Well, then, I suppose I'll cut to the chase, eh?" As he moved to set his goblet aside, two of his guards reached for it. He dropped it into their hands and leaned forward, his eyes on Tikran. "Gohar now belongs to Dilovar. I think that much is clear. Rest assured, it will thrive under Dilovar's dominion. I intend to allow Gohar to have its own jurisdiction, including its own mage —under my authority, of course." He nodded at Ayym and Bruneta. "Dilovar will be gracious in its guidance. I am no Delger. I will ensure everyone in Gohar is fed and that it is able to sustain itself." He leaned back, looking once again at Tikran. "The Gohari tribes clearly adore you, Freed Kingfisher. And since the last thing I need is an uprising, you will return to Anzor alive. I'll let the Anzori handle you." Bilguun paused, stroking his silky mustache. "Anzor will have one mage, appointed by me. This mage will answer to Dilovar and keep a close watch." His eyes shifted to Tanith. "As much as I hate breaking up your lovely little family, I think it's in our best interest for Mistress Tanith to serve as a mage of Gohar so I can keep an eye on her." Bilguun gave Tikran a smug look. "Congratulations, by the way. I hear you've sired a *daughter*."

"Thank you," Tikran answered smoothly, instantly feeling the women around him stiffen with indignation. They would have been reaching for their weapons at that moment if they'd had them, no question. "I couldn't be prouder." He tilted his head, his expression unchanged. "Will I be able to see my daughter and her mother?"

Bilguun waved his hand, as if the issue was of no consequence. "Yes, yes. I will have my men escort them to visit you, what, twice a year? Whatever you want."

A ponderous weight settled over Tikran. "And might I ask who you intend to appoint as Anzor's mage, Your Highness?" *Let it be Berk. I will wring his little neck the instant he sets foot in Anzor...*

Bilguun turned to look at Damir, who now stood at Bilguun's side, his face stoic. "Master Damir, I am demoting you. While I understand that you may have been acting out of fear for Berk's life in betraying me to help Anzor, I still find it difficult to forgive your actions. Had it not been for Berk, you might have been the deciding factor in this war." Bilguun's eyes flashed angrily. "As such, Berk will replace you as Dilovar's head mage. I am appointing you, Damir, as my mage in Anzor."

Oh, wow. Tikran nearly swayed on his feet, feeling as though he'd been struck by lightning. Damir's expression didn't flicker, even as he gazed steadily at Bilguun.

"I realize, of course," the Dilovari king continued, "that you have a preexisting relationship with the Freed Kingfisher, but Orxan made certain promises that he intends to keep, and I have little fear that you'll betray me. After all, doing so would be devastating for both you and King Tikran."

Tikran avoided looking at Damir. Orxan had made promises? To whom? And why?

"And Anzor's access to Gohar?" Coxani asked.

Bilguun chuckled. "Oh, Master Damir will ensure Anzor has enough Essence to sustain itself, but not more than that. It will certainly not be able to harvest slaves to feed its army anymore." Bilguun smirked. "Anzor will need a few generations to rebuild its forces, won't it, King Tikran?" A fierce glimmer shone in his eyes. "Now that the Manzakars are no more."

Even as Tikran's expression remained impassive, his heart lurched in his chest. The words echoed in his head thunderously.

The Manzakars are no more.

THE FULL MOON CAST A WARM, white light on the steppe. After a long day of recovering bodies and tending to the wounded, Tikran was finally alone. Breathing deeply, he kneeled on the torn earth, where so many of his comrades had died, and pulled Haydar's letter from his jacket pocket. He unfolded it with trembling hands and read it again, a lump in his throat.

Even if you lose this war, even if you lose all the wars...

He looked up at the sky, at the brilliant, tactile stars, and spoke aloud, his voice quavering and strained. "I've failed you, my lord. I've failed Gohar. I've failed Anzor." With a gasp, Tikran finally gave in to his need to cry. His body shook as he sobbed, all his anguish pouring from him. He set the letter down, afraid to stain it with his tears.

When a hand touched his shoulder, Tikran was too lost to care, his soldier's instincts suffocated by grief. Damir fell to his knees before Tikran and clasped him in a fierce embrace. Damir's warmth enveloped him, and the doctor's scent filled Tikran's nostrils. All of Tikran's senses were overcome by Damir and it was a salve on his soul. He sank into the doctor's arms, clutching him tightly.

"Tikran. Tikran." Damir stroked Tikran's hair, his deep voice soft and his breath warm against Tikran's ear. "I'm so sorry. I'm so very sorry."

The two men remained on their knees, their arms intertwined and bodies pressed together, for several minutes. Finally, Tikran pulled back a fraction, looking Damir in the face. In barely a whisper, he said, "What happens now?"

Damir ran his thumb along Tikran's cheek, his silver eyes brimming with love. "I don't know. But we will get through this." He smiled. "Together." Taking Tikran's palm against his, he weaved their fingers together slowly.

An unexpected tranquility flooded Tikran's body. He closed his eyes and rested his cheek against Damir's. He wasn't alone. He had Coxani, Naran, Tanith, and now, finally, he had Damir.

Tikran's eyes opened.

He was not done fighting.

Until Gohar was free, he would never stop fighting.

EPILOGUE

In the dimness of his cell, Vazha watched as a yellow, black-speckled spider crawled from between the grimy stones of the prison floor tentatively, the movement of its long legs making the prince shiver in disgust. The spider made its way toward him, where he sat on a cot. Once it was within striking distance, Vazha leaned on his cane, raised his good foot, and stomped down on the insect with force. He then scraped the bottom of his boot against the floor, smearing the crushed spider across stone.

Good and dead. Like Haydar.

The thought made Vazha smile, despite everything. He did not regret ending Haydar's life. He'd wanted to kill his father's accomplice for a long time. Yes, Haydar had laid a trap, using himself as bait, for Vazha. And yes, Vazha's grip on the throne of Anzor had slipped—for now. With any luck, it was a temporary setback.

He grit his teeth.

I will retake the throne of Anzor from that slave.

Vazha leaned gingerly against the wall, loath to touch anything in the dirty cell. He hadn't bathed in what felt like an eternity, but his filth was *royal Anzori* filth, after all. Even though he'd been imprisoned at Areg for a couple weeks now, he was confident that his time as a prisoner would come to an end soon. He was a prince and Cenk's most devoted apostle. Surely Haydar had underestimated the sway religion held over the people of Anzor. Besides, even if the Freed Kingfisher won this war, Vazha saw through his warrior's guise—Tikran had no taste for killing.

His lips twisted in that cruel smile again. *It will be his downfall.*

Urgent shouts rang out from outside the prison and Vazha tilted his head, trying to listen. When he heard the distinct consonants of Erdem spoken, his heart leaped in his chest. *Let it be true!* If the Dilovari were in Areg, it could only mean one thing. He got to his feet as quickly as he could and moved toward the iron bars of his cell, peering down the dark corridor to the prison's entrance. Several minutes passed before the doors swung open, letting in the blinding sunlight. The silhouette of a large Dilovari filled the entrance, his distinct helmet giving him away.

Vazha exhaled, feeling dizzy with relief.

Dilovar has won.

The big soldier strode into the prison, his voice booming. "Vazha! Where are you?"

"I'm here," Vazha answered, slipping his hand between the bars and waving. His eyes adjusted to the light and Orxan's face became clear as the Dilovari approached. Orxan stopped before Vazha's cell and stood in silence, his dark eyes assessing the prince critically. Vazha's heart pounded, his grip on the bars tightening.

"Prince Orxan," he said, "am I glad to see you."

Orxan remained silent for several more agonizing seconds. Finally, he said, "I understand that King Bilguun agreed to give you asylum in the case that you'd somehow lost Anzor's favor and Dilovar won the war." He scowled. "I don't like it. I would say that I don't trust you as far as I can throw you, but I'm certain that I can throw you far." He raised an eyebrow. "*Very* far."

Vazha cleared his throat. "Hopefully throwing me won't be necessary."

"Yes." Orxan's eyes glimmered with warning. "Hopefully."

With a sigh, he stepped back and gestured to one of his men. "Free him."

Vazha smiled slowly and stepped back as the door was unlocked. Lifting his chin, he said, "Neither you nor your father will regret this, Your Highness."

ALSO BY R. LAHAM

The Slave-Soldier Series

Manzakar

Freed Kingfisher

About the Author

I've done everything under the sun—I have a BA in archaeology from the University of Pennsylvania, a law degree from the University from Houston, and have worked as a graphic artist, romance editor, writer, UX designer, frontend developer... the list actually goes on. Yet through all these endeavors, I've always known my true calling was storytelling. I'm a huge nerd and draw my inspiration from actual history and RPGs, particularly video games (Dragon Age, Mass Effect, Horizon, Dark Souls...). I write "approachable" fantasy that is meant to be an escape from all of our real-world trials and tribulations while subtly (and not-so-subtly) challenging the status quo.

www.ingramcontent.com/pod-product-compliance
Lightning Source LLC
Chambersburg PA
CBHW030336010826
48973CB00004B/1024